BLACK OPS

"That's not why I'm here," Detective Abe Kennedy said. "Our forensics people were fortunate enough to get a print off it. The trouble is, when we ran the print through the AFIS computer, the ID on the print came back classified."

"I see, and that's why you wanted to meet?" Todd McCartney, National Security Advisor, asked, raising an eyebrow.

"Not exactly. I'm here because not only was the ID classified, but it was specifically coded under Black Ops."

"Slow down," McCartney said softly. He quickly looked around the room to make sure no one could hear them. Kennedy realized that he seemed to have that effect on people lately.

"That's a different story altogether. Anything regarding Black Ops is extremely sensitive. Technically I'm not supposed to acknowledge that such operations even exist. As a matter of policy we try to leave those matters to those with need to know . . . CIA, Defense Intelligence Agency . . . they have their own deals going."

"Meaning?"

"Meaning that a Black Op is a clandestine operation, generally backed by the CIA or one of the military intelligence services, operating covert, outside the usual chain of command and normal Congressional oversight. Unlike something as controversial as Iran-Contra, which required both a 'finding' from the National Security Council and an Executive Order from the President, a Black Op can proceed as part of a broad intelligence strategy when significant national imperatives are involved," he explained. "To sum it up, it is the most secretive type of operation there is."

"What kind of stuff are we talking here, assassinations, kidnapping? What?"

McCartney hesitated. "Abe, I'm not at liberty to be that specific."

CHINA CARD

THOMAS BLOOD

LEISURE BOOKS  NEW YORK CITY

To Colonel Thomas Blood (1917-1997)—
Father, Friend, Patriot

A LEISURE BOOK®

October 2000

Published by

Dorchester Publishing Co., Inc.
276 Fifth Avenue
New York, NY 10001

ISBN 0-8439-4782-9

Printed in the United States of America.

CHINA CARD

Prologue

To the old man, there was no greater seduction than walking the halls of the empty museum during the wee hours of the morning. For three decades he actually came to resent sleep, awakening each day before dawn without the aid of an alarm clock, rushing to relieve the man on the graveyard shift. Henri Claire was well liked, often arriving early with two steaming cups of coffee in hand, one for himself and the other for the security guard coming off duty. While it had started as a part-time job when he was young and had no love of art, for him, the love affair was inevitable, as the treasures held within the walls of the Louvre soon became his mistress. It was not long before Henri discovered that it was only in the brief solitude of morning, distracted only by the echo of his own footsteps in the cavernous chamber, that he could be alone with the works of the great masters. To him, Chagall, Matisse, and Monet weren't artists, they were modern-day prophets who gave the world a glimpse into man's soul. For most of the security staff it was a job, but for Henri it was a calling. Safeguarding these masterpieces was a privilege. He would have gladly done it for free.

As he began his rounds that morning, the sun had yet to rise over the city of lights. It would remain quiet for another hour or so, until the daily onslaught of cars and tourists filled the Champs-Elysées and surrounding thoroughfares. For most of his shift there was nothing unusual, except for a memo warning him of a pesky photographer that had been evicted by security the day before for snapping shots of an exclusive exhibit, the Weisel collection. Good taste, thought the aging security guard. The Weisel collection had long been dear to him, donated by a wealthy Berlin family after World War II. Included among its works were at least two dozen masterpieces constituting a virtual who's who of Impressionists. What made the collection even more extraordinary was that many in the Weisel family had died at the hands of the Nazis at Dachau. As it so often happened, most of their valuables, including their artwork, were confiscated by the SS. It was only after years of searching that the surviving family members were able to recover their lost treasures.

With a chuckle, Henri threw the memo in the trash, knowing that it was common for street hustlers to skirt the velvet ropes set up to keep a safe distance between the public and the masterpieces, in an attempt to get close-up photos of the works, which they would later sell to tourists. Around 6:45 A.M. he had almost finished his rounds when he turned the corner and approached the Weisel exhibit. Inexplicably, Henri began to feel anxious, as though he were being watched. This was impossible, he thought. One of the reasons the Louvre has only one guard making rounds at any given time is because it possesses one of the most sophisticated security systems in the world. The slightest movement in the wrong place would trigger a motion sensor that would immediately dispatch a hundred Paris police officers to the scene. The same was true with any sudden change in temperature or humidity. No, there could be no one else in the building without him knowing it. The possibility of theft was inconceivable.

But just in case, as Henri entered the vast anteroom housing the Weisel collection he removed his radio from its holster. He took a few more steps, nervously massaging the volume dial. As Henri got closer, his attention turned immediately to his favorite, a Manet entitled *Innocence*. But while his eyes tried to focus, his mind refused to embrace the atrocity before him. He looked first to his left, then panned across the room in the other direction, aghast at the wanton consistency of the desecration. For several seconds Henri Claire tried to regain his bearings, to make sure he wasn't having a terrible nightmare. Then, very nearly frozen in shock, he managed to lift the radio to his lips. As his eyes welled with tears, Henri clutched his chest with his free hand and tried to speak. His voice quivering, the old man could utter only, "Horror, horror . . ."

Chapter One

In a laboratory two hundred feet below the Yongbyon Nuclear Research Reactor, the floor of the otherwise sterile facility was awash with blood. The red torrent gushed from the intestines of the young Serb, creating a stark contrast with the fluorescent whiteness of the chamber. As he lay there, disemboweled, bleeding to death, his boss stood frozen with fear. He had been advised repeatedly against trying to make any last-minute changes in the arrangement. Tragically, he appeared to ignore those warnings. As a result, his bodyguard paid the price, receiving an unwelcome dose of North Korean hospitality. Standing over the body was the head of Pyongyang's dreaded Intelligence Service, still holding the bloody dagger. Looking on were the defense minister, several generals, and Kim Jong Il, the new leader of the Stalinist republic.

"Perhaps now we can stop playing games. Our government has paid your client a substantial sum of money. We have relied on your expertise, and instead of living up to your word, you deliver us defective merchandise. If this is some ploy to renegotiate your fee . . ." said the man holding the knife.

"Minister, don't be ridiculous, money has nothing to do with this," said Sam Belarus, freelancer extraordinaire in the world of illicit arms dealing. "As far as we know the device is in perfect working order. It was obtained only ten days ago from the Red Army nuclear installation in Chelyabinsk! I personally took delivery in Paris. It hasn't been out of my sight."

Kim Jong Il was furious. What should have been his moment of triumph had turned into humiliation. Raised since boyhood to fill the shoes of his late father, the feared dictator Kim Il Sung, the younger Kim sought to validate his claim to lead the totalitarian regime into the next century by doing the impossible, delivering North Korea's first nuclear bomb. It mattered not that it was a relatively small, tactical, "suitcase bomb." It was still ten times more powerful than the weapons that incinerated Hiroshima and Nagasaki. Ironically, he probably would have succeeded, had the damned thing worked.

Gaining membership in the "nuclear club" had long been an obsession for North Korea. Despite its million-man army, massive artillery, and hundreds of Scud missiles positioned just thirty-five miles from Seoul, the military power had failed miserably in attempting to develop its own bomb, producing less than ten pounds of plutonium to date, barely enough for a single weapon. What's more, since the demise of the Soviet Union, the clock was ticking. India and Pakistan had already preempted them. And Kim knew that without the Russians in their corner, they would never be able to stand up to enemies like the United States unless they acquired their own strategic nuclear capability. But unlike the holdovers from his father's cabinet, he didn't panic. Instead, he sensed an opportunity, knowing it would be only a matter of time before cash-poor Russia would have no choice but to broker its nuclear wares on the black market. The only thing he didn't count on was the incompetence of Sam Belarus.

"Mr. Belarus, let us assume for the moment that this device is in good working order . . ." began Kim Jong Il, breaking his silence. "Nevertheless, we are still unable to operate it. What would you have us do?" he said, diplomatically.

"Mr. Kim, you must understand that we have followed your instructions to the letter, going to great risks to acquire a device that would meet your exact specifications. Our only mistake has been in assuming that your people would have the expertise to operate it," he reasoned.

"Excuse me," interrupted one of the generals, taking offense. "The expertise of North Korean scientists is not the issue. You know full well that these kinds of tactical nukes cannot be armed without bypassing each weapon's 'Permissive Action Lock.' Otherwise they are virtually useless!"

Kim Jong Il was growing impatient. "How difficult would it be to reprogram the weapon?" he asked his generals.

"Dear Leader, I must be honest with you, reprogramming such a weapon is almost impossible. Without the PALs or a bypass program, it could take us years. But the greater concern is the chance of accidental explosion if we input a code that simultaneously arms the weapon and triggers the detonation sequence . . ." said one of the generals.

"How could that happen?" asked the incredulous Kim.

"The Soviets had thousands of weapons with so-called 'failsafe triggers,' " began the defense minister. "The Red Army generals reasoned that, if under attack, they might only have time to arm their weapons, but not to launch or detonate them. So they invented a way that if you arm it, the weapon will automatically detonate within a specified period of time. Unfortunately, I must agree with the general. Reprogramming the weapon is out of the question. What's more, any attempt to decipher either the PAL or activation codes runs the risk of blowing our own country off the map."

"Well that's it then, Mr. Belarus? You leave us with very little choice," said Kim, signaling his intelligence chief, who immediately put the knife to the arms dealer's throat. "It's sad really. This could have been a profitable relationship for both of us," he said, turning to walk away.

"Wait, wait!" gasped Belarus, squeezing the words out as the blade pressed against his larynx.

"Yes, what is it?" said Kim impatiently.

"I-I think I know someone that can help you with your problem."

"I suppose you have somebody in Lubyanka that will just give you the PAL for this weapon if you ask for it? Or some friends in the Leipzig Mob? And let's not forget your comrades in Mitrovica?" he asked skeptically. "From what I understand, they'll sell anything to anybody."

Belarus knew that this was his last chance. If Kim didn't believe him, he would have him gutted, just like his aide. "No," he said nervously. "There's only one man who has access to the PALs, but he's not a Russian. In fact, he works out of Langley, Virginia . . ."

"Are saying that this man is CIA?"

"Yeah, in a manner of speaking. At least once upon a time . . ."

Part One

"The only thing you can't survive in politics is getting caught with a dead woman or a live boy."

—Lyndon Johnson

Chapter Two

In the end, there was absolute clarity. It was all about power. In Washington, power is everything. The irony is, the business of politics is still all about buying and selling. In some cities people pay in cash, in the nation's capital they trade in favors—a well-timed handshake here, a slice of pork there. You scratch my back, I'll scratch yours, just be careful while it's turned. In a city where the game is about power, and the winners take all, she was tossed into the big leagues. And it cost her.

It was fitting that she died bound to an antique four-poster bed in one of the city's poshest hotel suites. She was exposed and completely helpless. The finely sculpted features of her schoolgirl face were battered and bruised, and her flaxen hair was speckled with blood. Her swollen eyes showed no defiance now, only terror. She was only seventeen years old, but she knew he wasn't playing games this time.

She looked around wildly for help. Heavy brocade curtains blacked out the windows and CNN blared from the large-screen television. As for him, he was very drunk and out of control, having consumed a half dozen martinis aboard the Concord during his return from Paris. In his fury, he had already smashed a crystal decanter and two bottles of Chateau Margeaux, but the walls were thick. Like the jacked up charges for hotel operator calls, the room rate came with a heavy privacy premium. She knew help wouldn't arrive until it was too late.

He raged on, cursing her. His rancid, meaty breath and spittle were hot against her skin. Her weak pleas only frenzied him more, and he punched her over and over again. She desperately thrashed about to avoid the blows.

In her last moments, she tried to focus on the people she loved, tried to forgive them for what they had done to her. The pain triggered images of famous and powerful men whose secret lives, those they concealed so carefully from family and friends, would die with her.

She begged him to spare her life, but she knew it was futile as she stared into his bloodshot eyes. She strained against the ties one last time as his fist rose and fell to crush her larynx. As she died, her lips moved silently. "Okay Mommy, I'll do it for you."

Chapter Three

The headquarters of the D.C. Homicide squad is hardly what you would call a cheery place. Cramped for space, with olive-green walls that old-timers swear used to be white, the third floor housed the thirty-two detectives in the busiest division in the Metropolitan Police Department. Cold in the winter and hot in the summer, it contained a large bullpen with a hodgepodge assortment of sixteen desks—one for every detective on each shift, some wooden, some metal, some broken, giving the space a feel akin to that of a garage sale rather than a suite of offices. Nevertheless, for the Homicide squad and the rest of the cops at the 7th Precinct it was home, and tonight there was reason to celebrate.

"What the hell does a black man have to do to get a decent cup of coffee in the United States of America?" bellowed Abe Kennedy with a grin on his face as wide as the Potomac. With that comment things returned to normal in the unit for the first time in almost a year. Nearly twelve months to the day, on a bitterly cold Halloween night, senior detective Abe Kennedy took four bullets during a crack house ambush, two in the stomach, one in the leg, and another in the chest. The latter, which was still lodged just below his left lung, remained an inoperable reminder of his mortality. That he survived the attack at all was incredible, that he made it back to active duty was nothing short of a miracle. But Kennedy, a bulky, muscular man, with mahogany skin and salt and pepper hair, seemed to specialize in miracles. Ironically, as a result of the intense regimen of physical therapy mandated by his doctors, he was in the best shape of his life, despite his wounds. To his fellow detectives, Kennedy was a precinct house legend, dubbed "the human polygraph" by admiring colleagues in tribute to his investigative skills and conviction rate. He was also known for his irreverent wit, as well as his chronic complaining about the squad's coffee, or "witch's brew," as he liked to call it.

Perhaps the only one who wasn't surprised at Kennedy's recovery was his partner, Ira Murray. Murray, the senior member of the squad, was proud of being the other half of the department's "odd couple." Twenty years older, tall and lanky, all long arms and legs, with a high forehead culminating in a widow's peak and dark brown eyes that radiated wisdom, Ira Murray was the squad's resident rabbi, priest, and to some, surrogate father. Fifteen years ago the two men had been paired as the department's first interracial team and had partnered together ever since. And if Ira was sure of one thing, it was that for Abe Kennedy, his recovery was meaningless without a return to duty. So certain was Murrary of this fact, that he delayed his own retirement long enough to work one last case with his partner. No matter what the case, no matter how the investigation turned out, this was the moment the two had been anticipating for months. It was Abe's first case back, and the last of Ira's career.

It was that fact that made the squad's reaction to Detective Kennedy's return somewhat odd. Instead of getting the big welcome he expected as he made his grand entrance, not a single detective even looked up from his desk when he arrived. Not even Ira Murray. Feeling strange, he tried again. "I said, what has a black man got to do to get a decent cup of coffee in the United States of America?" Again, no reaction. Abe was understandably spooked. It wasn't as though he anticipated a marching band and streamers, but a friendly "hello" or "welcome back, Abe" wasn't unreasonable. After waiting for a few awkward seconds, he made his way to his desk, which had been cleared by the watch-commander in anticipation of his return. Before taking his jacket off and sitting down, he looked around, taking measure of those in the room. All the faces were familiar—Beckett, Alvarez, Lindstrom, even Damani. These people were supposed to be his friends. What on earth could be wrong? Setting down his briefcase, he went instead to the kitchen and poured himself a cup of the thickest black, tarlike coffee he'd ever seen. Taking a whiff, he recoiled at the harsh aroma, thinking that the "witch's brew" was far worse than he remembered. Looking around and finding no sugar, Sweet 'n Low, or creamer to safeguard his palate, he reluctantly returned to his desk amid the awkward silence of his fellow detectives. Maybe they didn't want him back. After all, he'd survived wounds that should have killed him twice over. Cops are a superstitious bunch. Maybe they thought a dead man walking was bad karma.

Slowly Abe unpacked his briefcase and tried mightily to sip his coffee. "So, Ira, how's Freda doing?" said Abe, referring to his partner's wife. Murray, who was sitting directly across from him, had his nose buried in a case file and didn't look up. One detective called out aloud about the upcoming Redskins-Giants game. Abe tried to join in, "This is our year, I'm tellin' you . . ." But almost as soon as he opened his mouth, they changed the subject. By this time he was totally confused, on the verge of panic.

Abe sat there hoping that the phone would ring, that the captain would summon him to his office, that there would be a bomb scare, anything to get him out of there. And then it happened.

Alvarez was first. Reaching into the bottom drawer of his desk he ever so carefully removed a small bag. Giving his fellow detectives the most subtle of telling glances he rose and walked slowly in Abe's direction. As he passed each detective they looked up from whatever they were pretending to be doing, eager with anticipation. Finally, as he made the last few tentative steps toward Abe's desk, the senior detective noticed, immensely pleased that someone was trying to make contact with him. "Hey, Alvarez, que pasa? How ya been?" he said.

Instead of responding, Alvarez lifted the bag and methodically removed its contents, setting it down on Kennedy's desk. With a stern look on his face, he said only, "Decaf Hazelnut Latte with a sprinkle of nutmeg." Without ceremony, he turned and walked away. Next up was Damani, who followed Alverez's lead to a tee. "Cappuccino, extra foam, with just a hint of cinnamon."

Bobby Lindstrom, who had made detective on Kennedy's recommendation, ran full throttle to Abe's desk. Once there, however, he was so choked up he could bearly utter his assigned words, "Arabian-Mocha Java . . ."

And so it went. By the time they were done, Detective Abe Kennedy had a desk full of piping hot cups of Caffe Americano, Caramel Macchiato, Decaf Sulawesi, Guatemalan Antigua, Narino Supremo, African Sanani, and another ten selections from Starbucks, Hannibals, Vie de France and any other place the Homicide unit could find that sold coffee. Finally, it was Ira Murray's turn. Standing tall, he stood over his partner, half laughing and half trying not to cry. Despite the fact that everyone in the precinct was in on the joke but Abe, they were all on the edge of their seats. "Double Espresso with a twist of lemon. Axel Foley sends his regards," he said. "Welcome back, Detective!"

With his eyes welling with tears, Abe leaped to his feet and grabbed his partner in the tightest bear hug he could manage. "Thanks, Ira," was all he could say with the golf ball–sized lump in his throat.

Pulling back to face Abe, Murray responded, "No, partner. Thank you. Thank you for not giving up. Thank you for coming back to help us do our job. How ya doin' anyway? You feelin' all right?"

"Waddaya kiddin'? All of a sudden I feel great!"

"Well, your colon won't be doing so good after you drink all that caffeine," chimed in Lindstrom.

"That's right. And we expect you to drink all of it. Tonight!" said Murray.

"In your dreams. Hey, as long as we're on the subject, can I buy anybody a cup of coffee?" he called out, relishing the very experience of being back among cops. Having been cleansed of any doubts about Abe, the Homicide squad mercifully took him up on his offer, reveling in his return. For the better part of an hour they took the time to get reacquainted, bring Abe up to speed, and just get some of their old "flow" back.

After a while, Murray raised his cup of espresso and said, "To

Abe Kennedy. Our brother is home. We are a family again!"

As will always happen, no matter how warm and genuine the event, its interruption by real police work was inevitable. But this time it wasn't an APB or a multiple homicide or any of the circumstances that typically filled the nights of Murder City. Rather it was a simple two-page fax. Lindstrom, who happened to be standing by the machine, was the first to see it. "Hey guys," he called out over the din of the detectives' collective banter. "Listen to this." After waiting a few seconds for the squad to quiet down, Lindstrom continued. "INTERPOL ALERT. Paris police report that an unprecedented act of terror occurred late Saturday evening or early Sunday morning at the Louvre. According to police sources, at least two dozen priceless Impressionist masterpieces were mutilated by a knife-wielding assailant or assailants. All of the paintings in the prestigious Weisel collection, with an estimated value exceeding twenty-five million dollars, were damaged beyond salvage in this city's worst act of vandalism. Police are looking for a suspect that was seen earlier in the week. He is described as a white male in his early thirties, with light brown hair and a slight build. Authorities believe he may be a photographer. Any information or inquiries on this matter should be referred to Inspector Claude Moleier at INTERPOL at 011-322-6651."

"How on earth could anybody hate art enough to do something like that?" asked one detective.

"Maybe it's an insurance scam?" posited another.

"So Abe, waddaya think?" asked Damani.

Abe smiled, enjoying the give and take. "Hell man, I'm a homicide detective. What do I know about art? Unless that nut starts cutting up pictures of dogs playing poker, I have no comment." As the squad erupted in laughter, the captain emerged from his glass-enclosed office.

"Detective Kennedy, it's good to see you," said the captain, a former Marine drill instructor and Lou Gossett Jr. look-alike who had sported a shaved head long before it was fashionable.

"Good to be back, Captain."

"Anything you need . . . besides a cup of coffee that is?"

"No, no. I'm fine."

"That's good, 'cause there's plenty of work to do. Speaking of which, if any of you have any interest in real police work, we just got a call from dispatch. Any takers?"

Almost as if they were scripted, no one said a word. Murray and the crew had hoped that the captain would just assign the case like he always did, but they were ready if he asked for volunteers. "Come on people, doesn't anybody wanna catch the bad guys? How about it, Damani?"

"I'm swamped, Captain."

"Alvarez?"

"I'm helping out Damani."

After about a minute, Murray spoke up. "I can handle one more, Cappy."

"Ira, I thought you were about to retire?" said the Captain.

"Uh . . . he is. . . . But I'm not. And let's face it. My caseload is a little light right now," injected Abe.

The captain studied Kennedy. There was a time when he wished he could give all of his investigations to the detective. But that somehow seemed like a lifetime away. There was just no way to know how Abe's skills had deteriorated or how he would perform on the street. "I don't know, Abe, this one sounds pretty ugly."

"Give me a break, Captain. I've been doing this a long time and I can't remember any of 'em that were pretty," said Abe.

"You're missing my point."

"And you're missing mine. Somebody's dead and we're wasting time while their killer is getting away. These guys here are all jammed up. I'm available. Let me do my job," he demanded.

Although Abe didn't really catch on, he had exactly the reaction the captain was hoping for. He had planned on assigning the case to Kennedy anyway. He just wanted him to want it a little bit. "Fine, you want it, you got it," he said as he turned and walked away.

"All right!" shouted Murray. "Back in business."

Abe stood and quickly put on his jacket, running after the captain. "So what are the details, Cappy?"

"Possible homicide at the Capital Pavilion. Officers on the scene say it's pretty gruesome. Go check it out."

With that Detective Abe Kennedy, at long last, went back to work.

* * *

The ten o'clock local news was wrapping up as the detectives stepped around a splintered Queen Anne chair and peered into the bedroom of suite 701 at the Capital Pavilion, one of Washington's oldest and most elegant hotels.

Kennedy had seen a lot in his twenty years on the force, but he was still shocked at what was waiting inside. A shattered colonial mirror on the opposite wall presented him with a jagged view of the room. The furniture had been tossed around and smashed, and the peach walls were streaked with blood like rotten fruit laid open and oozing. The crime unit was silently working around the carnage, stepping over broken glass to collect evidence. In the middle of it all was the dead girl; naked, hands and feet tied to the bedposts. The bright white sheets were soaked with blood, especially around the girl's hips. Kennedy and Murray exchanged glances.

"They'll need a rape kit," said Kennedy, and Murray nodded slowly.

It had been so long since Kennedy had inspected a crime scene that he found himself relying more on instinct than on method. Cautiously, he moved closer to the body as Murray, ever protective of his partner, hung back, monitoring Abe's every move. Even before his wounding, Kennedy's gait was somewhat awkward, his physique fooling many a suspect who took a quick look at him and chose to run when he yelled stop. More than once the detective made perpetrators pay for confusing big with slow.

As Kennedy got closer to the bed, he saw how bruised and battered her body was, and noticed a large tuft of hair pulled cleanly out of her scalp. From the blue discoloration of her lips, he estimated that she had died within the last two hours. He circled the bed, stopping to examine the purple necklace of bruises around her crushed neck. He shook his head in disgust and pity. The Captain wasn't kidding when he said it would be gruesome.

Kennedy had worked the streets of D.C. for most of his adult life. He had investigated hundreds of murders and seen just as many dead bodies. Usually, the deceased were young black men, victims of gang violence and drug turf wars. He viewed the drug boys and gang bangers with pure hate. They were a cancer feeding off their own families and communities. Where there had once been starter homes and shiny new stores full of hope and pride, the bangers and boys left burned-out voids. Fourteenth Street, where Kennedy grew up, had once been the heart of D.C.'s growing African-American middle class. Now it was a festering alley of shooting galleries and chop shops. The tempoed roll of jazz band drums that once filled the night had long since been replaced by sporadic metallic claps of gunfire.

Tonight, however, Kennedy was working downtown Northwest, in one of the nice neighborhoods. He already knew this murder would make the papers, and he also knew that Division would be watching his every move as he headed up the investigation.

"Okay, fellas, wadda we got here?" Kennedy asked.

"Female, probably a minor, but no ID on her, not even a purse. Caucasian," said a young uniformed officer. "The hotel manager is in the next room waiting to be questioned, but I don't think we'll get too much information from him. A housekeeper was making the nightly rounds, heard the TV blasting away, and saw the door open. That's what she found." He pointed to the girl. "I've already asked for a complete guest list, and we'll be making the rounds, asking if anyone in the other rooms heard anything."

Kennedy nodded in approval and looked up to see Murray leaning against a wall. He didn't have to ask what was wrong. Of all the cases for Ira to draw, this was the absolute worst. "You all right over there, partner?"

Murray shrugged his shoulders wearily. He wanted to be there for Abe, but as he looked over at the battered body, he thought of his own daughters and wondered how he had spent a lifetime examining such violent death. He sighed. "I'm just going to take a look at the rest of the suite," he told Kennedy.

"Sure, Detective," Kennedy said as a concerned look flashed across his face.

Kennedy and Murray originally called each other "Detective" when they first started out. Thousands of arrests later, they still used the greeting as a gesture of respect. In a town that manufactures laws, respect for the law was hard to come by. Kennedy and his colleagues saw it every day, from the senators' wives who thought fire hydrants made excellent parking places, to the Hill staffers who believed police lines were only for interns and tourists. So when Kennedy found someone worthy of respect, he held onto them, protected them like melting ice. He knew how a case like this would affect Ira, and he also knew that his partner, whether he would admit it or not, couldn't help but take the murder of a teenage girl personally. Kennedy would do anything for Ira. Together they would solve his last case.

When Ira left, Kennedy studied the room, trying to get a feel for what had happened. It was a bloodbath, the type of thing he usually saw when a drug buy went bad. But he saw no signs of drug use, no signs of gunfire. The detective wondered if the girl knew her killer. He watched the crime scene techs rhythmically dust the rooms from top to bottom with black carbon dusting powder. These were the guys who got to pick up the mess, piece together a jigsaw puzzle of fingerprints, carpet fibers, blood samples, and dirt under fingernails. As the detective stepped aside to let the crime unit photographer videotape the scene, a booming voice broke the silence.

"So Charles Manson, the Son of Sam, and Andrew Cunannan walk into a bar . . ."

Startled, Kennedy looked up to see Dr. Julian Cole of the Forensics Division of the MPD standing in the doorway.

"Oh, we're in a serious mood, aren't we, Abe? No mood for jokes, I assume," Cole said.

Kennedy shook his head at his old friend. "Not tonight, Julian. Come over here and take a look at the victim." Cole was known for having the worst sense of humor in the department, but he was also the best medical examiner with whom Kennedy had ever worked.

As Cole approached the girl, his mood turned somber. "Geezus, this guy played rough."

"He sure did," Kennedy said.

"Well, let's see what happened to her," Cole said, as he pulled a rectal thermometer out of his bag. "Do you have any theories?"

"Nothing much yet," Kennedy admitted.

"Actually, I think I might have one," said Murray, finally emerging from the bathroom.

"Hey, Ira, how are you doing over there?" asked Kennedy.

Murray didn't answer. He just walked over to the two men and held out his hand. "Look at what I found in the bathroom." He opened the handkerchief in his hand, revealing a single gold cuff link. An ordinary piece of men's jewelry in this town. However, as Kennedy came closer, he saw what made this ordinary cuff link so special. Instead of jewels or monograms or some other design, the cuff link bore a rather unusual fashion statement:

The seal of the President of the United States.

Chapter Four

Mike Hanson waited impatiently for an elevator to take him up to the headquarters of the Joe Albert for President campaign on the building's seventh floor. He was running late as usual. He paced back and forth across the lobby, pressed the button for the elevator again, and checked his watch. Griff was going to kill him.

The hell with the elevators. Hanson headed for the stairs. He took the steps two at a time in the sticky heat of the unairconditioned stairwell, and sweat started to drip down the back of his neck by the third floor. By the time he reached the seventh floor and popped out the door to the campaign, his face was flushed, and the press was coming off his clothes. The receptionist, Martha, looked up, glad to see Hanson as he stood there wiping the perspiration from his brow. Hanson was in his late thirties, slightly over six feet tall, with a mop of brown hair and loads of attitude. He winked at Martha and she beamed at him.

"So, what's the latest?" he asked. Martha was his best source of office gossip.

Martha smiled a half smile, trying not to look scared. "Is it true, Mr. Hanson?"

Hanson grimaced. He hadn't been at the office ten seconds and the questions were starting. "Yes, Martha. I'm afraid it is. . . ."

"But I thought that they ended the investigation two years ago."

Knowing there was no good answer to her question, he said, "What can I tell you? Impeachment wasn't enough. *They* control both houses of Congress. It's an election year. *They* changed their minds."

"Rumors are flying all over this place," Martha said.

"That's what I like to hear, especially since I'm the one who starts most of 'em," said Hanson as he moved on, whizzing right by the security guard. The guard checked the I.D. of each and every person who entered the suite, but was so accustomed to Hanson's comings and goings that he had long ago stopped bothering him for his jail pass, as I.D.s were known in the campaign.

Having joined the campaign following a tortured three-year stint running the much-maligned, debt-ridden Presidential Legal Defense Fund, Hanson was no stranger to scandal. It seemed that everywhere Hanson went—the Democratic National Committee, the White House, the Defense Fund—an investigation was sure to follow. His downtown office had become known in the press as "subpoena central." "Hell, even my dog is taking the fifth," he was fond of saying. Friends and foes alike were suggesting that it was time to relinquish his role as party lightning rod and sit out the 2000 presidential race, but Hanson wouldn't hear of it. While his new business card may have read, "Deputy Campaign Manager," he and everyone else on the seventh floor knew that his title was purely ceremonial. Mike Hanson was a fund-raiser and damned proud of it. Defiant as ever, he cemented himself early on as a key player in Vice President Albert's presidential campaign, delivering 90 percent of the major donors from the '96 reelect. Suffice to say, in a town contaminated with the rarefied air of impeachment, this was no easy feat. As it turned out, Hanson's faith was rewarded as Joe Albert, once uncomfortable in the spotlight, proved to be a formidable campaigner, the genuine article, eventually fending off a brutal primary challenge from a tall, Rhodes Scholar, ex-senator to claim the nomination.

As Hanson walked down the corridor, he noticed that the halls were abuzz with activity. Good. He had ordered a deputy to circulate a memo several days ago that advised staffers to clean up their offices, straighten their desks, and wear ties and business suits all week. From his vantage point, it looked as if the memo had worked. Several staffers shot him inquisitive looks, and Hanson knew that Martha was right. Rumors about the Republicans' latest ploy—restarting the campaign finance hearings with only weeks to go before the election—had obviously spread up and down the seventh floor. It was a political dirty trick of the first order, completely without merit, in direct conflict with the best interests of the country and, in Hanson's opinion, a stroke of pure genius. As much as he hated to admit it, if the situation were reversed and the Dems had the chance to stick it to the Repos this way, they would have jumped at the chance. After all, this was politics, not some weenie profession like cardiac surgery or pro hockey. In presidential politics, there is more to the game than just winning. Anything short of total annihilation of your enemy is considered failure.

Hanson knew that there were other rumors swirling around. The one that had the most buzz was about the major donor summit being held in the chairman's office. Hanson assumed it was his memo that started it all. Circulating such memos was common when key constituents or interest group bigwigs came to town. But with so little time left, there weren't a whole lot of bigwigs out there left to impress. Every conceivable natural ally of the campaign had already been invited in to hear the Dems' dog and donkey show. This late in the game, the staffers knew that it could only be one thing—the money men were in town.

Hanson smiled to himself. He knew how quickly news traveled in Washington, particularly around election time. All campaigns are hotbeds of paranoia, as staffers young and old alike are instantly panicked by any shift in the prevailing winds—but this was worse than anything he'd ever seen. Hanson guessed that the troops were probably nervous about the solvency of the campaign, wanting to know why major donors were being brought in so late in the race. He also suspected that they were at least as worried about what he intended to do about it. The fact was, they had reason to be concerned. As Hanson was all too aware, despite all the charges, countercharges, and proposed reforms, in the year 2000, soft money donations were still the lifeblood of politics. Direct contributions to a candidate carried all sorts of Federal

Election Commission strings and donation limitations. In contrast, soft money, passed through the national party to individual campaigns, is fund-raising's mother of all loopholes, allowing the sophisticated political contributor an open checkbook to a specific campaign. Hanson sympathized with the staff, knowing full well how things looked. An eleventh-hour meeting of the campaign's financial gurus not only implied that a big cash infusion was needed to keep their horse in the race, but would trigger the inevitable onslaught of reporters on the headquarters. Even worse, for the veterans of the sordid endeavor of 1996, the unmistakable air of scandal was in the wind.

Hanson moved too quickly down the hallway to encourage any idle conversation. He was headed to see Tom Griffin, his best friend for over fifteen years. Griffin, aka "the Faith Healer," aka "the Messiah of Money," was the campaign's Finance Chairman and the best fund-raiser in either party, so nicknamed because insiders said the only thing that Griffin couldn't raise was the dead. Many believed that was only because he hadn't tried. His secluded office was located at the far end of a long corridor dubbed "no man's land" by young staffers foolish enough to try to get near it. With process servers waiting around every corner, for legal reasons, it was strategically located in an area sublet by the DNC from the campaign proper. Despite this, Griffin's office was the nerve center of the organization and everyone knew it.

Griffin's door was shut, but Hanson opened it without knocking and breezed in with his briefcase in one hand and his laptop slung over his shoulder. As always, he paused for a second to admire Griffin's "wall of fame." Unlike most brag walls, which included stiffly posed photos with the President and other members of the administration, Griffin's was different, displaying candid shots of the Messiah and Hanson huddled in the 1996 "war room" with the President, either discussing various campaign strategies, or just yukking it up to break the tension. And instead of the typical autopen signatures, Griffin's candids bore good-natured references to the Messiah's girth, or to Hanson's assorted vices. Griffin's two favorite photos were displayed prominently. On one, a photo of Griffin and the President standing over a conference table, the Chief Executive had written, "It takes a big man—and I mean a really BIG man—to have pulled this off." The other captured Hanson and the President laughing. The President was inspired enough by the memory to write "Griffin, I couldn't have done it without you . . . though there were days when I would have been glad to try." Hanson smiled. Notwithstanding the fact that most of his own photos were still in a shoebox somewhere under his bed, he couldn't help but reminisce about the 1996 campaign. Griffin and Hanson and a team of the best fund-raisers ever assembled raised a record amount of dollars, but this had come at a terrible cost, with most of the key players on the Democratic side, including the dynamic duo of Hanson and Griffin, now each owing more in legal fees than they would earn in a decade. Together the two men adopted a rather unusual response to what had become a never-ending investigation. After years of depositions, grand jury appearances, and congressional testimony, it had become unmistakably clear that this wasn't going to end anytime soon. So, instead of crawling back into the woodwork like so many of their friends, Hanson and Griffin did something completely unexpected. After a long night of assaulting their brain cells with all kinds of firewater, the two made a pact. It was fine if everybody else wanted to go down in flames, but not these two guys. Together, they would fight back. Screw the Select Committee. Screw the Independent Counsel. And screw anybody else that didn't like it. Treating every committee or grand jury appearance like an audition, Hanson and Griffin evolved into walking sound bites. They were determined to survive.

Hanson looked around the spacious suite, more than three times the size of the other offices on the floor. Griffin stood at his desk across the room, talking quietly on the phone, but he motioned for Hanson to come in. A man of gargantuan proportions, ruddy skin, and wavy dark hair, Griffin had spent his college years anchoring the Harvard Crimson's defense as an All Ivy League middle linebacker. The Messiah eventually traded in his helmet and pads for horn-rims and bowties, and often said that his years on the gridiron were the ideal proving ground for a career in politics. His massive desk was always hopelessly cluttered with documents and newspapers. But even from across the room, Hanson could see Griffin's priorities. Enough space was cleared for his daily call sheet, a list of thirty-five new donors on his radar screen that required special handling. Hanson guessed that Griffin had come in early enough this morning to call each and every one of them.

Griffin's guests sat, chatting and eating lunch at the oblong conference table next to the windows. For strategic meetings such as these, Griffin always made sure the heavy curtains were closed; you could never be too careful. He also kept a conspicuous but vitally important paper shredder by his desk.

"Hi folks," Hanson said, and started shaking hands with the financial angels: Al Heflin from the AFL-CIO, representing the unions; Cynthia Miles from SARA's List, the powerful pro-choice womens' PAC Sisters Actively Raising Assets; Rabbi Alex Meyer of the Progressive Jewish Coalition and chairman of the U.S. Holocaust Museum; David "Bundlemeister" Falcone of the Litigation Council; and last but not least, legendary Hollywood agent Zev Horwitz, representing the entertainment industry. All were regulars at the exclusive New Year's retreat known as the Renaissance Weekend, Lincoln bedroom slumber parties, and enough White House coffees to have Starbucks worried. Exclusive didn't begin to describe this private club, each of whom hailed from their own zip code of the rich and famous. Not only had each raised a million dollars for the party a dozen times over, but they all made it look easy. At first glance, the group appeared quite like other players on the Washington power scene, with their fat checkbooks, Range Rovers, and Rolexs. But Mike Hanson knew better. Nothing was easy in this business. These were the bag men, the junkyard dogs of politics, the go-to guys that candidates turn to when their backs are to the wall. They might look and smell pretty, but major donor fund-raisers have always been a breed apart, the people that make the trains run on time—or, more accurately, the people who keep the checks from bouncing. In the year 2000, the money men controlled Washington like never before—and they knew it.

From across the room, Griffin shook his head at Hanson's tardiness but smiled as he watched him work the room and greet the money men. Hanson had a well-earned reputation as the campaign's perennial bad boy. Fortunately for him, he was also the only fund-raiser in the party that could put up comparable numbers with those of the Faith Healer, a fact that made many, including the White House, overlook his foibles.

"Nice to see you, Mr. Hanson," said Griffin as he hung up the phone.

"Nice to be seen, Mr. Chairman," retorted Hanson.

"You're late, Michael."

"I know, I know. Fucking traffic in this town."

"Michael, to the best of my knowledge you haven't been on time for a meeting since the Dukakis campaign. In Little Rock you were practically a missing person. In New Hampshire you were more difficult to track down than an Orrin Hatch delegate. I don't even want to talk about the Convention . . ."

"Let's not go there . . ."

The money men laughed and dug back into their food.

"Jokes, right, Griff? Like at my expense, huh?" said Hanson, grinning. Looking at the buffet, he said, "What, no Peking Duck?"

Griffin just shook his head, trying to keep a straight face. Griffin and Hanson's easy camaraderie developed when they first met years before as mere rookies, working advance for the ill-fated Gary Hart campaign. As first mates on what became the political equivalent of the *Titanic*, the politicos became best friends. "Everybody, you all know our deputy campaign manager, Mike Hanson. Michael, this is everybody. Everybody, Michael," he said. "Michael, why don't you grab some food?"

Hanson gamely took his seat, dropping his bags and grabbing a plate. He knew that Griffin always liked to get lunch over with before he talked business. He filled his plate high with grilled Mediterranean vegetables on focaccia with goat cheese, braised fennel, and roasted rosemary potatoes in olive oil. This was a long way from the rubber chicken circuit, he thought as he admired the feast. "Excuse me, Griff, would you pass the Grey Poupon?" he asked loudly.

Griffin tilted his head, considering several retorts. But now, though razzing Hanson was one of his greatest joys, Griffin knew it was time to get down to business. This would be a make-or-break presentation. "Okay, okay, let's get started," said Griffin, smiling. "People, as you know, we've all been at this for almost two years now. Unlike '96, when we had a sitting president running unopposed in the primaries, this time we had a tougher campaign than anybody expected. Impeachment virtually eliminated any bump we should have gotten from incumbency . . ."

"What's that expression? 'Once you're impeached you're always impeached,' " said Hanson, unable to resist the opening.

"Thanks for sharing, Michael. Honestly," shot back Griffin in an exasperated tone. "Anyway, as I was saying, it's been a tough season. The fact that the Select Committee has trashed the Vice President at every turn hasn't helped much. But despite all that, the people seated at this table rallied around Joe Albert. Together we not only beat back that tall bastard, but along the way we managed to hold our own with the Republicans who, I'm sad to say, beat our '96 record. We did this despite the fact that the "Prescott for President" campaign has done everything humanly possible to scare off every Democratic contributor in America. I've said it before and I'll say it again: You are the reason the Veep won the nomination and is going to be our next president. As I'm sure he's told each one of you personally, our guy is fully aware of your efforts and is forever in your debt."

As Griffin bobbed and weaved his way through the pep talk, Hanson discreetly glanced around the room at the money men. Over the last two years, he had heard his buddy make the same speech—tweaked ever so slighty depending on his audience—at least a thousand times. But Hanson knew that this time was different. It was one of the rare occasions when Griffin wasn't just working people. He was actually being sincere, a sin worthy of a scarlet letter in a town like Washington. Hanson almost laughed out loud at the irony of it all. But for Griffin's sake, and the good of the campaign, he munched the focaccia with goat cheese instead and listened intently as Griffin recounted the accomplishments of the campaign's finance plan. Every now and then, Hanson's eyes wandered over to the other side of the room, where Griffin's two televisions played side by side, with one flickering an image of an obscure Congressional debate somewhere in a state with a lot of cows and the other the First Lady greeting children at a drug-free school. Though the sound was muted, Griffin never turned the televisions off when he was in the room. One was set to CNN and the other ran C-SPAN all day. Both Griffin and Hanson always liked to know exactly what was going on in the world.

Hanson watched Griffin's earnest face as he spoke about the plan. Nicknamed "Search and Destroy," it was hatched two years before at Hanson's law office and almost everyone around today's table was there that day or conferenced in. It was brilliant in its simplicity. For a badly bloodied Vice President to have any chance at the Presidency, it was vital to minimize damage during the primaries. It didn't really matter whether he had the nomination locked up before the convention, just that he made it to the convention in one piece. Ironically, the best way to avoid damage was with money—lots of it. The good news was that the strategy worked, ultimately defunding the opposition. But given that there was only so much money on the Democratic side to go around, the bad news was that general elections are a whole lot more expensive than the primaries, and the campaign was now coming up just a little short.

"Just how short is a little short?" demanded impeccably dressed Zev Horwitz, conspicuous among the group with his unnaturally orange tan. Hanson noted that even his completely bald head glowed with a copper tint under the fluorescent lights.

"Now, hold on, Zev. I know what this sounds like, and I know we've asked a lot from each of you," began Griffin.

Hanson smiled, but began to worry as he watched Griffin squirm.

"Answer the question," demanded Cynthia Miles. "And don't play games with us. There's no such thing in presidential politics as being a little short."

"Yeah, that's sort of like being a little bit pregnant," said David Falcone, known throughout Washington as the Bundlemeister in deference to his unsurpassed reputation in the art of "bundling," a widely practiced strategy to avoid federal contribution limits. Because an individual can only give a maximum of two thousand dollars per candidate in federal races, bundling money is an essential strategy for anyone who wants to have a major impact on a campaign and hence an elected official. Hanson knew that for Falcone, who represented about a million trial lawyers nationally, it wasn't uncommon to go to lunch with the managing partner of a 200-person law firm and leave before dessert was served with an envelope containing two hundred individual checks for a thousand dollars each.

"Either we have the money to win this thing or we don't." Rabbi Meyer's voice was rising.

"Rabbi, please," said Griffin. "People, you're not hearing me. We are up by seven points in the *Wall Street Journal*-CNN poll, and we all know the *Journal* hates us. That's outside the margin of error."

"A number, Tom. Please, just give us a number," said Horwitz.

Griffin paused and looked over to Hanson for help. It wasn't often that Hanson saw Griffin flustered, but what had just occurred was the inevitable train wreck that Hanson had seen take place in virtually every campaign. Sometimes it's press, other times it's advance, still other times it's delegate selection, but the one thing that is certain is that every campaign has at least one train wreck along the way. Hanson's eyes met Griffin's and he called out, "Fifteen million," loudly and firmly.

"Fifteen million? Where the hell does that come from?" Al Heflin screamed.

There was a moment of silence in the room.

Cynthia Miles, a former Miss Pennsylvania in her early forties who was still attractive except for the fact that she never smiled, chose this moment to break ranks and light up a cigarette, a huge violation of decorum among Democrats. Heflin and Horwitz quickly followed suit. Not a good sign, Hanson observed, particularly for a campaign that refused to take money from the tobacco lobby.

"Would someone mind telling me how the campaign ends up fifteen fucking million dollars in the hole after all the goddamn money we've raised?" she asked in her gravelly voice.

Hanson's eyes narrowed. "Actually, we're not in the hole. But we need the money for a media buy," said Hanson.

"What media buy?" sputtered Rabbi Meyer.

"Please, not this again. They're still investigating '96 . . ."

Hanson slipped effortlessly into the role of attack dog for Griff, just as he had so many times before. He was confident he could persuade the group to accept the new plan. He just needed one of the money men to accept his challenge. "We've decided to go for a huge media buy. We'll run tons of TV ads in selected markets in states deemed critical to the outcome of the election: California, Michigan, Ohio, Florida, New York, New Jersey, and Pennsylvania to be exact."

"But what ads are we going to run? I haven't heard anything about any new ads," Horwitz said.

Hanson just stared at Zev. Since when do we have to clear our new attack ads with you, Hanson thought. The super-agent's ego had been looming out of control for some time. Hanson sighed and he willed himself to stay calm. At this stage of the campaign, everyone was on edge. "That's because they haven't been shot yet, Zev," he said, trying to be diplomatic. "But not to worry, our media consultants have offered to shoot them on spec. And I promise you, everything will be clean."

"But that's not the problem," interrupted Griffin. "As you know, you can't buy political time on margin like you can commercial time. So we've got to be able to give the networks the cash up front—lots of cash. Let's face it, political campaigns don't exactly have 'A' credit with affiliates. It's pay as you go or nothing."

"And what if we don't do the buy?" Cynthia asked.

"Then the Republicans, who still have fifty million in their kitty, run their ads unanswered for a week before the election in at least six key states totaling a hundred and ten electoral votes," Hanson said, letting his voice drift off and flipping his pen down in frustration. "Translation, Cynthia: kiss the fucking election goodbye!" He spun his chair around 180 degrees and stared at the curtain covering the window. The room was silent.

With Hanson's dark forecast ringing in everyone's ears, Griffin chose this moment to regain control of the meeting. "So this is how it breaks down. I know it's a tall order, but I need each of you to deliver three million by Friday, soft money only," he said. "Mr. Hanson, I expect double that from you, just to create a little cushion."

"Three million soft. Are you insane? Have you forgotten 1996? What do you suppose the Select Commitee would have to say about this?" the Rabbi asked.

"I'll know soon enough, Rabbi. I got my subpoena over the weekend," said Griffin.

"Forget the goddamn hearings, everybody I know is tapped out!" Horwitz said.

"Look, people, we haven't got a lot of options here. It would take us six months to raise fifteen million federal. We just don't have the time. I promise the ads will be broad enough that they'll fly with the FEC."

"And if they don't?"

"Aw c'mon, guys, how the hell bad can it get? We've lived through an impeachment inquiry, for chrissakes. I mean honestly, same shit different day. What the hell is a little fine anyway?" said Hanson. "Besides, the Repos got nailed for doing the same thing back in '96."

"You've got to be kidding," Zev said.

"I'm serious as a heart attack. The new committee doesn't give a damn about us. They want the Veep," Hanson explained.

"I can make it happen if you get me either of the principals for an event either here or in New York," Cynthia said.

Hanson rolled his eyes. Impossible.

"No way," Griffin said. "Neither the POTUS nor the VPOTUS can do an event between now and the election. And don't even mention the First Lady."

"We're not talking heavy lifting here, Tom. Just a cocktail party in somebody's home. My people can work fast . . ."

"I'm sure they can," Griffin said, "but try telling that to the schedulers. Last time I checked, we still had a country to run."

"I'm with Mike on this one," said Griff. "The press is watching Albert's every move. I'm not taking any chances. I'm not letting any Buddhist Temple screw-ups bite us in the ass this time," he said, almost shouting. "Read my lips, there is no availability between now and the election. Understand, we need your help, but you're going to have to rely on good old-fashioned strong-arming to get it done. Right, Hef?"

"That's right, Tom," said the grizzled old labor organizer. "Frankly, I didn't know there was any other way."

"I hear you. So that's it, kids. The Prescott campaign's got the Select Committee, the NRA, the Christian Coalition, and every fucking tobacco company in America. Rumor has it that they're about to cut a deal with the third-party candidate, Ben Thurman. All I've got is you. The two-minute warning has sounded, we're leading by a field goal and we're on their one-yard line. This is the final push. Either you guys come through for a win, or the other side, who's bigger, meaner, and better-financed, will march all the fucking way down the field and score with only seconds left on the clock. The choice is yours," said Griffin.

"Three million in a week," the Bundlemeister said. "I can do that with my eyes closed. I'm in."

Hanson breathed out heavily with relief. Both he and Griffin grinned at each other.

"So, who else wants to elect a president?" asked Hanson, knowing victory was at hand.

One by one, everyone got on board, even the skeptical Cynthia Miles.

"Okay, now, everyone knows the drill. We need three million by the third. Individuals and corps, U.S. citizens, please. Make sure all the checks get made out to the party's nonfederal account," Griffin said.

"Not the coordinated campaign?" Horwitz asked.

"Sure, if you want it reported and want to have your donor's name appear in the *Post*," said Hanson.

Shaking his head, Griffin jumped in. "Trust me, this is the only way to go," he said. "And don't worry about getting windowed. One trick I learned from the Republicans. Even when it's reported, it won't be until next quarter, long after the election's over."

"That's why they call you the Messiah of Money," the Bundlemeister said. "No offense, Rabbi."

"None taken."

Griffin began to speak, but was interrupted by an electronic beep from his intercom. His secretary's voice filled the room. "Griff, the Vice President's holding on line one for you. He's calling from a plane and says it's important."

"Mr. President," said Griffin, taking the call on speaker. "Flying commercial, I assume."

"Hey, I could get used to the sound of that. But let me tell you, the cost of jet fuel is no bargain. Hey, Tom, I hate to interrupt, but if it's okay with you, I'd like to just tell everybody there just how much I appreciate all their hard work. . . ."

The shamelessness of the stunt was not lost on Hanson, who once again, for the sake of his friend as well as the campaign, bit his tongue and kept a straight face.

Chapter Five

As soon as the meeting broke up, Hanson and Griffin started down the hallway to Hanson's office for their next meeting. Falcone came up behind them.

"Mind if I walk with you guys?"

"Hey, Bundles, now isn't the best time. We've got to go to war with a deadbeat," Hanson said. But when he saw the look on the Bundlemeister's face, he said, "Let's talk while we walk."

As they walked down the hallway, Hanson had the strangest feeling of déjà vu. After all, this was recycled office space, used first by the Hart campaign in '84, then Dukakis in '88 and the current President in '92 and '96. Hanson had been through four of his five presidentials and never changed addresses. From his vantage point, the only things that changed were the haircuts of the volunteers and the wall posters. Twenty years ago, it was "Stop Nuclear Power!", followed by "Free Mandela," then "We Are the World," and "Fight the Power," then a whole lot of stuff about Generation X. And while he steadfastly refused to admit he was pushing forty, Hanson was acutely aware that this was the first time in a campaign that almost everyone instinctively referred to him as "sir" or "Mr." Hanson.

"So how you guys holdin' up? Any butterflies?" asked the Bundlemeister.

"Not really. I mean what the fuck can the committee ask us this time that they didn't two years ago? Typical election year bullshit!" Hanson said.

"When do you testify?"

"I go at four today. Mike doesn't get the chair until tomorrow," joked Griffin.

Falcone was genuinely concerned. "Word has it that they're all hung up on the China thing again. You know, all that Los Alamos bullshit."

"No big deal. Been there, done that."

Guys, just be careful to keep your stories straight. Whatever you do, don't contradict your earlier testimony."

"Bundles, since when do you let the Repos get under your skin?"

"Ever since they decided that impeachment was an effective substitute for the Electoral College. Mike, make no mistake about it, I've been through this before. It's *hunting season* in good ole D.C. They don't get you the first time so they bring you back just to trip you up, to make you perjure yourself. Just remember the three rules of surviving a Congressional investigation: admit nothing; deny everything; if backed into a corner, attack with countercharges!" Falcone said, in a deadly serious tone.

"Yes, father."

"Hey guys, maybe it's just me, but does anyone mind if we change the fucking subject!" roared an exasperated Griffin.

"Gladly," the Bundlemeister said with a smile. "Per your request for the three large. What would you say if I told you that I got a head start?"

Griffin and Hanson stopped abruptly. "I'd say I want to have your child!" Griffin said.

"You can't," said Hanson. "I saw him first. Bundlemeister, you really are the man. And thanks for your help back there. We were losing them."

"Guys, the party ain't over yet," said Falcone, handing a fat envelope to Griffin.

Taking it in his enormous hand, Griffin felt it carefully, as if to weigh the parcel. "So Bundles, what do we have here? Are we talking six figures?"

"Keep going . . ."

Griffin's eyes lit up.

"Don't tell me we got a telephone number here, Bundles," said Griffin, barely able to contain his enthusiasm. "Because, if you do, I'm making the switch, and you and I are going on a moonlight cruise."

"Try long distance," the Bundlemeister said proudly. Hanson and Griffin exchanged looks.

"Geezus Christ, Bundles, what did you do, start bundling soft money?" asked Hanson, incredulously. "Nobody bundles soft money."

The Bundlemeister just turned and started to walk away. He looked back once. "There are checks in there from fifty of the biggest law firms in the country. The smallest check is for twenty-five grand. Never forget who loves you."

Falcone disappeared around the corner with Griffin and Hanson staring in amazement. "I honestly love that guy," Hanson said.

"A truly great American," said Griffin.

"Come on. Next victim," Hanson said as he opened the door to his office. This wouldn't be so pleasant. Hanson had no respect for the grossly overweight man sitting alone inside. Leonard Lynch ran the government relations shop for Monarch Oil, one of the largest oil companies in the world, and also happened to be a Republican who thought he was smart enough to play both sides of the street. The trouble was, he tended to run his mouth and make promises he had no way of keeping. Hanson decided to play hardball today and dispense with all greetings.

"Okay, Lenny, what's so fucking urgent? Let me guess. You want me to set up another appointment with the POTUS so you can prove to him all over again how full of shit you are," said Hanson.

Lynch looked up, shocked. "Michael, what's with the attitude? I've delivered you guys a helluva lot of money over the years," he whined, wringing his hands.

"Exactly wrong!" Griffin boomed. "As far as I'm concerned, you haven't done shit for us. Do you have any idea how badly you embarrassed Michael with the President?"

"Why the fuck does he care? The guy is a lame duck. Hell, you can't get a whole lot lamer than the President. I mean that guy ought to be grateful that anyone will give him the time of day."

"You watch your goddamn mouth, motherfucker! Don't think you can come into my house and talk that kind of trash," Hanson warned. "The President is my friend." He paused and looked at Griff.

"Correction. He's our friend," said Griffin. "Don't forget it, Lenny. As for business, you came to us and said that Monarch was going to do two hundred fifty grand this year. So, where is it? Huh?" he said, looking at Lynch expectantly.

"It's not that simple. I've got to get clearance from our board," Lynch said.

Hanson knew this was a waste of time. "Board clearance my ass, Lenny. You don't think we've got friends over at the RNC? We know you guys gave almost a million to the fucking Republicans. So what gives?"

Lynch started to sweat, knowing he'd been caught. "Guys, here's the problem. We've given you about ninety-five thousand this year."

"Yeah, which makes you around a hundred and fifty short."

"Hold on, let me explain. See, every time the *Washington Post* or some other paper or magazine does a piece on campaign finance, they only publish the names of the donors over a hundred grand."

"So, what else is fucking new?" said Hanson, knowing exactly where this was leading.

"See, Monarch Oil doesn't want to be windowed, you know . . . on record as giving that much to the Democrats."

"But it's all right to get windowed supporting the GOP?"

"We're an oil company, for chrissakes. Our shareholders expect that," he said. "But look. I think I figured out a way to make good on Monarch's commitment."

Hanson and Griffin both rolled their eyes. "We're listening," Griffin said.

"You guys ever hear of the National Wholesale Meat Distributors Association?"

"Yeah, the NWMDA, about as Republican an association as they come," said Hanson.

"Well, they want to get in the game. They are prepared to make good on the balance of our commitment."

"Lenny, that's what's known as a phantom-conduit. Have you been asleep for the last two years? It's borderline illegal." Hanson said.

"Only if you get caught," said Lynch.

"Lenny, we're the Democrats, for chrissakes. We always get caught!"

"This stinks just like the Teamsters deal," Griff said. "You wearing a wire, Lenny?"

"God, you people are a paranoid bunch. Unless the FEC can prove the money came from us, everything's kosher. Am I right?"

Hanson knew what Lynch failed to realize. Even if Griffin green-lighted the deal, things would never be kosher again between Lynch and the Dems. He tried to screw them over, and they knew it.

"And the NWMDA doesn't mind being windowed?" Griffin asked.

"They couldn't care less. But there's only one hitch . . ."

"I knew it," said Hanson, exasperated. "All right, let's have it."

"Okay, here it goes. The NWMDA has given a lot of money to a certain leadership PAC in town that has been pretty heavily investigated, and well, they don't want to give any more until the heat dies down."

"Let me guess, you pick up their slack and they write a fat check to us covering your ass. So, who is it Lenny?" Hanson demanded.

In a timid voice, Lynch said the words softly. "The Family Research Council."

Hanson watched as Griffin blew up.

"The FRC? I hate the FRC! No deal. If you want to give to those bastards, go ahead, I can't stop you. But tell your friends to keep their fucking money. If I have to cut that deal to get a lousy one fifty, I'm in the wrong line of work," Griffin said, his face turning redder and redder. "I'm outta here!"

As Griffin stormed out of Hanson's office and slammed the door, Hanson listened to Lynch desperately pleading his case.

"Mike, please. We want to make things right with the President.

What do I have to do? We'll make the whole thing out to the Legal Defense Fund if that's what you want!"

Hanson looked at Lynch, realizing that this would be easy. "Lenny, I really don't know what to say. Forget about the Defense Fund. You and I both know that the Fund has a ten-thousand-dollar limit. What we're trying to do here is win an election. But you've burned us once and now you want us to accept a bullshit arrangement, while your company is giving a goddamn boatload to our enemy. Worst of all, you want us to like it. As for Griff, everyone knows he's a true believer, he takes this shit real seriously."

"Can't you think of anything?"

Hanson fell silent and looked up at the ceiling. After several awkward seconds, he said, "Well Lenny, it might help if you and the meat guys closed the gap a little bit."

"How much closer does it have to be?"

"I'd say at this point you gotta meet us more than halfway if I'm going to be able to sell it to Griff. You tell your meat guys that the number is a half a million. Deliver it and all is forgiven."

"But what if they can't go that high?"

"Oh, I got a feeling they can, particularly since Monarch's gotta be giving at least that much to GOPAC. That's the deal. Take it or leave it," Hanson said.

For a moment Lynch just sat there like a prize fighter who'd just been counted out. Then, with defeat in his eyes, he got up, waved a meek goodbye to Hanson, and started for the door.

"And by the way, Lenny, two more things. No money changes hands between Monarch and the meat guys. That's money laundering. If you bastards want to cover the other's commitments, that's got nothing to do with us. So if you are wearing a wire, tell the fucking committee or the special prosecutor that we will only except the money with your assurance that you fellas aren't funneling it back and forth. Got it?"

Still feeling the effects of the earlier tongue-lashing, Lenny meekly said, "What's the other condition?"

"We want the check here by close of business tomorrow. Got it?"

About thirty seconds after Lynch exited Hanson's office, his phone rang. "So did he buy it?"

"Hook, line, and sinker. Got them up to a half a mill," said Hanson.

"Do you believe that fucking guy?" Griffin asked. "I mean coming right out and suggesting a phantom conduit. With all the shit that's going on. Man, do you think he was setting us up?"

"Who knows. But don't worry, I handled it. . . ."

"Never a doubt in my mind, ole buddy. Like I always say, we didn't write the lyrics to this song, Mike, we just sing them better than anyone else in town," Griffin said. "All things considered though, a job well done, huh, buddy?"

"Not bad. Not bad at all."

"So, waddaya say we celebrate after work. How does Nathan's sound to you?"

"How about I catch up with you about nine-ish. I gotta meet Adam Melrose for a drink about seven . . ."

Griff took a deep sigh. The very sound of Adam's name made him cringe. "Mike, how many times do I have to warn you to just steer clear of that guy? He is nothin' but trouble."

"Griff, that guy has also bailed you and me out at least a dozen times when we came up short. And not just with his checkbook . . ."

"His daddy's checkbook, Michael."

"Whatever. The point is, he's our friend and you and I can use all of those we can get."

"Don't remind me. All right, do what you want, Mr. Good Samaritan. Just remember, we don't need any surprises. Okay?"

"Gotcha."

"See ya about nine."

"Sounds like a plan," said Hanson, and he hung up the phone.

Chapter Six

Only at the Atlantic Flyer Lounge in the Delta terminal at Reagan National Airport could the improbable mixture of neon, chrome, Corinthian leather, and Berber carpet sprinkled with remnants of free chicken wings equate to interior design. Notwithstanding the facts that the drinks were ridiculously watered down and the bar contained enough secondhand smoke to make your lungs bleed, the cheesy decor offered a backdrop to a rare venue in Washington—a place where reporters almost never showed their faces. While most of the local press corps had spent years staking out every watering hole in town—especially those frequented by the likes of Hanson and Griffin—they had somehow missed this joint. That its clientele was made up largely of nomadic travelers, mostly salesmen with no interest in politics, was a plus. Another was a beaten-up television that ran a close-captioned version of CNN twenty-four hours a day, reportedly the result of a theft of the remote control by a busboy in 1993.

"Is this Naugahyde?" Hanson asked.

"No. It's leather," said the cocktail waitress, a frazzled blonde sporting way too much eyeliner.

"No, this is definitely Naugahyde. My parents' entire house was Naugahyde. It was really big in the 70's."

"I wouldn't know, sir. I wasn't even born in the 70's," she retorted, having no way of knowing that she had struck Hanson below the belt with the dreaded "sir" comment. "Sir, may I get you something?"

Virtually certain she wasn't going to ask him for his I.D. a disgusted Hanson said, "Cutty on the rocks, make it a double. And bring me a vodka gimlet for my perennially tardy guest."

As he waited there for Adam to make an appearance, he kept hearing Griffin's warning over and over in his mind, "Mike, whatever you do, just steer clear of Adam Melrose." Hanson laughed aloud. Steer clear of Adam Melrose? Griff had to be kidding. Adam, the scion of the wealthiest family in Delaware and fledgling congressional candidate, was in D.C. every week trying to drum up PAC money. When he wasn't in D.C. he was in New York for more of the same. Avoiding Adam was next to impossible. So when he called the night before in a panic, Hanson felt it was better to just get it over with. Knowing Adam would be heading up to New York that evening, Hanson suggested the airport lounge, figuring it was as good a place as any to hear all the gory details of the latest crisis de jour in the life of his ethically challenged friend.

Almost as if by instinct, Adam made his grand entrance at the same moment the drinks arrived. "Michael, you saint. You absolutely shouldn't have."

Hanson, fully acquainted with Adam's vices, responded, "Obviously *you* have. Hit a couple of fund-raisers on the way over, huh, bud?"

Adam smiled his characteristically devilish smile. Handing the waitress a fifty and waving her away dismissively, he said, "Nice to see you too, Michael." Then, raising his glass, he offered, "Cheers. To the only friend I have left in this city."

This is weird, Hanson thought. Adam lived his life like Peter Pan, he just didn't get this morose. Whatever it was, it must be bad. "Cut the sweet talk, fuckhead. You're still buyin'."

"I'm deeply moved by your concern."

Hanson knew from experience that for every drink Adam ingested, the essence of his story would be amplified tenfold. With this in mind, Hanson cut to the chase. "Okay, big guy, what's goin' on? Did the committee subpoena you or something?"

"I wish," snapped Adam as he hoisted his drink, swallowing it in one gulp. "There's a lot to be said for testifying in public. You know, free air time and all."

"Somehow I don't think that would be all that helpful."

"Don't underestimate the value of name recognition, Michael. At this point I'll take anything I can get."

Hanson took a moment and studied Adam, who was now holding his empty glass aloft to signal the waitress for a refill. In a matter of seconds the blonde arrived with another round. Something about his friend's WASP good looks, Canali suits, and fifty-dollar tips always seemed to inspire good service. On the outside it was the same old Adam, all six feet three inches of him, so perennially tan it was as if skin cancer didn't exist. And thanks to his hairdresser, his thinning hair was still blond. Ever fit and meticulously groomed, Adam was, as usual, well on his way to inebriation. But it was clear that this time something was very wrong. The fact was that Adam, having ignored the stern warnings of Hanson, Griffin, and just about everybody that knew him, was absolutely determined to become the next congressman from Delaware's third district.

While many considered him to be a competent party operative, few people took him seriously as a candidate, especially not Hanson, who regarded him as more of a wayward little brother. But over the last several months, Adam Melrose had proved everyone wrong, spending months in the trenches of a brutal primary campaign, ultimately coming out on top. With only weeks to go until the election, he was sitting comfortably on an eight-point lead. This despite the fact that he had been called by the Independent Counsel to testify before the grand jury on three separate occasions. Each time the team of prosecutors subjected him to twelve-hour marathon sessions focusing on Hanson's connections to the White House. Each time Adam stood his ground, steadfastly refusing to implicate Hanson in anything shady. Hanson knew that Adam refused to roll over despite the fact that he cared about this race more than anything in the world. For him to even joke about getting a subpoena from the Committee in the last weeks of his campaign was simply bizarre. For once in his life Adam Melrose wasn't just crying wolf. Hanson took a long sip of his drink and leaned over the table.

"Listen, ole buddy, I've got a lot on my plate. And you've gotta catch a flight. I want to be helpful. So just how much trouble are you in?"

"Deep, deep shit," Adam said, turning his head away, unable to look Hanson in the eye.

"How bad could it be? Did Larry Flynt get some anonymous tip that you're playing hide the salami with some alderman's wife or something?"

For several seconds Adam tried to speak but was unable to get the words out. Finally, he said, "Michael, it's worse. Much worse than that. . . ."

"Geez, would you lighten up? The only thing worse than getting caught boning another guy's wife this close to an election is getting caught boning another guy," joked Hanson. "So come on, let's have it."

Adam tossed down his drink, again giving the signal for a refill. "Michael, I'd say you're getting pretty warm."

Hanson stared at Adam, taken aback. For several seconds, as the waitress delivered the next round and stood there, determined to weasel out another outrageous tip, he recalled all the rumors dating back to the Mondale campaign, how he dismissed them, never thinking in a million years that Adam would keep something so important from him. But there, as he waited for the young blonde to walk out of earshot, he could see that the truth was written all over Adam's face. "Holy shit! You're not kidding. Does the other side know?"

"I don't think so. Not yet anyway. But see, there's this reporter . . ."

"Oh shit, I knew it. Who's the bastard?"

"Rick Seltzer," said Adam.

"Rick Seltzer. That asshole we ran into in Chicago? Who does he write for, the *Blade* or one of those gay rags?"

"Yeah. But Rick is also a big player in Queer Nation. A big player! I think I'm about to be outed."

Hanson took a deep breath and took a look around to make sure there were no eavesdroppers. This was bad. The Dems were in a position to take back control of the House for the first time in years. They just couldn't afford to lose another seat, especially not this one. If this wasn't handled right, Adam would be front-page news, labeled a fraud and a liar. "So, old friend. What the hell did you do to piss off Seltzcr?"

Nervously, Adam squirmed in his seat, trying to muster the nerve to tell Hanson the truth. He looked at his watch. "You know, this Rolex always runs slow. I don't want to miss my flight. I really gotta start wearing my Rado . . ."

It was obvious to Hanson that he was getting near the root of the problem. "Adam, you're giving me a coronary over here. Tell me what you did to this guy?"

"Well, I don't know exactly. In fact, I thought we were friends. But then I get this call yesterday, and he starts telling me that he's sick of my elitist attitude and that he can't protect me any longer. He says it is his obligation as a journalist to report the news regardless of who gets hurt."

Hanson was skeptical. He remembered how miserably Adam treated women in the old days. He couldn't be that much better to men. "Bullshit. I'm gonna give you three seconds to tell me what happened. After that I'm gone. . . ."

"It's just like I told you . . ."

"THREE!"

"All right goddamn it, Rick and I were involved. Is that what you wanted to hear?"

"What a shock. So are you telling me that this is some sort of lovers' quarrel?"

"Apparently so. Rick doesn't like me spending so much time with Antonio."

"Antonio. Who the fuck is Antonio?"

"My driver."

"Ah Geeze . . ."

"He's a wonderful guy. You'd love him."

"Uh, Adam, let's not go there. Let's try to focus on the problem. First, I just gotta know, has this been going on for a while?"

Hanson's question immediately put Adam on the defensive. "Why does it matter?"

"It matters because the longer you've been out there looking for Mr. Right, the more chance that another Rick Seltzer will come out of the woodwork."

Adam took a last gulp of his drink, finally having had his fill. Then, for the next ten minutes, he bared his soul, confessing in excruciating detail how for more than a decade he'd lived the life of a closeted gay man, terrified that his secret would be discovered. He told of his liberal use of escort services, of falling in love with a young employee in his family's business, of wild summers in Rehobeth and Fire Island, winters in Key West and finally, a regular pattern of cruising the gay bar scene in whatever city he happened to be in.

As for Hanson, a million thoughts were swirling through his head. The exposure was enormous. The Democratic National Committee had sunk a ton of cash into Melrose for Congress. Worse, Griff was certain to go ballistic. But none of that mattered to Hanson at the moment. Adam was his friend and his friend was in trouble. "Adam, my boy, believe it or not, this is your lucky day."

"How's that?"

"As we both know, there are few guys in town with my first-hand experience in managing sex scandals . . ."

"Or that will admit to it."

"Whatever. But the bottom line is that this is familiar territory for me," Hanson said. "Of course, you do realize this gives me the absolute right to give you shit for the rest of your life, don't you?"

"Yes, I am well aware of that, Michael. I don't know which is worse. Being publicly humiliated à la Marv Albert or having to deal with you," Adam said, with the hint of a smile lighting up his glum face.

"I don't know. There's a lot to be said for private humiliation, too. But let's not get ahead of ourselves. I'm pretty sure I can put the kibosh on this if I can get to Seltzer soon."

"How?"

"That doesn't concern you. Just promise me that you won't speak to him until I do. Got it?"

"Whatever you say . . ."

About this time, they were interrupted by the boarding call for the eight o'clock shuttle to LaGuardia. "You better get going," said Hanson as he stood up.

"Michael, I don't know what to say . . ." he began, his eyes welling up with tears.

"Adam, just relax. I'll kick Seltzer's ass if I have to. Believe me. It's handled," he said, extending his hand.

As they shook hands, Adam said, "Thank you so much, Michael."

By this time, Hanson was grinning with embarrassment. "Will you just get on the fucking plane, you idiot? And don't hit on the pilot."

With that, Adam gave Hanson the kind of dirty look that only brothers can give each other and get away with it. He turned and started for the gate certain of the fact that Hanson would indeed silence Rick Seltzer, and that he would hear about it every day for the rest of his life.

Hanson arrived at Nathan's, a turn-of-the-century-style saloon in the heart of Georgetown, just past ten o'clock, right as the Redskins turned the ball over on their own nine-yard line. The place was filled with dozens of drunken, angry fans. None of them, however, were drunker or angrier than Tom Griffin.

"Fuck you, ref!" shouted Griffin, giving the television the finger. "He was down, he was down, you asshole!"

Hanson could recognize that sound of agony anywhere.

"Blow me, you fucking zebra!"

Hanson looked up at the television as he navigated through the crowd. Bad news. The referee had just tagged a Redskins linebacker with a personal foul, a fifteen-yard unsportsmanlike penalty.

"Eat shit!" came Griffin's unmistakable roar.

Hanson was getting close. Finally arriving at the television, he found Griffin.

"Redskins suck!" Hanson said.

Griffin turned, ready to defend the honor of the home team. When he saw Hanson, his look of outrage melted into a broad grin. "Hey Mike, where the hell you been?" he said, slapping Hanson high five. "So how did it go with Adam?"

"Ask me in about eight drinks."

"Works for me."

"So how did it go before the Committee?" Hanson asked.

"Let me quote a wise man I once met. Ask me in about eight drinks."

Hanson laughed. "It looks like you've already had eight drinks."

"Nine, but who's counting?" retorted Griffin. "Hey, check out this game, we're getting our asses kicked."

"How much time is left?"

"Thirty seconds."

"What's the score?"

"37–20, New York."

"I like the action. I'll give you the Skins and sixteen," said Hanson.

"You're a real fucking comedian, Mike. I get one night off in two years and the Skins blow it. It's not fair."

"I agree. It's not fair, you shouldn't get any nights off. How the hell are we gonna elect a president with you out getting hammered?" he said, provoking a dirty look from Griffin. "All right, relax. Let me buy you a drink."

"That'll work." They headed for the bar as the crowd thinned out. "Where the hell's everyone going?"

"Home. Unlike us, these people have real homes and real jobs to go to in the morning," Hanson explained.

"Poor bastards."

"I hear you," Hanson agreed as they sat down at the bar. "That's the great thing about politics, the hours are long."

"But the pay sucks," said Griffin, finishing his friend's thought. "Make mine a double."

"Two double Glenmorangies on the rocks," Hanson said to the bartender. "So Griff, it looks like I gave you an excuse to get out and howl a little?"

"No shit, between Bundlemeister and the way we worked Lenny, we might pull this race out . . ."

"You sound a little shaky, big man," Hanson said, sensing that something was amiss.

Griff took a long gulp of his drink. "Hell, Mike, I'm just nervous as hell about the fifteen million. I mean, I'm not worried about you and Bundles. But the others, I'm not so sure."

"They're the best in the business, Griff," Hanson said, trying to be upbeat.

"You and I know our base is tapped out. I can't blame the

angels if the money just ain't there. Our only hope now is that fucking Thurman will just stay in the race."

Hanson lowered his voice, always on the alert for eavesdroppers. "What's the word?"

Griffin leaned forward, almost spilling his drink on Hanson, and whispered, "We just got the new numbers in. Hardly anybody's seen them. With Thurman's third party in the race, we're up by about four points according to our own poll. Without him, we're dead in the water."

"Any word from our spies?"

"The deal is about 90 percent done."

"So what else is new? Just once I'd like to be in a campaign where the fucking Republicans couldn't outspend us ten to one. Just once."

"What the hell. Without our Republican buddies, we'd be out of jobs. Besides, I suppose things could be worse. Think how bad it would be if Oliver Devon was stirring the pot," said Griffin.

"Devon? The 'Repo Man'? Are you kidding me? We'd be screwed, blewed, and tattooed. I still can't believe he's sitting this one out," Hanson said. Whenever Devon's name came up, it meant trouble for the Democrats.

"Let's just be grateful that after Forbes got shellacked on Super Tuesday, Devon picked up his ball, as well as his money, and went home. The guy just can't stomach a 'kinder, gentler' Republican Party."

"Thank God!" Hanson said. "Is that all we know?"

"Yep, but I'll keep looking into it. There's nothing we can do until the Repos show their hand."

Business as usual in good old D.C., thought Hanson. Changing the subject, he said, "Griff, in all seriousness. How did it go today?"

Griffin began to move his huge neck from side to side as if it were getting stiff. He looked around for any signs of electronic eavesdropping, as if anybody could overhear anything above the din of crowd noise. Taking a moment to gulp down the last of his drink, he said, "Mike, if you want to know the truth, they ripped me a new asshole."

"About what?" asked a stunned Hanson. "Did they come up with anything new?"

"No, not exactly. I really couldn't tell," Griffin said. "They got this new chief counsel who is an absolute ball buster."

"Who is he?"

"It's a she. Her name is Danielle Harris."

"Danielle Harris is the new chief counsel?" Hanson asked quizzically.

"Yeah, you know her?"

"Not really. But a lot of my friends do. About ten years ago all I ever heard was Danielle Harris this and Danielle Harris that. I mean they made her out to be this living saint for chrissakes. For years they told me that if I ever wanted to meet a really nice girl that they would set me up."

"So what was the problem?" said Griffin.

"If you recall, in those days I had no interest in meeting a nice girl."

"Well lemme tell you, she wasn't so nice today."

Hanson was intrigued. "Are you sure she's a Republican?"

"Mikey, I don't know what she is, just that she kicked my ass today. If I were you, I'd be on guard tomorrow," Griff warned, shaking his head in frustration.

"Thanks for the heads-up."

"So, how's the Jag running?" asked the Messiah, knowing that after politics, Hanson's favorite subject was his new car. It didn't hurt that he received the Jaguar, a sixty-thousand-dollar black beauty, as part of his divorce settlement with his ex-wife.

"As a matter of fact, it's running great. I put the new plates on yesterday."

"What do they say?"

" 'BAGMAN,' what else?"

Griffin laughed. "Man, you're unbelievable. I remember when you couldn't pay your Visa bill, and now you drive a nicer car than the fucking POTUS."

"The POTUS isn't allowed to drive, you drunken moron."

Feeling no pain by this time, Griffin responded, "On behalf of the next president of the United States I resent being called a drunken moron. A drunken consultant, often. A drunken fundraiser, whenever possible, but you'd have trouble proving it. A drunken lover, without question. But a drunken moron, never!"

Hanson laughed. After this grueling day, they both deserved a few drinks. He downed his drink and finally felt on the verge of loosening up. Then he saw Paul Angelo.

"Sleazebags!" Angelo yelled from across the bar. He started to make his way over to them with a young blonde at least thirty years his junior on his arm.

Hanson bristled. He, like most Georgetown locals, had known Angelo for years and considered him a sleaze of unprecedented dimension. Angelo, a local pub owner, was also a loudmouth, who dished out his insults indiscriminately. Hanson had always found it fascinating that Angelo himself was virtually impossible to insult; he had skin thicker than an alligator's.

"So, how are you two felons doing?"

"Felons? Get it right, you fucking fossil, we are unindicted coconspirators," said Hanson, enjoying the abuse. He smiled menacingly at Angelo. Griffin knew exactly what he was thinking and grabbed him firmly by the elbow.

"Take it easy, Mikey, we only got a few more days."

Hanson nodded. Turning his attention to Angelo, he said, "Sleazeballs, felons? Griff, is it that obvious we're Democrats?"

"Bartender, get my two sleazeball friends a round of drinks, on me. I want you two boys to enjoy your last days of freedom. Once we get the White House back, we're gonna indict the whole lot of you."

The girl on Angelo's arm giggled.

"So Paul, what's up with that Viagra, anyway?" Hanson asked.

The blonde's sugary smile disappeared and she scowled at Hanson.

"Babe, why don't you go get us a table while I get our drinks?" Angelo said. She left compliantly, attracting stares as she sauntered away.

Hanson rolled his eyes and the drinks arrived. "Drink up, losers," Angelo said, gloating.

"On behalf of Democrats everywhere, we thank you," said Griffin.

Angelo missed the sarcasm. "Hey, you guys hear about the trouble over at the Pavilion?"

"What kind of trouble?" Griffin asked.

"Man, it was crazy!" he said, shaking his head. "There was a party on the seventh floor last night, you guys know what I mean.

Anyway, one of the girls either OD'd or got beat up real bad. Guys were flying out of there like rats, and I think the girl died. The place was crawling with cops."

"You sound like you were there," Hanson said.

"No, but friends of mine were," he said. "Hey Mike, come to think of it, doesn't your ex work those parties?"

"My ex lives in L.A.," said Hanson, growing uncomfortable.

"No, no, not that ex . . . your high school sweetheart, CeCe."

Hanson, his back turned to Angelo, facing the bar, said, "What's your point?" Angelo was beginning to enjoy himself.

"Hanson, don't tell me you're still carrying a torch for CeCe—she's a fucking hooker! That bitch got one of her girls killed last night."

That did it. He'd been dealing with all sorts of shit today and wasn't about to take any more. Angelo wouldn't utter another syllable. Hanson didn't even bother to turn around. Instead, wheeling around to his right, he backhanded Angelo across the right side of his face. Even though he held a little back, the blow was plenty hard enough to send Angelo tumbling back across the dance floor. Hanson then got up slowly from his barstool, expecting retaliation, but there was none. It was one of the few times that Paul Angelo ever acted his age. He stayed on the floor, dazed, furious, and scared. Hanson shook his head in disgust. Angelo might have wanted to pick a fight, but he certainly wasn't up to finishing one.

Griffin ordered another round from the annoyed bartender, and he and Hanson watched as Angelo was helped up off the bar floor.

Angelo walked toward Hanson, but not as close as before. "That's assault, you sonofabitch! I could sue your ass."

"The way I saw it, it was self-defense," Hanson said.

"No question. You threw the first punch, Paul. I saw it," said Griffin. "You sure you're okay, Mike?"

Hanson was still angry. "Paul, why don't you get the fuck out of here before I double your pleasure?"

With some encouragement from his date, Angelo finally left, yelling threats as he exited onto Wisconsin Avenue. As often happens after a brawl, Nathan's had nearly emptied, leaving Hanson and Griff to close the place.

"Last call, *gentlemen*," yelled the bartender in a weary, jaded voice.

"Two Remys. Make them doubles," Griff said, knowing that Hanson needed a nightcap. "Don't let that prick upset you. He's a has-been and he knows it."

As they sat there sipping their drinks, Hanson couldn't shake a vague sense of unease. He wondered about the incident at the Pavilion. Was CeCe really involved? And who was the girl? Most of all, he wondered, who killed her?

Chapter Seven

Twenty-four hours after the young girl was murdered, Kennedy came back to the scene of the crime, and sat alone in the only chair left intact in Suite 701. Yesterday forensics had hauled the body away to the coroner's lab to be further violated, and the crime scene unit was through. Kennedy wanted to be alone in the room. He wanted to look around and get a sense of what had happened here last night. The horror was even more apparent without the body: broken glass shards glittered dangerously, and the blood had dried on the walls to a dull reddish brown. The solitude was broken only by the soft whoosh of air as the room's ventilation system clicked on, followed by the coughing sputter as it clicked off.

Kennedy's gloved hand flipped over the small, pink, numbered evidence tag hanging from the victim's pocketbook. In his haste, or perhaps out of fear, the killer must have tossed it into a large green Dumpster behind the flashing neon sign of a dancing bull and hen at an all-night steak and egg joint, just two doors away from the Capital Pavilion and a block from the White House. A uniformed Secret Service officer found the bag when he was called to break up a fight between two winos in Lafayette Park, the small, decorative meadow directly in front of the White House. The officer knew the two winos well. They, along with many other homeless people, made the park their personal campground. The homeless were drawn to this pocket of green because the tight security around the White House made it a safe place to flop. During the day, it was full of idealistic protesters and generous tourists, easy marks for handouts. At night, the park filled with homeless people who came to bed down on benches and on the ground under the lights of the White House looming before them.

Unlike most cities, which have but one police force, Washington D.C. is policed by no less than four uniformed police departments. Even though Lafayette Park is technically the jurisdiction of the National Park Service rangers, its proximity to the White House and its potential to harbor threats to the safety of the President put it also within the jurisdiction of the uniformed Secret Service. D.C. is like that, everyone has some claim on someone else's turf.

The officer who came upon the purse had been assigned to "walk the green," as the service called it. In his two months as a glorified park ranger, he had become familiar with the park's residents. Among the bench crowd, two stood out: a tall gangly recluse with wild matted hair, and his drinking buddy, known as "Mad Dog" because of his penchant for the booze by the same name. Most nights, the officer found this odd twosome fighting over a bottle, but tonight they wrestled on the ground, tugging at the woman's purse tangled up between them. After threats of being hauled away on a robbery rap, the two were fast to tell their tale, to distance themselves from the bounty they had fought over moments before. In slurred, excited voices, they told the officer how they found it while looking for dinner in the Dumpster.

The girl's killer was either an amateur or the murder wasn't planned in advance, Kennedy thought, or the purse would never have been found. He must have panicked. For the first time, Kennedy felt he had a chance of solving this case.

The small black quilted purse with gold chain strap now emitted the heavy, sour odor of fast food grease. The contents felt slick to the touch, so slick that he found them hard to handle and they kept slipping from his grasp.

Kennedy was a voyeur with a purpose. Each item was a window into what was, until a few hours ago, a life. The victim chewed spearmint gum, perhaps to stop smoking the Marlboros he found in a side pocket. She had clipped an old, yellowing article from *Cosmo* magazine recommending ten things to do to relax in stressful social situations. She wore Burgundy Compulsion lipstick, rode the metro, and had a rail card with eighty cents left unused. Tonight the city was eighty cents richer.

The other contents spoke of a less innocent existence. Assorted condoms—she was either a safety-first modern woman, or a pro. The tube of K-Y Jelly and the amyl nitrate poppers said the latter. Party girls just weren't both that careful and that careless at once. Her expensive but worn wallet contained one hundred and fourteen dollars in cash, American Express, Visa, and Diner's Club cards, and a D.C. driver's license. He hoped that at least the I.D. would stick, or she would probably end up as Jane Doe number 109 this year.

Kennedy stared down at the Ivory girl portrait on the license. Ariel Fairchild, seventeen years old, was too young to drive after 9 P.M. alone, but not too young to wind up on the wrong side of a body bag zipper. There was little resemblance between the frozen, seen-it-all face of the corpse and this freshly scrubbed beauty, whose long blond ponytail and wide natural smile resisted even the harshness of a DMV mug shot. Whoever killed her liked them young, really young, he thought.

Once upon a time, back when he was a rookie, Kennedy might have wondered how this seventeen-year-old could have ended up in an expensive hotel room like this one. But his naivete had long since given way to cynicism. Each time he left his house and family to rub elbows with the gutter, a little more of the grime rubbed off on him. It was only after taking three bullets to the chest one night last year as he and Ira were trying to serve an arrest warrant that Kennedy's hard outlook began to soften. This change of heart was short-lived, however, as the sight of Ariel Fairchild's contorted young body jolted him back to reality. He hated to admit it, but deep down he knew the truth. Beauty and youthful dreams aside, you couldn't avoid the way things were. The betting odds were that she was a pro; a pro with connections to the White House, no less.

Using tweezers, Kennedy emptied the wallet, pulling out the illegible scraps of paper that had once carried phone numbers or lists of things to do. Then he pulled out the deck of credit cards. The cards had been well-used, run through scanners so often that the numbers were worn down to shadows. Stuck to the back of one of the cards was a tattered piece of paper, about the size of a business card. This was good. It could be the name of a john or the phone number for her service. Anything would be helpful. He carefully separated it from the plastic. What he found wasn't what he had in mind, but it was a start. The personal data card had probably come with the wallet and it, too, bore signs of use.

Paydirt! He whistled under his breath. Barely legible under the heading "In Case of Emergency Please Contact" was a name and a phone number.

Chapter Eight

When Mike Hanson first heard the knocking at his front door, he thought he was dreaming. His head was pounding and his tongue lay thick in his parched throat. How many scotches did he drink last night, anyway?

Hanson couldn't imagine who the hell would be knocking at this hour. Fuck them. He turned over and tried to get back to sleep.

The knocking continued, louder and louder. "Who the fuck is it? Do you have any idea what time it is?" Hanson yelled.

"Metropolitan Police. Would you please open the door, sir?"

"Police?" Hanson was confused. Why were they bothering him? For a second he wondered what he did after drinking with Griff last night. Nothing he could recall. Reassured, he yelled, "I didn't call the police!"

"I know, sir. Would you please open the door?"

Hanson gave up. He waded to the door and opened it to the two detectives standing on his front steps. He felt them staring at him, which reminded him that he was standing there naked except for a University of Virginia baseball cap and boxer shorts. He knew he reeked of booze.

Indignantly and more than a bit embarrassed, he asked, "What's the problem?"

"I'm Detective Kennedy from the Metropolitan Police, and this is Detective Murray. We're looking for a Michael Hanson. Are you Michael Hanson, sir?"

Hanson was in a daze. What were the cops doing at his house? He hadn't had any brushes with the law since some long-forgotten fraternity antics in his college years. "Yes, I'm Mike Hanson."

"Mr. Hanson, I'm afraid I have some bad news."

"Bad news?" he asked, wondering who he knew that could be in trouble. A surge of fear swelled in his stomach, and he suddenly felt nauseous.

"Yes, sir. Mr. Hanson, do you know an Ariel Fairchild?" Kennedy asked.

Now Hanson was confused. Fairchild. "No, that doesn't sound familiar. Why?"

"Miss Fairchild was murdered Saturday night. Are you sure you don't know her?"

Hanson was wide awake now. "Yes, I'm sure I don't know her. Come to think of it, why are you asking me these questions, Detective?"

"Mr. Hanson, you should be aware that documents found among the victim's personal effects have you listed as her next of kin."

Hanson heard the words but they didn't register. For just a second he was thrown, as the room spun. Methodically, he slowly inhaled a deep breath, trying to get his head straight.

"Mr. Hanson, did you hear what I said, sir?"

Hanson took another deep breath. "Yes, I heard you, Detective, but I don't know any Ariel Fairchild. What am I supposed to be, some long-lost cousin or something?"

Kennedy and Murray exchanged glances. Kennedy was famous on the force for his ability to know when someone was lying a mile away, but he wasn't quite sure about this guy—not yet, anyway.

"No, Mr. Hanson. According to documents in the victim's possession at the time of her death, she claims you are her . . ."

"Her what?"

"Her father, sir. She's identified you as her father."

Hanson went numb. Despite the cold morning air, he suddenly began to sweat.

"Are you okay, Mr. Hanson?"

His head still spinning, Hanson asked, "How did she die?"

"Well, actually," said Kennedy, as both detectives stepped into Hanson's foyer, "I was hoping you could tell me."

Part Two

"Politics is supposed to be the second oldest profession. Since coming to Washington, I have come to realize that it bears a very close resemblance to the first."

—Ronald Reagan

Chapter Nine

Lufthansa Flight 563 touched down at Kennedy Airport at roughly four o'clock, a few minutes ahead of schedule. The flight crew was relieved, as the two Austrian nationals in first class were proving more than they could handle. Since the layover in Miami, the two had consumed roughly twice their weight in vodka, schnapps, and whatever else was left in the wet bar, making sure to proposition every flight attendant on board. As far as anyone knew, they had no takers.

What the flight crew couldn't possibly know was the level of exhaustion, boredom, and plain old cabin fever the two men were experiencing. It had been a long trip, an extremely long trip. It began in Moscow, where the orders first came in from the Investors. From there it was a car ride to Minsk, where they picked up the cargo, a medium-sized briefcase. The only instructions: do not open the briefcase and under no circumstances let it be examined by airport X ray. After that it was an Aeroflot flight directly to Munich. Unfortunately, in Munich they encountered some difficulty with, of all things, the German Environmental Ministry. It seems that there had been a rash of attempts by Bavarian businessmen, Croatian nationals, and Russian black marketeers to smuggle nuclear contraband out of the former Soviet Union. According to Ministry officials, the illicit trafficking ranged from a few flakes of uranium to materials as volatile as highly enriched weapons-grade plutonium.

Luckily for the Austrians, the matter was handled by one of their close contacts in the Office of Customs Enforcement, who vouched for them, maintaining that they were diplomatic couriers in the employ of the Austrian government. Word came down that the visitors should be treated with the utmost respect. Once in the air, the two drank a toast to the old days. As two of the most feared agents in Stasi, the old East German KGB, it was good to know they still had some friends they could count on.

Both men were pros, as efficient and ruthless as East German strongman Erich Honnecker's "Dark Legion" had to offer. With resumes that included surveillance and cryptology instruction at Lubyanka, a tour with the dreaded Bulgarian KGB, as well as paramilitary training in Algeria, there was very little that was outside their scope of expertise. Even so, they were grateful to get the mission. With the fall of the Berlin Wall and subsequent reunification with the West, freelance opportunities were few and far between for ex-Stasi types. They had colleagues who once arrested Soviet Jews for trying to escape to the West, who now ran charters helping them immigrate to Israel. Others were in the import-export business, brokering human organs in Guatemala and Brazil. Still others weren't doing much of anything.

No sooner had the pilot parked the plane at the gateway than the two men sprinted off the plane and headed for the terminal, luggage in hand, asking impatiently for directions to 'diplomatic customs.' Once there, they passed through the security checkpoints unmolested. Although both men were born and raised just outside of Berlin, their cover as Austrian nationals once again served them well.

Waiting for them at the Avis rent-a-car booth was a late-model Lincoln Towncar in the name of Belarus. After using their counterfeit American I.D.s to pick up the car, they headed due east on the Seaford–Oyster Bay expressway toward Montauk. Their destination was Long Island Sound. With traffic, they had about a two-hour drive ahead of them.

The ride itself was uneventful, as they kept their speed down, given their level of alcohol consumption during the flight. This wasn't the Autobahn and the last thing they needed was to be pulled over by some redneck American cop. Along the way, the man in the passenger seat reassembled his weapon, a plastic Glock nine-millimeter pistol. For the most part, it was the perfect gun for their line of work, virtually undetectable by X ray, and hence airport security. The trouble was the metal slide and firing pin, which the man had carefully stashed in a lead cigarette case designed specifically for that purpose.

The men passed the time by talking about the many ways they intended to spend the $250,000, that the Investors had agreed upon. They had already received a $50,000 down payment via wire transfer to an offshore bank in the Caymans, with the balance due upon delivery of the cargo. The conversation helped them keep their minds off what exactly was in the locked suitcase that they were to deliver to the American clients, known to them only as the Investors. If the Investors were willing to front that much money for the cargo's delivery, then whatever it was, it must be worth millions. Being businessmen themselves, they couldn't help but wonder how much their client would pay for safe return of the cargo if somehow it didn't quite make it to its destination. But this was only a passing thought, as they were well aware of the consequences of trying to double-cross the Investors; both men would be dead within hours.

It was dusk. The sign up ahead read MONTAUK, POINTS NORTH, 2 MILES. This was it. Their orders were to turn off on the coastal highway and head north until signaled. When it came, they were to pull over on the shoulder and wait. Darkness was moving in quickly as they turned onto the highway. After a few minutes they began to wonder if they had overshot the drop-off point. Just then a light began to flash from a trawler about five hundred yards offshore. At first they were alarmed, thinking it was the Coast Guard. But despite the growing darkness, there was still just enough light to see that it was a fishing boat.

"What are they signaling?" the driver asked. "Is it Morse code?"

"No, not from what I can see. The mate is just flashing the light at us . . . no message. Pull over, this must be it. If nobody shows up, we'll start driving again."

The two ex-Stasi operatives didn't have to worry. No sooner had the driver come to a stop than another vehicle, a late-model Range Rover, pulled up behind them. The passenger readied his weapon as they both got out of the car. There were two men seated in the front of the truck. After a few seconds, the man on the passenger's side got out. Slowly he walked toward them carrying a metal briefcase.

"I'm Belarus. Do you have the cargo?"

"Yes. It's right here. Do you have the money?"

Belarus was irritated by the question. "Yeah. Right here. Now get the cargo."

"Not 'til we see the money," said the man holding the pistol.

"What do you guys think this is, some fucking drug deal? You work for us. Now get the merchandise before I have my friend back in the truck end this negotiation," he warned.

Both men looked past Belarus to see that the driver of the Range Rover was standing outside of the truck by now. It was too dark to see him clearly, but they could see the red light of his laser gunsight trained on them. Under the circumstances, they relented, handing over the cargo.

Belarus took the briefcase. "Here, take your money," he said, handing it to them. "Now I want you to go sit in your car and count it. I'm going back to the truck and check this out. If all is as it should be, we will drive off in that direction," he said, pointing south. "Wait until we're out of sight, then start driving north for about another ten miles. After that, you're on your own. But do not, I repeat, do not attempt to drive away until we are out of sight. Got it?"

The two men followed instructions and returned to the Lincoln. It was all quite simple. More than that, as they discovered when they began to count their money, it was profitable. It was all there, every penny of it. This was good news. Over the years, some clients had proven somewhat untrustworthy in making full payment for services rendered. The men were glad to see that the Investors were men of their word.

Belarus sat in the backseat of the Range Rover, inspecting the cargo. He was the only one with a key to the briefcase. Opening it carefully, he found a large pouch along with a thick, leather-bound notebook with an unbroken wax seal bearing the imprint of the Sword and the Shield, the infamous logo of the KGB. This was what he was told to look for. "It's all here," he said. "Let's get moving." The driver of the truck gunned the engine and pulled a U-turn, heading south on the coastal highway. After about thirty seconds, Belarus said, "Call the boat, tell them I said to take 'em out."

"But Sam, what about the money?"

"Forget about it. Do as I said! And step on the gas, I want a little distance between us and our German friends."

The driver complied, calling the fishing boat. The captain on board didn't really understand why, but he wasn't there to question orders. Within seconds, a mate appeared on deck with a shoulder-mounted stinger missile and took aim at the Lincoln, which had just started moving. "Fire!" ordered the captain.

The missile streamed through the dark fog that had just rolled in, striking the Lincoln in the gas tank, causing it to explode into a fireball that lit up the night sky like a second moon. The car went out of control, tumbling down the embankment toward the sea. As it fell, the horrific noise of metal twisting, glass breaking, and of men dying was muffled by the sound of the waves crashing into the shore.

As he watched the fireball in the rearview mirror, Belarus muttered aloud, "Auf Wiedersehen, you bastards."

Chapter Ten

Oliver Devon was stretched out in the backseat of the black limousine on 13th Street, parked outside the National Press Building. His young aide waited on the pavement, fidgeting spasmodically. The aide had promised to deliver Devon on time today, and they were already ten minutes late. But Devon, phone glued to his ear, showed no signs of moving too quickly. A light mist began to fall, and the aide covered his head with a newspaper.

The truth was, Oliver Devon was having a very bad morning. In the last twenty-four hours he'd received devastating news, the kind that would make most men recoil in self-pity or bury themselves in a bottle. But not Devon. He had an agenda and nothing, absolutely nothing would undermine his progress. "Clay, partner, how is that darling niece of yours? Is she enjoying her new job at the RNC? Don't mention it, it's the least the party could do for our whip. No, I'm not calling about the Telecom Bill today, just checking in on the family front. But now that you mention it, let's have lunch this week and go over the license auction. You know, my clients are very interested in how the bidding comes out. Great, how's Thursday?"

The aide leaned in to pull Devon out, but the older man's hands were too fast. No sooner had he clicked off with one call, than he pulled up a new number on his pocket electronic organizer and speed-dialed onto the next call. Oliver Devon's Rolodex was legendary among Washington insiders. When he went from the paper desk version to the pocket minicomputer, he had to have extra memory built in so that the small device could handle the thousands of detailed entries. Devon's database went well beyond names and numbers. For every person listed, the notes covered everything from favorite restaurants to musical tastes. Devon's aide kept copious notes on all his interactions with Washington's elite, and these notes were then programmed into this little intelligence source. When Devon had to see a particular agency head to smooth over a federal contract, what better way to make a meeting than to show up with four tickets to the Bullets when the Knicks were in town? When a Congresswoman's vote carried the day on a particular bill, a bouquet of flowers just seemed to appear at her Georgetown door. The typewritten note may have just said "Thanks," but she knew whose handwriting was all over it.

Unlike some people, who are easily pigeonholed at cocktail parties by their jobs—meet Sam, he's an attorney—Oliver Devon's job lacked any simple description. He was the consummate insider with a hand in every pot. Oliver Devon's father had made a fortune in the 1950's, building a vast import-export business based in postwar Europe. In the late 1970's, as his father's health slowly failed, Oliver Devon sold the lucrative family business to embark on more heady adventures. Following the advice of the young rogue traders with whom he ran in New York's fast new-money social scene, he threw all of the profits into the newly emerging junk bond markets and made a killing on the bulls of the 80's. The junk bond markets had prospered by interlocking circles of personal relationships, with insiders parlaying friendships into cash, lots of it. Devon had learned from this experience, and when he decided that making money was too pedestrian for his tastes, he decided to apply these skills in the political realm. Devon became a quick darling of the go-go political world of the Reagan Revolution. With fat pockets to make contributions to local and national Republican causes, he was a veritable poster child for the "It's morning in America" set.

This fact was not lost upon the politicians who came to call for cash. Soon the invitations to the Rose Garden parties began to pile up. He chopped wood with Reagan on the President's four-day weekends at Camp David and lunched with Nancy at the Jockey Club. The domino effect was swift. He found his way onto legions of corporate boards, gaining access to even more closely held secrets and fatter wads of spoils. Like a huge legal pyramid game, he built layer upon layer of connections. And he was ruthless in both extending his influence and guarding his power. When a rival sought a slot on a federal advisory board making new rules for biotechnology—he held vast shares in this emerging industry—Devon was quick to give the kiss of death to the man's candidacy. It was amazing what the talk of an affair with a staffer could do, and all it had taken was the offhand remark to the nice lady from the *Washington Standard* seated next to him at a dinner for the Prime Minister of Japan.

But all of Devon's ruthlessness was concealed behind a facade so refined and genteel that when the Reagan revolution ended and George Bush came to power, Devon had no trouble in schmoozing even the consummate national grandfather. With a thousand points of light flickering in the background, Devon too evolved. As scrutiny over political gifts and boondoggles grew, Devon burrowed down deeper, began making even more elaborate bank shots, using his networks to conceal three transactions deep what had once gone on so openly. Now, payoffs to Congressional members occurred through intermediaries and fronts. He bankrolled college courses, taught by the Speaker of the House, on winning back the Congress—the ultimate twist on a liberal arts education. He made sure that all the right people's sons and daughters found jobs in all the right places. He was a deal-maker extraordinaire. When a politician needed a biographer, he had a list waiting. When a company needed access to Russian markets, he had the phone numbers for the finance minister's weekend love dacha at his fingertips.

Finally, fifteen minutes late, Devon left the car and, aide in tow, headed up the elevator to the banquet room of the National Press Club. He straightened his Hermes tie and ran a distracted hand through his dark, wiry hair. Devon stood exactly six feet tall and exuded power and confidence. His lightly tanned face was amazingly unlined for his fifty-six years. His blue eyes never stood still, but always wandered about, taking everything in and measuring all. They moved constantly, leaving people around him feeling as though he wasn't listening to them. But Devon never missed anything, one of the many traits that got him to where he was today. He stretched his lips into his power-smile and exited the elevator.

The National Press Club is part country club and part forum. The Club's membership is a who's who of the fourth estate. News makers from all corners of the industry have come here to have their voices heard, to reach out through the wires and words of the media to put some notion into the minds of the American people. The place is, quite simply, an incubator for what eventually becomes the prevailing wisdom. The talk at the club's Wednesday happy hour about who is up and who is down will be chewed over on the front and editorial pages of papers, and be spoken by the talking heads of news anchors over the week ahead. News makers are invited here for christening or crucifixion; there is no middle ground.

The board of the Press Club had wanted Devon's christening to be a dinner, but Devon insisted on lunch so as to make the network news deadlines and still leave him time to tape a segment for "Nightline." He had the game down to an art. Devon and his aide were greeted at the elevator bank by the exasperated president of the Press Club, who remarked pointedly that not even presidents kept the full club's membership waiting. As they walked into the banquet room, Devon apologized profusely, explaining that he just couldn't get the Majority Leader to shut up—"It's the damned Select Committee nonsense again. . . . I told him I have put that part of my life behind me, but apparently he's a little hard of hearing." The Club's president stopped nagging and leaned in to hear the juicy bits, which were more than payoff enough for twenty minutes off schedule.

The large oak-walled banquet room was filled to capacity. In the back, a two-tiered riser was packed with camera crews from CNN, C-SPAN, and all the major networks. The chime of crystal and the clink of china echoed about the room as the fourth estate made quick work of their tasteless farm-raised salmon lunches.

Devon walked past the seat reserved for him at the head table, directly to the podium. He paused long enough to allow the startled pencil press types to find their pads, and to let the camera crews adjust their light levels off the white of his shirt. The room's noise fell to a low murmur. Then he began in a solid, measured voice.

"Ladies and gentleman, my name is Oliver Devon. I know that all of you have come here expecting to hear me make some major announcement on some political topic. Some of you are speculating that it has to do with the ongoing criminal investigations concerning the 1996 campaign finances. Others have called me to get the scoop on what you believe will be remarks about the coming election, or the budget battles. If these are your expectations, I am sorry, but I will disappoint you. I have come here today to talk about a more pressing problem for our nation: homelessness."

A startled murmur spread throughout the hall. A bald columnist from a liberal Chicago daily chortled out loud at the notion of Oliver Devon worried about the homeless.

Devon raised his hand for silence and then continued. "Homelessness is no laughing matter. We as a nation talk a great game of common ideals and values. We like to think of ourselves as special, and yet every day we step over those of us who are less fortunate. We pay the sidewalk tax of a dime or a quarter into their outstretched cups and feel we have done our part," he said, gesturing to the crowd as he held up a quarter. "For over two decades, those of us in the Republican party have struggled to reduce the powers and burdens of the federal government, believing that the more our government tries to help us with federally funded social programs, the more our government ends up hurting us. We have railed about the problems of handout dependence, and argued that no program can help those who are not willing to help themselves. But those of us who have fought against these programs have done little to address the realities of our society. We are a society founded upon Judeo-Christian beliefs that tell us we owe each other more than a cold shoulder. If we are to remove the federal safety net, we have to be willing to replace that net with a bridge of hands that can carry our less fortunate members out of the misery and sorrows of poverty and powerlessness. Today I am here to announce such a bridge. Today I am announcing the formation of a two-hundred-million-dollar endowment to combat homelessness, called the Devon Foundation. And I am calling upon my friends in the private sector to join me in this crusade to end homelessness by the end of the decade. Our goal is to put in place, by the end of next year, a ten-billion-dollar fund to put people back on their feet and to put roofs over their heads. Thank you." Devon stepped away from the mike and began glad-handing in the VIP seating.

The crowd stared in disbelief. Even the media could not comprehend what was occurring before their very eyes. From the back of the room, a lone pair of hands began clapping. Even the cynics could not resist the temptation to salute the largest private initiative ever announced to combat a social problem. Not since Robert Kennedy's Bedford-Stuyvesent renewal plan had there been a social program of this magnitude, and even the press rose to their feet and clapped wildly in support.

The chorus of the applause was quickly broken as the first unapologetic microphone wielder pushed through the crowds to get the first interview. Soon the room became a cacophony of screamed questions and grunts as news people elbowed their way into better positions.

"Mr. Devon, are you going to testify again before the Select Committee?"

"Do you plan to serve in the next cabinet?"

Devon knew the cardinal rule: leave them wanting more. The plan was to make a clean getaway without so much as a word. But as Devon followed his aide out the main door of the room in the direction of a waiting elevator, one question got his attention.

"Oliver, are you still Beijing's man in Washington?"

To Devon, the very sound of the question was like chalk screeching on a chalkboard. Like so many after the '96 election, he had spent well over a year under the magnifying glass of the first Select Committee, his every move watched, his every word questioned. In any other year, Devon's Republican pedigree and the fact that he controlled more political money than anyone in history would have afforded him some measure of insulation from the witch hunt. But this wasn't just any year. Unfortunately for Devon, the chairman of the Select Committee was determined to find proof of a conspiracy by the People's Republic of China to steal the U.S. Presidential election. And, as anybody in Washington knew, no matter what the reason, you simply couldn't deal with the Chinese on any level without running across Oliver Devon. It was only an eleventh-hour grant of immunity that kept Devon from a choice between a prison sentence and an unauthorized flight to avoid prosecution. "Young man, you must be confusing me with someone else," said the unflappable power broker.

"Are you saying that you are no longer a registered foreign agent for The People's Republic?" blurted the reporter, completely unaware that he was only a phone call away from doing obituaries in Wilkes-Barre.

Devon took a moment and studied his prey. The entire day had been carefully orchestrated, and he had to be careful not to let an unchecked display of emotion undermine the bigger agenda. "Son," he said, smiling, "I've been out of the lobbying business for three years, and I've never been happier. I lead an unexciting life. As you can see, I occasionally do some charity work. Otherwise, I'm just a simple art collector."

"But honestly, Mr. Devon. With the espionage arrests at Los Alamos, as well as FBI findings of Chinese nationals illegally funneling money into party committees, can you really deny that there is a China connection to the Oval Office?"

"As a Republican, I really have no comment on that," he said with a smile. With that, Devon finally made his way to the elevators as more questions came.

"Mr. Devon. Any comment on the Presidential election?"

Once safely inside the elevator, Devon called out, "Don't forget to vote . . ." By the time they hit the curb, the car door was opened, and they were on the road.

Devon turned quickly to his aide. "Any word on how the hearings are going?"

"Yesterday they ate Tom Griffin alive. Unfortunately, she's really pushing the Chinese connection again. There is a rumor that she's got a smoking gun, supposedly somebody in the West Wing that has gone over to the other side."

"Damn! I was afraid of that."

"Do you want us to take any action?" the aide asked.

"Absolutely not. Anything else?"

"Nothing else is scheduled until later this afternoon."

"Otherwise how is she doing?"

"So far she's holding her own. I assume that's how you want it?"

"Yes . . . at least for the time being. We are being careful to avoid any fingerprints, aren't we?"

"None of the info will trace back to us. No, no fingerprints at all."

Devon reclined into the car seat's soft leather and pulled on the Cohiba his aide lit for him. It was all in a day's work.

Chapter Eleven

Right smack in the middle of the busiest week of the campaign, hangover still hammering in his head, and Hanson had to take the morning off to go and look at the corpse of a stranger. He stood next to Kennedy at the morgue at the D.C. Medical Examiner's Office, barely containing his frustration, but he wanted to prove to Kennedy that he didn't know the dead girl. He didn't like the way Kennedy looked at him when he asked him questions. Kennedy didn't believe him, and Hanson knew it.

The detective got straight down to business. "Mr. Hanson, have you ever seen a dead body?"

"Yeah. A couple of times."

"Mr. Hanson, I want you to be prepared for what you're about to see. Your daughter is in pretty bad shape."

"Detective," said Hanson, exasperated, "I don't have a daughter. I don't even know this girl. Are we clear on that?"

Kennedy looked noncommittal. "Sure. Let's say we have a look anyway."

The detective signed them in at the guard desk and motioned for Hanson to follow him down the hallway.

The lingering smell of formaldehyde burned the nostrils of both men as they entered the coroner's lab, and the sudden drop in temperature made the hair on Hanson's arms stand on end. Row upon row of shiny steel pull-out storage lockers, stacked three high and twelve wide, lined the far wall of the room.

They came to a door marked AR-1. "This way," said Kennedy.

The inside of AR-1 had the antiseptic look of a hospital operating room, but the instruments were cruder, lacking the high technology that has come to dominate modern medicine. In here, there was no need for electrocardiogram monitors or oxygen units. By the time a person reached this place, there was no life to sustain or revive, just death to analyze.

The harsh fluorescent light gave the room a bluish tinge that only exacerbated the institutionalized feel of death. In the middle of the room, a minimalist steel table sat holding a body covered by a white sheet. Alongside the larger table stood a smaller steel instrument table covered with spreaders, scalpels, scissors, mallets, and a meat slicer. The real menaces loomed from above, and Hanson's eye was drawn to them involuntarily. Cutting and sawing devices hung down over the body from a central instrument panel. The glint off the teeth of the shiny steel blade of a radial saw struck Hanson's eye and he shivered.

"Miss Fairchild is scheduled for an autopsy later this morning," said Kennedy.

Hanson wasn't sure why, but he was suddenly nervous. He had no idea what was happening to him, much less why. As he approached the table, his nerves gave over to a raw fear, like a child's paralyzing fear of the dark. He hesitated.

Kennedy grabbed the sheet. "Ready?" he asked.

Hanson nodded, his eyes focused on the table as Kennedy lifted the sheet. He knew he didn't have a daughter, and he couldn't place Ariel Fairchild no matter how hard he tried. Just the same, he was terrified that he might recognize her anyway.

The girl's ashen skin contrasted with the unearthly blue of her lips. Her throat was crushed, and her face and body were mottled with bruises. Only her blond hair looked remotely human, but it too lacked the luster of life. She was so young, just a baby. Who could have done something like this? He looked away in horror.

Hanson realized he had never really seen a dead body, at least not one like this. The body lying on the concrete slab bore little resemblance to the well-coifed faces of death he had seen while paying last respects at funeral homes. The bodies at the city coroner's office looked anything but peaceful. Virtually all had met violent deaths: beating, gunshot, sexual assault, or in the case of Ariel, all of the above.

"We think someone strangled her, probably breaking her neck," Kennedy said. "There's also the possibility that she choked on her own vomit. On the other hand, the killer might have done it slowly, smothering her. We'll know more in a few hours, after the coroner is through with her."

Hanson felt the detective studying him for any reaction.

"She was only seventeen years old. Did you know that, Mr. Hanson?"

Hanson said nothing, just stared rigidly at the wall across the room, his eyes slowly welling up with tears.

"Mr. Hanson, were you aware that she was a call girl? Imagine that. A prostitute at her age. Please look more closely at her, please try to identify her."

Hanson turned to him with despair in his eyes. "I've told you. I'm not her father!"

"Okay, you're not her father. What were you then, a friend?"

Hanson turned away. "Don't push me, Detective!"

"A customer?"

Hanson stared at the detective, seething with outrage. He was trying not to lose his temper, trying not to let the detective get to him, no matter what. It was proving to be more difficult than he had expected. Hanson looked back to the girl. He was having trouble breathing, and the room's antiseptic death smell left him light-headed and confused. Focusing on her eyes, Hanson felt for a moment that he was looking into a mirror. He looked off, trying to break the hold of the reflective gaze, but looking away was not enough. What he saw under the bruises, the abrasions, the white and blue skin, was unbelievable yet undeniable. Ariel Fairchild was blonder and more fair-skinned than him. Otherwise, he was looking down at his own features, inexplicably seeing his own face.

"Are you sure you've never seen her before?"

"I'm absolutely, one hundred percent certain. I've never seen her before in my life," Hanson said. It was the perfect spin, an art he had practiced all his life. What he had said was true, but the truth served only to obfuscate what went unsaid. Like an art critic viewing a never before seen work, and knowing immediately from whose hand it came, Hanson had never seen her before, but he knew what had made her.

"Okay," Kennedy said, pulling the sheet back up over the corpse. "I believe you."

Unwittingly, the next of kin had given the detective exactly what he wanted.

No one, not even Kennedy, could have spotted the man in the late-model black sedan that had followed him since he left the Pavilion early that morning. He was the best surveillance man on the east coast, and waited patiently across the street until Kennedy and Hanson came back out of the building.

Grabbing his cell phone, he immediately dialed the number. The phone rang several times. Finally, a voice came to the phone. "Yes?"

"It's me," the man said.

"Yes, what do you have?"

"Per your instructions, I've been tailing the cops since last night."

"Who's heading up the investigation?"

"His name is Abe Kennedy."

The voice was silent for a moment. "Anything else?"

"I'm at the morgue. I've been following Kennedy for hours. He went from the Capital Pavilion, to the coroner's lab, to his precinct. I figured next he'd head home and get some sleep. But instead he stops by this townhouse in Georgetown and picks up this guy and heads back to the morgue. I'm there now."

"Do you have a name?"

"Hanson . . . Mike Hanson. I'll have a background check completed by noon."

It took a few seconds for the name to register. This was the last thing he expected.

"Has anyone located CeCe yet?"

"Not as of yet, sir," the man replied.

"What about the Chief?"

"Nothing, sir. What should I do about Hanson?"

"Nothing for now. I'll take care of Mr. Hanson personally," Devon said, then he hung up the phone.

Chapter Twelve

For three decades The Devon Group had occupied the top of 800 Lafayette Place, located at the corner of 15th and H Streets, looking down on the White House. As the building's largest tenant and principal owner, Oliver Devon was constantly urged by his advisors to name the building "Devon Place" or "Devon Square," anything with "Devon" in it. Despite their persistence, however, this was an option that he absolutely refused to consider. It was tough enough for his organization to maintain a low profile without turning one's self into a billboard. Although he never publicly would admit it, the site was selected with the sole purpose of sending a message. Simply put, notwithstanding the party affiliation, poll ratings, or national stature of any particular resident of the Executive Mansion, every man or woman that sits in the Oval Office eventually has to deal with Oliver Devon.

When the Chief arrived, he parked in a dark corner of the underground lot and took a secure elevator to the penthouse level. No sooner did the doors open to a foyer laden with Italian marble accented by track lighting, than he was met by a security aide whose job was to escort him directly to his meeting. On the way, they passed a bubbling freshwater fountain filled with tropical fish that looked more predatory than exotic. It was encircled by Devon's meticulously pruned indoor Bonsai garden, a gift from the Japanese ambassador. Finally, they arrived at a private entrance to Devon's outer office, the one he used when dealing with underlings or his lawyers or anybody else he felt no need to impress. While it was lavish by most standards, the decor was designed to say as little about the man as possible. Other than the fact that it was all very expensive, the outer office was almost sterile in its composition. Desk, chair, credenza, and conference table were all contemporary in design, the unusual plants in each corner offering the only signs of personality. Conspicuously absent from Devon's walls were any photos of loved ones, and other than an original Dali hanging over a fireplace, no artwork to speak of. More than a little strange for a man whose passion for art preceded him. Rather than stimulate small talk, the outer office was designed to minimize distractions and prompt people to focus on the matter at hand. Some found this unnerving, surprised to learn that despite his very public persona, Devon was a very private man, quite particular about his associations. "Business is business and friendship is friendship. Rarely do the two cross paths," he was fond of saying.

"He's been waiting for you," the aide said as they entered the suite.

Devon was seated behind his desk, his eyes glued to the monitor of his computer. Every few seconds he would type in some kind of response to the database, occasionally muttering some profanity aloud to the screen. Without looking up, he asked, "Need a drink, Sam?"

The Chief was surprised by the offer, not used to such hospitality from Devon. "Well, given the fact that I haven't been to bed yet, my biological clock thinks it's happy hour . . ."

"Don't make excuses, Sam. If a man wants a drink, he should have a drink. My guess is you probably could use one about now."

"What the hell, gimme a Stoli, straight up."

Devon was all too willing to comply, nodding to the aide standing at the rear of the office who quickly fetched drinks for both men before exiting. Devon was well aware that the Chief was a man enslaved by excess, an immensely talented operative, yet completely unable to resist even the slightest temptation. Ironically, this vulnerability met with the approval of the Investors, as it was his addiction to a myriad of vices that included prostitutes of either sex, cocaine, and strong drink that allowed them to "handle" this mole of virtually unmatched ruthlessness. "So, I trust we had a safe trip?"

"Well, some of us did. Some others didn't."

"Was that really necessary? I mean, those two might have been useful on another project sometime down the road."

"Just following instructions per the Investors. I was told to leave no loose ends. The Germans were loose ends."

"I suppose. . . . So what happened in Yangbon?"

Belarus took a moment to sip his drink, well aware that it might be his last. After a long sip that burned his throat going down, he said, "The good news is that when I showed my hand, the North Koreans bit hard, I mean they want this thing, big time! The bad news is that we lost a man in the operation."

"Too bad. Unfortunately, sometimes it is the cost of doing business," Devon said in a plaintive tone. "And the status of the cargo?"

"The cargo was received on time and is presently secure."

"And where might that be?"

The Chief smiled. Devon was well aware of the security protocols, but still loved to ignore them. "Mr. Devon, as you are aware, I am not authorized to disclose the whereabouts of the cargo to you until twenty-four hours prior to transfer."

"What about verification?"

"My team should complete verification of authenticity in about two days."

"Good. Once we are ready to move I don't want any delays."

"Do you mind if I ask how soon you want to begin transfer?"

Devon paused and took a sip of his drink. "Very soon, Sam, very soon. Certainly before the elections. Right now, I'm watching the hearings just to make sure no one accidentally mentions my name."

"That makes sense."

"So, any progress on ECHELON?"

"Some," he began, knowing that this was Devon's hot button. "We've been able to determine that both the Yahoo and eBay attacks back in February were ECHELON operations. Some kind of a test run . . ."

"Or a warning."

"Very possible, but it is important that we know that it was more than just cyberpunks screwing around with the Net. ECHELON is very real."

"I agree," said Devon as he leaned back in his chair. "Do we have any kind of a back plan if they pick up our trail?"

"So far we've been able to identify ECHELON monitoring stations in Herndon, Virginia, and another just outside Los Angeles. Worst case scenario is we can take one of them out with a H.E.R.F."

"H.E.R.F.?" Devon said. "What the hell is a H.E.R.F.?"

The Chief smiled. He enjoyed being one step ahead of his boss. "High Energy Radio Frequency weapon. A single device can shut down telecommunications in a large city for up to a year."

"You never cease to amaze me, Sam. But let's hold that one in reserve for now. In the meantime, alert your people. For the remainder of the operation I want no communications via e-mail or fax. Only face to face or hard copy."

"Understood," said the Chief. "Anything else?"

Devon studied his security director, unsure of his veracity. "Sam, you should know that I'm dealing with a personal matter. CeCe had some trouble with the service over the weekend. I'm sure you heard about it . . ."

The Chief felt nervous. For some reason, Devon was probing, suspicious about something. Whatever was going on, he wanted Devon off of his trail. "No, actually, I've been in New York for several days coordinating the arrival of the cargo. What happened?"

Devon could barely utter the words. "It was Ariel. She . . . she's dead."

The Chief, who'd trained in paramilitary camps in Algeria and gone one on one with the best guerilla fighters in the world, nearly pissed in his pants. "Good God! How?"

"She was murdered."

"Are you certain? I'm so sorry," he said. "You know you can count on me. Is there anything I can do?"

For a moment Devon was touched by the Chief's show of

humanity. "No, at least not with this phase of the investigation. I have our people all over it. Between the police and our personnel, we'll identify the killer in a matter of days. Who knows, maybe then you can be helpful."

The Chief sat there, not knowing what to say.

"By the way, there is one thing you can do."

"Anything."

"We're having trouble tracking down CeCe. I'd appreciate anything you could do to help locate her."

"Consider it done," he said, standing. "I'll keep you posted on what I find."

"Thanks for your help, Sam," Devon said, wheeling back around to his computer, not even looking back at the Chief. "You know the way out."

After waiting several seconds, Devon pressed the intercom buzzer.

"Yes sir?"

"Have my scheduler check into the Chief's travel logs for the last ten days. Be sure to check any and all aliases that he uses. Also, check his phone usage to see if there are any roaming charges during the last week."

"We'll get right on it, sir."

As Devon sat there he thought of how alone he was. The Chief, while unstable, had always been his most loyal operative. He hated not being able to trust him. But unfortunately, in the wake of Ariel's murder, everyone was a suspect. If the Chief had been out of town, there would be some kind of trail no matter how he tried to cover his tracks. On the other hand, if he were lying, there would be no trail at all and Devon would have found the killer.

Chapter Thirteen

Leaving the fluorescent light of the morgue, Hanson squinted as the late-morning rays of the sun glared down at him. Today's weather called for highs in the low fifties, but it already felt like those temperatures had been well-eclipsed. Unlike other cities, where autumn ushers out the burn of summer, Washington's autumn cooling is unpredictable, slow to bring relief from summer's deep fry. Today's temporal highs did little for Hanson's low spirits, and helped the waves of hangover come faster and deeper. His stomach rolled with acid and a shimmer of sweat glazed his brow.

After Kennedy followed Hanson out the polished steel doors of the morgue, he noted Hanson's eyes. The detective wondered if it was the sun or the weight of lies that caused his companion to squint. Kennedy's intuition, sharpened by decades of observing lying and desperate men, told him that no matter how much the sun played on Hanson's eyes, the real squint came from inside the man.

"I would highly recommend that you stay in town, Mr. Hanson. We'll be needing to question you further." With that, Kennedy stepped into his car and left Hanson standing alone on the sidewalk.

Hanson's head was reeling. He hailed a cab and told the driver to take him to his home in Georgetown. The taxi fought traffic across downtown, and the driver complained about how the new lobbying laws were killing his business. Hanson just nodded away, hoping to keep conversation to a minimum. As they passed through downtown's "K Street corridor"—home to more lawyers per square block than anywhere else in the country—the roads opened up and they crossed into Georgetown. Even though the new academic year had recently brought a fresh flock of college kids to town, M Street seemed strangely quiet on this midweek morning. Only a few well-scrubbed students in crisp Georgetown University T-shirts strolled about, making purchases on parental charge accounts. The quiet gave Hanson an opportunity to think. Like a tongue that keeps probing the tenderness of a new cavity, his mind kept coming back to Ariel Fairchild. Ariel's features were strikingly similar to Hanson's, but she had inherited her mother's blue eyes and fair hair. Her mother . . . CeCe Farentino. Hanson plunged down deep into the seat, hiding himself from the day, and sighed audibly. She must have changed her name to Fairchild when she upscaled her business. His head pounded harder.

CeCe and Hanson had gone their separate ways years ago. More than seventeen years ago, Hanson realized with a jolt. CeCe was his high school sweetheart. Back then, he hadn't realized that CeCe's family hid secrets of abuse and perversion. CeCe never let on, somehow managing to always show up at school with a sweet smile and a ready laugh. They broke up when Hanson came home from college for Christmas break during his sophomore year. He simply couldn't forgive CeCe for the choices she had made while he was away. Sleeping with men for money. He'd been shocked, disgusted. Now, many years later, he realized that while he was off playing BMOC, blowing off his books for fraternity parties, CeCe was surviving the only way she could. Hanson had long since forgiven her, and he was ashamed that he couldn't understand at the time what she was going through. He still occasionally wondered if he could have helped her, if she had just let him know how bad things really were.

Now he wondered if she kept Ariel's birth a secret to protect him and his sunny political future from the sordidness of her life.

Even back then, Hanson's path to the political limelight lay out before him like his own yellow brick road: president of his high school class, captain of the baseball team, a who's who selection among American college students, and so on. The demands of such a steadfast and unwavering path were only now becoming clear to him, and he was beginning to realize how his political aspirations had wreaked havoc on the lives of those close to him. In shielding him, had CeCe made her daughter one more sacrifice on the altar of politics? Now he might never know. He'd heard she had turned into a hard, bitter woman, but he still couldn't imagine her letting her daughter—maybe even his daughter—work as a prostitute.

His emotions hit him all at once. Hanson suddenly wanted to cry for the dead girl lying in the morgue. He abruptly told the cab driver to stop so that he could get some fresh air. Perhaps it would clear his head. Muttering in an unrecognizable language, the cabbie fought his way to the curb. Hanson paid the fare with a twenty, fresh from the cash machine, making the driver all the more miserable.

Hanson stepped from the taxi to the curb across the street from Nathan's, but the bar's dark comfort and cigar smoke–stained walls were unappealing to him now. He walked up Wisconsin Avenue, first past the trendy stores and boutiques that lined its lower blocks. Then he traversed its midsection of knockoff stores and street vendors selling designer ripoffs at higher than bargain rates. Years ago, when the city built its metro system, the residents of Georgetown successfully rallied against having a subway stop located in their neighborhood. They kept the metro out because they feared public transportation would let the riffraff descend upon them. Now, this garish zone was the unwelcome reminder to the residents of Georgetown that, metro or no metro, a different existence played out each day just beyond the gates of their enclosed gardens. As Hanson walked through, a deeply tanned man in a neon silk shirt and sloppy linen trousers stood in front of a small clothes store, hawking the leather jackets inside. He thrust a paper flyer at Hanson, who shook his head and kept walking.

Soon the stores ended and he was among the neighborhood shops and supermarkets of Burleith and Glover Park. Cresting the

Georgetown hill, he continued on, walking past the spectacular National Cathedral. Hanson looked up at its steeples as they pierced the clouds, but felt no peace. Ariel was dead. Maybe she was his daughter and maybe she wasn't. He walked past the exclusive St. Anselm and Sidwell Friends schools that had educated presidents, diplomats, and senators, and then educated their children. Bitterly, he realized that these were breaks Ariel never had. When he could no longer fight the ache in his feet and the hunger gnawing at his stomach, he stopped at Cafe Deluxe for lunch. For the next two hours, he hid in its cool, dim interior and thought about everything except Ariel. Under the slowly circling blades of a ceiling fan, he consumed a western omelette, side fries, endless cups of coffee, two bloody marys, and every section of the *New York Times* and the *Washington Post*. Strange, he thought, though the *Post* had a strong crime desk, there wasn't a single word about the murder at the Capital Pavilion. Then he realized it made sense. In a week filled with presidential campaign news, the murder of a young hooker would hardly rate as newsworthy.

When the burn of the liquor began to take the edge off his cognitive abilities, he felt fortified enough to face his empty Georgetown townhouse. He stepped outside once again into the bright sunlight and hailed an empty taxi. The ride was short, but he needed only a few moments to make his decision. He had to testify in less than two hours. Normally he would meet with his lawyer first to go over strategy, but right now he needed sleep. He could handle this, he told himself. He always did. Tomorrow he had to be back on top of things at the campaign. Less than thirty days until the election—perhaps the most important thirty days of his life. Until yesterday, he hadn't even known he had a daughter. Now the poor girl was dead and he couldn't do anything for her—it was the police's job from here. He would go home, grab a nap, and forget about it. He just couldn't handle thinking about any of it now.

The cab deposited him on the front walk of his three-story brick townhouse, and he stood for a moment looking at his home and street. It was one of a row of distinguished houses with tiny but manicured front lawns bordering on the tree-lined sidewalk. In the spring the cherry trees blossomed pink and white, and in the summer the broad leaves of the tall magnolias umbrellaed over the homes and sheltered them from the heat. Now all the leaves were still gloriously ablaze in autumn splendor. Behind the houses, away from prying eyes, beautiful gardens gave owners an oasis from the city. Except for an occasional cocktail party that got a bit out of hand, or the times that Hanson and his friends came home drunk and messy, it was always quiet on this street. His neighbors looked down on anyone or anything that interrupted their very civilized existences.

Hanson opened his front gate, glad to be home. On top of everything, weighing heavily in the mix was the fact that the campaign simply didn't need any more bad press right before the election. The potential headlines screamed through his head. He could hear how the pundits on "The McLaughlin Group" and "Crossfire" would take great pleasure in rehashing his demise over and over again. It would destroy everything he had. Moreover, if things continued to go south, a sex-murder scandal could destroy everything he was working for, even costing the Dems the presidency.

From the gate, Hanson noticed that his front door wasn't completely closed. Did he leave it open on his way to the morgue this morning? He walked quickly to the door and, ducking like a fighter, pushed it open. As his eyes took it all in, he stood up slowly, arms falling limp at his sides. He was in shock, speechless. The front hall and dining room had been destroyed: his two favorite paintings slashed, decorative plates broken, stuffing hanging out of his ripped sofa, his belongings strewn all over the place.

Hanson slumped against the door frame, leaning his head on his bent arm. He looked around frantically. Who would have donc something like this? Should he call the police? Then he remembered Kennedy's endless questions and unbelieving eyes. Never. His heart began to pound louder and louder as he whirled and grabbed a fireplace poker from the floor. With adrenaline rushing through him, he ran upstairs, taking the steps two at a time. He raced through rooms, looking into closets and under beds to make sure the house was empty. Someone had gone through every drawer and cabinet, and tossed his clothing, papers, books, everything all over the place. When he found his stereo, VCR, and cameras all untouched, his fear solidified in a molten ball in his stomach. Whoever did all this damage wasn't trying to rob him. So what could they want?

Hanson cautiously returned downstairs in search of comfort, which he found in a bottle of Dewars. He picked it off the floor, uncapped it, and took an unhealthy swig. Sitting on his ruined sofa, he thought carefully about the events of the day. Who hated him enough to do this to him? Hanson's mind raced through names of old political rivals and childhood enemies. He even thought briefly of Paul Angelo, but dismissed him as too weak. Try as he might, Hanson couldn't come up with any answers. He was so overwhelmed, so tired. Sleep. He needed some sleep to get things straight in his head. Unfortunately, he remembered his appointment with the committee scheduled for later that day at the campaign. He sighed and got up slowly. He moved through the house with a near-drunken awkwardness, double-checking the door and window locks. Finally, he headed upstairs and barricaded himself in the bedroom with the fireplace poker and his bottle. Unsteadily, he set his alarm for 3:15 P.M. Then, just to make sure, he moved his desk in front of the bedroom door as he began to regret not calling the police. For the first time since childhood, he was terrified to be alone, but his fear and exhaustion soon dragged him into a deep alcoholic slumber. When the phone rang downstairs, he was lost in nightmares of a once innocent girl turned madam and her still-innocent daughter beaten and slaughtered.

Chapter Fourteen

CeCe wondered if he would recognize her voice after so many years. She was nervous, trying desperately not to sound hysterical when she called him. Sitting alone behind the wheel of her late-model Mercedes, CeCe gunned her engine every few seconds to get the most out of the heater. Despite the unseasonably high temperatures, she couldn't get warm. Parked in a wooded area less than a hundred feet from the Jefferson Memorial, she saw the first drops of rain fall on the still waters of the Tidal Basin as the sky clouded up. She shivered, and her hands trembled as she tried to guide the white-lined pocket mirror to her waiting nostril. After taking several hits, she realized it was no use. Drugs couldn't numb her pain anymore. CeCe Fairchild's worst nightmare had come true.

Though CeCe Fairchild was never invited to ribbon cuttings or socialite charity balls, she frequently hobnobbed with some of Washington's wealthiest and most powerful men at ultra-private social gatherings that rarely made the papers. CeCe's modeling agency served as a front for a high-class escort service called Exotica. She was successful and wealthy, and the secrets she held made her powerful. But all that was over now. Life as she knew it would never be the same. She was exhausted, strung out, close to a nervous breakdown. Physically, she had aged years in the past several days, and her perfect ash-blond hair was now stringy and streaked with gray.

As much as she tried to stop it, CeCe's mind kept flashing back to her party at the hotel. Because of the upcoming presidential elections, the Washington press corps was relentlessly chasing down even the slightest rumor of impropriety. As reporters staked out singles bars, topless joints, and the condos of selected mistresses of the city's power brokers, CeCe's customers decided to lay low. Finally, CeCe became tired of this Potomac paranoia. Marketing in the world's oldest profession meant finding a way to put the buyers with the sellers. Booze and hormones would do the rest. A party would be just the right thing, a trade convention of sorts.

CeCe set the stage with a cocktail party Sunday night in the presidential suite of the Capital Pavilion Hotel. She had provided her best front-room girls, the best scotch, bourbon, and cognac that money could buy, and an ample supply of cocaine and ecstasy for her clients' consumption. To be on the safe side, she also rented most of the rooms on the corridor leading up to the suite.

No one knew her clientele better than CeCe did. When she looked around the room, she saw the usual doctors, lawyers, real estate developers from the suburbs, a few politicos, a former Superbowl MVP, and, of course, the diplomats. CeCe's clients trusted her guarantee of complete confidentiality. Also, as one client put it, "Why should I care if anyone sees me here? They're here too. What are they going to do to me?" All the same, CeCe always provided two entrances. One was for the diplomats and businessmen. Elected officials or men with equally recognizable faces used the other private entrance.

Tonight, both entrances were busy, and all was going perfectly. No one blinked an eye at the $1000 cover to gain admission, and CeCe knew the party would be a big moneymaker. The Investors would be pleased. The room was awash in a mix of shimmery silk and Lycra, coupled neatly with conservative gray and blue wool suits. Champagne corks popped, and CeCe noticed that the small *talk and laughter was getting louder as the night progressed. She noted with satisfaction that her girls looked gorgeous as they paired off with men twice their age. CeCe was just beginning to relax and believe the night would be a complete success. Then the uninvited guest called.*

It was the Chief calling from his car to say he wanted to drop by. She recoiled and walked down an empty hallway to take the call on her room phone. "What can I do for you, Chief?"

"Sounds like you got one hell of a party going on there, CeCe."

"What can I say?" she said. CeCe hated and feared the Chief more than anyone alive. He was the worst kind of man, more cruel than anyone she'd ever known.

"Okay, if you're gonna have an attitude, then I'll cut to the chase," said the Chief.

"What is it you want?"

He could hear the disgust in her voice, and it pleased him. It was always fun making her crawl. "You know exactly what I want, CeCe. Is she there?"

He made her sick. "Yes, she happens to be here, but only in case your boss shows up."

"Great, I'm about twenty minutes away. Have her ready, wearing something white."

"Look, Chief, I'm serious, you can't do this again. You have got to leave her alone. First of all, I won't allow it. More importantly, Devon will kill you if he finds out," she said.

The threats were lost on the Chief. He had stopped caring if he lived or died years ago. "Listen, if you don't have her ready in twenty minutes, I'll call the boss myself. I'll tell him I've already had some fun with her—and that you gave me the go-ahead." He laughed. "You know he'll blame you. God only knows what he'll do to you. You know how he's obsessed with her."

CeCe knew deep down that the Chief would not hesitate to pass on his lies. His newfound power over her made her nauseous with fear. And though Devon would punish the Chief, he would blame her for allowing it to happen. At best, he would shut her down. She would rather not think about what else he might do to teach her a lesson. She had no choice.

"Okay, but whatever you do, don't come to the main suite. Go to suite 717," she said, clipping her words and swallowing her spite. "Ariel will be waiting for you. And Chief, I'm warning you,

no rough stuff. Nothing weird. You got it?" She thought hard for a moment. "And if you hurt her this time, I swear I'll kill you myself."

The Chief hung up without bothering to respond. He turned to his rider in the passenger seat, "Man, you just wait, you've never had anything like this."

CeCe found herself shaking. She asked one of the other girls, a tall blonde in a leather miniskirt and little else, to find Ariel and bring her to suite 717. She then went to the bar and poured herself a tumbler of vodka before going there herself. When Ariel showed up, looking as beautiful as ever in a simple black evening gown, CeCe decided this would have to be the last time she would let the Chief near her daughter. If he wouldn't leave Ariel alone, CeCe would go to Devon herself, no matter what the consequences.

Ariel asked, "So, is Devon coming by?"

CeCe avoided the question. She felt a lump in her throat. "The Chief called . . ." She never got to finish her sentence. Ariel started to cry.

"How could you do this to me? You promised me I'd never have to speak to him again!"

"Ariel, I know how you feel—"

"No! You don't either," Ariel sobbed. She raised a finger and pointed it in her mother's face. "You don't know how he put a plastic bag over my head and nearly killed me."

CeCe stared at her daughter. It took a lot to shock her, but she was horrified. She liked to say that when you play hard, it's smart to die young and leave a pretty corpse. At this moment, she really believed it. She'd been in the business for almost twenty years, and she had reached the end of her rope. Devon was always promising that he would take care of her and Ariel. Then they could shut down the agency and she could retire. But that day never seemed to come. Meanwhile, she was getting too old and too tired to take care of things when they got out of hand.

"The Chief said he would tell Devon everything. He said he would tell Devon that I put you up to it, and that you wanted to fuck him." CeCe's voice was loud and imploring.

Ariel stared through her tears at her mother. "Mom, the Chief grabbed me as I walked down the hallway. Then he attacked me—

against my will. He raped me. You had nothing to do with it." Ariel's face was taut with apprehension.

CeCe stepped towards her, taking Ariel's hands into her own. "I know, I know, but it doesn't matter. Devon will still blame me. Then I don't know what will happen to us."

Ariel could feel the strength leave her body like air passing on each breath. Slowly she collapsed to the floor, kneeling, her arms wrapped tightly around her body. But she knew her mother was desperate. "Promise this is the last time," she said.

CeCe nodded and lowered herself to comfort her daughter. As they hugged, CeCe whispered, "We'll work this out. It's going to be okay. I promise, honey, I'll never ask you to do anything like this again."

A sudden crash of thunder over the Jefferson Memorial jolted CeCe back to reality. As she stared out the window into the darkness, she wouldn't let herself remembe what happened later in the suite. What nobody else knew but her. She kept thinking of the frightened look on Ariel's face. And most of all, CeCe kept thinking of Ariel's words:

"Okay, Mommy. I love you, I'll do it for you."

Chapter Fifteen

The ornate caucus room on the ground floor of the Dirksen Senate Office Building was aglow with the blinding glare of video camera lights and flashbulbs as the chairman of the Select Committee on Campaign Finance called the hearing to order. For Hanson, seated only a few feet away at the witness table, the barrage of lights was certain to propel his already pounding headache from mere hangover to full-fledged migraine. As he sat there, his hair still wet from a last-minute shower, he did his best to focus his blurred vision and regain his bearings. He listened dutifully as the chairman, Senator Del Cutler, began his remarks. The senator, a tall stately figure, with a deep tan and slicked-back white hair, affected a down-home aw shucks manner that could only have been scripted by a media consultant. Gone this time was the shrill, prosecutorial demeanor that had backfired in the first set of hearings. If only the House Managers had taken heed, some thought.

"I'd like to start by thanking my colleagues on both sides of the aisle for agreeing to participate in what I hope will be the last set of hearings on campaign finance abuses during the last presidential election cycle," began the senator. "I know that some of you all are up for reelection and would prefer to be back home with your constituents. For the record, I sympathize with your situation, but I ask that the voters understand that we are dealing with a matter of vital national importance. Any further delay in this investigation is likely to result in the loss of evidence and to undermine the ability of key witnesses to have full recollection of events that occurred several years ago," he drawled.

So this is how it was going to be, thought Hanson. The chairman was going to play the role of Senator Sincere, so sweet and kindly that everyone within earshot ran the risk of hyperglycemia. Meanwhile, he would assign the job of henchman to some other member of the committee. Once again, Hanson had to hand it to the Republicans. Their strategy was perfect.

"Now, after consultation with both sides, we have agreed to expedite these proceedings by having our respective counsels handle the bulk of the questioning. I think we all agree that time is of the essence and that the sooner we get to the facts the sooner we can adjourn. Do I have a motion to that effect?"

"Motion," said a colleague to the chairman's right.

"Is there a second?" asked the Senator, looking to the Democratic side, hoping for any sign of support. Seeing nothing but stone-faced grimaces, he looked back the other way, where several senators of his own ilk willingly obliged.

"Motion carried," he said, banging down the gavel. "All right, according to our agenda, our first witness today will be Michael Hanson. For the record, Mr. Hanson is the deputy campaign manager of the Albert for President campaign and served as the deputy finance chairman of the 1996 reelection effort. In that capacity, Mr. Hanson has testified on five prior occasions before this committee. Mr. Hanson, thank you for agreeing to appear on such short notice. I assume you have an opening statement, sir?"

Hanson fidgeted in his seat for several seconds. To all who observed him, this was a very different witness than the man who'd testified so many times back in '97 and '98. Back then, while everyone else was panicked, hurrying to line up the best legal talent in the city, Hanson viewed his chance to testify as an opportunity, joking that it was the ultimate audition. Besides his very pricey lawyer, he bragged openly that he also hired a personal trainer and a publicist. He knew that in a war of sound bites, he had to maintain a propaganda advantage. Every time the committee leaked some tidbit about his testimony, he was ready to strike back. And for a time it worked. He may have been driven to the brink of insolvency by the investigation, but his reputation, while dubious to some, remained largely intact.

To the members of the committee, to the reporters in the press pool, Hanson had long been known as the man who never met a microphone he didn't like. But today he seemed out of sorts. Normally dapper, his suit was wrinkled, his skin pale. While no one in the hearing room could have had any idea of the kind of morning he'd had—starting with Detective Kennedy's early-morning wake-up call and their subsequent visit to the morgue—few would have actually given a damn. In Washington, there is nothing people enjoy more than seeing someone crash and burn. To many, Hanson was practically invincible, but today he looked as though he'd finally cracked under the pressure. The buzz was clear: The sharks smelled blood. For the first time since the scandal broke, Mike Hanson looked guilty.

"Mr. Hanson?" the Senator repeated.

Hanson turned to his counsel, a $500-an-hour pit bull who was a veteran of ABSCAM, Iran-Contra, and Filegate named Nick Lombardi. "So what do I do?" he asked.

Lombardi, a stout man with bulging eyes whose olive skin would turn bright red when he was angry, was none too pleased with his client for missing their strategy meeting earlier in the day. His tone was emphatic. "You do nothing. You have no prepared statement, so you do nothing. Just answer all their questions."

"Nick, I see your point. It's just that there are a few things that I really want to get off my chest."

Lombardi looked at Hanson, his cheeks getting flushed. "Not today you don't."

"How about I just wing it?"

"How about you do five years in Allenwood for perjury? Michael, I am dead serious. You cannot just give an off-the-cuff statement to these bastards. They'll destroy you."

The senator was growing impatient. "Gentlemen, can we get started? Does the witness have an opening statement or not?"

Hanson turned away and faced the panel. "Uh, Senator, the truth is that I really didn't plan on giving an opening statement.

In fact my counsel has strongly advised against it. But after listening to your opening remarks I do have a few comments, if it pleases the committee."

"Go ahead. Remember you are under oath."

"How could I forget?" he said, causing some laughter among the crowd. As Lombardi slumped in his seat, rubbing his brow between his fingers, his blood pressure skyrocketing, Hanson continued. "First, I want to commend the chairman for his gracious manner, particularly concerning the inconvenience caused by the timing of these hearings. I'm sure your fellow committee members are grateful for your concern." Stopping for a moment to take a sip of water, Hanson studied the panel, particularly the chairman. It was obvious they had no idea where he was going with this. "As I said, I very much want to commend you, Mr. Chairman. But the trouble is, as I look at the makeup of the committee, I can't help but notice that seven out of eight Democrats on it are up for reelection, while only one of the Republican members has a race this year. . . ."

"Mr. Hanson, is there some relevant point you're trying to make?" snapped the senator.

Hanson felt bad. The senator was basically a good guy who was trying his best to be fair in a toxically partisan climate. "Well, Mr. Chairman, I'm just curious if the timing of these hearings has anything to do with the GOP's plan to hold its majority in the Senate? I mean, how can these folks campaign when they're stuck here in Washington?"

The senator was furious. He may have been a pawn in his party's "takedown" strategy against the White House, but he was well known as a man of integrity. "Mr. Hanson, I strongly resent the implication that the timing of these hearings is in any way related to election-year politics. . . ."

Amid an explosion of flashbulbs, the senator spent the next several minutes on a tirade defending the objectivity of the hearings. As he carried on, he began to appear ridiculous even to members of his own party. This was Washington, where special investigations and select committees are a way of life. Every four years the party out of power will, without fail, find a reason to investigate the Executive Branch. The closer to the Oval Office the better. This time around, the Senate, an institution that normally thrives on high drama, was still trying to recover from its post-impeachment hangover. Timingwise, it was the best chance the Repos had in years. The setting was near perfect—election-year politics at its best, a televised Congressional hearing featuring a tough committee counsel grilling a tortured witness in search of the ever-elusive smoking gun.

As Hanson listened, he could feel Lombardi's angry scowl trained on him. He looked over to see his counsel shaking his head in disgust. The hearing was less than five minutes old and Hanson had already pissed off the chairman in a major way. It was going to be a very, very long day.

". . . So having put that matter to rest, let's begin the first round of questions for the witness. "Ms. Harris, you have the floor," the chairman said.

Although Hanson had no way of knowing it, this was the moment everyone in the hearing room had been waiting for. Danielle Harris was tall, blond, and brilliant, the kind of woman that all men claim to want but of whom they are secretly terrified. Harvard-educated, with five years as a federal prosecutor under her belt, she had obliterated Tom Griffin the day before, leaving the normally composed Messiah so tongue-tied that he could hardly explain the difference between soft money and soft ice cream. As for this afternoon's showdown, it pitted the committee's one-woman Dream Team versus Mr. Sound Bite. The fact that a seemingly vulnerable Hanson had already drawn first blood was of great relief to the crowd of media, who were banking on the fact that today's hearings would offer enough fireworks to be thc lcad story on thc evening's network news.

Despite having a vague recollection of Danielle Harris, Hanson didn't quite make the connection. As a rule, committee counsels of either sex do not tend to be the most attractive individuals in town. Overworked and underpaid, most have never seen the inside of a gym, let alone a beauty salon. "Makeovers waiting to happen" was the joke. Although the Danielle Harris he remembered was attractive enough and very decent, she was nothing like the Allure cover girl seated only a few feet from him. How could anybody age this well? Hanson wondered.

Dressed in a classically cut teal suit that seemed to accentuate her healthy tan, Danielle took a seat next to the chairman. After first adjusting the microphone and donning her half-rimmed glasses, she took a moment to review her notes. Then, very slowly, she looked up and made eye contact with her prey for the first time. "Mr. Hanson, again, on behalf of the committee, thank you for coming. We are well aware of the enormous strain your numerous appearances have put on you professionally. And while some on the committee have found your demeanor to be somewhat irreverent, the consensus among the panel is that you have been mostly forthcoming," she said solicitously. "As for today's line of questioning, it will focus on the activities of Vice President Albert as they specifically pertain to fund-raising strategy during the 1996 campaign. . . ."

"The hell it will," snapped Hanson.

"Excuse me, Mr. Hanson. What did you just say?"

Hanson took a drink of water, amazed at how warm it had become under the blaze of lights. Over and over he thought of the Bundlemeister's mantra: Admit nothing; Deny everything; When cornered, attack with countercharges. "I said, the hell it will."

"Mr. Hanson, let me remind you that you have voluntarily accepted a lawful subpoena from this committee—"

Nick Lombardi, having serious doubts as to his client's sanity by this time, quickly intervened. "Mr. Hanson is well aware of that and apologizes to the committee—"

In an instant, Hanson covered the microphone with his hand. "Nick, if you ever do that again, you're fired, got it?"

"Mike, you are out of control."

"It's about time somebody was," Hanson said as he turned back to the panel. "As I was saying, Ms. Harris, there is no way I'm going to discuss the Vice President's involvement in the '96 fund-raising plan. I've already testified chapter and verse on the subject. I simply have nothing more to add. Besides, didn't the Justice Department pass on this one?"

"Mr. Hanson, would it surprise you to learn that you are currently the official target of an investigation by the Special Prosecutor?"

"Which one?" he retorted. "HUD, Agriculture, Energy? Or is that independent counsel still out there winning friends and influencing people?"

"Take your pick," said Danielle.

Hanson chuckled. After what he had been through, being named an official target of an investigation was no big deal. Some of his friends had even told him that it might be a blessing in disguise, having the ironic benefit of triggering the Federal Adjudication Compensation Act, which provided funds for the legal bills of private citizens targeted by federal investigations. Amazingly, as his lawyers' fees continued to mount, Hanson actually found himself hoping that he would be named an official target. But alas, there was one hitch: to collect you had to be found innocent in a court of law or officially exonerated by the special prosecutor. Hanson knew that the truth was that in this climate the chances of either were slim or none. There was no getting around it. He was stuck. The Republicans had him right where they wanted. "Look, counsel, I really don't give a damn whether I'm a target or not," he began, somehow managing to maintain his gameface. "Since these hearings began I've told you everything I know about the '96 fund-raising operation. To my knowledge your investigators have questioned everyone I have ever known, including my own mother. The fact is that I'm just burned out. More to the point, I don't remember much more than I've already told you. . . ."

True to form, Mike Hanson was living up to his reputation for being a defiant, incorrigible ham that played to the media. That much was expected. But what Danielle Harris didn't anticipate was that the star witness also appeared to be a man who had nothing to lose. It was obvious to her that with the election so close, he was willing to risk almost anything, a contempt of Congress citation, even jail time, rather than offer up any kind of a comment that would hurt his candidate. Hanson was a true believer, and that made him dangerous. He was media-savvy, a real pro. As for Danielle, this was her first time at the dance. This was the closest thing to an audition you get in politics. Any kind of setback this early in the game would prove fatal. She had to win at all costs. It was time to go for the jugular.

"Mr. Hanson, believe it or not, I sympathize with your position. No one in their right mind would trade places with you. You say you are burned out, and I say fair enough. After all, who could blame you? A dozen depositions, grand jury appearances, six months fighting the impeachment of the President, not to mention your dealings with this committee. It's a wonder that even you can tell when you're telling the truth or not!"

Her last comment gave Hanson pause. Up to that point he was enjoying having the undivided attention of a beautiful woman. This beautiful woman. All of a sudden he remembered what it was about Danielle Harris that stuck in his mind all these years. It was her sincerity, her obnoxious, sincere sincerity. Unfortunately, the whole thing had the unmistakable feel of a setup. "Uh, Ms. Harris. I really don't know what to say. . . . Thanks, I guess . . ."

Danielle looked at Hanson with pity. He was likable, a lot like the guys that would come over to hang out with her older brother. Big, funny, wiseguy jocks with an unmistakable crush on little sister. Destroying him wasn't going to be fun. "Mr. Hanson, let's focus on the issue of your recollection."

"Fine."

"Your full recollection."

"Whatever."

"What would you say if I told you that a senior party official describes your relationship with the White House as 'indispensable'? That during the campaign both the President and Vice President 'absolutely refused to make a move without checking with you first?' "

"I'd say that person was somewhat deluded."

"What would you say if I told you that the person who made those statements was Tom Griffin?"

On the inside Hanson was numb. On the outside, the surface of his skin was red-hot, a lot like the feeling people get when they get pulled over by a cop, or get dumped, or when someone dies. He remembered the night before at Nathan's how Griffin had avoided the subject when Hanson brought up the hearings. He had written it off to the Messiah's generally lousy mood that night, never thinking that there could have been something more behind his silence.

"Tom Griffin gives me way too much credit," he began awkwardly. "As I told you, it was all a long time ago. My memory . . ."

"Mr. Hanson," Danielle snapped, "I must say at this point that

I find your testimony somewhat disingenuous. Isn't it true that you were not only an advisor to the Reelect, but were in fact the chief architect of the '96 fund-raising plan, including the effort to mobilize wealthy Asian donors, Asian donors who were directly linked to the theft of classified U.S. nuclear technology at Los Alamos Nuclear Laboratories?"

By now it was obvious to Hanson and everyone else in the Committee Room that Danielle Harris had cultivated one hell of an ability to get under people's skin. "Counsel, do you really want to talk about being disingenuous? I mean particularly after your party's stellar showing at the impeachment trial. Do you really want to go there, Ms. Harris?"

"I and the American people want answers, Mr. Hanson. And by the way, as long as we're at it, the truth about you and the China connection would be nice," she said.

By now Hanson was fuming. All at once the bile in the pit of his stomach from the meeting with Leonard Lynch, Adam's revelation, the run-in with Paul Angelo, and Detective Kennedy's wild accusations boiled to the surface. "Counsel, you want truth. Great. Let's talk about the truth. The truth is that this committee has been investigating campaign finance for over three years now. The truth is that this whole thing has cost the taxpayer over thirty million dollars. The truth is that this committee has issued over a thousand subpoenas with all but fifty targeted at Democrats. All this after the honorable chairman pledged to conduct an honest and balanced investigation."

The chairman, who had been content up to this point to sit back and let Danielle do his bidding, quickly pounded his gavel in an attempt to regain order. "Mr. Hanson, you are dangerously close to being in contempt. I instruct you to wait until counsel has asked you a direct question before you begin spewing reckless accusations to this panel—"

"I'm just getting started, Mr. Chairman."

"Mr. Hanson, isn't it a fact that the Democratic Party has had to return over three million dollars in illegally raised soft money?" injected Danielle.

Hanson was unfazed by the question. "Yeah, that sounds about right. Almost the same number as the Republicans, who, by the way, outraised us last year by over seventy-five million dollars."

"So your position would be that since everybody's doing it, then it's okay?"

"No, counsel, my position is that the system is so broken it can't work. No amount of reform will help as long as the gutless wonders in this chamber constantly campaign against PACs and special interest money and whatever else is convenient."

"Mr. Hanson, you, sir, are in contempt—" began the chairman, stopping in midsentence as Danielle squeezed his arm tight enough to restrict his circulation. He turned and looked at his counsel. Her eyes said it all. She saw an opening and wanted to go in for the kill.

Danielle took a moment to collect herself. Her senior members of the committee, including the chairman, had wanted a lengthy, brutal interrogation of this witness. Instead she would opt for a high-risk strategy. If it worked she would deliver Hanson's head on a platter. If it backfired, the game, and maybe even the election, would be over. "Excuse me, Mr. Chairman, but I think we owe the witness the courtesy of at least hearing him out."

"Very well. Continue, Mr. Hanson, but keep a civil tongue in your head."

For the first time that afternoon, Hanson felt encouraged. It was always a good sign when the opposition bickered among themselves. "Look, let's say General Motors gives a hundred grand to one of the political parties. They've got at least a hundred thousand employees. That works out to about a dollar an employee. Big deal! The trouble is that nobody wants to admit the truth. I mean hell, getting elected in this country is more expensive than any place on earth, but we still have to operate under spending limits set up twenty-five years ago. Lemme tell you, every single consumer item in America has gone up exponentially in cost over the last twenty-five years—cars, houses, food, medicine, you name it. But in politics we still have to work with limits set up in 1974. Do you have any idea how long ago 1974 was? Rap music hadn't even been invented in 1974! Neither had the fax machine. My god, in 1974 the Ford Maverick was the car of the year!"

With the last comment the chamber erupted in loud, sustained laughter. Until then, Hanson was doing a good job of digging his own grave. Unfortunately for Danielle and the committee, he saved himself at the last moment with the sound bite of the day. She had to counterattack and she had to do it quickly. After studying him for several seconds, it came to her. "Mr. Hanson, are you, as a senior Democratic campaign official, saying that campaign finance reform isn't necessary?"

Maybe it was the heat from the camera lights, or his splitting headache, but Hanson completely missed the deftly loaded question. "No, Counsel. I'm saying that campaign finance reform won't work. It is a waste of time so long as there are fifty thousand lawyers in this town who would like nothing more than a chance to show their clients a way around it."

Perfect, thought Danielle. Hanson had given her almost everything she wanted. "Mr. Hanson, I'd say that I'm just about done here. I have only one more question. As to your position that campaign finance reform is a waste of time. Does the People's Republic of China agree with you?"

Almost instantly the barrage of flashbulbs repeated itself as everyone with a camera trained their lenses on Hanson's face to gauge his reaction. Hanson sat there stunned, the sweat beading up on his upper lip, amazed at how he had been sandbagged by Danielle Harris. For a moment he was frozen, certain that whatever he said could only do further damage.

Danielle used the lull in the action to sharpen her blade. She had already drawn blood, it was time to go for the kill. "Did you hear me all right, Mr. Hanson?"

"I heard you just fine, counsel."

"What about the Vice President, Mr. Hanson? Does the Democratic nominee for president agree with your position that campaign finance reform is a waste of time?"

Amid the sounds of camera shutters and the bustle of reporters attempting to get closer, Hanson glared at Danielle with a feeling of sheer contempt so palpable that it made him feel physically sick. Then, as the chamber grew silent once again, he was fully aware that everyone in the hearing room was tilting on his response. He said only, "Nice try, Counsel . . . nice try."

Knowing that his side had taken the day, the chairman slammed down the gavel. "The committee will recess until ten A.M. tomorrow morning," he said.

Part Three

"Success in this town depends on how much they fear you. It's just that simple."

—Richard Nixon

Chapter Sixteen

The emergency 911 pages started coming in on Hanson's digital pager before sunrise. All were from Tom Griffin, who was both boiling mad and scared for his buddy all at the same time. Hanson, famous for pulling disappearing acts on the campaign trail—usually a woman was involved—had missed a long-scheduled Tuesday night dinner with several of the party's biggest contributors. Griff couldn't help but feel concerned. To pull a stunt like this with the election less than thirty days off was way out in left field, even for the man-child Mike Hanson. The word on the street was that Hanson had gotten pretty roughed up during his testimony. But having gone through the same thing the day before, Griffin could only have so much sympathy. No, there had to be more. Otherwise, Griffin thought, the deputy campaign manager was going to have a very bad day.

As for Hanson, he was fortunate enough to leave his pager on tone, the silence of which allowed him to sleep through most of Griffin's messages and nurse the killer hangover that was brewing inside his head. It was only after the twentieth or so attempt that the pager vibrated enough to fall off a nearby table, crashing onto the hardwood floor, the sound of which woke Hanson.

When he arrived at the campaign, tie untied, hair still wet from his shower, he found Griffin sitting alone in his spacious office reviewing FEC reports.

"Well, if it isn't the ghost of fucking Mike Hanson. Sit down, Mike, sit down," Griffin said. "Can I get you anything? Coffee, tea? A good lawyer, perhaps?"

Hanson sat down, watching Griffin closely. Despite the sarcasm, Griffin seemed pretty calm on the surface, but his voice was strained and he looked exhausted. Smart money said to hold off spilling his guts and let the Messiah make the first move.

For several seconds no one said a word. This was by design. Hanson knew his loquacious friend was a chatterbox and sitting in silence would make him just uncomfortable enough to start talking away when given the opportunity. Roughly a minute passed. Then Griff, leaning back in his chair and staring out the window, said, "So what's going on, Mike?"

Hanson shrugged his shoulders. Nothing happened in this town without Griffin catching wind of it. He had to have heard about his performance before the committee. The only question was whether he'd been tipped off about the murder investigation.

Griffin tilted his head. "Is there anything you want to tell me?"

Hanson shook his head and rubbed his bloodshot eyes.

"Well then," Griffin said, his voice starting to boom, "I would like to know why you were impossible to get ahold of yesterday? And why you missed dinner last night? I figured you were dead. But obviously you are not. Frankly, at this moment I'm not sure if that is a good or a bad thing. So I'll ask you again. What's going on here, Mike?" Griffin went on. "We're running a presidential campaign here. We're in the last lap, the race is neck and neck, and my right hand man isn't anywhere to be found!"

"What can I say, Griff? I guess I was just too busy being indispensable to the fucking White House."

Griffin rolled his eyes.

"I was just so caught up thinking of ways to funnel Asian money into the campaign . . . or shapely young interns into the Oval Office. Better yet, how about funneling shapely young interns into the campaign?"

"Okay, okay. I get the point. Now I understand why you're pissed. I guess I deserved that. Although that last suggestion is certainly intriguing," he said. "But for the record, Mikey, that lady lawyer twisted my words. Everything I said about you I meant as a compliment."

"Right, like the part about me being the chief architect of the Chinese connection."

"I never said that, you can check the committee transcript," Griffin explained.

"You can count on it."

Despite Griffin's valiant attempts at mea culpa, Hanson was buying none of it. The two had been through more campaigns together than they could count and had never turned on each other, not even once. Until now. Of all the rotten things he'd gone through since '96, this was the worst.

"Mike, I honestly can't believe you'd think that I would sell you out."

Hanson looked at his best friend with disdain. "I honestly can't believe you could be such a fucking pussy."

"Goddamn it, Mike. It's just that fucking Danielle Harris. She can make you say anything that she damn well pleases."

"Tell me about it."

"So are we still speaking?"

"Sure, Griff, no problem. At least until after the election," Hanson snapped.

Sensing that the worst was over, Griffin asked, "Is this why you blew off our meetings?"

Hanson took a deep breath. "No, no, not really. I just had a rough day yesterday," Hanson said, trying to explain. "Personal stuff I had to attend to. An emergency came up."

"Does it concern your daughter?" Griffin said, looking at Hanson knowingly.

Hanson blew up. This was all he needed. "Griff, what the fuck are you talking about?" Blood rushed to his face and pounded in his ears. "Where the hell did you hear that garbage?"

"Mike, take it easy, it had to be a huge blow to find out that CeCe never told you about your daughter," Griffin began, loving the chance to play amateur psychologist. "And then to find out she'd been murdered?"

"Griff!" Hanson screamed.

"Mike, buddy. I'm here to help, honest."

"Griff, if you want to help, just go back to being an asshole like you usually are and let me handle this my way."

"Well, that's a little difficult, Mike, with police detectives and reporters from the *Washington Post* breathing down my neck." Griffin sat back in his chair, crossed his arms, and looked expectantly at Hanson. "What I really want to know is why you didn't think you could tell me what was going on?"

Hanson was floored. Griffin really looked hurt. "Tell me about the police."

"A homicide detective named Kennedy stopped by to check your alibi and ask a few questions. He seemed like a good guy. I didn't get the impression that he was trying to link you to your daughter's murder."

"Griff, for the last time, I don't have a daughter. Frankly, I have no goddamn idea why any of this is happening. How much does the *Post* know?" Hanson asked.

"So far not much. I spoke with Eleanore Savoy from their national desk. It seemed like she was sniffing around for dirt, to see if any Ds might have been at the Pavilion that night. So far she hasn't mentioned your name. You weren't there that night, were you, Mike?"

Griffin was really pissing Hanson off and it showed in his face.

"All right, goddamn it. I'll lay off. But you should have told me just the same."

"I know, I know. I just tried to keep it quiet because I thought it could hurt the campaign."

Griffin rolled his eyes. "Well, you have hurt us by missing an entire day of meetings yesterday. But what the fuck, it's only money, we'll raise more. So as long as you're here in my presence, is there any more to this story?"

Hanson smiled bitterly. "Oh, you'd be surprised." And he began to tell his friend. When he was done, Griffin's mouth hung open in amazement.

"Mike, is there any way I can help?"

Hanson just shook his head.

"Do you think you're in real danger?" Griffin asked. "We could hire you a security guard—I could even stick close, keep an eye on things."

Hanson considered all that had happened to him. "No, I think up to now how, it's just harassment. To rattle my cage. And lemme tell ya, it's working. If these bastards wanted to really hurt me they've had plenty of chances. I'm also not totally convinced that my house being ransacked wasn't just a coincidence." Hanson shook his head. "If I can just get past the election, things should just work themselves out."

"Mike, in light of everything that has been going on . . . I mean, shit, the atmosphere in this town has become simply paranoid! Maybe you should take a few days off," Griffin said gently.

"No way," Hanson said, and heard his voice rise. Griffin couldn't take the campaign away from him. "This campaign is as much mine as it is yours, Griff. I've got work to do. Besides, you need me, especially if Thurman decides to endorse Prescott."

Griffin was silent, considering it for only a few seconds. "Okay," he said, and pointed at Hanson. "But if you're in the game, you're in it 100 percent. It's crunch time and we need your undivided attention. You have to make a decision: either get your head back in the game or get out now."

Hanson didn't hesitate. "I'm in."

"Good," Griffin barked. "Although you might want to change your mind after you hear the latest. We got a call from Public Voice, that citizen's action group that's been snooping around our finances. I'm worried."

"Don't worry about it; we haven't done anything," Hanson said.

"Well, who's to say what's right and wrong these days?" Griffin replied, clearly distracted, running a hand through his hair.

Hanson stared at his friend. Griffin usually didn't know the meaning of pessimism. What was going on?

"Well, Mike, you might as well know the real bad news," Griffin said. "I got final confirmation from my sources that Thurman is definitely pulling out of the race."

Hanson whistled softly. He felt like he was just punched in the stomach. "Shit," he muttered. As it was, the race was neck and neck. Without the split Republican vote, the Dems were in serious trouble. "Shit, Shit, Shit, Shit, Shit!" he said louder.

"That's not the worst of it," Griffin continued. "His campaign is so saddled with debt that it's likely to endorse whichever side will offer them a better deal—that includes debt retirement."

"That's bullshit," Hanson interrupted. "So it all comes down to whoever has more cash to pay them off."

"Yep. Mike, we're talking with Thurman's people, but the truth is, we've still got to pay for this campaign. I don't see how we can compete with the Repos. He needs to retire his campaign debt, pure and simple. And that's out of our league."

"That gives us about . . . uh . . . four days. Fund two campaigns in four days. A cake walk." Hanson was trying hard to control his anger.

Griffin looked grim. "And so the dance begins."

Hanson thought for a moment, tired of being a victim, and got a sudden burst of determination. "We're not dead in the water yet. We'll make it work, Griff, we always do."

Griffin nodded and flashed his big Irish smile for the first time that morning. "Now that's what I like to hear. Okay, let's get back to work. You and I have a lunch date at the Palm at twelve-thirty."

"With who?"

"With nobody. Actually, that's only half true. See, my spies tell me that Gopey Taylor is setting up a daisy chain in six big electoral states. The Repos are trying to funnel a shitload of cash into key state races, trying to create a reverse coattail effect."

"Where do we come in?"

"Word has it that Gopey is taking a couple of Republican 'Eagles' to lunch at the Palm today to close the deal," said Griffin, referring to the term—a magnificent bird of prey—that the GOP uses to label their biggest supporters.

"Don't you think that's a little indiscreet, even for Gopey?" Hanson asked. Griffin's longtime nemesis, GOP finance chairman Richard "Gopey" Taylor, was a tall, skinny North Carolinian who bore a striking resemblance to Ron Howard, or a grown-up Opie Taylor. Years ago, during a joint appearance of Griffin and Taylor on "Crossfire," Griffin figured that given his counterpart's affiliation with the GOP and his looks, he had a moral obligation to anoint him with the nickname "GOPey." Suffice it to say, the former Richard Taylor, a lover of the limelight and a true publicity hound, was none too pleased to have his identity transformed à la sound bite on national television. Before long the name stuck. Everyone, including fellow Republicans, even his own wife, began calling him Gopey. For that he had no one other than his arch enemy, Tom Griffin, to blame.

"Mike, don't you get it? Gopey is doing this just to stick it in our face. To send us a signal that we're through. He knows we eat at the Palm all the time."

Hanson laughed. Griffin loved this part of the game more than anybody. Winning was one thing, but mixing it up face to face reminded him of his football days. "So what's the plan?"

"You and I pop over there just after noon and crash his party. I've called Bundlemeister, he's meeting us with a mystery guest."

"Why am I not surprised?"

"You shouldn't be. Hey listen, before you go, don't forget, tonight is the First Lady's birthday party at the White House. It will be her last one at the White House. And bring a present for a change."

Hanson was grateful for the reminder. With all that was going on, he not only would have failed to bring a present but would have forgotten about the party altogether. "Gotcha. Anything else?"

A hint of a smile crossed Griffin's face and he looked questioningly at Hanson. "One more thing. You weren't by any chance thinking of jumping ship, abandoning us poor Democrats, were you?"

"What are you talking about?"

Griffin held a pink telephone message slip in his hands. "This is for you. Oliver Devon wants to have drinks with you later on today."

Hanson was flabbergasted. "With me? He's a billionaire. Not to mention a Republican. I'm, well, I'm not exactly in his league."

"Such a gift for understatement. . . ."

"Come on, Griff. Why the fuck would Oliver Devon want to have drinks with me?"

Griffin handed Hanson the message slip. "Why don't you find out?"

Chapter Seventeen

Kennedy slammed down the phone and twisted the cord between his fingers. Hanson was telling the truth about at least one thing: He didn't kill Ariel Fairchild. On the night of the murder, Hanson was at a AFL-CIO fund-raiser at the Sequoia restaurant. Kennedy just wasted two hours of his time sitting in this noisy, overheated station house, calling a who's who list of big wheel politicos and union leaders who all told him the same thing. While Ariel Fairchild was being murdered, they were sucking down scotches with Kennedy's one and only suspect.

Kennedy seethed with frustration. He had no suspects, and the trail was icing over. He knew the statistics by heart; murders were solved quickly or they weren't solved at all. Kennedy hated to fail at anything, and he knew Division would never let him forget it if he couldn't solve this case. Already a reporter from the *Post* had left a message for him; soon the networks would be running their stories about an investigation going nowhere. The pressure for answers would build, and, as things stood, he had none to give.

A large shadow passed over his desk and hovered there, blocking the light. He looked up into another detective's eyes.

"Kennedy, Captain wants to see you," said the detective. "Pronto. He's raging mad."

"Great," Kennedy said. "I guess I know what this is about."

"Yeah, well," the detective said. "Any solid leads yet?"

Kennedy shook his head and rose slowly from his chair. When his beeper began to vibrate, he pulled the number off the display and quickly dialed it.

"Kennedy here."

"It's Ira."

"What's up, Detective?"

"Abe, you're not gonna believe this one."

"What'cha got?"

"DOA, another kid," said Murray. "Same profession. But this time it's not a girl."

"Shit," Kennedy said, pounding the desk. "Where are you at?"

"The Westin, off P Street."

"I'll be right there." Kennedy grabbed his gray sports jacket and headed for the door. The other detective watched him disbelievingly. Kennedy paused at the door and spun around, "Tell the captain I'll get with him when I get back."

The detective held his hands up and said, "You're gonna have to tell him that yourself."

Kennedy ran out to his car. He pulled out of the lot, tossing the red bubble light onto the unmarked black sedan's roof. It bottomed out leaving the lot, and Kennedy swerved onto the street.

Another kid, murdered, thought the detective as he weaved his way across town. Contrary to precinct house legend, Detective Abe Kennedy cared about some things in life more than just catching criminals. He was raised from birth to be a role model for the other black children in the neighborhood. His father was a schoolteacher, as stern a taskmaster as you could find. And no mother ever loved a son more than Mama Kennedy loved young Abe. Over her husband's vehement objection, she insisted on naming him after this country's sixteenth president. Of course, at the time, no one could have foreseen that the lad would someday share a surname with another of this country's beloved presidents.

Young Abe made a habit of exceeding people's expectations. All-Met Quarterback in high school, student body president, full scholarship to Howard University. Above all, this young man was a leader. To hear his father tell it, with a name like Abe Kennedy, there was no question that his son would grow up to be the country's first black president. Everyone in the neighborhood agreed, the kid had it all. Unfortunately, there were two things no one counted on: Vietnam, and a druglord named Andre Moten.

The summer after his freshman year, knowing he was prime draft bait, Abe didn't even bother returning to school. Before the leaves turned color he'd received his induction notice. And by the time Thanksgiving rolled around, Pfc. Kennedy was leading point for an infantry unit somewhere in a jungle south of the Laotian border.

Fortunately, as with everything else in his life, Abe Kennedy succeeded in war—that is, if your definition of success is coming back in one piece with a chest full of medals. With a bronze star and a Purple Heart in hand, Kennedy returned home to the shock of his life. He could hardly recognize the neighborhood he dreamt about every night for two years, a close-knit community where the residents looked out for each other's children. To Kennedy's horror, his old neighborhood had become infested with druglords competing over turf.

The most ruthless of these was a New York dealer named Andre Moten. Word on the street had it that Moten was sent down by a Harlem gang to set up operations and take over the D.C. heroin trade. Almost overnight, Kennedy's old stomping grounds were filled with small-time pushers and whores. Robberies, break-ins, and muggings by the junkies Moten created happened almost daily. It got so bad that young kids couldn't walk to school without finding syringes or used condoms lying in the middle of the sidewalk.

Worst of all, just days before Kennedy returned, three of his high school teammates were brutally gunned down in a shootout less than fifty feet from his parents' home, some of the bullets shattering the windows of their living room. Everybody knew it was Moten, apparently in retaliation for some argument over a woman. Among the dead was Abe's sixteen-year-old cousin.

Once he learned of the killings, Kennedy immediately swore revenge, promising personally to bring Moten down. It didn't take long, though, for him to see that the problem was bigger than just

Andre Moten. Which is why, only hours after his cousin's funeral, Kennedy went down to the District Building and, breaking his father's heart, made out an application to join the Metropolitan Police. Abe Kennedy was going to get Moten all right, but he was going to do it his way.

Kennedy made homicide detective in less than five years, considered by most to be some kind of a department record. As luck would have it, one of the first homicide investigations Kennedy ever worked on was the murder of one Andre Moten. The detective made no secret of his anger that some lucky bastard got Moten before Abe had his chance.

That was almost two decades ago, and Detective Kennedy never regretted his decision. He was committed to holding the line against the druglords for as long as he was still a cop. While he couldn't save the whole city, he still had his family to worry about, especially his fourteen-year-old son, A. J.

Earlier in the week, Kennedy's wife, Marlene, told Kennedy that A. J. was proving to be more than she could handle. Marlene was scared. It was bad enough before Abe was wounded, but since the shooting A. J. was a different person, determined to tempt fate at every chance. Abe's decision to return to the job seemed to only make matters worse.

Like many parents, the Kennedys made every effort to find a refuge for their family from the epidemic of drugs and violence that was plaguing the city, settling in a small house on Capitol Hill, a half-gentrified neighborhood of tiny parks, turn-of-the-century row houses, and a famous weekend outdoor market. On Kennedy's block, congressional staffers, lawyers, and lobbyists raised families and tended gardens. But only three blocks down, a crack house did business all day, everyday, including Christmas. Kennedy's neighborhood, sadly, was a buffer zone between two clashing worlds.

For official purposes, Washington is divided into four quadrants, but in reality it is a town divided between the haves of Northwest, and the have-nots of the rest of the city. Northwest is home to the luxury hotels, baronial homes, museums, and monuments. The other three sections are patchworks of housing projects, burned-out tenements, deserted industrial zones, and the occasional neighborhood struggling to survive. Except for sight-seeing side trips to the Capitol and thruway shortcuts out of town, few visitors, and still fewer residents, ever venture beyond the relative safety of Northwest. Kennedy and his wife loved their neighborhood and their neighbors, but even they were slowly being worn down by the drug posses and the nightly bursts of gunfire. And like many of the kids on their quiet, gentrified block, their son was mesmerized by the gangsta lifestyle. A. J. was suddenly becoming secretive and resentful of his parents' attempts to draw him out. He stayed out late after school. His grades were slipping so dramatically that together the Kennedys had taken him to a child psychologist for evaluation. What's more, Marlene didn't like the new crowd he was running with. She told her husband that they had gang banger written all over them.

Kennedy was enraged—and full of guilt. He felt like a complete failure. He hated the rap on black men that they weren't there for their children. Yet he couldn't help but wonder if he was falling into the stereotype. It was obvious that A. J. was having problems, and suddenly, only three days back on active duty, Kennedy couldn't even find an hour to talk to his own son.

As he fought his way through the one-way, clogged streets, Kennedy vowed to call home as soon as he could get away from this crime scene. Even though he had made it back, he was determined not to get caught up in the twenty-hour-a-day marathon cycles of so many investigations. As soon as he solved this case he would take a couple of personal days, spend them with his family, and make things right again.

He saw the Westin up ahead, and spied the squad car in the alley. As he pulled up to the service entrance, he could see Murray and two uniformed officers standing behind an industrial-sized Dumpster. Good, he'd arrived even before the crime scene team. The uniforms were just beginning to get the yellow tape out to block off the area. Even so, several busboys and a housekeeper in a pink uniform were standing outside the hotel's back entrance, peering toward the body.

Murray had a handkerchief over his mouth and nose, and Kennedy wondered how long the body had been there, decomposing in the sun.

"Damn, partner, you're white as a ghost," he called to Murray as he got out of the car. He took the keys and locked the doors as he left. Car thefts, even of police vehicles, were on the rise.

"Sorry I can't say the same," Murray said, his brow furrowed. "Take a look at this, Detective."

Kennedy approached the body. He sniffed, delicately, then pulled out his own handkerchief. The body had been there awhile. Two uniformed officers stood nearby, chatting, completely disinterested.

The victim, a male about twenty years old, lay atop a pile of garbage in the Dumpster. He wore nothing except torn jeans and sneakers. No shirt, no socks. His blood had congealed in the stab wounds all over his torso. His head fell at a decidedly unnatural angle to the rest of the body. Like Ariel Fairchild, his throat was crushed and encircled with bruises and abrasions.

Kennedy looked closer at the victim's face, more that of a boy than a man. The eyes stared straight ahead in horror. The detective closed the boy's eyes and observed that once again, the violence couldn't completely hide the innocence of youth. The boy's face was all angles and cheekbones. Fair skin, green eyes. He must have been a handsome kid—maybe too handsome for his own good, Kennedy thought ruefully. But now, like Ariel Fairchild, he was dead.

"Talk to me, Ira."

Murray picked up the boy's arm and pointed to the needle tracks running up and down the otherwise unblemished skin. "Detective, what we have here is a deceased male by the name of Rene La Salle aka Rick Lewis. Caucasian, approximately eighteen years of age; occupation—escort; health—lately not so good. Some preliminary indications are that he was violated anally and probably had oral sex shortly before his demise. Killed somewhere else and dumped here."

"Dumped like the pocketbook," Kennedy said softly. "Cause of death?"

"Crushed larynx, broken neck, multiple stab wounds . . . hard to tell yet which ultimately did him in. That's not all, either."

"What else?"

Murray grimaced and ran his hand through his hair. "His . . . ahh . . . well, his penis was severed at its base."

"Geezus," said Kennedy, somewhat startled. "Have we found it?"

"Not yet," Murray said, his cheeks sucked inward with revulsion.

"What else you got?"

Murray motioned for Kennedy to come closer. "The victim had almost nothing on his person. About a dollar's worth of change and an empty film canister."

"Drugs?"

"Like I said, it was empty. Forensics will check for any residue."

"Anything else?"

"Take a look at this."

Kennedy then saw the tattered piece of paper thumbtacked to the victim's jeans.

"A note?"

"Actually, it's a page from a personal telephone directory. Probably from the victim's trick book."

"Any sign of it?"

"Right there in his jacket pocket. Oh, by the way, you probably want to look under F." Kennedy flipped through until he found "CeCe Fairchild/Exotica."

"Have any idea what kind of place Exotica is?" Murray asked, but didn't really expect an answer. "Anyway, the page tacked to the body matches a missing section in the trick book—I, J, and K." he said. Using tweezers, Murray carefully removed the thumbtack and held up the page so Abe could read it. "Looks like the kid was servicing some heavyweight talent."

There were about six names on the K side of the page. Some of them were familiar. But one name, circled in bold red ink, stood out. Kennedy recognized the name immediately. He hoped it was just a coincidence, but unfortunately, he recognized the phone number as having one of the three prefixes reserved for Capitol Hill. There was no mistake. The name read:

"Malcolm Kassendine" -202-555-3452
-202-224-9999

Murray watched for Kennedy's reaction. "So, what do you make of this?"

Kennedy knew something wasn't right. They would have to be

cautious. Someone was trying to use the police to send a message, or a challenge. Maybe it was just a sick joke, he thought with little hope. He waited for a second to make sure the uniformed officers were out of earshot.

"Ira . . . we gotta keep this very quiet. Also, Captain's already on our case. He'll be waiting for us when we get back to the precinct."

Murray looked miserable and pointed to the circled name. "Is this guy who I think he is?"

Kennedy nodded yes. "Listen, have any of the uniforms seen this page?"

"Not up close."

"Let's make sure it stays that way."

"I was afraid that's what you were gonna say. So what's our next move?" asked Murray.

"We pay a visit to Senator Malcolm Kassendine . . . just like the killer wants us to."

Chapter Eighteen

With lunch booked, a late-afternoon meeting with Oliver Devon penciled in, and a White House party scheduled for that night, Hanson decided to use what precious little time he had left to handle the Adam Melrose problem. As it was, Hanson was certain that the Messiah was now hell bent on cramming his schedule to 150 percent of capacity for the last month of the campaign. Griff was the master at gaining leverage over people, and Hanson's disappearing act over the last few days had offered a golden opportunity to guilt trip him into an insane commitment of time. The truth was that Hanson didn't blame him, knowing that regardless of the polls or money, Griffin had every intention of winning this election. If he had to work himself and Hanson and everybody else into an early grave, then so be it. The good news for Hanson was that he still had two free hours that morning to get Rick Seltzer's mind right. And, while it was hardly enough time to deal with a streetwise reporter with an axe to grind, Hanson would make do. The fact was, he didn't have much choice.

When Hanson arrived at the office of the *Washington Blade*, the city's foremost alternative newspaper, he was surprised at just how much the people milling about looked, for lack of a better term, like him.

"What did you expect, a fucking 'Dream Girls' review?" snarled Rick Seltzer as he leaned back in his chair, arms folded, his Timberland boots propped up on his desk. Seltzer was all of six feet four inches, muscular, his goateed face accented by half a dozen or so small scars from countless rugby matches. His head was shaved clean, yet somehow managed to shine despite the dim gray office light. More noticeable though was the unmistakable chip on his shoulder. He reminded Hanson of his high school football coach, a likable enough guy, but so irrationally competitive that he alienated most of his own players. For Hanson, Seltzer was easy to size up. He was your basic hard case. Winning was good, but obliterating the enemy was better.

"Actually, Rick, I guess I expected your crew to be a whole lot more hip."

"Sorry, Hanson. Not every fag is a poster boy for Donatella Versace."

"I realize that, Rick," said Hanson. "But honestly, your whole staff is vintage Drew Carey."

"Not that there's anything wrong with that," Seltzer joked.

As Hanson sat across from Adam's ex, he sought to uncover the source of his hostility. Anger toward Adam Melrose was a fairly common phenomenon, and Hanson had come to expect that sort of reaction from people. But Seltzer's hostility was palpable, way past anything he had seen before. "So tell me, Rick, are you mad at Adam or just plain mad at the world?"

"What are you, my psychiatrist?" he snapped. "Cut the bullshit. I know why you're here. You can forget it. My mind is made up. I'm giving Adam an ultimatum tonight. Either he comes clean or we go public with his whole story," said the reporter.

"Will you calm down already?" Hanson pleaded. "I'm not here to change your mind. I've advised our mutual friend to take the high road. That it's time to end the charade."

"You have, huh?"

"Damned right. Although I personally have no earthly idea why the gay community would want to claim Adam Melrose as one of their own. But that's not really my problem."

Seltzer was amused. "I've asked myself that question several times. So why the hell are you here?"

"Career counseling."

"Excuse me?"

"Yeah. From what I know of you, you're a really bright guy with an extra shitty attitude. Which explains why your career is stuck in neutral, writing for a small-time rag like this."

Seltzer immediately took the challenge. "Hanson, assuming that you didn't come down here just to insult me, where the hell is this going?"

"The question, my friend, is where are you going? What are you, thirty-five, thirty-six? Is outing a congressional candidate your idea of a making journalistic history? For chrissakes, Rick, you oughta be with one of the big papers, chasing big stories."

"Cool. Big stories, like the impeachment of the fornicator in chief, or maybe the latest campaign finance investigation?"

"You're hysterical, do you know that? The point is that you oughta be out there winning Pulitzers instead of writing a politically correct gossip column."

"Maybe I like what I'm doing."

"Right. You like making forty a year. You like knowing that the only people that read your stuff already agree with you. You like watching the talk shows and seeing young little shits on TV who you can write rings around getting all that media exposure. Don't bullshit a bullshitter, Seltzer. You'd love to have a regular byline with the *Post* or the *Times*, making six figures a year, getting to play pundit from time to time. And groupies, don't forget groupies."

Seltzer rolled his eyes. Hanson was a real piece of work. "And lemme guess, you are here to help me?"

"Goddamn right I am."

"And why would you do that?"

"Because I would do absolutely anything to help Adam Melrose. Anything."

Seltzer was a little startled by Hanson's resolve. "I gotta ask you something. Why? I mean Adam is such a complete jerk."

Hanson knew he couldn't very well disagree with Seltzer's statement. "Actually, it's a little hard to explain. Part of it is that Adam and I go back so many years. Part of it is that I'm probably the only one he hasn't screwed over. Who knows? But the bottom line is that I'll do whatever it takes to stop you from hurting him.

And you and I both know that with the election so close, I haven't got a whole lotta options."

"Hanson, I appreciate loyalty as much as the next guy. But you gotta understand that I'm not afraid of you. I don't give a damn about politics and I don't give a damn about this president. So that leaves kicking my ass, which I don't think you can do."

Hanson smiled. He knew that the encounter would eventually turn in this direction. "Rick, this isn't about me kicking your ass. It's about the whole Melrose dynasty coming down so hard on you that you'll wish you were never born. The bottom line is that you can't win. You need to understand that if you go after Adam, it's the same as going after the whole Melrose family. Make no mistake about it, no matter how they feel about Adam's lifestyle, they will view this as a declaration of war. And lemme tell you, they are the most vindictive bunch of old-monied WASPs I've ever seen. If it hasn't dawned on you yet, don't forget that his old man owns television stations and a couple of newspapers back in Delaware. He sits on the boards of a dozen of the biggest corporations in the country. They will bury you . . . count on it!"

"You know Adam's whole life is a lie . . ."

"I'm beginning to understand that. But when he comes out, he'll do it when he's ready, on his own time."

"He doesn't deserve a friend like you."

"He probably doesn't deserve a friend like either of us. But he doesn't deserve to have his life ruined either."

Selzter took several deep breaths, much like a boxer about to enter the ring. He stood up. Hanson half expected him to lunge across the desk at him. Fortunately he turned instead and reached to a nearby bookshelf and grabbed a bottle of Wild Turkey and two small glasses. "Drink?"

"Absolutely," Hanson said.

Seltzer poured them both about two fingers of bourbon and slid a glass across the desk towards Hanson. After a long pause, Seltzer downed the liquid in one gulp. "So, you really know people at the *Post*?"

"Only the entire political desk," bragged Hanson as he raised his glass in salute to his nemesis. "I'll start making calls tomorrow."

* * *

Gopey Taylor was busy working his targets by the time Messrs. Hanson and Griffin arrived at the Palm. The restaurant, besides serving the best lobster and stiffest drinks in town, was well known for its trademark walls covered with hundreds of caricatures of its more prominent patrons—including presidents, first ladies, senators, publishers, and occasional movie stars. Today, courtesy of Gopey Taylor's greasing of the maitre d', the walls of the Palm boasted two new additions, Canfield Rittenour, a wealthy oilman from Galveston, and Xavier Peña, the richest man in Miami's Little Havana.

The Palm was a classic Washington contradiction—a loud, brassy joint boasting pridefully obnoxious waiters and the best service in town. If there was a more indiscreet meeting place in Washington no one knew about it. But the fact is, everyone who is anyone in Washington lunches or dines at the Palm. While other establishments offer more refined atmospheres, including Lennox china, Buccelatti silver, freshly cut orchids, not to mention quiet, the one thing diners at the Palm could count on was that no one, absolutely no one, could possibly eavesdrop on their conversation over the noisy din of the noontime lunch crowd. So if you didn't mind being just seen—and Gopey Taylor very much wanted to be seen and not heard—it provided the perfect venue.

"Why, that thing doesn't look a damned bit like me," said the oil baron as he looked across the table at his picture, strategically place in his field of vision.

"Canfield, it's uh, not supposed to. None of the pictures at the Palm are supposed to look like the real people," Gopey explained.

"Ross Perot's does. Looks just like the little fella!"

"Ross Perot is a caricature," said Peña, joking. "So, Gopey, explain this to me one more time, this 'daisy chain' idea of yours."

Gopey was quick to correct him. "Xavier, first, a 'daisy chain' isn't a term I would be comfortable using. That's for the Justice Department and suggests conspiracy or bid rigging, of all things. This is different. It isn't about profit. This is about winning the White House back not only from a president who can't keep it in his pants, but from the liberals who support him. Say you want to help our boy, Prescott, and, coincidentally, you also want to help out our Senate candidate in Florida. Great. But the law says you can only give a thousand to each man in the primary and a thousand in the general."

"Hell, I can't even do that in the presidential," Rittenour blurted.

"That's right. Not if our candidate is accepting federal matching funds. But that doesn't mean there isn't more you can do to help. Let's suppose besides the presidential and the Senate races, there's an important race for state attorney general. The GOP cares just as much about that race as any of the others," he said with the sincerity of a televangelist, knowing, in fact, that the national party didn't give two shits about who was the attorney general in Florida. "So the way you help out is by writing us another check, say in the neighborhood of two hundred fifty thousand dollars."

"And then you boys cut a check to the state party for the same amount?"

Gopey had to be careful here. In Washington you never know who's under investigation. "More or less. Of course, it depends on a number of factors."

"Like if the Senate candidate or the guy running for attorney general agrees with our presidential candidate. That's the point, isn't it, Gopey?" said Peña rather directly. He'd obviously done this dance before, and wanted Taylor to commit himself if he was going to pony up a quarter of a million dollars.

"Yes, Xavier, that would certainly be one of the considerations. Yes."

"And it wouldn't much matter if the Florida state party used the money to buy local ad time to run thirty-second spots on the key issues affecting the state races."

"Right. And if the state party's position happens to coincide with that of our presidential nominee, then so much the better," Gopey said enthusiastically.

"And this is supposed to be legal?" asked Peña, proving to be a tough nut to crack.

"It's one of those things that's not legal or illegal. It falls in between the cracks. Any election law type will tell you that tracing the DNA of soft money is damned near impossible."

"I still don't get it," said Rittenour, who was already working on his second Bloody Mary.

Gopey was frustrated with this yokel. "Here, let me show you," he said as he drew the diagram of a 'daisy chain' on a cocktail napkin. And then, like a huge explosion, a voice thundered over the crowd noise of the Palm.

"*Gopey!* Gopey Taylor? Why, as I live and breathe, what on earth are you doing here in my neck of the woods," screamed Tom Griffin at the top of his lungs. Leaning in to the table with Hanson in tow, Griffin slapped Gopey on the back, hard enough that the sound resonated throughout the nonsmoking section. "Hey fellas, how y'all doin'? Tom Griffin, Joe Albert for President, good to meet you," he repeated quickly, extending his mammoth hand to Gopey's guests. As he did so, both Rittenour and Peña recoiled in their seats. Gopey, meanwhile, was virtually speechless as Griffin refused to let up, pulling up a chair and taking a seat. "You boys know my partner in crime, Mike Hanson?"

Hanson, who basically felt sorry for Gopey, tried to be as polite as possible. "Hi guys, welcome to Washington. How you doing there, Richard?"

Gopey looked up, and despite Griffin's onslaught, almost smiled. He liked Hanson. After all, he was the only one in town who had enough consideration to still call him by his given name. "Hey, Mike. Don't you think you guys should check on your table?"

"Ah, screw our table. We'll eat when we're ready," said Griffin. "What about you guys? Do you see anything you like on the menu? Lemme guess, you guys are in the mood for pork. Well, you came to the right place. Just ask Gopey. Me, I'm a steak kinda guy. The rarer the better."

"Honestly, Griff. Do you mind? I'm conducting a business meeting here," he retorted.

Although to onlookers at surrounding tables the scene appeared to be just a friendly, good-natured encounter between rivals, Hanson could tell things were about to get ugly. Gopey would only take Griffin's antagonism for so long, and as for Griff, he was going to keep pushing and pushing until Gopey stood up to him or backed down, humiliated. Both men's claws were out. It was just the latest round in D.C.'s "Battle of the Swinging Dicks." Hanson had reason for concern.

"Hey, lemme give you guys my card," he said, handing his

business card to Rittenour and Peña, who each reluctantly accepted one without even looking up from the table. "If this putz doesn't treat you right, call me anytime."

By this time, Gopey was fed up. He stood, looking positively emaciated in Griffin's shadow. "All right, Tom, what's it gonna take to make you go away?"

Griffin, as expected, completely ignored Gopey's threat. "So what about you guys, you guys got cards?"

Gopey's guests squirmed, not knowing what they had gotten themselves into. "No-no, I don't have any on me. . . ."

"Me either," said the Texan. "I'm fresh out."

At this point Hanson felt that it was time to cut their losses. Griffin's goal, juvenile in every respect, was to disrupt Gopey's meeting. Clearly, mission accomplished. If Gopey had set up the luncheon to send the Dems a signal, it had backfired. There could be no doubt in his mind that Griffin had no intention of throwing in the towel. Unfortunately, Griffin wasn't done. "That's okay. Write your numbers down for me. Here, use this," he said as he grabbed Gopey's cocktail napkin. "Hey, what's this? Look, Mike, our old friend Gopey is an artist. Good lord, Gopey, what other talents have you been hiding from us?" he said, twisting the knife.

The GOP money man's face was redder than the Palm's best six-pound lobster. "Gimme that, you sonofabitch!"

Hanson tried desperately to intervene, but it was no use. These two men genuinely hated each other, and in Washington people sometimes get a little carried away. Fortunately, before they came to blows, a friendly face appeared. "This is kind of like Netanyahu and Arafat having dinner together," said the Bundlemeister.

Hanson was never happier to see anybody in his life.

"Bundles. Fancy meeting you here," said Griffin. "Who's your friend?"

The Bundlemeister tried to keep a straight face, not wanting his arrival to come off as too staged. "Oh, forgive me. I'm just a rude sonofagun. Mike, Griff, Gopey, this is an old law school buddy of mine. George Kress from the Justice Department, these are the guys."

At this point, as the Democrats shook hands and made small talk, the Texas oilman and Miami's best money man looked at Gopey with contempt, like they'd been set up. In truth they had been, but not by their host. With all the subtlety of a bond trader, Gopey signaled the waiter for the check. For several seconds, the men squirmed in their seats as they awaited its arrival. Finally, Gopey blurted out, "This is ridiculous. Let's get out of here."

Almost in unison, Gopey and party got up and walked away from the table, quickly exiting the restaurant, leaving Griffin's card on the table.

"Don't worry, guys, the drinks are on me," screamed Griff, laughing aloud. "Boy, I actually enjoyed that," he continued, looking at Hanson, who wasn't laughing. "What, what'd I do?"

"You're incorrigible. Completely incorrigible."

"We'll be lucky if this doesn't make the papers, you know," said the Bundlemeister.

"You guys worry too much."

"Someone has to," Hanson said.

Out of nowhere, the maitre d' appeared. "Mr. Griffin, if your party is all here, your table's ready."

"Forget about it, we'll take this one," Griffin said, looking at Hanson for some sign of approval.

Hanson, for his part, was both furious with Griff and grateful to him at the same time. He felt that pissing all over Gopey was completely unnecessary, yet after the week he'd had, a little comic relief was more than welcome. "You heard the man. Sit on down, guys. Griff's buyin'!" he said as he started to walk away.

"Where the hell are you goin', Mike?"

"What do you want from my life? Nature calls," said Hanson. "Order me a double Chivas."

"You got it."

Hanson proceeded to navigate his way through a maze of tables, dodging waiter after waiter, each carrying a tray filled with an assortment of grilled tenderloin au poivre, blackened sea bass, Cobb salads, and an inordinate amount of booze. Along the way he encountered scads of familiar faces en route to the men's room. Some were lobbyists, some were big contributors, almost all were lawyers. To Hanson they were mostly self-impressed pains in the ass who didn't hesitate for a moment as they offered their two cents on his testimony the previous day. "Hang in there, Mike," said one. "Tell your lawyer to get in the game," said another as he handed over his business card. To Hanson, it was amazing how Washingtonians felt the strange compulsion to inject themselves into the daily psycho-dramas of the city's politicos. Public humiliation had long been the most popular spectator sport in town and, like it or not, guys like Hanson were the marquee players.

As any mental health professional will attest, something is amiss when a person begins to regard a public restroom as some sort of safe harbor. But, unfortunately, that is exactly how Hanson felt. He honestly couldn't remember the last time he had to relieve his bladder, only that every hour or so he felt the uncontrollable need to hide out in a place so unpleasant that even a *Washington Post* reporter would be offended. This was such an occasion. Between Gopey's arrogance and Griff's immaturity, the nearest john seemed a more than adequate refuge. After listening to the last possible bit of unsolicited advice, the sanctity of the men's room called to him like a siren. Privacy was only footsteps away. Then it happened. There she was, sitting all alone at the bar, wearing a tight-fitting linen jacket, black leggings, and shoes with toes and heels narrow enough for a man to notice, sipping a glass of Merlot.

"Miss Harris?" he said, shocked not only at seeing his arch nemisis in his favorite restaurant but that this extraordinary specimen was roaming the town unescorted.

"Mr. Hanson. I didn't expect to see you," said Danielle Harris, as the tiniest bit of wine rested on her lips.

"You gotta be kidding!" Hanson said. "I eat here practically every day. Didn't your investigators tell you that?"

"No, actually. Your eating habits never came up."

"Carnivorous, born and raised."

"I'll make a note of it."

Relishing the chance to give Danielle some grief without some senator banging a gavel, Hanson asked, "So counsel, forgive me for being curious, but what the hell are you doing here alone?"

Knowing that any answer was the wrong answer, that Hanson was going to fuck with her no matter what she said, Danielle cut to the chase, hoping to just get it over with. "I'm waiting for my date. He's late."

"Lemme guess. Rich, Republican, at least ten years older than you, and best of all, he absolutely, positively swears he's not married."

"Right on all counts, Hanson," she said. "And by the way, how the hell did you become so cynical?"

"I was born in Washington, raised in Washington, and I live in Washington. Give it time, Ms. Harris. A few more months in town and I'm sure you'll relate."

"Thanks for the vote of confidence," she said.

"Don't mention it," said Hanson. "So, what are you having, counsel, filet of Democrat?"

"No, Mr. Hanson, actually I've had my fill for the week."

"Try the steak tartare. It's still moving."

"Funny."

"I like to think so," he said, laughing aloud at his own joke.

Danielle made an unsuccessful attempt to be discreet as she glanced at her watch before taking a long sip of her Merlot. Sitting alone at a bar was bad enough, but running into a serial wiseass like Mike Hanson in public was about as bad as it got. "You know, Mr. Hanson, I feel awful about what I put you through."

"That makes two of us."

"You held your own pretty well."

"That's what they told Custer."

"Believe it or not, I honestly agree with a lot of what you had to say."

"Yeah. And you sure showed it."

"I'm not being nice. But you more than anyone should understand that the committee has a job to do. The American people deserve some answers."

"What is with you people, anyway? First, there's that charming ol' independent prosecutor, then those wacky House Managers. Talk about guys I'd like to party with . . . and now you. You claim to be so damned worried about the American people, but we both know better. If yesterday had a fucking thing to do with the American people, you might have listened to one of the ten thousand polls on the subject. Shit, you and I both know that we were just extras in another campaign infomercial. You want a scandal, open your eyes. The only scandal here is what passes for legal. Unfortunately that's the way this town operates. Reagan did it. Bush did it. When my guy does it, you all suddenly get religion."

"Mr. Hanson," she began, putting down her drink. "As far as fund-raising goes, your guy, as you put it, broke the sound barrier, cured cancer, and won the World Series. He's going to Disney World. The way I see it, he is either the most charming man since Cary Grant or the mother of all influence peddlers . . . and don't even get me started on impeachment."

Hanson was actually enjoying this. Getting under Danielle Harris's skin wasn't easy, but once the mission was accomplished, it was kind of fun. "First, call me Mike. Second, do you really believe that any of the fat cats that gave money to the Dems were buying access? My god, where are you from, Mayberry? Trust me on this one, all the people you think were buying access have already had access for years, even decades. That's the way Washington works."

"I find that hard to believe."

"Come see for yourself."

"I doubt that opportunity will present itself."

"Don't bet on it. Tonight I'm going to an event at the big house. It starts around seven. Every money man in the country will be there. You can come as my guest."

"Mr Hanson . . ."

"Mike."

"Okay, Mike. Are you hitting on me, Mike?"

"Of course I am. I'm a Democrat for godsake, I can't help myself. But I'm also offering you a proposition."

"Even better."

"You come with me tonight to the First Lady's birthday party. It will be the President's last hurrah. If you, in your own judgment, really think that anybody is conducting business or doing anything shady, then I'll . . . I'll answer every conceivable question you have . . ."

"Under oath."

"Good lord, you are a ball buster."

"Do we have a deal or not?"

"Deal."

"And wear something sexy. The President likes blondes," he said as he started to walk away.

"Are all Democrats pigs like you?" she called to him.

"No, only the ones with power and money," he said as he headed for the restroom.

Chapter Nineteen

There was an eerie calm on Capitol Hill that afternoon. With the exception of the Select Committee, Congress had been in recess for more than a week. With the entire House and a third of the Senate up for reelection, the place was virtually deserted. Menacing clouds were rolling in over the Capitol building and a cool breeze was rising, breaking the heat and stirring up piles of fallen leaves along the streets.

When Detectives Kennedy and Murray walked into the Russell Senate Office Building, they encountered a lone security guard who was failing miserably in an attempt to stave off sleep. He perked up when the detectives flashed their badges. All kinds of people passed through the security gate each day: tourists, students, reporters, lobbyists—the guard saw it all. But try as he might, he couldn't remember the last time two homicide cops showed up. "Can I help you, gentlemen?" he asked.

"We're looking for Senator Kassendine's office," said Murray.

"Might I inquire as to the nature of your visit?"

"I'm sorry, I thought I made myself clear. We're looking for Senator Kassendine's office."

"Congress is in recess, I'll have to check if the senator's here."

Kennedy was growing impatient. "We called ahead. He's here. He's expecting us."

"Well, I'll have to get verification."

Normally relations between the Metropolitan and Capitol Hill police departments were positive, but they had no time today for bureaucratic bullshit.

"Okay, enough of this. I'm Detective Kennedy, Metro Police, and I'm on my way up to see Senator Kassendine. If you have any questions, why don't you call the Sergeant at Arms and mention my name. He's an old friend of mine."

The guard ignored him, but picked up the phone.

"Fine. Oh, by the way, be sure to tell him that you're being taken into custody."

This finally got the guard's attention, and he sneered at Kennedy. "On exactly what charge?"

"Interfering with a police officer during the lawful execution of his duties," said Murray.

"You guys don't scare me."

"Another word and it's resisting. Go ahead. If we don't scare you, I'll bet you'll just love the guys down at lockup," Kennedy said. "Now, which way is Kassendine's office?"

The guard sniffed and pointed to the left. Begrudgingly he said, "It's on the third floor. Room 2–315."

"Thanks so much for your cooperation," Kennedy said.

The two started for the elevators as the guard called out, "You'll have to check your guns at the desk."

"Yeah, right. Call a cop," said Murray.

Though the building was almost empty, the elevator never arrived, forcing the two men to take the stairs to the third floor. As they approached Kassendine's office, they marveled at the silence. Their voices echoed through the cavernous hallways of the stately old chamber. Russell was normally a hub of activity, with eager, clean-cut interns and staffers running up and down the hallways. Today, with everyone gone, the building didn't just appear empty, it seemed somehow asleep.

Arriving at suite 2–315, the two were met by a lone aide. Kennedy noticed that he didn't look too happy to be stuck babysitting the senator during recess. All over the Hill, just about everybody who counted was either back home campaigning or off somewhere on vacation—except for Senator Malcolm Kassendine. Kennedy wondered why.

The aide barely made eye contact with the detectives as he walked them back to the senator's private office. He said nothing, avoiding even the most basic of pleasantries such as an offer of coffee or any indication that the senator's arrival was imminent. Kennedy took notice of this, concluding that the aide had been instructed to keep his nose out of the matter. While they waited for the senator, the detectives had the time to look around the office and get a feel for the man. The walls of the office were cluttered with letters of gratitude from at least three former occupants of the White House, as well one Nobel Prize winner. Squeezed in were campaign posters from past elections: KASSENDINE FOR GOVERNOR, KASSENDINE FOR CONGRESS, and of course, REELECT SENATOR KASSENDINE.

"Look at this one, Abe," Murray said. The red faded letters across a tattered poster read KASSENDINE FOR PRESIDENT.

"Detectives, it is a rare pleasure indeed to meet with two of this city's centurions. How may I be of service?" said the senator as he entered the room.

"Senator, I'm Detective Kennedy," Kennedy said, extending his hand. "This is my partner, Detective Murray. Thank you for seeing us."

"Don't mention it. No trouble at all. Please have a seat." After waiting for them to get settled, the senator continued. "So what can I do for you gentlemen?"

Kennedy watched the senator closely. He was tall and lean and exuded health and vigor, as though he'd just come from the gym. His hair was silver-white and contrasted sharply with his darkly tanned matinee idol face. Though Kennedy's immediate impressions were of a stately and distinguished older gentleman, when he looked closer he noticed that the senator was too tan, too lean. Even his hair seemed too white. There was something slick and insincere about the senator, Kennedy thought, but he couldn't put his finger on exactly what it was. Perhaps his movie-star smile and flashing white teeth, or the way he greeted two homicide detectives so happily at the door.

"Senator, this is kind of awkward for us. Detective Murray and I are conducting a homicide investigation."

"A homicide investigation? My Lord, Detective, I've been accused of a lot of things in my day, but never murder." The senator laughed. "Although I can think of a couple of Democrats that could inspire me to consider assault."

This guy is good, damned good, thought Kennedy. "All kidding aside, sir, we need to ask you some rather personal questions concerning our investigation."

"No problem. Fire away." The senator smiled affably at them.

"Fine. Senator, do you by chance know a man named Rene LaSalle?"

"He also goes by Rick Lewis," added Murray.

"I'm sorry. Doesn't ring a bell. What about him?"

"He was murdered last night. We found his body lying next to a Dumpster near Georgetown," Kennedy said.

"How awful," said the senator, appearing to be genuinely affected by the news. "But what's any of this got to do with me? Was he a constituent of mine?"

"Senator, there's no easy way to say this," said Kennedy, wondering if they had made a huge mistake. "Senator, Rene LaSalle was a hustler. A male prostitute. What this has to do with you is that we have the late Mr. LaSalle's trick book, and well, sir, your name is in it."

For several excruciating seconds no one spoke. The detective used the time to study the senator, but couldn't tell what he was thinking. Typical, Kennedy thought. Like most politicians, the senator would believe his own bullshit.

"Detective, this doesn't have anything to do with that Larry Flynt person, does it?" Kassendine asked.

The detective chuckled. "Nah, Senator, we haven't heard from ol' Larry on this one. No, here it looks like someone took great pains to make sure that the police would have no trouble finding the page with your name on it."

Kennedy's last comment seemed to do the trick. With his memory sufficiently jogged, the senator responded, "Ah yes, now it's all coming back to me. I think I met him at a fund-raiser. He was a photographer or something. He expressed a strong interest in my campaign and, well, I always do my best to encourage young people."

"Of course," Kennedy began. "Hey Senator, let me ask you.

Almost everybody here is gone. What are you still doing here?"

The senator looked surprised at the question. "I'm not up for reelection, Detective."

"Yes, but one would think that a man of your stature would be wanted back in his home state campaigning for his colleagues," said the detective, gesturing to the presidential campaign poster.

Kassendine paused, and Kennedy saw a brief flash of pain shoot through the senator's eyes. "Yes, Detective, one would think. But things don't always turn out how you would think. I've devoted my life to serving others, but I don't think I'm wanted anymore on the campaign trail."

The senator sounded resigned, not angry. Kennedy decided to wrap it up. "Well, I guess that about does it. Let's go, Ira."

As the senator showed them out, he said, "It's really a tragedy about the young man. I mean, who would do something so horrible?"

"Lots of people, Senator," Murray said. "This is Washington, D.C."

"I know what you mean. The rules of engagement have completely changed since the impeachment."

"I don't know about all that," Kennedy said. "I'm just a cop."

"I have a feeling you know a lot more than you're letting on, Detective," offered Senator Kassendine.

As they reached the hallway, Kennedy turned around and watched the senator's profile as he looked at his old campaign posters. He was no longer a tall, larger-than-life figure. His back was now hunched and his face was sunken. It occurred to Kennedy that the slickness he had observed in the senator was a facade to hide the fact that he was a lonely old man.

"Senator, before I go, I can't help but ask, aren't you the least bit concerned about your name being in a gay hooker's trick book?" pressed Kennedy, impulsively.

"Detective, I've been in politics for thirty years. As you might expect, I've made a few enemies in my time."

"Enemies are one thing, Senator. But would anyone hate you enough to implicate you in a murder?"

Kassendine straightened a picture and a plaque. Stopping at the

KASSENDINE FOR PRESIDENT poster, he paused, touching it for a moment.

"The answer to your question is easy, Detective. There's only one person in the world who hates me enough to frame me for murder . . . and his name is Mike Hanson."

Chapter Twenty

"Good afternoon, detectives. How very nice of you two to stop by to see us." The commissioner's beefy face was redder than usual as he motioned Kennedy and Murray to come in and sit down.

Kennedy and Murray had just arrived back at the station house, only to be hustled up to the watch commander's office by a young, fresh-faced detective who warned them that the commissioner was loaded for bear. As they walked into the office, their captain sat tensely on the edge of his seat, refusing to make eye contact with them. Seated next to him was a small, mustachioed man, whom the detectives didn't recognize. Something was up.

The commissioner wasted no time. "So what exactly have you two been up to?"

"We got a call about another murder," Kennedy started to explain.

"I know *exactly* what call you got—another prostitute murdered. So this means we've got two unsolved hooker murders in three days, even better."

The captain spoke up, trying to steer the discussion. "Are they related?"

"Well, this one was a guy, a hustler. He had his trick book with him when he was killed," Murray said, leaving out the part about Kassendine and the missing page. "Under 'F' he had the dead girl's mother listed. Also, despite the fact that he was sexually mutilated, the medical examiner thinks the cause of death was a crushed larynx. Also, he was beat up pretty badly before he was killed."

The commissioner's eyes narrowed. "Same as the girl. So, it looks like we might have a serial killer out there. Just wonderful. Of course, if you two had done your job, he wouldn't have gotten the chance to move up the ranks to serial status. Instead this looney is on his way to being the next Andrew Cunanan!" He slapped the side of his mahogany desk for emphasis. "The press is gonna go *crazy* with this. I want to know exactly how you're gonna solve these murders."

Kennedy groaned inwardly. The commissioner had a reputation as being a fair man, though he was also known for being more interested in promoting good public relations than in truly solving the city's crime problems, particularly in the poor black neighborhoods. His temper was legendary, but neither Kennedy nor Murray had ever borne the brunt of it. Usually, the commissioner didn't bother himself with cops who spent most of their time working drug-related homicides.

The last thing Kennedy felt like doing was explaining that one suspect had an airtight alibi and the other was a U.S. Senator. He suddenly felt exhausted, defeated. His first day back on the job had turned into a thirty-six-hour shift, and it didn't look like he was going to get to sleep anytime soon. He looked away and down at the floor, glancing over to see Murray doing the same. The carpet was a deep blue and bore the insignia of the department. Kennedy figured it must have cost the same as a new squad car or two.

When he finally looked up, he saw the commissioner whispering something in the ear of the stranger with the mustache, who was copiously taking notes. After a few moments, he stopped and pointed at Kennedy. "And what's going on with that cuff link you found?" he demanded. "Any prints yet?"

"Forensics has it. We should be hearing any time now."

"Well, tell those lazy assholes that we need to know *now*!"

demanded the commissioner. His face was growing hotter and hotter.

Kennedy knew that any response would only prolong the commissioner's tirade. Feeling boxed in, he looked to his captain for help. But the captain was too smart to join the fray. He knew that in this case silence was golden, and he refused to make eye contact with his detective, focusing his stare on the lint that danced in front of a fan whirling and rattling in the corner of the room. Several seconds passed before Kennedy realized he was on his own. Having no choice, the detective cleared his throat and began to speak. "Uh, Commissioner, we are—"

"Pardon me, Detective, was there anything unusual in the dead man's personal effects?" said the man with the mustache.

Normally, Kennedy would have found the interruption somewhat rude, but given the circumstances he welcomed any sort of distraction. "And you would be?"

"This is Henry Lisagor from the U.S. Postal Inspector's Office," the captain explained, confident that the tirade was over for the moment. "He's offered his assistance to the homicide division."

"Postal inspector?" exclaimed Kennedy, incredulous. "Commissioner, with all due respect, what the hell can a postal inspector do to help us on a murder investigation?"

The commissioner glared at Kennedy. He didn't care whether or not Abe had fought his way back from a near-fatal wounding. As far as he was concerned, the detective was on thin ice. "Inspector Lisagor is working on an investigation that could well be related to the hooker murders. For now, that's all you need to know."

"But sir, honestly, how are we supposed to do our jobs if we don't have all the facts—"

Lisagor leaned forward and, half raising his hand, said, "Uh, excuse me, if I can jump in for a second. Commissioner, I really don't have a problem filling in the detectives on some of the details of my investigation."

"What a sport," Kennedy muttered sarcastically.

"Go ahead, be my guest," said the commissioner.

"Detectives, as you know, I'm a postal inspector. For the last five years I've been following an art forgery ring that has been operating in several European capitals. They specialize in Impressionist masterpieces. Over the last couple of years their fakes have started showing up in the U.S., a number of prominent collectors have been burned . . ."

"That's real interesting, Inspector. But I still don't see—"

"A few days ago, some madman slashed over a dozen masterpieces at the Louvre. Within hours the same thing happened in London, Brussels, San Francisco, and New York."

"I know, we heard about it," Ira said.

"But what hasn't been reported is that in each case surveillance cameras spotted suspicious individuals taking an unusual number of photos of the masterpieces shortly before the attacks."

"So?"

"In every case those photographers were found dead within hours of the desecrations."

"So you think that this forgery ring was destroying evidence?" asked the captain.

"Could have been a lot of things—covering their tracks, insurance payoffs . . ."

"What's this got to do with us?" Kennedy asked.

"All of the dead men had purchased round-trip airline tickets within the last two weeks. All of their flights originated out of Washington, D.C."

"Okay, so that explains why you're here," Kennedy said. "But why are you talking to us?"

"Frankly, Detective, because the trail has run cold."

"Well, unfortunately we haven't had any trouble at the National Gallery or the Hirshorn."

"Have you found anything unusual in either of the victim's backgrounds? Have either of them spent time recently in Paris or London?"

"That phase of the investigation is still underway. There is one thing, though . . ."

"Please, Detective. Anything would help."

"One witness has suggested that Rene LaSalle may have had some interest in photography," Detective Kennedy said. "But unless we can link him to one of the museum incidents, the trail you're chasin' ain't gonna get any warmer. I'm sorry."

Finally, the captain spoke up. "Detectives, I want an immediate search of every airline and railway passenger database for the last month. If the names Rene LaSalle or Rick Lewis show up anywhere, I want you to notify me immediately."

"You read my mind, Captain," Abe said.

The commissioner, who had exercised uncharacteristic restraint up to this point, said, "You know what I'm thinking? I think that everyone in this room has hit a brick wall. Both investigations are stalled."

"Commissioner, aren't you being just a tad pessimistic?" asked the captain.

"I don't think so," he said. "No, the truth is that together these investigators have a lead. It's time to combine forces."

"Meaning?"

"Meaning that effective immediately I want Inspector Lisagor to start riding with Detectives Kennedy and Murray. Inspector, I want you on our lead investigative team."

Kennedy was irate. "Excuse me, Commissioner. Forgetting for just a second about jurisdictional issues, what possible purpose could it serve to add another face to the mix?"

"Detective Kennedy, do I have to remind you that you've been back on the job only three days? It goes without saying that your investigative skills are a little rusty."

"Excuse me?"

"Commissioner, this really isn't necessary," Lisagor said.

"Actually, Inspector, this is absolutely necessary," he said. "I want you riding with the detectives for the duration of this investigation. What do the MBAs call it?"

"Synergy?" said Ira.

"Synergy my ass," Kennedy said.

The commissioner's burgundy leather chair let out a catlike squeal as his 250 pounds sat bolt upright. "So, then we are all agreed. A little healthy competition never hurt anybody."

The captain studied his troops. It was obvious that they hated the commissioner and his officious penchant for pulling rank. Nevertheless, the die was cast. What the brass wanted they usually got. "We'll make it work, Commissioner. Right fellas?" he said.

Both Kennedy and Murray gave the weakest of nods, as if there were a competition between the two men to see who could come off the most insincere. Together, they glanced at Lisagor, who looked at them apologetically. The postal inspector obviously had no idea what he was getting into.

"Good. And one more thing," the commissioner said as he looked into eyes of the detectives. "I don't want one word about the cuff link getting out to the press—or to anyone." His hand came down hard on the desktop and pens toppled out of his silver Policemen's Benevolent Association mug. "I just know that I want an arrest made by this time tomorrow. Whoever's committing these murders is running around right under our noses, just waiting to get caught. If you need extra manpower to stake out the hotels, then fine, I'll authorize it. Hell, if you need extra money to call the Psychic Friends Network, I'll give you that too. But I want results, goddamn it! Now get the fuck out of here and catch me a killer!"

The two detectives got up silently and exited the room. They didn't say a word to each other until they were back at their desks. Word of the commissioner's displeasure had obviously spread, and everyone around paused to look at them and give them tentative smiles of support. Kennedy was fuming. The commissioner and the other political appointees called all the shots, but their expectations were completely unrealistic, and they were ignorant about the streets, about investigative work, about his job. What was worse was that even those who had come up through the ranks were too scared of the commissioner to open their mouths in protest. Kennedy wondered if they had all been lobotomized when the gold braid was stuck onto their caps.

"So what do you think, Abe?"

Kennedy looked up at his partner. Murray looked as miserable as Kennedy felt.

"Well, for starters, Detective, I think there's way more going on than they're telling us. My gut tells me the big guy smells a huge PR opportunity and he doesn't give a damn about our case. That makes us expendable."

Murray nodded thoughtfully. "Exactly what I'm thinking."

"Well, they want a suspect, I'm gonna give 'em a suspect . . . Mr. Michael Hanson."

"You're not serious. What do we really know about the guy?" Murray asked skeptically.

"Like it or not, the guy seems to be tied into both of the murders . . . maybe more. Even if he didn't do it, he can help us fill in the blanks. He's the link," reasoned Kennedy. "Look, partner, you go home. I just got a couple of things to do here and then I'll meet you back here bright and early."

Murray just nodded wearily and turned to leave. "Bye, partner."

Kennedy nodded back. "Bye, partner," he said.

It didn't take Kennedy long to figure out exactly what kind of operation Exotica was. Five minutes on the computer and three phone calls. Exotica: an upper-end, exclusive escort service. A wine-and-dine front for prostitution. Owned by CeCe Fairchild, a woman who had enough cold cash to own a three-bedroom apartment in the Watergate, but who rented out her seventeen-year-old daughter as a prostitute.

What kind of woman could do something like that? More importantly, where was she? Kennedy intended to find out.

Chapter Twenty-one

Hanson arrived for drinks at six sharp. Upon his arrival he was met by two Devon Group employees, one of whom valeted his car, while the other escorted Hanson to the penthouse. No sooner did the doors of the elevator open than he was met by a third aide and escorted through a private entrance to Devon's suite. "He's just finishing up a meeting. It'll just be a few minutes," said the aide as they entered the lavish office.

"No sweat," Hanson said.

Together the two men walked the length of a sixty-foot antique Persian rug, entering the most eclectic collection of work spaces Hanson had ever seen. This was Devon's inner sanctum, physically separated from the other executive offices of the Devon Group. Laid out like a loft, Devon's personal suite encompassed at least half the entire penthouse floor. On the far side was a telecommunications workstation with a computer that looked like it could intercept the space shuttle. The aide explained that it was connected to a transponder located on the roof. Only a few feet away was a Quotron so Devon could instantly monitor changes in the financial markets. In the opposite corner was a drafting table strewn with architectural blueprints. In the near corner a complete law library. And, of course, the fourth angle of Devon's domain was completed by a fully stocked, beautifully sculpted mahogany bar complete with leather couches and nearby humidors. Most striking of all, however, was the circular, glass-enclosed chamber in the center of the suite, directly below the skylight. This cylindrical enclosure served as Devon's office. As they passed by, Hanson got a glimpse of some type of meeting going on, but couldn't tell much more than that. "Does Devon use all this space?" he asked.

"Every inch of it. He never stops working. Never," said the aide.

"I'll bet."

Once they arrived at the bar, the aide said, "You wait here. Mr. Devon will be along shortly. Fix yourself a drink. We have every kind of scotch ever made. Mr. Devon recommends the Isle of Skye."

"How did you know I was a scotch drinker?" Hanson asked, a little surprised.

"I didn't, Mr. Devon did," said the aide as he walked away.

It didn't take long for Hanson to take advantage of the Devon Group's hospitality. I have entered the lion's den, he thought. From his vantage point behind the bar, he could see Devon about thirty feet away. He was sitting behind a classic, Louis XIV desk. Although Hanson couldn't hear anything—obviously the chamber was soundproof—it appeared that Devon was deep in conversation with another man, a nondescript fellow, fortyish, still wearing his overcoat. Hanson's guess was that the meeting wouldn't last that long.

Inside the glass walls, Devon was conducting something less like a meeting and more akin to an inquisition. The private detective retained by Devon to track down the whereabouts of CeCe Fairchild had no idea that his assignment was doomed from the get-go. "You know, if I could rely on my head of security, there would be no need for your services," Devon said.

"I'm aware of that. But given the circumstances, I have to assume that I bear some utility to your organization."

Devon leaned back in his chair and looked up at the skylight. "That remains to be seen. So what have you got for me? Any word on CeCe?"

"The last thing we have is a credit card trace at a Mobil station off Reservoir Road on Monday morning," said the private investigator.

"So where the fuck has she been staying, in her car for godsake?"

"Mr. Devon. Believe it or not, there are still places in town that accept cash and don't ask questions. It is my understanding that at the time of CeCe Fairchild's disappearance, she could easily have been in the possession of several thousand dollars in cash."

Devon was irritated. How difficult could it be to track down a desperate call girl whose face was known to every concierge in every hotel in Washington? "So that's it? That's all you have?"

The private investigator took a deep breath. Washington is the kind of town where killing the messenger is considered sport. "Mr. Devon. I gotta tell you, this is weird. I'm getting a little concerned about foul play. There is no other way to say this, but Ms. Fairchild appears to have disappeared. Completely."

"I find that hard to believe. I've known CeCe for over ten years. She wouldn't have the first clue about going underground."

"With all due respect sir, given the backgrounds of some of the people she ran with, any number of them could have helped her pull this off. The question I would be asking is why?"

Devon looked intently at the private investigator. It was his hope that he would offer some theory, unsolicited, to explain the disappearances. That way, Devon figured, he could get some validation of his suspicions. But after several seconds, no theory was offered. Only awkward silence. "Okay then, that's it. Well, thanks so much for your time. You send us an invoice and we'll take care of it," said Devon. It was becoming increasingly clear that CeCe was on the run. For all Devon knew, the Chief was helping her. She had done something wrong, horribly wrong, and knew that, for her sins, she would ultimately have to answer to Devon. CeCe, like so many in Devon's web, knew that any fate—even death—was preferable to facing Devon's unrelenting wrath. Devon stood. "Now if you'll excuse me, I have another engagement. Wait here and someone will escort you out."

"Mr. Devon, I'd be happy to keep working on the case . . ." the private investigator said.

"That won't be necessary," said Devon brusquely as he exited the glass chamber and headed to the bar to meet his guest.

Hanson, who was still fumbling around behind the rail, looked up to see the fifty-something power broker fast approaching. He looked almost regal, and had the air of an ambassador presenting his credentials. Typical for Devon, he wore a charcoal-gray double-breasted suit that was carefully tapered to his lean frame. He wore a starched blue shirt with a white collar and french cuffs, a Hermes original tie, and a Tiffany tie bar that glistened every time he moved. If nothing else, this guy was well put together, thought Hanson.

"Mr. Hanson, good to see you," Devon said, extending his hand. "I see you've already made yourself at home."

"I was told to help myself."

"And are you always so obedient, Mr. Hanson?"

"Rarely."

"Good. Neither am I. Can't stand yes men. So what are you looking for back there behind my bar?" Devon asked.

"Your aide suggested a scotch. Isle of Skye. I can't seem to find it."

"We're out. Don't worry about it, I'll send you a case next time I'm in Scotland. Meanwhile, since you're already back there, why don't you pour us a couple of Chivases and take a seat over here so we can get started."

Hanson had no idea what to expect from this meeting, or how he ended up playing bartender, but assumed he would soon find out. After pouring both men a drink Hanson walked over and joined Devon in the sitting area.

"Here ya go. Rocks okay?"

"Perfect. Please, please take a seat. Would you like a cigar?" Devon asked, gesturing to the box on the coffee table.

"No thanks. They tend to make me sick," said Hanson.

Devon laughed. Hanson was nothing if not candid. "Well I love 'em, and since I built this fucking building I think I might indulge myself," he said, snipping off the tip of an Esplandido. "Honestly, if you mind . . ."

"Go ahead. Knock yourself out," Hanson said, instantly admiring Devon's self-assured but homey demeanor. As Devon lit up, Hanson couldn't help but look past him, spotting the original

Dali hanging on a nearby wall, the surreal nature of the work accentuated by the wafts of smoke rising from Devon's freshly lit cigar. It was only one of at least a half dozen masterpieces adorning the walls of the suite.

Devon leaned forward. "Listen, I want you to know that I appreciate your taking the time to meet with me, particularly with the election coming up so quickly."

"Not a problem," Hanson replied. What the hell, between murder investigations and presidential campaigns, he always had time for another meeting. "I know you've been quite busy yourself," he added, pointedly.

Devon nodded and smiled knowingly. "So what do you think of my digs?"

Pausing first to take a long sip of his drink, Hanson said, "I'd say you've combined the concepts of efficiency and beauty better than anyone since Cindy Crawford's parents." Both men laughed at Hanson's attempt at humor. "But all kidding aside. If the guys at the DNC knew you had this setup they would have all thrown in the towel a long time ago."

"So how's your drink?"

"As a matter of fact, outstanding. I'm not much of drinker though," Hanson said, lying through his teeth. "But I enjoy an occasional glass."

Devon just smiled again, knowing his guest was full of shit. "Well, it had better taste pretty damned good. That Chivas you poured us isn't the twelve-year-old pisswater that they serve in restaurants. It's my thirty-year-old private stock. Costs me over two hundred dollars a bottle."

"Two hundred dollars. Good god. That's more than I paid for my first car."

"What was it?"

"A 1968 Covair," boasted Hanson.

"A 1968 Corvair? What was it that Nader said, unsafe at any speed?" Devon asked.

"That's right. The second he said it, I just had to own one."

"How did it run?" asked Devon.

"Come to think of it, pretty lousy. But that wasn't the point. It drove all my liberal friends nuts. Believe me, it was worth all the trips to the mechanic." Both men laughed, and Hanson was surprised. Not everyone caught the symbolism of the Corvair, and he was shocked that Oliver Devon would even know what a Corvair was. He was also shocked that Devon could be so charming. He took another sip of his drink and leaned back in his chair, starting to relax.

"I really am glad you could make it. I just thought since we're on the verge of electing a new president, I'd have myself a powwow with a real live Democrat."

Hanson's eyes narrowed and he took a deep breath to control his temper. "As long as you're buying the drinks, I know dozens of Democrats who would gladly powwow with you. But honestly, Mr. Devon, you must have gotten to know some of us during the last eight years."

"None that impressed me. And call me Oliver. Seriously though, what's your read on the election?" asked Devon.

"I've learned not to try to predict anything in this town before it occurs," Hanson said, hedging. "Nothing's ever a sure thing, especially not this year."

"I can understand that," Devon said.

Hanson sat back and waited to see where the bizarre rendezvous took him. He studied Devon, trying to place his finger on how the man exuded such power and self-assurance. "But as long as you asked, this is my read. So long as Thurman stays in the race, we win. If he pulls out, it's anybody's guess. But if he endorses the Republicans, well, we're fucked."

"Tell me a little about yourself," Devon said, changing the subject.

"Well, let's see. I've been in politics for about fifteen years, give or take. I started back in 1984 during the Mondale campaign," he began.

"What kind of stuff did you do?"

"Mainly fund-raising. Once in a while I'd write a speech. 'Where's the beef?' was my line," said Hanson.

"Clearly the high point in the campaign."

"You have no idea. Believe it or not, I thought that turned the corner, but we all know how that turned out."

"What did you do next?" Devon asked.

"From there I went to law school, like almost every other young guy in the campaign."

"Where?"

"The University of Virginia," he said.

"Damned fine law school. Not Ivy League, mind you. But still top-notch as far as state schools go," said Devon.

Hanson was starting to get just a little angry at the inquisition, as well as wasting his time—he had to be at the White House within the hour. He thought of his humble beginnings and how proud he was of being a Virginia Law grad. "I'm so glad it meets with your approval. Anyway, when I graduated, I did a stint on the Senate Judiciary Committee."

"I know some people over there. Who did you work for?"

This was just great, thought Hanson. The one subject he wanted to avoid was his service on the committee. He'd been down the same road a hundred times. He was continually amazed that one incident over ten years ago could continue to haunt him. "Malcolm Kassendine," he said softly.

Devon burst out laughing, almost spilling his drink on himself. "No kidding, you actually worked for that fucking asshole? What a small world!"

Hanson had no idea what to make of this. Either he was being set up, or there must be a full moon or something. Playing dumber than dumb, he asked, "Do you know the senator?"

"Know him? I went to Yale with the sonofabitch. We were in the same fraternity."

"Well, I didn't leave the committee on the best of terms. I had what could best be described as a personality conflict with the senator."

Once again Devon burst out laughing. And once again Hanson didn't understand why.

"Personality conflict? Who doesn't have a personality conflict with that prick? Michael, let me tell you, if you didn't have a conflict with Kassendine then I'd be worried about you. We tried to blackball him out of the fraternity every semester."

"Did you succeed?"

"Shit no. . . . The bastard was a legacy. It's tough to blackball someone with four generations of history with a fraternity."

"I'll bet."

"Kassendine gives new meaning to the word *shithead*. I remember a few years ago he pissed off one of his aides so bad that the guy kicked the absolute shit out of him. Put him in the hospital for weeks, I heard."

"Hmm, no kidding. Well anyway, as I was saying. After the committee I moved around, running a couple of different PACs until I opened my own firm in '88," Hanson continued, speeding up to finish this conversation.

"What's it called?"

"Hanson and Associates."

"Catchy."

"Yeah, kind of like the Devon Group," Hanson answered.

"Touché. So what kind of stuff do you do?"

"Mostly I'm a money guy. As you are aware, I'm working the money angles for the Presidential right now."

Devon sipped his drink. "Very aware. So basically you're a bag man?"

In the old days Hanson would have recoiled at such a characterization. But as the years passed and the political wars came and went, he'd come to grips with his identity. He also knew that for all Devon's money and influence, he was really just a bag man, albeit on a grander scale. "Guilty as charged. However, I prefer the term *operative*."

"I suppose you're right, *operative* does sound more expensive," Devon said, giving both men a laugh. "Listen, Mike, don't take this the wrong way, but in a way it's encouraging to meet someone who survived the investigations intact. I hear they roughed you up pretty good."

Hanson smiled. Either this guy was his long-lost mentor or the second coming of E. Howard Hunt. "What about you?"

"What about me?" said Devon defensively.

"The way I heard it, the committee did a number on you as well."

"Well, suffice to say I've had more pleasant experiences. But in my case the Select Committee only knew what I allowed them to know. The credibility of the investigation required a couple of sacrificial Republicans. So I obliged them."

Hanson was amazed at how nonchalantly his host referred to his involvement in the campaign finance scandal. Devon had been publicly attacked by members of his own party during televised committee hearings. It was only after a grant of full immunity that he agreed to cooperate, handing over some of the biggest fish in the Republican sea—a Korean banking magnate, a top fund-raiser, even implicating the national chairman of the GOP in soliciting off-shore contributions. Anyone else would have been disgraced, labeled a turncoat. But not Devon. Instead, he was lauded by the K Street crowd for sending an unmistakable signal to his enemies that he held all the cards, that he would bury anyone that got in his way. Still, Hanson had doubts. "But word had it that right after that you quit politics."

"I was planning on quitting anyway. The nonsense with the investigation just gave me an excuse."

"So what about the Devon Group?" Hanson asked, changing the subject.

Devon looked at him with surprise. He was used to asking the questions, not being asked. "What do you want to know about the Devon Group?"

Hanson, feeling ballsy, was determined to delve into uncharted waters. Devon had grilled him about his company. He felt he had the right to do the same.

"For starters, what the hell is it?. . . . I mean, what does it do?"

"Well, Michael, the Devon Group is actually a holding company. It contains a number of subsidiaries: Devon Capital, which is our investment bank, Devon Consulting, which is more of a management consulting operation, and Devon Development, which handles all of our real estate holdings."

"Real estate. Tough business. I know a lot of people who lost their asses when the recession hit back in '89," said Hanson.

"Well, I probably don't know those people, but my guess is they got hurt because they're a bunch of goddamned pussies. My company has made a fortune the last five years," Devon replied. "Do you know why?"

"Not a clue," said Hanson.

"Because we conduct business just like our ancestors."

"Excuse me?"

"Very simple. Just like the men who settled this country, when we see the land we want, we take it. We don't ask nicely if it's okay. We do whatever it takes to make it ours. The founding fathers didn't give a shit about the Indians and we don't give a shit about the competition. We always win, by whatever means necessary."

Hanson was taken aback. He felt like the older man was testing him. "So, I suppose you believe in survival of the fittest," he said.

"Absolutely."

Hanson was fascinated. Oliver Devon was too much.

"Michael, do you mind if I share something with you?"

"No. Go ahead," said Hanson.

Devon leaned in. "For several years now, people in this town have viewed me as this big Republican."

Hanson simply nodded, knowing that his host's words were a ludicrous understatement. To say that Oliver Devon was a big Republican was like saying the Pope had good connections at the Vatican. For years Devon owned this town and everyone knew it.

"But the truth is, I don't really care who the hell is in the White House. If a Republican is in office, then I'm a Republican. If a Democrat is in office, I work with the Democrats. Ultimately, I don't really give a shit."

While Hanson didn't doubt the sincerity of Devon's words, he wasn't about to be the one to tell him different. More than that, the man was as ruthless as he was charming. For some reason, he was working Hanson, setting him up. As for Hanson, he still had no clue why he was even there. "Well, Oliver, from the look of things, I'd say that was a very profitable attitude," he said. "So is there something specific you want to talk about?"

Devon smiled. "Yes, Michael there is. First, understand that when I told you that I was glad that you landed on your feet after the Select Committee went after you, I meant it. And, while I understand that these investigations are just part of the game of politics, I think this has gotten way out of control. Personally, I detested the impeachment and everyone associated with the whole sorry episode. Bad for the country."

"All I know is that it has been bad for my wallet," joked Hanson.

As for Devon, he was in no mood for jokes. "That's exactly what I'm talking about. Me, I can afford this for as long as it takes. I pay lawyers big fat retainers all the time and I have no idea what they do. But this goddamn committee, they've ruined so many people's lives that it is absolutely unconscionable. And the worst part is that they're gearing up to do it all over again."

"Hey, Oliver, I gotta ask you one question. What do you care? I mean, you have immunity."

"I care because I'm an American, Michael. I intend to stop this witch hunt once and for all. And I want you to help me."

Hanson was shocked. The last thing he expected was an offer of an unholy alliance with 'the Repo man.' "Oliver, just what in the hell are you talking about?"

Try as he might to conceal it, Devon's face betrayed a very self-satisfied smile. Hanson was a rarity in the nation's capital. Magnificent in his zeal and expertise, yet truly pathetic in his naivete. "Michael, what I am talking about are special prosecutors, independent counsels, and select committees. People with absolutely no accountability. People that make it impossible for guys like you and me to do our jobs."

"Oliver, I feel that I should make you aware that I am still under subpoena. Frankly, almost anything you might say could be viewed as obstruction."

"Michael, my immunity deal is pretty broad. Even if I get tricked up, I'm probably covered."

"Still, I can't imagine how on earth I could be of any help to you."

"You can start by helping yourself," said Devon.

"That would be a nice change. How do you mean?"

"Michael, whether you know it or not, you're being positioned to be the fall guy in this investigation."

"That's not exactly news. Everyone in town knows the committee is after my scalp."

"I'm not talking about the committee, I'm talking about the White House."

Hanson was taken aback by the comment. "The White House?" he exclaimed.

"Michael, you're probably not old enough to remember Watergate, but one thing we learned back then was that when an investigation gets legs, the only way to survive it is to offer up some kind of sacrifice. If you have to give up your chief of staff you give up your chief of staff. If it takes a cabinet member, then that's just the fucking price you pay to protect the President.

Unfortunately, the White House didn't learn this lesson until it was too late. Impeachment was a fait accompli by the time they got wise. Trust me, no one over there wants to go through that again."

"And you're telling me that the White House is offering me up to the committee?"

"I can prove it. Danielle Harris has moles all over the West Wing. They've been feeding her dope on you for months."

Hanson was puzzled. "Why me? As you pointed out, I'm just a bag man."

"Because you bridge the gap between the old scandal and what may be the new administration. Make no mistake about it, your guy doesn't want to start out his first term with this investigation haunting him. He wants it over with. Besides that, you're expendable."

"So the White House green-lights a bloodletting?" said Hanson, feeling more violated than surprised.

"Exactly."

"Where do you get your information?"

"Michael, I'm Oliver Devon. I have spies everywhere. In the White House. On the committee, in every campaign. Trust me on this one, son, you are being hung out to dry, and Danielle Harris is playing the role of executioner."

Hanson stood and walked to the bar. Without asking, he poured himself a refill. Bottle in hand, he returned to his seat, gulping down his drink in the process. "So what are you proposing?"

"I'm proposing that you counterattack. That, together, we destroy Danielle Harris," Devon said bluntly.

"You know, Oliver, while I wouldn't put anything past the Veep's staff, it's a little hard for me to believe that Danielle Harris has this kind of agenda. I'll admit that she nuked me pretty good yesterday, but that's her job."

"How well do you know her, Michael?"

"Well, hardly at all. But we have a number of mutual friends. By all accounts she is universally loved. I can't believe you have such a jaded view of her."

"Believe me, I have my reasons. Here, it's all in this dossier. It'll provide you with all the ammunition you'll need." Devon slid the sealed envelope across the table, but Hanson didn't touch it.

"I have no doubt," Hanson said. It was obvious that Devon intended to tell him as little as possible. But Hanson wanted to know. What was Devon up to? This wasn't good. Hanson was already angry at himself for even listening to the proposition. He understood better than anybody how a person's career could be destroyed by some unnamed, unseen enemy. Some special interest that just happens to decide that you're not right for the job. But this was even worse. Devon was asking him to torpedo the reputation of someone who was just a notch below sainthood. "What am I supposed to do with this?"

"Read it and draw your own conclusions. If you are satisfied with the evidence, there is a prepared statement detailing how she is working hand in hand with several ultraconservative groups and a few disgruntled White House staffers to build a case against you."

"A good old-fashioned right-wing conspiracy."

"Right wing, left wing, they're coming after you from both sides, son. All you have to do is read the statement into the record and it's over for her."

"And I hurt the President and I kill the Veep's chances of winning the election."

"Personally, if I were you, I wouldn't care. It's you or them. But if you are still such a damned true believer, demand a closed hearing, which is your right. There is no way the committee will leak it, because it would be too embarrassing. And by the time the White House gets wind of it, the election will be long over. They'll know they can't fuck with you."

"Sounds like a perfect plan."

"Believe me, it is. And it's your only option."

Hanson was beginning to get the sense that Devon's beef with Danielle Harris went far beyond the normal everyday internecine warfare of Washington politics. "Look, Oliver, I have to tell you, I appreciate the drinks. But the fact is, this isn't my thing. I would be uncomfortable doing something like this."

"Bullshit!" said Devon, obviously not used to people rejecting his ideas. "If you don't go after her, your career is finished. Believe me, one way or the other, she's dead in this town. You couldn't save her if you wanted to. Win or lose, someone's going to profit on her demise, and it might as well be you."

The perverse sense of logic that runs Washington, thought Hanson. "But why me?" he asked, wondering why Devon would choose him.

"Because I know you can do it. Look, I know you're out there trying to raise a quick fifteen million for a media buy. What's your pleasure, Michael? What's it gonna take to get you on my team? A fat check to the Party? Or to your lawyers? If you want it made out to Mike Hanson, just tell me," Devon implored.

Hanson was in shock. How on earth could Devon have gotten wind of their strategy? "Oliver, it's more complicated than that. But it doesn't matter. Thanks for the heads-up and all, it's just that I don't operate like this," he said, trying to hand the package back to Devon.

Devon stared at Hanson. "Michael, your integrity is impressive. However, I live in a world where everything is negotiable and everything is for sale. It all comes down to a matter of price. Everyone has one and believe it or not, so do you. My guess is before too long you'll come around to my way of thinking. The truth is that Danielle Harris and the committee have to be stopped for the good of the country. Plain and simple."

Hanson shook his head firmly. "There is no amount of money you can offer me, Oliver. Conversation over."

Devon looked at his watch, a European model with two faces for dual time zones. "Unfortunately, Michael, I have to go to another appointment. You hold on to that. Take the next couple of days, mull it over. But I want you to consider what I said. After you have a chance to think it over, give me a call. By the way, I wouldn't lose that, your fee's in there," he said.

Devon stood to leave. "If you need more financial incentive to clear your head, just let me know. Anytime. Just remember that I have money to burn and I intend to see this happen—by you or by someone else."

Hanson shook his head again.

As Devon started to walk away, he turned to Hanson. "Are you by any chance going to be attending the gala for the First Lady's birthday tonight at the White House?"

Hanson just nodded.

"Good," Devon said. "Wish her my best. My aide will be along shortly to show you out. And Michael, one last thing . . . trust no one. Absolutely no one." With that, Devon walked away and out one of the suite's many doors.

Hanson's mouth hung open. Devon knew more about his life than he did. Minutes passed while Hanson nursed the coffee brought earlier. He had to compose himself, he had the First Lady's birthday party in a matter of minutes. Worse, Danielle Harris was going to be his date. Part of him wanted to just leave the envelope on the table unopened and never look back. But he'd gone this far and questions kept gnawing at him. What was Devon's problem with this lady? Why would he choose Hanson for his dirty work? Hanson had to know. Slowly he picked up the envelope. With a minimum of dexterity, Hanson tried to open the package without tearing it. Inside, he found a memorandum at least thirty pages in length providing extensive background on Danielle Harris, some law journal articles written under her name, as well as several photos of her with a who's who of the Republican right—tobacco types, pro-life activists, and Sung Yoon, the very same Korean banking magnate that Devon had implicated as part of his immunity deal. Hanson studied them, trying to understand Devon's angle. What if Devon was actually telling the truth?

Finally, there was yet another envelope with Hanson's name typed neatly on it. Knowing it was too late to turn back, he slowly opened it. Inside he saw something that made his heart pound like a jackhammer: a wire transfer receipt to the personal account of Michael J. Hanson in the amount of one million dollars.

"Jesus Christ! This bastard means business!" he muttered to himself.

Chapter Twenty-two

The temperature had plunged earlier in the evening, but tourists bundled up in layers of sweatshirts and windbreakers still wandered by the White House to see it lit up at night. They stood on the sidewalk, gaping and pointing at the late-arriving guests. Some stopped to take pictures for friends back home. As Hanson hurried across the sidewalk, they parted to allow him access to the small East gatehouse. Hanson was a little embarrassed as a few figured him to be someone important as their cameras clicked away. When the flashes caught his profile, he spun and gave them a hearty wave, but this was as much ham as he could muster. His quick shower and shave after drinks with Devon had been too short to completely quiet the drum solo raging in his head. Hanson regretted pouring their drinks so stiff almost as much as he did finishing two bottles of wine with Griff at lunch. His hands were thick and clumsy while he had gotten dressed, and by the time he was able to tie his tie, the clammy "I'm late and in trouble" sweats were already starting. Rushing only made things worse. By the time his shoes and socks were on, he was racing for the door. He had no time to pause to see the small red light blinking menacingly on his answering machine.

The East Visitors' Gate was manned with the standard array of uniformed secret service officers in their black and white uniforms. Hanson spied one of the regular old-timers, a perennially cheerful balding man whose pants sagged under his massive gut.

"Hey, Pete, how are you doing?" Hanson asked.

Pete grinned. "Pretty well, Mr. Hanson. I haven't seen you around here in a while."

"Well, I've been pretty busy lately with the campaign," said Hanson, his voice wavering for a split second. "Among other things," he continued, thinking of Ariel Fairchild. Quickly he stopped himself, trying his hardest not to think about it until the election was over. "So, Pete, hit the links lately, or taking a break for the winter?"

The officer laughed gruffly, "No way. I find a way to play all winter. Went out with the big guy's detail to California last week for an event," he said pointing over his shoulder at the official portrait of the President that stands guard over every federal building's lobby. "I got in two good rounds. I'm getting closer and closer to breaking a hundred."

"Well, you're off my list of people to play with then," Hanson said, extending his driver's license to the guard, who then typed his information into the computer, and found him on a list of persons prescreened for the First Lady's birthday party.

"Uh, Mr. Hanson, there's a note here in the computer telling me to verify some information about your guest."

Hanson stopped in his tracks, suddenly realizing that he should have anticipated the paranoia of the White House. "Sure, Pete. What gives?"

"According to the computer, your guest is one Danielle Harris, DOB 8-8-67, Social 199-01-7963."

"I really wouldn't know all that. But she is *my guest*. Is there a problem?" asked Hanson.

"No, but there are instructions asking you to touch base with the Chief of Staff as soon as you are inside."

"Not a problem," he said. "I gotta talk to him anyway."

"Give my regards to the missus. Wish her a happy birthday for me," said Pete, handing back Hanson's driver's license to him.

"If I'm sober enough I will."

"Want me to call you a cab now?" the officer asked, chuckling, as Hanson stepped through the turnstile and onto the official grounds of the world's most prestigious address, 1600 Pennsylvania Avenue.

Hanson passed through metal detectors manned by two uniformed officers and was greeted by a plainclothed agent of the elite of the Secret Service. The agent was tall and imposing, with a military-issue buzz cut and sharp eyes. Hanson silently admired his trim Italian suit. The lean styling of the presidential protection detail was most impressive, Hanson thought, considering that the suit hid a gun heavy enough to blow through steel and a self-sustaining communications system that rivaled that of a Navy Seal unit. The agent escorted him to a door manned by a Marine lance corporal in full dress blues. Light danced off the guard's polished brass buttons and insignias. As Hanson stepped within the officially designated distance of three feet, the marine guard snapped to attention with an echoing click of steel heel plates. The guard delivered a crisp regulation salute, and in a fluid sweeping motion of pure pomp and circumstance, he opened the door allowing Hanson and the agent to pass through without needing to break stride even the slightest bit. Welcome to never-never land, Hanson thought.

Hanson was escorted through the lavish Blue Room, past the portrait of Jackie Kennedy and into the State Room. The Navy band played an orchestral version of Simon and Garfunkel's "Bridge Over Troubled Waters," a favorite of the President. The room was filled with over one hundred and fifty of the First Lady's closest and dearest friends, all dressed in fashionable business attire. The party was a casual event for the First Family, no cameras, no press, no black tie, mostly an occasion the outgoing administration was using to rally the faithful behind the Democratic nominee. Hanson spied Griffin in a corner, talking to a matronly blonde in a red Chanel suit who gestured excitedly, her arms at times seeming to miss Griffin's body by a mere whiff. Poor Tom, Hanson thought. He caught Griff's eye and watched as he disengaged himself with some difficulty and sidled over to where Hanson stood.

"Hey, sorry I'm late."

Griffin just shook his head. "Incorrigible."

Hanson laughed and picked up a glass of champagne from the

tray of a passing formally attired waiter. "I love this administration. Everyone knows that the President's running late, but as usual they'll just offer us more and more food and booze until they think we don't notice."

"Actually, I never notice what time he arrives," Griffin said.

"See what I mean?" said Hanson, grinning.

"So, how was your meeting with Oliver Devon? Are you a Republican yet?" joked Griffin.

"Damned close. Damned fucking close," Hanson said. "That is one impressive guy. Scary as hell. But still impressive."

"Tell me everything. Leave nothing out!" demanded Griffin, sounding like a schoolgirl.

"All in good time, my gargantuan friend. At the moment I am battling a walking hangover. My immediate priority is finding a real drink," said Hanson, who felt surprisingly on his guard after Devon's warning.

Taking heed, Griffin used his height and arm reach to get the attention of a steward, who arrived immediately with two double Chivases on the rocks.

"Goddamn it, Griff, can they read your mind?"

"No, but for some reason when I give them a wave, they come a-runnin'."

"I don't know about you, but I can think of forty million reasons. . . ."

Together they laughed aloud at a joke both had heard many times over. "Listen Mike, this probably isn't the best time to tell you, but I've got some bad news," Griffin said, his face hardening.

Hanson took a deep breath. Deep furrows ran across Griffin's forehead, and his face was unusually red. He knew to prepare himself for the worst, but he didn't know how much more bad news he could handle today.

"It's about the Independent Party. I got word about an hour ago that Thurman is definitely withdrawing from the race.

"Fuck!"

"It gets worse. Supposedly, Gopey et al cut a deal with the Thurman camp on debt retirement. They're picking up the whole goddamn tab for Thurman. The bastard's agreed to endorse the Republican ticket. The announcement could come as soon as Monday."

The news went through Hanson like a knife. Even so, he knew it had to be worse for Griffin, who likened this kind of a defeat to slow death. "Can't we offer him some kind of deal? Maybe a cabinet post, or an ambassador gig? I've set my sights on Bermuda, but I'd be willing to settle for my second pick . . . say, Polynesia," he said, trying to lighten things up a little.

Griffin laughed briefly, knowing his best friend meant well. "The last thing we're going to do is hand you the keys to a nation of bikinis and Bacardi."

Hanson watched Griffin's fading smile. "Griff, are you sure about Thurman?"

"Yup. It's done. In a word, we're fucked."

"Come on, man. We still got a few weeks. There must be something we can do."

Griffin took a long sip of his drink, almost finishing it. "Mike, we've been friends too long to bullshit each other. The fucking Republicans have so much money they'd have killed us with their ads anyway. We might have held on, but who knows? What the hell, with all that's happened since the last election, maybe it's better this way."

"And our ads won't do any good?"

"Our goddamn ads are still being shot for chrissakes! And then there's still that annoying little issue of paying for the air time. Even without Thurman in their pocket we were in for a rough ride," he said.

Hanson crumpled his napkin and tossed it down on a waiter's silver tray. The napkin bounced off onto the plush red carpet, sending the waiter scurrying to pick it up. "There must be something we can do."

Griffin took a deep breath. The subject was wearing on him. "Oh sure, Mike, if you've got a spare fifty million laying around, we could buy every bit of goddamn air time the networks got. You know, keep the fucking Republicans off the air. That would just about do it," said the Messiah, knowing it was a pipe dream.

Hanson was perplexed, not able to tell if Griffin was serious or not. "If our ads aren't in the can yet, what would we run?"

Griffin laughed. His buddy cared so much that he actually was taking this seriously. "Mike, don't you get it? We could run goddamn Bugs Bunny cartoons for all I fucking care. If we keep the Repos off the air, then we win. Period."

"Fifty million?"

"Yeah. More than we spent on the entire fucking primary campaign," said Griff, incredulous. "My turn for a refill. You need anything?"

"No, I'm good," said Hanson, thinking he should let Griff be on his own for a little while. As the finance chairman lumbered over to the bar, Hanson wondered what they would do next. Over two years of work for nothing. The perfect ending to this day. In disgust, he spun to a bar on the other side of the State Room, hoping to make it to another cocktail without being pulled into chatting with some high roller from the West Coast who wanted to discuss the latest opinion polls. He moved surreptitiously across the room until Chief of Staff John Brigham grabbed his arm.

"Mike, mind if I have a word with you?" said Brigham as he ushered Hanson into a corner.

Hanson turned to face officious, prematurely graying Brigham. The fact that there was no love lost between the two men was apparent to all who knew them. Brigham was the fourth chief of staff to serve in the administration's second term and was by far the least popular. As for Hanson, he made it no secret that he felt there could be no more irrelevant position than that of chief of staff to a lame duck politician. He viewed Brigham as a lightweight and all around pain in the ass. "Hey if it isn't Deep Sphincter."

"Cut the wisecracks, Hanson. This is serious!" warned Brigham. "The POTUS knows about your latest stunt, and take my word for it, he's none too pleased."

Hanson turned to Brigham and looked at him and laughed. "Gosh, I'm shaking in my boots. What's he gonna do, not talk to me for two months?"

"Don't fuck with me, you piece of shit! I don't know what you could have been thinking bringing that bitch here."

"Good lord, John-boy, if I didn't know better I'd swear you sound like you have something to hide."

"I'm warning you, Hanson, bag men like you are a dime a dozen . . ."

Hanson began to interrupt when his eyes spotted a familiar-looking woman across the room. For just a moment he froze as his heart dropped, a little embarrassed at his double-take. Danielle Harris was walking right towards him. "So, Ms. Harris, packing any subpoenas?" he said.

Startled, Brigham swirled, turning his attention to the new arrival. "Ms. Harris, welcome, welcome. Mi casa, su casa," said the COS in a lame effort to be charming.

"Last time I checked, it was the taxpayers' casa," retorted Danielle.

"Excuse me, but just what the hell is a casa?" asked Hanson sarcastically.

Although John Brigham didn't drink, he summoned over the first steward he saw and grabbed a flute of champagne. Dealing with Hanson was bad enough. But now he had to contend with a young Republican bombshell who was by all accounts out to get the President. "Honestly, Ms. Harris, I hope you're enjoying your visit to the White House. Is it everything that you expected?"

"Everything and more," said Danielle.

Not knowing quite how to take her response, the chief of staff decided to extricate himself from the situation. "Uh, it has been very nice meeting you," he began. "Unfortunately, I have to kibbitz with some other guests," he said, extending his hand.

"Nice meeting you as well," said Danielle, taking his hand.

As the chief of staff practically sprinted away, Hanson noticed the grimace on Danielle's face. "Like shaking hands with a flounder, huh?" he said.

She looked at him. "Oh my god, he is so sweaty I think I need to go wash up."

"Not to mention that vice grip of his."

"How did a guy like that make it in politics? A wormy, weak handshake. And he wouldn't even look me in the eye!" said Danielle.

"I honestly don't know. For some reason this town has more than its share of reptilian yes men."

"I thought you Democrats prided yourself on being virile and sexy?"

"Danielle, I'm shocked. Most women think John Brigham is an animal, walking testosterone. Well, it's your loss. Now I'm sorry I gave him your home phone number," he joked.

"Hanson, you don't even know my phone number, and aren't likely to get it."

Undeterred, Hanson continued. "But how am I supposed to call you from prison?"

Danielle looked at him. Hanson was a strange one all right, a deft practitioner of gallows humor even when his own head was on the chopping block. "Michael, the committee isn't trying to send you to prison. We just want some answers."

There was an awkward pause and Hanson recklessly rushed in to fill the silence. "That's a relief, I thought for sure I was a condemned man. So, come here often?"

"Yeah, every four years or so," she said, smiling, glad for some reason that Hanson didn't hate her.

Hate was the last thing Hanson was feeling at that moment. Despite the fact that Danielle Harris was his judge, jury, and possible executioner, he was absolutely dazzled by her smile, her wit, not to mention her looks. He simply couldn't believe this was the woman whom Devon wanted him to destroy. "So have you had a chance to observe all the influence peddling going on tonight?"

She laughed. "Well, not quite yet. But the night is still young."

"Let me make it easy for you. About half the people here tonight are contributors. Major supporters. Two hundred fifty thousand dollars and up. Most of them have been in the game for more than a decade."

"Okay, but that's not exactly a newsflash."

"No, but that's not the point. What the committee and the rest of you Repos refuse to acknowledge is that almost all the people you claim are buying access have already had access for years. I mean, look around you. Almost everybody in this room is talking to each other, not the President."

"Michael, it's a little hard to believe that with all the coffees and sleepovers that some people didn't get some special favors."

"Danielle, believe me when I tell you that the only thing this White House ever sold was ego-fuel, plain and simple. Just ask your boss. He knows the drill."

Sensing a little hostility, Danielle pulled away. "Look, maybe this wasn't such a good idea, I probably shouldn't be here."

"Come on now, don't get all ethical on me. Aren't you enjoying the fact that everyone here is gossiping about us?"

"No, not particularly," she said, still annoyed.

Why is this happening? thought Hanson. I'm liking this woman like crazy and I can't say one intelligent thing. "Let's start over," he began. "Can I get you a drink?"

"Got one."

"Then how about a car, a condominium. A racehorse perhaps."

"Not necessary," she said, smiling as she looked around the room. "Besides, I'd have to go back and change all the financial disclosure forms I've filled out. It would be a nightmare." She smiled at him once more, as if to decide it was time to let him off the hotseat for a bit.

Suddenly an honor guard's voice boomed from across the State Room, "Ladies and gentlemen, the President of the United States, accompanied by the First Lady." The band struck up "Hail to the Chief," as the first family reentered the ballroom. After their entry there was confusion, as people pressed to be at the head of the receiving line, and Hanson lost Harris amid the chaos. He cursed under his breath. He could hardly believe he'd let her out of his sight.

After everyone had shaken the President and First Lady's hands, the party moved toward the pink and white three-tiered cake. Hanson and Griffin stood together and watched the President toast the First Lady. As she blew out all five candles on the cake, Hanson scanned the crowd while everyone boisterously sang "Happy Birthday."

The President then turned to the bandleader and drawled, "Tommy, this is a birthday party, not a wake. Give us something I can spin her to."

The President was clearly enjoying a night off, Hanson thought. Tommy brought the band into a brassy version of "In the Mood," and Hanson stood watching couples fill the dance floor.

"Dance with me?" she asked, tugging on his hand.

"Dance? You mean here, with you? Danielle, are you sure we're ready for this? It's a big step."

"C'mon, I'll lead," she said, shaking her head, but still smiling.

Fortunately for Hanson, Danielle knew exactly how to lead, and he followed, hoping it would camouflage his rusty dance moves. Danielle was poised and graceful on the dance floor. Hanson felt her body sway next to his in rhythmic harmony with the music. Her movements were fluid, and he felt the contours of her back as she moved him along to the muted wail of a sax, felt her long blond hair dance along his hand as he pressed against the center of her lightly muscled back. Hanson was proud to be dancing with this beautiful woman.

Not long into the set Hanson was beginning to tire; it had been quite some time since his last dance marathon. "How about a drink?" he asked, hoping for a break.

"I'd love one."

'Fuckin' A, thought Hanson. Finally a breakthrough.

The rest of the night moved in slow motion, as Hanson felt the weight of the day melt away as he danced with Danielle. With each song came another chorus of stares, forcing them to steal away in search of ever more remote locations in the White House. "You know, I never realized how the goddamn Secret Service can really cramp a person's style," he remarked. Sure, there would be the inevitable blurb in tomorrow's *Post*, as well as the jokes from his colleagues about sleeping with the enemy. But Hanson knew it was mostly just envy. For all his troubles, any guy at the party would gladly have switched places with him. Finally, when the President and First Lady had left, the band struck up "Strangers in the Night."

"One last dance," he asked her.

When she nodded, Hanson took her in his arms and said, "This time I lead."

Danielle looked into his eyes, wondering what she'd gotten herself into. "Michael, you seem rather good at this. Should I be worried?" she said, smiling.

This woman is perfect, Hanson thought as he pulled her closer.

"So, are we having fun yet?" she asked.

"Danielle, I'm so way past having fun it's scary," Hanson said. "And yes, I assure you, you should be worried." He was looking into her eyes when suddenly a pretty young redhead grabbed him. "Mr. Hanson! I can't believe it's you."

Danielle looked at Hanson with a trace of a smile on her lips, "Friend of yours?" Hanson just shrugged his shoulders, confused and not placing the girl at first. Then he realized who it was.

"Julie?" he said. "My God, you've grown up. What the hell are you doing here?"

"I'm the head of the National College Democrats."

"No kidding, that's fantastic!"

"Uh, excuse me," said Danielle.

"Oh sorry," said Hanson. "Danielle, this is Julie Blumenthal. Julie was one of my interns from years ago. Julie this is Danielle Harris, she's investigating me and everyone I know."

Danielle rolled her eyes at Hanson. "Pleased to meet you," she said, shaking Julie's hand.

"So Julie, the last time I checked, you had braces, were really into 'General Hospital,' and had a huge crush on Leonardo DiCaprio. Bring me up to date," Hanson said.

"I can't believe you remember all that," said Julie. "Well, after I left Hanson and Associates, I went back to Brown, got elected student council president, and now I'm in my last year at Georgetown Law. I have no idea what's happening on 'General Hospital,' but I've accepted a position at the Justice Department, Civil Rights Division, beginning in the fall, and I owe it all to you!"

"Me? That's crazy, I've never violated your civil rights, and even if I did, I was probably drunk," he said. Danielle rolled her eyes and smiled as Hanson and Julie laughed.

"No, seriously," Julie said. "If it wasn't for you, I would've given up on politics and I definitely would never have applied to law school. You showed me how important it was for people to get involved in the process, that one person really could make a difference."

Hanson was moved, and a little embarrassed by her words. He felt Danielle's eyes on him, studying him. Danielle was wondering if underneath that cynical exterior lay the heart of an actual human being.

"I remember that no matter which issue you gave me to work on, you always told me the same thing—that no matter what the media or anybody else says, politics isn't about money or power or special interests. It's about people, period. That every regulation, law, or bill that gets passed affects peoples' lives," she said emotionally, tears suddenly welling up in her eyes. "You really changed my life!"

Hanson was completely mortified. He hated compliments. "Aw

shucks, come over here and give Uncle Mikey a hug," he said. Everyone laughed. Wiping away Julie's tears, he went on. "Now I want you to promise to eat all your vegetables and get plenty of sleep, and most of all, don't get too successful, or else you'll become a Republican, like Ms. Harris here."

"Not likely," Julie said, and gave Hanson her new work phone number. "I have to get back over to the other side of the room to meet some people. It was really nice to meet you, Danielle."

When Julie had moved on, Danielle leaned in to whisper in Hanson's ear. "Your intern, Michael? What is it with you Democrats?"

"Please, no jokes, Danielle," he begged. "I assure you, she and I never had sex, regardless of the definition. What can I say? Must be a case of mistaken identity."

"Shut up, Mr. Hanson," she said, throwing both arms around his neck and kissing him lightly on the cheek. She left her arms there after the kiss.

Shocked, Hanson tried to make the moment last as long as possible despite the presence of a hundred onlookers, wondering if this was the first and last time he would be kissed by this beautiful woman. He was speechless as he looked into her unwavering eyes. Finally, Danielle tilted her head and whispered in his ear, "So, you wanna get out of here?"

"I thought you'd never ask. Your place or mine?" he said, biting his tongue, forgetting in his excitement that his home was in shambles.

"Slow down, Michael. I thought maybe we'd go somewhere and have a drink and see where the night takes us," said Danielle. She looked at him and smiled coyly. "Don't worry, I have a room at the Hamilton tonight, in case you get lucky."

"No problem. Hell, I'm a Democrat, rejection is a way of life with me," Hanson said, smiling his most winning smile at her.

"Let's get out of here," she said.

"Promise you'll be gentle with me," he teased, leading her out of the ballroom.

Chapter Twenty-three

The two wasted no time once inside the hotel room. Hanson grabbed Danielle, kissing her first on the mouth, then down her neck and shoulders. She responded, unbuttoning his shirt and kissing his chest softly. "What, no chest hair?" she asked.

"I'm a founding member of the chest-hair club for men."

"You're quick, Hanson, I'll give you that," she said.

"Gosh, for your sake I hope not," Hanson said, maneuvering her towards the bed. He began kissing her again, slipping his hand under her blouse.

"Uh, Michael . . . I hate to ruin the moment, but before we go any further I have . . ."

". . . To go to the bathroom," he said, finishing her sentence.

Danielle smirked, then said "I won't ask how you knew that. I'll be right back." Before closing the bathroom door, Danielle turned and said, "Would you mind terribly if we turned the lights down a little?"

"No problem at all," Hanson said. The truth was, she was doing him a favor. He was relieved that the dark would spare him explaining the five extra pounds of fast food and beers that he had added to his waistline since the campaign started. He vowed that after tonight he would get back on a workout routine. When was the last time he had seen the inside of his gym? Besides, he rationalized, the real problem with the lights was that he desperately needed a tan. No, the cover of darkness suited him just fine. While Danielle was in the bathroom, Hanson raided the honor bar, and turned on the television to pass the time.

When the bathroom door opened, Hanson looked up. Danielle stood in the doorway, her image illuminated only by the starlight sneaking through the window and the glimmer of the television. In the dim light, he could see this tall beauty, in a black lace bra and panties that contrasted sharply with the milky whiteness of her skin. Skin that seemed to almost shine in the darkness as she moved toward him. He started to stand, but stopped as she crawled to him on the bed. Their lips met in the first of many long, wet kisses. While he loved the lingerie, it was only seconds before he unhooked her bra and took her breasts in his mouth, first one, then the other. He licked her breasts until Danielle's neck bent back and she began to rasp. But he had no intention of stopping there.

She held his head in her hands as he suckled her breasts, her nipples growing incredibly erect. Hanson put his hand between her legs, feeling her grow hotter and more wet with every touch. Danielle continued to moan. She reached for him. But as much as he was dying for her to touch him, he had other plans.

"I want you inside me," Danielle whispered in his ear, tonguing it as she spoke.

"Not yet," said Hanson. "We've got all night." He followed the contours of her body, kissing every inch of her stomach, then her hips, and then finally arriving at his destination, he teased her with his tongue, massaging her clitoris with his fingers. After a few minutes, Danielle was at the threshold. "My god, Michael, where did you learn to do this?"

"I confess. I caddied for a year on the LPGA. You wouldn't believe some of the pointers I got . . ."

"Michael . . ."

"Honestly, I'm a lesbian inside a man's body."

"Shh," she said, giving him a light tap on the top of his head.

This went on for over an hour, as Hanson repeatedly held her at the peak of excitement, let her dance over the line for a moment, and then brought her back down. Finally, as CNN's overnight coverage was closing out its third airing of the same campaign segment, Danielle was ready.

"Rumors continue that Thurman, the first Independent since Ross Perot to make a national run for the White House, may be leaving the race," the CNN political correspondent intoned.

"Oh my God! M-Michael, p-p-please, don't stop!" Harris yelled, digging her nails into Hanson's shoulders.

"The latest federal election reports show that the Thurman campaign remains heavily in debt and has failed to make major progress in its recent fund-raising push in the west."

"*There! There!* Slower, slower!"

"Some campaign staffers have reported that they have yet to be paid for last month. Meanwhile at the White House, the President greeted a gathering of the Democratic Party's biggest supporters as the campaign heads into the home stretch. There, he had this to say . . .

" 'How ya'll feelin' tonight?"

"*Now! Now!*" screamed Danielle.

At this point Hanson wasn't exactly sure why what he was doing was working, but he was determined to keep doing it.

" 'Well, ya'll came to the right place if you're lookin' for a party, I'll tell you that right now . . .' "

"*Yes! Yes!* That's *it*!" she screamed.

Danielle lay in Hanson's arms for several minutes, her heart pounding. Hanson tried to listen to the speech, once again amazed at the effect the President had on female voters. The guy oughta give his lawyers a raise, he thought.

After a while, Danielle sat up, and looked at him. "Okay, Mr. Hanson, it's your turn," she said, kissing him passionately. "What do you want? Just tell me, let me please you."

What did he want? Since the second Hanson laid eyes on Danielle he wanted to be so far inside her that paramedics couldn't pull him out with the jaws of life. "Just lie back, beautiful," he said.

That was the last request Hanson had to make. For the better part of the next hour Danielle tried to please him every way he could imagine, and then some. It was as though she had a sixth sense, able to anticipate his every desire before he did. In all his years, he had never felt such a level of arousal. She was incredible. Several times he was on the verge of climax, able to maintain control only with the help of three scotches and plenty of latex.

After trying out every position in the Kama Sutra, Danielle mounted Hanson, wrapping her well-sculpted legs around him as he took her supple breasts in his mouth. Finally, he couldn't hold back any longer, erupting inside her. As Danielle felt him dissolve, she looked down to see Hanson's face filled with ecstasy, relief, and exhaustion all at once. She was proud of herself. Although she couldn't pinpoint it, there was something exceptional about this man, and she wanted to satisfy him.

Together they lay in the darkness with only the sounds of the CNN business report in the background. Neither would say it aloud, but both of them knew something special had happened. Hanson's guess was that Danielle didn't do this sort of thing every day. For him, on the other hand, this was far more than a casual interlude. Over the years he'd had countless liaisons with beautiful women. Seduction was one of the few things he was good at. But this was different.

Danielle was the first to break the silence. "You know, you really touched her," she said.

"Touched who?" he said.

"You know, Julie."

"I told you, despite the fact that she was my intern, I never laid a hand on her," Hanson said with a short laugh.

She rolled over and faced him. "Come on, you know what I mean. You touched her heart, she looks up to you."

"That's stretching it," he began. "All I know is, every year hundreds of young people flock to this town, each with the same idea. They want to get involved, to make a difference. Some of them really want to change the world. They have this incredible energy level . . . that is just amazing. The trouble is that most of them run into all these burned-out old farts that are just collecting their paychecks. After a while most of these kids get discouraged and give up," he said. "It's just such a waste."

"Were you one of those kids, Michael?" she asked.

He was surprised by the question. "Me? You gotta be kidding."

"No, of course not," said Danielle, as sarcastically as Hanson.

"Look, I stopped being a true believer years ago, but despite that, I still don't think there's anything wrong with being a little idealistic once in a while, particularly when someone is just a kid starting out. A person ought to able to dream a little without being derided by a bunch of cynics."

"So you protected her?"

"I don't know. Mostly, I just took her seriously."

"Maybe it's the cynics that deserve the bad rap. What about your dreams, Michael?" asked Danielle.

"Get out of here! Guys like me don't have dreams . . . we have fantasies." Hanson looked away, and then said, "Like tonight."

"You're a good egg, Hanson," she said, hugging him.

"You're just saying that because you want to use me for sex."

"What can I say? You're the guy who knows where the bodies are buried. One way or the other I was out to fuck you. Either in the committee or in the bedroom."

"Oh, I get it now. It's pillow talk you're after," he said, smiling.

"That's right, and you can't believe where I'm hiding the wire," she joked.

"You have a dirty mind, woman."

"I'm just getting started," said Danielle in a devilish tone. "But honestly, Michael, I'm the first one to admit that I had an ulterior motive tonight. Didn't you?"

"How's that?"

"By inviting me tonight you sent out the signal to the committee, to the media, to all of your enemies that you won't be intimidated, that the administration has nothing to hide. It was a brilliant move, despite the fact that the First Lady's party was the most innocuous, Milquetoast event in eight years."

"And how would you know that?"

"Come on, Michael, don't play dumb. We have videotape, Secret Service logs, as well as the official guest lists on every event this administration has ever had. Tonight's party is no different. We'll have everything we need by morning."

"Okay, I'm busted. What's your angle?"

"You know damned well what my angle is, Michael," she snapped. "This administration would make Beijing the fifty-first state if they had their way. I want information, and one way or the other, I intend to get it."

Hanson was growing irritated. He knew he was being used, but had hoped that some part of the night was real. "Look, I hate to disappoint you, but this seduction scene doesn't cut it with me. I've told everything I know to Justice, the independent counsel, and now your committee."

"Everything?"

"That's right, Danielle, everything! Sorry, I guess you're just going to have to fuck some other guy to get the answers you're after."

"That's not fair."

"None of this is fair, Danielle."

"I made love with you because I wanted to."

"Making love. I've heard of that. I wonder what it must be like," he said as he felt the bile rise in the back of his throat. "I gotta get going. Suddenly, I feel like I want a shower." Hanson slid his legs off the side of the bed and began to put on his trousers. As he did so, Danielle threw her arms around his back.

"Michael, please don't be angry."

"I'm not angry, Danielle. Just disgusted. Disgusted with this town, disgusted with politics, most of all I'm disgusted with myself," he said, standing up abruptly, knocking her back as he did so. Quickly he grabbed his shirt and looked around for his tie.

"Michael, we can help each other. . . ."

"I seriously doubt that. See, I'm done talkin', Danielle, and believe it or not, I've been helped enough for one night. Amazing as it may seem, even a bag man like me has too much pride to stick around while a beautiful woman fucks me to get information."

"I told you, I made love to you because I wanted to. . . . I still want to," she said, taking his hand.

"Like I said, I gotta get goin'," said Hanson, grabbing his suit jacket and heading for the door.

"Michael, the White House is setting you up for a big fall!"

Suddenly Hanson stopped dead in his tracks. His bruised ego was inflamed by a sense of violation. But somehow Danielle had spoken the only words that would make him hear her out. He turned to her. "What the fuck are you talking about?"

"Stay the night and I'll tell you. . . ."

* * *

Kennedy finally headed home for a couple hours of sleep. As he pulled into his driveway, he ran into A. J., coming home in his football uniform, helmet under his arm.

"A. J., just coming home from practice now? What's up?"

"Nothing much, Dad." A. J. ducked around his father and walked into the house. Kennedy followed, frowning. A. J. went straight for the refrigerator, rummaging around for the leftovers his mother had left aside for him and his father.

"Hey, leave some for me," Kennedy said, grinning, as A. J. scarfed down a huge helping of chicken pot pie. "Slow down. Why don't you sit down and eat with me?"

Kennedy saw that A. J. was less than thrilled, but he was determined to spend some time with his son. Marlene was also happy to sit down with her husband and son for a rare meal, even if it was after eleven at night. Over pot luck and potato salad, Kennedy worked on drawing his son out, and proposed a father-son fishing trip.

"What do you think, does it sound like a good idea?" Kennedy asked.

A. J. looked skeptical at first, then grudgingly relented. "We should try fishing that stream we found the last time we were out on the river. I think we might get lucky there."

Kennedy smiled. "Sounds good to me." He felt like he was actually making progress with A. J., though every now and then when he looked at his son, he couldn't help but be reminded of the faces of Ariel Fairchild and Rene LaSalle. He was going to get the killer, no matter what it took—even if it made life extremely unpleasant for Mike Hanson.

Kennedy looked at his watch. His friend, District Attorney David Kincaid, had once told him it was never too late to call if he needed a favor. Kennedy picked up the phone and dialed a number ingrained in his memory.

"Dave, it's Abe Kennedy. Sorry to call so late. . . . How you doin'?. . . . Not bad, not bad. Listen, I need a huge favor, I need your help getting an arrest warrant on a perp. . . . Murder One, yeah, that's right. Good, I'll be right over if that's okay with you. . . . His name, yeah . . . Hanson, Mike Hanson . . . that's right, s-o-n . . . Hanson."

Part Four

"There are people in this town who see politics as a cutthroat game, and a lot of 'em don't mind holding the knife."

—David Gergen
Former White House
Communications Director

Chapter Twenty-four

Kennedy had hoped that a few hours sleep would leave him refreshed, but when his alarm went off at 5:15 A.M., he was already awake, wondering when and where the killer would strike again. He jumped out of bed, showered, and was headed back to the station before 6 A.M. to attack the backlog of paperwork related to the murders. No sooner had he arrived at the station than he found a message on his desk from Marlene reminding him that they had a three o'clock follow-up appointment with A. J.'s psychologist. Thank god for that woman, he thought.

As he made his way to the pantry for the first of what was certain to be several cups of witch's brew, he got the buzz from the graveyard shift. The night had been particularly quiet, with the exception of one shooting near a crack house in the Adams Morgan neighborhood. The victim was a twelve-year-old boy. Kennedy couldn't help but wonder how much the commissioner would care about finding the killers of that child. Still, this was a quiet night in Murder City, just like Kennedy hoped it would be. Even serial killers need their rest from time to time.

Kennedy was at his desk reviewing his notes when his line rang. Wondering if it was the commissioner calling to check up on him, he almost didn't answer it. Then he reconsidered. It could be Marlene. Or Ira. He picked up.

"Abe, is that you?" Kennedy could barely recognize Julian Cole's half-whispering voice.

"Julian?"

"Yeah, I really have to talk to you." The forensic pathologist sounded uncharacteristically subdued.

"Fire away, buddy. Have you gotten any prints off the cuff link?"

"I think maybe we should meet somewhere and get some breakfast," he said, his voice quivering at the ends of the words.

"Julian, I really need to know about the print. Did you get a match?"

"Why don't you meet me at the Stars and Stripes Diner up on Wisconsin Avenue?"

Cole sounded spooked. This case was getting more and more strange, Kennedy thought. Well, only one way to find out. Anyway, he was starving, and greasy eggs at his favorite twenty-four-hour dive sounded awfully good right now. "I'll be there in twenty minutes."

The second Kennedy arrived, Julian caught the eye of a waitress and ordered the special for both of them. Waiting until she reached the grill to call in their order, Julian got to the point. "We sent the print into AFIS," he said, referring to the Automatic Fingerprint Identification System run out of Quantico, Virginia. "Within hours the computer recognized it."

"Fantastic. Let's have the name."

"It's not that simple, Abe. That's why I asked you to come down here."

"Yes, Julian, it's that simple. See, the way this works is you give me the name that matches up with the print, and then I go catch me a bad guy. See, simple!" he said, trying to get Cole to lighten up.

"Abe, I really don't know how to begin explaining this to you."

Kennedy stared at his friend, for the first time feeling a bit nervous about what Cole had found. Cole was fidgeting, and his eyes kept scanning the street through the grimy window smudged with yesterday's grease and fingerprints. "Why don't you start at the beginning?" Kennedy prompted.

"Here, wiseass, read the printout yourself," Cole said, sliding a copy over the chipped Formica table.

Kennedy picked it up and studied it for a moment. He whistled, a low, disbelieving sound that released all the air out of his chest and left him feeling shaky. "Holy Shit! Now everything's beginning to make sense. Who else knows about this?"

"There's a record of the search somewhere in the computer morass, but apart from that nobody, just us. That's why I wanted to tell you in person," Cole said.

"Good. For now let's just keep this between us, okay?"

"Oh, as far as I'm concerned, that's not a problem," Cole said, sitting way back in the orange plastic chair.

"What about the cuff link itself, where is it?"

"Actually," Cole said, a bit of a gleam coming back to his eyes. "I was planning on returning it to the evidence locker as soon as I was done . . ."

"And?"

"Well, I was in such a rush to get to you, I guess I just must have forgotten." He grinned. "It just happens to be in the trunk of my car."

Kennedy threw down a twenty on the table and started toward the door. "Don't bother going back to the office, Julian. Why don't you go home and get a few hours of sleep? I would be more than happy to bring it back there for you."

"I'll bet you can, Abe," seeing the look in Kennedy's eye. "I don't have to tell you what will happen if the cuff link doesn't make it to the evidence lockup, do I?"

"Julian, I'm shocked. You don't actually think I'd misplace it on the way back?"

"In a heartbeat," Cole said, smiling. Then he turned serious. "Abe, I trust you more than anyone I know on the force. But whatever hunch you're playing better be right. This is a dangerous game." He handed over the car keys. "Be careful, Abe."

Chapter Twenty-five

As Kennedy jumped back into his car with his new precious cargo, he knew that only one person could help him. Someone from way back, someone he trusted, someone who owed Kennedy his life. He decided not to call from his car phone—cells could be tapped by anyone—but to stop at a pay phone. "Hey, Todd, it's Abe. Do you have a moment?"

"Abe, I always have time for you. How's Marlene and A. J.?"

"Marlene's great, except she's a little worried about A. J. He's hanging out with the wrong crowd. Trouble in school. I really don't know exactly what to do. I try and try to make time to sit down and talk with him, but I'm on this big case and I don't know when I'm going to be able to find the time."

"What's A. J. doing tonight?" The calm, concerned voice reassured Kennedy. Everything would work out. "I'll take him out for dinner, have a little talk with him. After all, he's my only godchild."

"Are you sure? I know you're busy, especially with all that's been going down in K, and the elections around the corner."

"Well, *my boss* wants to have things nailed down before he leaves office, but I always have time for A. J."

Kennedy hesitated and felt a stab of guilt. Maybe it would be wrong to involve his old friend in this mess. But he had no one else to turn to. "I was also wondering if you had some time to talk to me about a rather delicate matter. It's pretty urgent."

"Where are you?"

"Connecticut Avenue, up by Woodley Park. I was headed back to headquarters."

"Why don't you meet me at Starbucks on Pennsylvania by the Old Executive Office Building on your way back? I could use a caffeine break anyway."

Kennedy was relieved already. "I'll be right there."

The detective entered the trendy coffee bar and immediately starting longing for the grease-caked Stars and Bars Diner. A handful of men and women in suits, with security passes hanging around their necks and tucked into their pockets, were trying to be conspicuously inconspicuous as they ordered coffees that went by exotic names in other languages, reminding Abe of his welcome on his first day back at the homicide squad. Kennedy glanced around at the spotless, shiny chrome room and spotted his old friend sitting on a tall, narrow stool. Todd McCartney, National Security Advisor, was a tall, broad-shouldered African-American. He was as fit as ever, and his salt-and-pepper hair cropped close to his head didn't make him look older, only more distinguished. McCartney stood up, and the two men embraced warmly.

The NSC advisor had grown up in D.C. only six blocks away from Kennedy. But the two didn't meet until they were practically grown men in a foreign land half a world away. Vietnam was a place neither of them spoke about much, even now, almost twenty-five years later. Even so, their time in-country left a permanent impression on both and was forever imbedded in their memory. In such an uncertain, dangerous land, with no warning when death would strike, friendships grew fast. Kennedy and McCartney bonded immediately, telling stories about the old neighborhood, calling each other brother, and swearing to always, always look out for each other. The slightly older McCartney took Kennedy under his wing and watched out for the new recruit until their roles were reversed one steamy, cloudless afternoon, when Kennedy risked his life to save McCartney's.

Both wounded, they were sent back home to the States, heroes in a heroless war. They stayed in touch, even though McCartney reupped to return to Nam and Kennedy's uniform was mothballed, never again to leave the closet. McCartney rose through the ranks of the U.S. Army as Kennedy chose another field of battle. The two men remained close, bonding through their decisions to lead lives dedicated to duty and honor, and Kennedy had chosen McCartney to be A. J.'s godfather.

McCartney now passed Kennedy a tall, skinny latte, a cup of designer coffee priced nearly four times as much as the Stars and Bars's plain cup. Kennedy assumed there were no free refills here either. But he gulped it down gratefully.

"Abe, how are you?" McCartney's brow was furrowed, and he looked concerned. "So what's going on?"

Kennedy sighed and leaned in towards his friend. "Well, this is going to sound mighty strange, but I'm conducting a murder investigation, and we have reason to believe that one of your people might be involved."

"One of my people?" McCartney stared at Kennedy with incredulous eyes. "What do you mean by that? Military? White House staff?"

Kennedy shrugged. "Yes. Or someone close to the President."

McCartney's reaction said it all. He thought his friend had finally lost it. "Abe, that's a serious charge. I hope you're prepared to back it up."

"Absolutely," he said, placing the bag with the cuff link on the marble tabletop. "This was found at the murder scene. Have you ever seen anything like that before?"

Staring at the bag, McCartney asked, "May I?"

"Go ahead, just please don't take it out of the bag. It's evidence, and I really shouldn't even have it on me."

McCartney picked it up and examined it through the plastic, holding it close, as if trying to read something. "You know, over the last four years I've seen the President give out at least a hundred pairs of these. He's even given me a pair. Does that make me a suspect?" McCartney smiled, but looked uneasy.

Kennedy shook his head and felt a pang of guilt. He shouldn't have dragged McCartney into this mess.

McCartney read the engraved signature on the back of the link.

"You know, Abe, this isn't even one of ours. It's from another administration."

"Yes, I'm aware of that. But that's not why I'm here," Kennedy continued. "Our forensics people were fortunate enough to get a print off it. The trouble is, when we ran the print through the AFIS computer, the I.D. on the print came back classified."

"I see, and that's why you wanted to meet?" McCartney asked, raising an eyebrow.

"Not exactly. I'm here because not only was the I.D. classified, but it was specifically coded under Black Ops."

"Slow down," McCartney said softly. He quickly looked around the room to make sure no one could hear them. Kennedy realized that he seemed to have that effect on people lately.

"That's a different story altogether. Anything regarding Black Ops is extremely sensitive. Technically I'm not supposed to acknowledge that such operations even exist. As a matter of policy, we try to leave those matters to those with need to know—CIA, Defense Intelligence Agency—they have their own deals going."

"Meaning?"

"Meaning that a Black Op is a clandestine operation, generally backed by the CIA or one of the military intelligence services, operating covert, outside the usual chain of command and normal Congressional oversight. Unlike something as controversial as Iran-Contra, which required both a 'finding' from the National Security Council and an Executive Order from the President, a Black Op can proceed as part of a broad intelligence strategy when significant national imperatives are involved," he explained. "Even Congress, which loves to micromanage, thinks it's too hot to handle. Congress signs the checks, budgets money each year for Black Ops, but only a handful of the leadership even knows how much is budgeted. To sum it up, it is the most secretive type of operation there is."

"What kind of stuff are we talking here, assassinations, kidnappings? What?"

McCartney hesitated. "Abe, I'm not at liberty to be that specific."

"Are Black Operations legal?"

"So far. I mean, no one has ever had the bad judgment to

suggest that the Boland Amendment gives Congress jurisdiction or anything, if that's what you mean."

"So can you help me?"

"Well, that depends on what you're asking," McCartney said carefully.

"I need to know whose print is on this," he said, holding the glimmering link up. "Isn't there someone you can call, the Bureau, the CIA, whatever? After that, it's up to me. All I need is a name."

Leaning back in his chair, McCartney chose his words carefully. "Easier said than done. I can't just do that."

Kennedy stared at his friend disbelievingly. "Someone, who just happens to be involved in this highly classified Black Ops, which you yourself say is vital to national security, may well be going around killing teenage hookers right here in Washington, and you can't even help me I.D. the bastard?"

McCartney rubbed his face wearily. "Abe, try to think of this from my perspective. This cuff link came from a Republican administration. It's a month before the election. If I were to help you—and that's even if I were able to help you, and I'm honestly not sure I have the power to do so—the GOP would immediately accuse me of playing politics, which is the last thing this administration needs."

"With all due respect, old friend, isn't that what this White House does best?"

"Yes and no," said McCartney, pausing for a second to sip his java. "See, ever since the goddamn impeachment there's been a battle going on in the West Wing. The die-hards want to cut the Republicans off at the knees. On the other hand, the moderates, of which I consider myself a member, have been lobbying to take the high road. Just focus on running the country and the election will take care of itself. Unfortunately, we're losing the battle."

"Todd, the last thing I want to do is to make your job more difficult. I'm just running out of options," said the detective.

"Abe, my position with this administration is well known, but as a military officer, my job is nonpartisan, no favors, nothing. I serve the President in the interest of the nation, not in his political capacity. If I help you, they'll claim I'm using my office for political purposes. Then again, if I don't help you, you can accuse me of covering something up. I just can't win. What do you want me to do?"

"I need you to help me," Kennedy pleaded, "before this guy kills again."

"I simply cannot pursue any course of action that could possibly override the National Security Act." McCartney's voice was soft, but firm.

Kennedy's eyes narrowed. "Well, just because you can't give it to me doesn't mean it isn't out there. Lots of places have prints on file. If this guy is a lawyer, the D.C. Bar should have them. If he has ever applied for a securities license, served in the military, or was ever bonded, his print is on file somewhere."

"Abe, I honestly think you're too wrapped up in this case. Even if I start poking around in these matters, people will know. People will ask questions. If you do it, it could be really damaging—to you and to your department. I think you should take a step back. Maybe you could stand down temporarily, take a short vacation with your family."

Abe started to bristle, but he knew his friend was only looking out for him. "Todd, believe it or not, I hear you loud and clear. But you gotta hear me. This is our city, yours and mine. Most of those suits you work with, they may be good folks and all, but they're just passing through. As soon as this gig is over, they're outta here."

"Come on, Abe."

"You didn't see those dead bodies! They could have been A. J. Nothing is going to make me stop working on this case until I find the bastard who killed them."

McCartney started to say something, but thought better of it. He gave up and stood up to embrace his friend. "I have to get back over to the White House, I've got a meeting in fifteen minutes. Keep me informed, and be careful. Remember, if you start poking around and asking questions about Black Ops, people will know right away. It's suicide to stick your nose into national security affairs. This stuff is for keeps, no bullshit. When these guys play, it's no random drive-by deal. They're pros."

Kennedy just nodded and turned to leave. He shouldn't have involved his friend in this mess. But he wasn't going to give up.

For a few moments, the National Security Advisor sat alone in

Starbucks, sipping his latte and thinking intently. He walked slowly back to his office, thinking of the old days and how the complicated life he had chosen had changed his concepts of loyalty. When he got back to his office, he picked up the phone and dialed a number. He waited for the line on the other end to pick up, satisfied that he had no other choice.

"Mary, it's Colonel McCartney. Get me a safe line to Langley, the Director's office. It looks like we may have a problem."

Chapter Twenty-six

Hanson and Danielle Harris stayed up all night, devouring half of the items on the room service menu. Along the way, Hanson got a glimpse of the real Danielle Harris. He learned that she had wanted to be a lawyer ever since she was a lonely little girl growing up in an affluent Boston suburb. She had no brothers and sisters, and her mother died when she was eight years old. Her father was a renowned plastic surgeon who had operated on celebrities and foreign dignitaries. He was never completely comfortable around his daughter; Danielle always felt that she reminded him too much of her mother. Anyway, he wasn't around much, always on call, always catering to the demands of his patients.

At the same young age that Hanson decided he would go into politics to change the world, Danielle decided on a more down-to-earth goal—to become a prosecutor. Instead of chasing the almighty dollar, she made it her mission to chase bad guys. Just out of law school, she landed a job as an Assistant U.S. Attorney. Her turf was South Florida, where the drug culture quickly surrounded her every move. Based not far from the Overtown section of Miami, walking to her car was like traversing a combat zone.

On every corner were youngbloods armed to the hilt, assigned to be on the alert for "5–0," aka the cops. On their down time, these twelve- and thirteen-year-old boys served as order takers for the countless migrants from the suburbs who made the trek into no man's land to score dope.

Danielle recalled vividly how their fresh faces evolved right before her eyes. One moment they were babies eating ice cream cones, laughing, occasionally fronting to each other, pretending to be OGs. Then, in a matter of seconds, these same faces would be transformed—usually by gunfire—into the stark countenances of stone cold killers. And, as much as this broke her heart, she knew that the real cancer was the high-level dealers and wholesalers. She was determined to fight back, and fight back she did.

By the end of her five-year stint with the Feds, Danielle had become one of the bar's foremost experts in tracking the laundered profits from drug transactions. As the drug lords of South Florida and Cali eventually learned, there wasn't a sham transaction, a dummy corporation, or a numbered account that would escape her scrutiny. If a wiseguy had a pile of cash hidden somewhere in this hemisphere, Danielle Harris was bound to find every cent. And while she could never have foreseen it, this credential as a money laundering specialist made her the ideal counsel for the Select Committee on Campaign Finance. This also spelled trouble for Mike Hanson.

Despite this, Hanson found it impossible not to be impressed with Danielle. He admired her intelligence and quiet determination, and was charmed by her quick, self-deprecating wit. More than that, he felt completely disarmed by her. Several times he started to open up, but quickly retreated. He desperately wanted to tell her about what had happened to him during the past few days—Detective Kennedy's appearance on his doorstep, the destruction of his apartment, most of all how he was haunted by the ashen face of a dead seventeen-year-old girl. But each time he bit his tongue, reminding himself that even though he was sleeping with the enemy, Danielle was in fact still the enemy. "Listen, not that I'm not having a great time. But before I fall asleep or we, you know . . ."

"Suddenly, I'm blank," she said.

"Yeah, right. As I was saying, before we get distracted again, why don't you clue me in to this big White House conspiracy."

In an instant, Danielle's upbeat mood fizzled. She knew that sunrise was less than an hour away and whether she liked it or not, she was going to have to come clean. "First let me order us another pot of coffee," she said, running to the phone and dialing room service for the umpteenth time. "No, we haven't had enough. That's right, we're pulling an all-nighter. No, just the pot will be fine," she barked into the phone. "Thanks, see you in a few minutes."

"Okay, are we ready to talk now?" Hanson asked.

"Sure, just let me rinse off in the shower."

"No! Sit down!" he demanded.

"Michael, I'm not sure I like your tone," she said defensively.

While Hanson was the first one to admit that he'd loved every minute of their "date," his reservoir of patience was exhausted. "I apologize for my tone. But it isn't your ass on the line. It's mine!"

Danielle gave him a cold, indifferent stare. She knew she had no chance at winning this point. She just wanted to stall as long as possible. Finally, after several awkward seconds, she walked over to the bed and sat as far away from Hanson as possible, at the head of the mattress. "Okay, you wanna talk, let's talk."

"I'm listening . . ."

"I thought you'd never ask," she began. "Starting about three months ago, when the Republican leadership first started talking about reviving the committee, I began to get these anonymous e-mails. At first they were very gossipy, talking about which witnesses might cut deals and which ones would take the fifth. Some of the messages contained detailed breakdowns of the legal bills of some of the people on the committee's witness list. Eventually, they got more personal. One talked about how one senior campaign official was secretly on the payroll of the tobacco lobby and could be turned by the threat of exposure. Another told of how another witness had retaliated against the committee, or how that witness . . ."

"I assume that at that point you had not been hired. . . ."

"That's right. I was still at the U.S. Attorney's office. The chairman and I had only spoken briefly about me coming over."

"Sounds like they were trying to whet your appetite. What

makes you think it was coming from the White House?"

"At first I didn't have the first notion where the e-mails were coming from. But once I joined the committee, it was like I had a guardian angel on the inside. We'd subpoena some documents and the White House would drag its feet like always. But before they would respond, I'd get an e-mail telling me exactly what was coming over and what would be missing. This happened five or six times. My guardian angel was right every time."

"Okay, so you got someone on the inside working against the President. You know as well as I do this has happened at least a couple of times now."

"Not against the President, Michael. Against you."

"How do you mean?"

"Nothing ever came to me that could have done any more damage to the President than he has already suffered. On the other hand, the day before you testified, a courier delivered a package detailing your participation in every key finance meeting of '96. The coffees, the sleepovers, the Buddhist Temple affair. You name it."

"Big deal, everybody knows I was involved in some of that stuff."

"Not according to this. According to this, you were driving the train."

"Right."

"What I want to know is how you kept your name out of the Teamsters mess?"

"Mainly because I don't know any Teamsters."

"According to the file, you were who the union came to first. You signed off on the whole thing."

"Prove it."

"Michael, that's not the point. But what is interesting is why somebody would go to all this trouble to screw you."

"Does Tom Griffin's name show up anywhere?"

"Strangely enough, no it doesn't. What do you make of that?"

Suddenly Hanson remembered Devon's warning to trust no one. "I'm not sure. Nothing surprises me in this town anymore," he said, barely able to hide his disgust. "So, Danielle, while I appreciate the heads-up and all, I gotta ask you . . . why are you telling me all this? I mean, shouldn't you be using all this dirt to bury me?"

"Michael, I've been a prosecutor most of my professional life. I can honestly say that as much as I like you, if any of this added up, I'd hang you out to dry."

"That's comforting," he said sarcastically.

"Come on," she said laughing.

"I know, I know. Professional ethics and all. I've heard of that. . . ." Pausing to sip his coffee, he asked, "So are you saying that the evidence doesn't add up?"

"Michael, nobody could be as guilty as the file says you are. Practically the only thing that they haven't linked you to is the Kennedy assassination. It's a first-rate hatchet job. Fortunately for you, it's filled with inconsistencies."

"Like what?"

"Like placing you at two different meetings at the same time, or alleging that you were on a conference call when your cell phone records indicate that you were speaking with someone else."

Astonished, he asked, "You have my cell phone records?"

"Don't be so naive, Michael. We have everything."

"So what do you want from me?"

"I want you to help me find the mole inside the White House. This person obviously knows everything and has an axe to grind. You lead me to them and we'll find the smoking gun."

"Danielle, I don't mean to be rude, but are you out of your fucking mind? Why on earth would I help you, especially when everyone knows this is just a Hail Mary pass by the Repos, your last chance to bring down the President? In case you care, I like the fucking President. If there's a goddamn smoking gun, I don't wanna know about it!"

"Michael, the President is only going to be president for another two months. There really isn't much I or anybody else can do to hurt him. On the other hand, by exposing the mole, you can help both of us. Whoever this is, they aren't going to stop until they get you. I'm sure the same dossier is over at the Independent Counsel's office right now. You gotta get this bastard before he gets you."

"I'll take my chances."

"Suit yourself, Michael. But I'd think it over if I were you. My boss wants to call you back next week, and trust me, he intends to play rough," she said as she stood up and began to walk to the bathroom. "I'm gonna duck in the shower or I'll be late for work."

"What's up, have an early-morning execution scheduled?" snapped Hanson.

"Funny," she called from inside the bathroom.

While Danielle showered, Hanson drank rancid, room-temperature coffee and turned on the early-morning news. ABC was running its daily "Road to the White House" segment. "In today's ABC-Newsweek poll, voters reported that if the election were held today, it would be a virtual dead heat between Vice President Joe Albert and Texas Governor Richard Prescott. In a survey of over two hundred seventy-five registered voters, 38 percent supported Prescott while 37 percent said they would vote for Vice President Albert. Once again, the spoiler appears to be Independent candidate David Thurman, whose numbers appear to be hovering at around 22 percent. Rumors continue to fly that a deal is in the works in which Thurman will withdraw from the race and back one of the other candidates. . . ."

"Shit! Shit! Shit!" Hanson yelled. It was bad enough that the election was slipping right through the Democrats' fingers. He didn't have to be reminded of it every ten minutes. Finally, room service arrived with a fresh pot. Given that it wasn't his room, Hanson felt uncomfortable signing the bill, wanting instead to pay in cash. Unfortunately, he only had big bills, and the bellman, smelling a windfall, suddenly ran out of change. "Of course. Wait here," he said as he walked back to the bathroom. Knocking on the door before entering, he called out, "Uh, Danielle, do you have any small bills so I can tip the bellman?"

"In my wallet," came the muffled response, drowned out by the spray of the shower.

Hanson closed the door and grabbed her purse. He was uncomfortable going through it, and was glad to find her wallet sitting right on top. Removing enough for the coffee and the prescribed amount of tip, he handed it to the bellman, who was obviously disappointed that he hadn't made more of a profit. Once he left, Hanson started to return Danielle's wallet to its rightful place, but something strange caught his eye. At the very front of the wallet was a photograph of a younger Danielle embracing a handsome older gentleman as a dark-haired teenage boy looked on in the background. He studied the picture for a moment, not wanting to believe his eyes. There was no mistaking it. His worst fears were confirmed. The man in the photograph was Oliver Devon.

"Enjoying yourself?" said Danielle as she walked out of the bathroom, drying herself with a towel.

Startled, Hanson hurriedly returned the wallet to its rightful place. "Sorry, I just saw the picture. It's a great shot," he said, feigning innocence. Danielle was obviously Devon's mistress, just as he suspected.

"It's not that great, but it's the only one I have," she said, caught a little off guard.

"When was it taken?"

"About ten years ago."

"So who's the guy in the picture, some friend of the family?" he asked, playing dumb.

"What do you mean, who's the guy?"

"Just curious, that's all. Who is he?"

She went to him, the wetness of her skin practically soaking through her terry cloth robe, her hair wet and mussed. Softly, she put her hand on his cheek. "Michael, if you must know, the guy in the picture, as you put it, is my ex-husband."

Weird. Really, really weird, thought Hanson. "You were married to Oliver Devon?"

"Unfortunately, yes. Do you know him?" she asked nonchalantly as she began to brush her hair in the mirror.

"Danielle, everybody in town knows Oliver Devon."

"I suppose that's true. Is that a problem?" she said.

"No," said a shaken Hanson as he sat down on the bed, his head spinning. "Why would that be a problem?"

As they dressed, Hanson said little. By definition, he knew he could never trust Danielle, but he'd hoped to forge some bond based on mutual self-interest. But now his feelings were way past distrust. He was now afraid of her, not for her prosecutorial mind set, but because of the horrific notion that she could have ever loved a serpent like Oliver Devon. Danielle was either the most naive woman he'd ever met or a player with an unmatched political will the likes of which he'd never seen. Before leaving, they both agreed to keep their little encounter quiet, knowing that they each had a lot to lose if either of them went public. Hanson left the hotel feeling a mixture of elation and regret about the night before. He'd invited Danielle to the White House to prove a point. He'd seduced her to prove his manhood. Unfortunately, he'd exposed a whole lot more than he had ever intended. And so had Danielle.

Unfortunately, it didn't take Hanson long to realize what kind of day it would be. He jumped into a cab, and after several minutes, the driver suddenly stopped chatting.

"This is really strange," the driver said. "You got any friends who drive around town in a big black limo?" the driver asked, looking at Hanson in his rearview mirror.

Hanson, lost in thoughts of Danielle, looked back to see a limo following behind them closely on the twisting and turning Georgetown streets.

"No, I don't think so," he said, and a trickle of dread began winding up and down his spine.

"Well, he's been on my ass since we left the hotel. Tailgating me for more than ten minutes," he said. When Hanson was silent, the driver continued. "I sure as hell don't know anyone in a limo. Want me to go around the block a few times to see what he's up to?"

"Yeah, why don't you do that," Hanson said, fighting to keep his voice light as he remembered the violence and destruction wreaked upon his home. Were they coming back to finish him off? He knew he had to stay calm. He swallowed hard and gripped the hand strap that hung above the side window. Its loose screws fell from their holes and the strap dropped loosely into his hand.

His driver, seemingly enjoying the game, made several sharp left and right turns on the narrow, one-way streets, and Hanson slid from side to side over the glossy vinyl backseat. The limo followed. Finally, the driver turned the cab's wheels sharply and cut through an alley full of garages and garbage Dumpsters and came out on P Street, one of the last cobblestone streets in the city. He sped up, zooming past mansions, and they bumped across the old trolley tracks left there since the trolley system was dismantled in the 1940's. Hanson looked back, but the limo doggedly followed behind them, coming close to rear-ending them more than once.

"I can't believe this guy," the driver exclaimed. "He's trying to fuck with us, that's for sure. You want me to call in for help on the radio?"

Suddenly alert, Hanson became strangely calm. Although no genius, even he could see where this was headed. He would bet the farm that whoever was in that limo was Ariel Fairchild's killer. A slow, steady rage was building up inside him. "No, just take me to my home."

"Are you sure?" the driver said uncertainly. "The guy could be a nut."

"I guess this is my lucky day. Just drive me home." Hanson's voice was firm.

The driver pulled up to Hanson's house, shaking his head at his passenger's poor judgment. The limo pulled around Hanson's corner smoothly and silently, like any good predator, Hanson thought. It sat halfway down his block, its engine purring despite the rough ride they had just put it through. Hanson gave the driver two crisp twenties and opened the door of the cab. He stood up straight and suddenly whipped around on his heel and charged the limo. His fury made him brave. Whoever was in that limo had brutally murdered a poor, helpless teenager. Adrenaline raged though him; he would kill them, whoever they were.

"Who are you, you motherfuckers!" he screamed as he hurled himself toward the limo.

The limo lurched away from the curb, coming straight at him, and he threw himself back to avoid being hit. He slammed his back into the side mirror on a parked car and fell back across its hood, feeling sharp pain shoot up his spine, but desperately trying all the while to look into the limo as it sped by. The windows were darkly tinted and he could barely make out the driver's black hat. Hanson heard its wheels screech around the corner as he sat on the curb panting and shaking with rage. He had never felt so helpless in his life; it was almost paralyzing.

Hanson sat for a few moments, then slowly got up, eyes still tearing with anger, and walked inside his house, wondering if any of his neighbors had witnessed the scene. He contemplated calling the police and looked around for the phone. It was coiled around the legs of his armchair, and the lights on the answering machine were blinking furiously. Pressing the playback button, he listened to his messages while getting undressed, forcing himself to slow down, to concentrate. His ears perked up when he heard the woman's voice. It was harder, more clipped than he remembered, but he knew who it was immediately.

"Mike, please pick up. Look, I don't have much time. I don't blame you if you hate me, but I have to talk to you. Something terrible has happened and I think we're both in danger. I'm on the road. I'll call you."

Hanson listened grimly, wondering what the hell CeCe had gotten him into. No kidding, CeCe, I would agree that I'm in a little danger, he thought disgustedly, looking around at his living room. CeCe sounded terrible, hysterical. He prayed she would call back.

He punched the advance button.

The next call was a pleasant surprise. "Hey Hanson, you homophobic asshole, it's me, Seltzer. As much as it kills me to admit it, I want to thank you for making the call to the *Post*. The interview went super and I start the first of the month. On the national desk no less. Tell our buddy Adam to relax. I'll wait until he's really a big shot to ruin him. Only kidding. It goes without saying that I owe you a big one . . ."

"Boys will be boys," said Hanson to himself as he erased the message.

Unfortunately, more bad news was to follow. "Mr. Hanson, this is Eleanore Savoy from the *Post*. I would like to ask you a few questions. Please call me here at 555-8899."

Great, the press, Hanson thought. He pressed the erase button. No way was he speaking to any reporter.

The last message was all dead air and static, and Hanson was about to hit erase when he heard her desperate voice. It was thickly slurred and so hysterical that it was nearly impossible to comprehend.

"Michael, Michael, please pick up, it's me, CeCe. Michael I need to see you, I'm in horrible trouble. They killed my baby, the fucking animals! They killed her! Meet me at five o'clock today in Georgetown. I'll be under the gold dome in front of

Riggs bank at Wisconsin and M streets. Please Michael, don't tell anyone, just come alone. . . ."

Hanson played the tape over and over again. He sadly remembered the beautiful, fresh-faced girl he had once known. In his mind he debated the pros and cons of meeting her. Undoubtedly it would lead to more trouble, but CeCe was scared to death and needed help. Besides, he needed answers. He ticked things off in his head: Ariel Fairchild was murdered, a D.C. homicide detective breathing down his neck would love to charge him with murder, he was being stalked by psychopaths in limos, and his house had been ransacked. Maybe CeCe could give him some answers.

For Hanson, his decision boiled down to one thing—if he didn't meet CeCe, he might never know who killed Ariel. He could no longer run away from this, pretending he didn't care that she was murdered. Hanson just had to make sure that none of his actions would affect the campaign. Then, just as he was starting to relax, his digital pager suddenly lit up, interrupting his thoughts. He jumped up to read it. "Get your ass in here. NOW. 911. Griff."

"Shit," Hanson muttered. What now? He grabbed his wallet and darted out the front door. When he saw who was coming up his driveway, his heart sunk. It was his friendly neighborhood homicide detective, accompanied by a man he didn't know.

"Whoa, Hanson, where are you running off to so fast this morning?" Kennedy asked, his tone at once friendly and accusing.

"I have a meeting. And I'm late."

"Not so fast," Kennedy said slowly. "This is Postal Inspector Lisagor. He has a few questions for you." As Kennedy spoke, he did his best to maintain his game face. In truth, he didn't want Lisagor anywhere near his investigation. Unfortunately, the inspector had intercepted him during his last pit stop at the station house and insisted on tagging along.

Hanson started to sputter. "Postal inspector? I thought you guys were running a murder investigation?"

"Cut the wisecracks. Inspector Lisagor has been thoroughly briefed on your case."

"Mr. Hanson, I'm investigating a series of murders tied to an art forgery ring. I'm just trying to put a few leads together."

"Sorry to disappoint you. Not only do I know nothing about art, but I don't know anybody who does."

"What about your daughter? Did she have any special interest in art? Was she taking an art or photography class in school or something?"

Hanson glared at Kennedy. "Obviously you weren't all that well briefed, inspector. The dead girl is not my daughter. In fact, I have absolutely no idea who she is or who could possibly have done this to her!" As he finished that last sentence he felt a sudden twinge of nausea. Without meaning to, he had told a lie. He did know somebody in the art business, and that somebody was Oliver Devon.

"I apologize, Mr. Hanson. The detective said you were named next of kin. I must be confused."

"Join the club. So what's this all about?"

"We have evidence that links the murders to Washington."

"Sorry I can't help you. As I said, I know nothing."

"Well that ain't gonna cut it, Hanson," barked Kennedy. "Either we start getting a little cooperation or you are going to jail."

Before Hanson could answer, an elderly woman across the street opened her front door, poking her head out to find out what the shouting was all about. And kind of noise was a rare occurrence on the placid, tree-lined street, with its rows of ivy-shrouded townhouses. And while Hanson desperately hoped that Kennedy was bluffing, his more immediate concern was to avoid becoming the topic of neighborhood gossip. He didn't want the locals knowing he was a suspect in a murder investigation. He had to buy himself some time. Hanson had spent his entire career managing damage control for candidates and clients, but now he was his own client, and the stakes were considerably higher than passing a piece of legislation or winning an election. If he wasn't able to spin his way out of this one, it would cost him his career, perhaps even his life.

Hanson thought fast. CeCe was his only ticket. "Why don't you guys come on inside?" he said, motioning around. "Grab a seat if you can find anywhere to sit."

Kennedy and Lisagor's mouths fell open when they looked into his home. "What the hell happened here?" asked the detective.

Hanson started to talk, ignoring the question. "CeCe Fairchild,

Ariel's mother, just left a message on my answering machine," he began.

Lisagor jumped up to listen to it.

"Don't bother, I already erased it," Hanson said. "I didn't want to take any chances. Anyway, I have no idea why she called *me*, but she says she has information for me regarding Ariel's murder."

"Take us to her," demanded Kennedy.

"I can't. She's hiding out somewhere, scared to death. I'm supposed to meet her around five today in Georgetown. If anyone can lead us to the killer, she can," said Hanson.

"Five o'clock?" grimaced Kennedy, knowing Marlene would kill him if he missed the appointment with A. J.'s psychologist. "Where exactly in Georgetown are you meeting her?"

"Nice try, Detective, but that's none of your business," said Hanson, finally learning the game.

Kennedy was stumped. Somehow Hanson had gained some negotiating power by giving the Abe a much-needed break, even if it was less than the detective wanted. Still, it was a start. No time to be greedy. "Okay, Michael, you win this round. I guess you bought yourself just a little more time."

Chapter Twenty-seven

The fashionable Red Fox Inn has served Washington's elite and Virginia's gentry for over a century. Located outside of Middleburg, Virginia, in the shadow of the Blue Ridge mountains, the inn's regular patrons have included presidents, corporate moguls, and movie stars, all in need of a respite. They came for the rustic surroundings, the pampering service, and most importantly, the inn's reputation for maintaining the anonymity of its guests. It was the last place anyone would expect to find an aging madame with a cocaine problem, a murdered daughter, and a killer hunting her down.

CeCe sat alone in the elegant lounge, nursing her third Bloody Mary, anxiously waiting for the fourth to arrive. She stared mindlessly out the window at a spectacular view of the colorful quilt that made up the Virginia countryside, knowing that Devon would show up any minute. Her nerves were shot, and she was living on a steady diet of V & V—Valium and Vodka. She had dropped almost ten pounds, and her face was gaunt. CeCe wondered how much longer she could take this. The guilt was eating away at her. She was slowly killing herself with booze and drugs—and by going over that night over and over again in her head.

* * *

When the party began winding down and Ariel had still not reappeared after her liaison with the Chief, CeCe began to have doubts. She knew what the chief was capable of; she, more than any woman, knew all about man's evil side. And the chief was more diabolic than any man alive. She felt shaky and a bit confused from all the cocaine. She really shouldn't have washed it down with champagne. She called one of her girls over, was Leia her name? Yes, of course, it was Leia, and she was friends with Ariel. CeCe asked Leia if she had seen Ariel lately.

The girl shook her head and looked coldly through CeCe. Leia knew that CeCe had set her daughter up with a monster. CeCe started to panic. Her heart was fluttering and she knew it wasn't just the coke. She got on the hotel's service elevator and headed up to the suite.

When she got to the doorway, she hesitated, the vague, uneasy feeling solidifying fast in the pit of her stomach. Something wasn't right. She quickly pulled out the extra key she had wisely requested from the hotel management, and quietly pushed the door open and stepped inside. What she saw turned her blood cold.

She shut the door behind her and yelled, "What the hell are you doing to her?" Her voice came out shrill and weak.

"Get out, bitch!" He turned and started to approach her. She froze. "Get out!*" he growled at her. "I'm sick of you. You think you're so high and mighty, but you're just a whore. You're even worse than a whore—you send your own daughter out whoring for you."*

CeCe felt frozen to the spot. She simply couldn't move.

"I'm telling you one last time. Get out before I kill you." He looked at her, his face convulsed with emotions CeCe couldn't even begin to decipher. He took a step closer, and CeCe's heart tried to jump out of her body.

"Give me an excuse to kill you, you bitch."

She looked into his eyes and knew it was true as he slapped her and she fell to the floor, hitting her head on the door.

"Mom, just leave," Ariel pleaded from the bed. She started to whimper.

He raised his arm again toward CeCe and she knew that if she waited a second longer, she would be dead. She turned and fled, slamming the door behind her. As she ran down the hallway, she consoled herself with the thought that he wouldn't hurt Ariel too badly—or Devon would kill him.

CeCe wiped away tears from her eyes and looked up for the waiter only to see Devon walking right toward her, carrying her drink in his hand. She looked at her watch. Eleven-thirty, right on time as usual. "Well, look who they let in this place," she slurred in greeting.

Devon was shocked by CeCe's appearance. Normally well groomed and perfectly coifed, CeCe now looked like she hadn't showered in days. The bags under her eyes betrayed the fact that she hadn't slept either. Her once beautiful skin was practically ashen, her hair was greasy and matted, and her bloodshot eyes kept tearing over. "What have you done to yourself?" he asked, horrified and disgusted.

"I haven't done anything. The question is, what have you done?" she slurred back.

"You're drunk!"

"Wrong, Oliver. I'm pissed off! No, outraged is more like it! I gave myself to you when I was a girl. You got bored with me, no big deal. Hell, after all my years in this business, if there's one thing I understand it's that men have short attention spans. So I looked the other way for years while you fucked every bitch in my stable."

"Please try to control yourself. In case you haven't noticed, we're in a public place," he said sternly.

"You don't honestly think I give a shit, do you, Oliver?" CeCe's voice rose. "I trusted you, you bastard! I gave you my little girl . . . and now she's dead!"

Devon tried another tact. "Sweetheart, you're overwrought. But you aren't alone. I loved her too."

CeCe started to wail. Devon had expected it, and instructed the manager not to allow any other guests into the lounge. He said that CeCe had certain substance abuse problems and that he was going to try to convince her to seek help. The manager, having seen such scenes many times over, was only too happy to oblige and give them privacy. No need for the other guests to witness any ugliness. Now Devon's goal was to calm CeCe down, regain her trust, and get her back to Washington, where he could deal with the situation.

Devon cared about CeCe for only one reason. He wanted to know exactly who killed Ariel. Only CeCe could tell him. He also knew that if he was to learn anything about Ariel's death, he would have to play Daddy. He took her hand. "CeCe. I want you to listen to me very carefully. You are saying a lot of things. Dangerous things that just aren't true." He paused, handing her a handkerchief. "If you'll help me, maybe we can punish whoever killed her."

CeCe knew she had to be cautious. Normally she was sly as a fox, but she was finding it hard to concentrate today. If she told Devon that the Chief killed Ariel, he would blame her. He might even kill her. He certainly wouldn't need her anymore. On the other hand, if she didn't get his help, the Chief would eventually track her down. The Chief didn't want any witnesses, especially since he knew that Devon was after the killer.

"I don't know all that much."

"Just tell me what you know."

"Things have been slow with the service the last couple of months, so I got this idea to have a little get-together Saturday night. The girls all looked fantastic, especially Ariel, and the turn-out was great."

"CeCe, how could you! What was she even doing there?"

She was too tired to argue with him. Accepting her fate, she said, "Ariel was there in case you showed up."

Devon's face turned purple with rage, but he said nothing, just stared at her. CeCe shivered. She knew her punishment would be terrible.

"I've heard enough. Let's get out of here," he suddenly commanded.

"What makes you think I'm going anywhere with you?" she said defiantly, knowing that Devon was capable of anything, including killing her.

"Oh, you're coming with me all right," he said, grabbing her by the arm and dragging her out the back door of the inn to the waiting limousine. "Now get in the fucking car. I've got to get us back to Washington, where I can take care of this!"

"All right, Oliver, if I agree to go with you, what guarantee do I have that I won't end up like Ariel?"

Devon was way past negotiating with her. He grabbed her by the arms. "Now you listen to me, you ungrateful little whore. You got Ariel killed and I need to keep you alive long enough to use you as bait to catch the Chief. By the way, I also happen to be the only one who is capable of protecting you. Now get your worthless ass in the car!"

Both CeCe and Devon looked up as several of the inn's guests stopped to stare at the scene they were making.

CeCe looked at Devon as his grip relaxed on her arm. "Did you ever really love me?"

Devon just stared at her with cold eyes, filled with loathing and revulsion.

"I thought so!" screeched CeCe. She turned, sobbing, and broke away from him as the other guests watched.

"Should I go after her, Mr. Devon?" Devon's driver asked in a low voice.

"No, don't bother. There's nothing more we can do here," he said, watching her run frantically down the street. He had more important things to do. As CeCe finally disappeared around a corner, Devon knew that it would be only a matter of time before the Chief found her.

Chapter Twenty-eight

It was half past noon, and Hanson, having showered, shaved, and avoided arrest, had finally arrived at campaign headquarters. His head still in a fog, he opted to cab it instead of driving the Jag. As he exited the taxi, he slipped the driver a five, forgetting—as usual—to get a receipt. He started for the entrance with only one thought, how was he going to explain his tardiness to Griff . . . again? He passed by several limos sitting at the curb, paying them no attention. Then he heard his name called.

"Mr. Hanson."

Hanson stopped and looked up. He had expected to see Detective Kennedy, but instead a burly dark-haired man stood in front of him, head tilted expectantly at Hanson. His hair was slicked back and he was dressed in a spotless, tailored chauffeur's uniform. Hanson took one look at the man and could tell that he spent a lot of time in a gym. He stood with his shoulders thrown back and his huge muscled arms hanging down at his sides.

"Can I help you?" Hanson asked.

"Mr. Hanson, my name is Lonnie, I'm Mr. Devon's driver. Mr. Devon has sent me to pick you up," he said.

"Okay, Lonnie, tell Mr. Devon I'm very busy today and can't

make it," Hanson said, wondering if Lonnie was the same man who followed him and tried to run him down with the limousine.

"No sir, can't do that. Mr. Devon is waiting for you at his club. He told me to bring you there immediately. Not to leave without you. It's extremely important."

It was obvious to Hanson that Devon had trained Lonnie well. He followed instructions to the letter and did not question authority—all the traits one would want in a guard dog. There was no way Hanson was getting into a limo with this thug unless he had some sort of insurance. He thought for a second. "All right, Lonnie, I don't know what could be so goddamn urgent that I have to see Devon right this second, but just wait while I call my boss and tell him about my change of plans."

"Mr. Hanson, Mr. Devon has other pressing matters this afternoon. If you don't come immediately, he won't have time to see you."

Hanson sighed. Just by getting in the limo, he could disappear with no trace of his whereabouts. But Hanson had no choice. He had to smoke out Devon's real motive. He had to find out once and for all whether he was a mere pawn in the game or the target. "Okay, let's go."

As they drove to Devon's club, Hanson sat in the back of the limousine contemplating his meeting with his unlikely nemesis, not knowing whether Devon should be admired, loathed, or feared. Hanson knew he had to be careful not to let his doubts show. He would have to string this out a little while to find out what Devon wanted, and then would have to play Devon carefully. There was just no telling what Devon could do if he suspected a double-cross.

During the last few minutes of the ride, Hanson tried with little success to pick Lonnie's brain. "So Lonnie, have you worked for Mr. Devon long?"

"Yes sir, over seven years now."

"Do you like it? What is Mr. Devon like to work for?"

"Mr. Devon's a good man, treats me very well."

"So Lonnie, do you drive around Georgetown a lot?"

Lonnie looked at Hanson in the rearview mirror and answered in his monotone voice. "Yes, I've been driving around here for years."

Hanson resisted the urge to ask Lonnie if he liked to tear up sofas and slash through prints of impressionist paintings, and instead tried to find out more about Devon. "How about Mr. Devon's family? Does he have a wife, girlfriends? Do you drive them, too?"

Lonnie obviously became uncomfortable, and kept his eyes straight ahead on the road. "Mr. Devon ain't got no family, not no more. Don't really know nothing about that," he said as he exited the limousine and opened Hanson's door. "Mr. Devon is right in there waiting for you. Enjoy your lunch now, Mr. Hanson."

"Thanks for the ride," he said, meaning it more than Lonnie would ever know.

Chapter Twenty-nine

In Washington there is money and then there is old money. The Metropolitan Club is old money. As Hanson walked through its halls, he was struck by the unmistakable air of exclusive boarding schools, debutante balls, summering at Martha's Vineyard, and all kinds of other crap for which he had absolutely no use. Passing portrait of dead president after portrait of dead president, Hanson realized there was more to this club than just the antiques, the Persian rugs, and the best wine cellar in the city. These folks had money. Hanson had heard the jokes around town about the members of the Metropolitan Club being so rich that they have their nannies bronzed. But Hanson knew that wealth was only part of it. In D.C., making money is a piece of cake. All you need is some balls and a little bit of smarts. To get into this place, though, it took one hell of a pedigree.

When Hanson arrived at the table, Devon was already eating swordfish with a side of angel hair. He looked up at Hanson and shot him a cold stare.

"You're late," he snapped.

Hanson arched his eyebrows and gave his host a look of disdain. "How the hell can I be late for a meeting that wasn't scheduled?"

Devon just glared at Hanson as the waiter arrived to take Hanson's order.

"I'll start with a Bloody Mary, stiff," said Hanson. "And bring me a burger, medium rare."

Devon interrupted Hanson. "Rush that order. We're in a hurry." Devon waved the waiter away. "You look tired, Mike. Doesn't look like you got too much sleep last night."

The hair rose on Hanson's arms. Did Devon know where he was last night? He decided to ignore it. "Remember, Oliver, you're dealing with a Democrat. To us, swilling booze until all hours of the night is a way of life," he said as the waiter returned with his drink. Hanson downed half of it in one gulp. "What's so urgent, Oliver?"

"So, Mike, how do you guys feel about Thurman's decision?" Devon asked, a small smile playing around his lips.

"I think it's really shitty news," Hanson answered, looking straight into Devon's eyes. "Especially since you guys are bailing his ass out."

Devon laughed. "Don't act so self-righteous. You guys would have cut the same deal if you could've afforded it. It's not our fault you fellas don't have the cash. Sort of up shit creek without a paddle, wouldn't you say, Michael?" Devon leaned in towards Hanson, so close that Hanson could feel Devon's breath on his face. "But don't give up. You still might be able to figure something out."

Hanson contained his annoyance, but not his sarcasm. "Enjoy it while it lasts, Oliver. Tell your punk friends that the joke's on you. We got surplus bucks layin' around to buy enough air time to practically keep your whole fucking ticket off the air!"

Devon ignored the sarcasm. His eyes were filled with superiority. "You're bluffing, Michael. Everyone knows the Democrats are flat broke. But just out of curiosity, if this huge media buy is your last hope, how much money are you talking?"

"Why do you care, Oliver?" Hanson asked.

"Come on, Michael, give me a break. You know I'm not really supporting the Republican ticket this time around."

"I know, too liberal," chided Hanson.

"Well, too liberal to call themselves Republican, that's for sure. So come on. How much?"

Telling Devon couldn't hurt. It wasn't as if there were a chance in hell they could raise the money anyway. "About fifteen million bucks. We take Visa and Mastercard if that's easier for you."

Devon fell silent, and the two men stared at each other as the waiter brought Hanson another Bloody Mary. Devon was the first to break eye contact. "Indulge me just this once. Let's say you somehow got your hands on that kind of money. How would you get it into the campaign coffers?"

"I have no idea," he said, taking another sip of his drink. "But let's be honest. You and I both know that if presented with the opportunity, I'd figure something out."

"I have no doubt. So how would you spend it?"

"Like I said, mostly media. Unfortunately, the rules would force us to farm it out to the state parties and assorted interest groups."

"What kind of groups?"

"You know, women's groups, labor unions, environmental organizations. We shoot the ads, and they buy the time. At the end of the day, we win."

"What about gay organizations?" asked Devon quizzically.

"What about 'em?"

"Would the Albert campaign or the DNC ever funnel money to groups like that?"

Hanson set down his drink and looked Devon right in the eye. "Absolutely. Look, Oliver, it's no secret that the gay community is a huge source of campaign dollars for the Democrats, particularly in Hollywood. At some point, they'll want to be rewarded for their support."

Suddenly Devon's face turned sour, like he smelled something foul. "You know, Michael, I hear what you're telling me . . . but goddamn, it pisses me off."

"Well, I guess that depends on who you want to win. I gotta be honest with you, Oliver, if I had the money to spend, a whole shitload would go into ads targeted at gays. Not only do they vote, but they write big checks."

"Michael, even I understand that reality. What I'm talking about is the fact that these homo bastards think they can dictate policy. Gays in the military, health care, immigration. I mean, half the Internet is filled with queers trying to meet little boys, for chrissakes. What has happened to our society when a bunch of faggots can get away with this kind of shit?"

Hanson watched in amazement as Devon continued his diatribe. Mike knew there was plenty of homophobia in Washington, but this was ridiculous. The Repo Man was sounding like Bob Jones in an Armani suit. Fortunately, the waiter arrived with his burger, forcing Devon to contain himself. Quickly, Hanson tried to take a mouthful of burger to avoid responding, when he saw something that completely ruined his appetite. Walking right toward him from about twenty feet away was Adam Melrose. Hanson knew he had been spotted, that there was no way to avoid him. As usual, Adam's timing couldn't have been worse. He stood to greet his troublesome friend. "Adam, what brings you here?"

Instead of acknowledging Hanson, Adam leaned over, extending his hand to Devon, and said, "Hey there, old man. Adam Melrose, live and in person."

Devon reacted with his first smile of the meeting. "Congressman, I thought you weren't arriving until later."

"Change of plan, have some meetings scheduled," he began. "And by the way, I could get used to the sound of that." Then, turning to Hanson, he said, "Hello there, Michael. Running with a better class of client, I see."

Of all the things that had happened to Hanson during the past few days, this made the least amount of sense. In his wildest dreams he couldn't picture these two guys all buddy-buddy. "You two know each other?"

"We do now," Adam said.

"Obviously," said Hanson, curtly. "Adam, would you like to sit down?"

"Actually, I have to run. I have the media guys at two. But Michael, I wish you'd call me later so we can catch up?"

"Great. How long are you going to be in town?"

"I'll be at the Mayflower until tomorrow. And Oliver, I'll be seeing you about eight o'clock?" Adam said.

"I'll be there with my entourage, checkbooks in hand."

"Checkbooks?" queried Hanson.

"Yes. Oliver has been kind enough to ask some of his colleagues to attend a little fund-raiser I'm holding in my suite tonight. You're invited, of course, Michael. Suite 1133." He turned to Devon. "Oliver, thanks again," he said as the two shook hands.

As Adam walked away, Devon could tell by Hanson's expression that he was disturbed. "Michael, you worry too much. I called Adam for a reference on you. As it turned out, his old man and I have served on a number of boards together. He happened to mention that he was going to be in town, and I offered to help out. I figured it would be good for business and good for you. It was all quite innocent, I assure you."

Hanson knew that nothing in Washington was ever quite this innocent. "Oliver, I don't recall authorizing you to check any of my references."

"How interesting. I don't recall asking you for permission," he responded in a bullying tone. "Look, Michael, you do business with me, you do it my way, and if that means I feel like backgrounding one of my consultants, then I'm gonna do it. If that's a problem, then we can part company."

Hanson normally didn't take this kind of crap from anybody. But for some reason it seemed more important to learn Devon's motives than to save face. "No, it's not a problem . . . this time!" he said firmly. "But in the future," he began, stopping when he noticed Adam walking towards the restroom. "Listen, excuse me for one second. I gotta hit the men's room. Would you mind ordering me another drink?"

"Maybe I'll have one myself," blurted Devon, exasperated.

Hanson got up from the table and followed Adam. Once inside, he waited for a man to finish washing his hands. Once he left, Hanson locked the deadbolt and turned to Adam. "Do you mind telling me what's going on?"

"Michael, I'm sorry I didn't call you first. Devon and my father go way back, and he offered to raise some money for me. You know we need every cent we can get."

All Hanson could think about was Devon's tirade a few minutes before. "Forget about all that. Just listen to me carefully. Devon is one person you don't want to mess with. Whether you know it or not, you are in way over your head."

"Michael, if you are referring to my lifestyle, you can relax. I spoke with Rick and he said you were very persuasive. It must be that Irish charm and all. So there's no need to worry about that anymore. And by the way, thank you so much for handling it. I really had nowhere else to turn."

"Adam, please get it through your thick skull. The man is dangerous. If he thinks you've burned him, god only knows what he'll do."

"Geezus, Michael, you aren't kidding," said Adam, genuinely alarmed. "What do you think Devon's gonna do, break my legs?"

"For your sake, I hope that's all," said Hanson.

"Don't worry, I'm a big boy. I can handle this," he said as he unlocked the door and started to exit. "Call me later, okay?"

"Just be careful," Mike said as Adam walked out. For several seconds he stood alone by the sink trying to compose himself. Staring into the mirror, he wondered how he could possibly protect Adam now. Rick Seltzer was a puppy dog compared to Devon. This one was just about out of his hands.

"I thought you fell in," snapped Devon as Hanson returned to the table.

"I apologize. Sometimes nature calls and calls."

"Everything okay with you and Melrose?"

"Yeah, just fine," said Hanson.

"Good. I like him. If you had more like him in your party, you'd win Congress back."

Hanson was beginning to get fed up. "Ah, who needs Congress when we've got the White House?"

"For a couple more months anyway," gibed Devon.

"We will see, we will see."

Devon leaned over the table. "Look, back to our discussion. I'm prepared to help you out with the media buy."

Suddenly, Hanson was all ears.

"Let's start with ten million."

"Excuse me?"

"Let's see what you do with it. We'll trickle you the rest in increments over the next few weeks."

"Yeah, right. And for a billion dollars I'll whack the President."

"Michael, time is running out. You want to win an election and I want to neutralize Danielle Harris. She's getting way too close to the China connection. I have to back her off."

Finally, Devon was starting to show his hand. "I wasn't aware there was a China connection."

"Don't be coy with me, son. Unless you read her dossier into the record, you and I are both fucked. The offer is on the table. Take it or leave it," said Devon, an icy coldness to his tone.

Hanson paused, noticing that Devon wasn't laughing. "My God, you're serious," said Hanson, looking into Devon's eyes for any clue to the man. All he saw was hatred. Devon would do anything to destroy Danielle.

"Deadly serious," Devon replied as he stood up to leave. "And, Michael, one more thing. None of my money is to go to any gay organizations or candidates. Not a single cent. Are we clear?"

"Crystal," said Hanson.

Chapter Thirty

Hanson went back to his office after lunch at the Metropolitan Club and tried to keep his mind on the campaign. Most of all he waited for a call from CeCe, checking his messages at home and on his pager every fifteen minutes. The only link he had to her was her desperate plea on his machine, begging him to meet her at five o'clock. Hanson could only hope that CeCe would show as planned. He prayed she was still alive.

After about an hour Griff burst through his door, unannounced. Looking at his watch, he said, "Hell Mike, I gotta tell ya. This is progress. You're actually in your office working and the day's only half over. On behalf of the Vice President, I wanna thank you for showing up. Really, I mean it."

"All right, I deserved that. I admit it. Come on, let's get it over with," said Hanson, stoically.

"Forget it, Mikey. You aren't getting off that easy. First you fucking disappear at the FLOTUS's birthday gig, the campaign's in the crapper, and I can't even get you to return my calls. On top of all that there is a rumor that you are fucking Xena the Warrior Princess. This calls for a major guilt trip."

Hanson laughed, relishing Griffin's sense of humor in times of absolute crisis. "Are you aware how whining undermines that heterosexual facade of yours, Griff?"

"Painfully. But don't even try to change the subject."

"So what was so urgent this morning anyway?" asked Hanson.

"Well, you're not gonna like this, but that detective came by again this morning looking for you."

"You're kidding," he said, incredulous. He'd seen Kennedy only hours before and he hadn't mentioned it.

"Not on your life. He kept asking all these questions about you and Senator Kassendine?"

Hanson couldn't believe what he was hearing. His ten-year nightmare with his ex-boss just never seemed to end. "How the hell could Kennedy know about Kassendine?"

"I don't know, but he was digging pretty hard."

"So what did you say?" he asked, dreading Griff's answer.

"What did you expect me to do, Mike? I told him the truth, that a few years back you walked in on the good senator when he was trying to play hide the salami with a thirteen-year-old page, and that like the good Irishman you are, you kicked the living shit out of the bastard."

"Oh, god!"

"Relax. He seemed to really care when I told him how Kassendine and that thug Art Falmont tried to run you out of town, how you got blackballed and all."

"I'll bet," said Hanson, cringing at the sound of the name Falmont, the senator's pit bull attorney. "I'll bet."

Griffin felt badly. He hadn't meant to cause Hanson more worry. In truth, he didn't think his friend had anything to be ashamed of. No one deserved a beating more than Kassendine did that day. To those who knew the real truth, the senator got off way too easy. "Hey look, I just thought you should know. I've gotta get goin'. I've got a meeting at the White House in thirty minutes."

Hanson sat quietly. While he was still mad with Griff, it had nothing to do with this miserable excuse for a senator. It was just that once again, the ghost of Malcolm Kassendine—Hanson's own personal demon—still required exorcism. "Uh, Griff, before you go, I need to run something by you. Maybe you should close the door."

"This wouldn't have anything to do with your meeting with Devon by chance, would it?" he asked.

Griffin's reaction to news of a fifteen-million-dollar cash infusion to the campaign was not at all what Hanson expected. He didn't care that Devon was the source of the money, and stopped Hanson dead in his tracks when he offered the details of any quid pro quo connected to the contribution. The Messiah's position was the warrior's view—"Mike, this is war, plain and simple. I would do just about anything to beat those Republican bastards! Even so, I will not knowingly commit a crime, and as my deputy I expect you to follow suit. But if you have a way to get us fifteen million dollars that is legal, or at least appears legal, then I'm on board. Otherwise, you're on your own."

It was funny, Hanson thought. While Griff was taking the hard line, he wasn't being callous at all. In his own way, he was giving him as much latitude as he could to pull off a miracle without committing mail fraud.

By three in the afternoon, Hanson found himself too distracted to stay in the office any longer. Since the meeting was in Georgetown, he dropped by Nathan's to cool out for a while. He sat down at the bar, ordered a Bass, and marveled at the quiet. No Danielle, no Griffin, no Devon, and most of all, no Detective Kennedy. This was what life used to be like, he thought, before Kennedy showed up at his front door three days ago. Hanson felt strangely relaxed; everything was out of his hands now. He assumed he was under police surveillance, an assumption that was strangely comforting. And he knew that CeCe would have some answers. Most of all, he was enjoying the nearly empty bar. He'd been a regular here for over fifteen years, soliciting hundreds of phone numbers, downing thousands of beers, and a hundred gallons of scotch, but now it felt good just to be alone.

Hanson was so relaxed, he didn't notice the man sitting along in the corner booth. He had slipped quietly into the bar right after Hanson, and was sipping coffee and watching Hanson through steely blue eyes. The man knew that the meeting with CeCe would be taking place soon. Not a lot of time to waste. He got up from his seat and headed for the bar. When he was about ten feet from Hanson, he called out, "Mike? Mike Hanson?"

Hanson turned and looked at him, annoyed that someone dared to spoil his moment of silence. "Who's asking?"

"Walker, Jack Walker. We met at the San Francisco convention back in '84. Hart delegate, am I right? Mind if I sit down?" he asked.

With a sinking heart, Hanson looked the man over. He was a big guy, with just the beginnings of a tire around the middle, like an ex-jock, Hanson thought. The man's arms were heavily muscled, his eyes sharp, intelligent. He was balding and dressed in khaki pants and a navy blue golf shirt. He grinned away at Hanson, pleased that he recognized him. Hanson sighed.

"Sure, pull up a seat. Actually it was Mondale, not Hart. Uh, Jack, you'll forgive me, but I don't really remember you."

"No sweat. That was years ago and we sure as hell drank enough scotch in those days to make our memories a bit shaky. What have you been up to lately? I think I remember that you're a lobbyist or something?"

"Or something. Mainly, I'm a fund-raiser. And you?"

"Oh, same old thing. Project finance, you know, eastern Europe and the Pacific rim," said Walker.

Hanson still had absolutely no clue who the man was, but it wouldn't be the first time he didn't recall an old drinking buddy. "So, how's business?"

"Great, great. I'm in town handling a matter for one of my partners, Oliver Devon. Ever hear of him?" he asked.

Shit, Hanson thought. This guy had all the subtlety of a kick in the teeth. "Sure. Hasn't everybody?" Hanson said, turning his back on the man.

"So you don't know him personally then?" pressed Walker.

Whatever game this guy was playing, Hanson had enough. "Listen, Mr. Walker, or whatever the fuck your name is, if you're an international businessman, then I'm a big Republican. I don't know what you're up to, but I think it's time for you to move on."

"Mike, Mike, you're taking me all wrong," said the man urgently, lowering his voice. "Devon's involved in something that's, shall we say, just a little messy. With his clout, things will probably turn out fine . . . for him. But for some of the people around him, well, they could find themselves in some really deep shit," he explained. "And by the way, my name really is Walker."

Hanson was cautious. Knowing Devon, Walker could be a plant sent to conduct an idiot test on Hanson's loyalty. He could even be a cop working with Kennedy. On the other hand, this guy might be for real, in which case he should at least hear him out. Either way, the only strategy was to say as little as possible and let Walker do all the talking. "Let's say I do know him, what's all this got to do with me?"

Walker looked pleased. Checking first to make sure the bartender was at the far end of the rail, setting up for happy hour, he said, "Mike, Devon and I go back twenty years. I mean we've done more shit together than I can remember. Some of it's been clean and some of it's been, well, a little shaky, to say the least. But right now he's got himself into something which is way the hell over the line, even for Devon. Shit, I give the old bastard a lot of credit, he just might pull it off."

Hanson began to sweat. "Okay, so what if he's into some illegal shit. What do I care?" said Hanson.

"Don't you get it, son? You're the fly in the ointment."

"Mr. Walker . . . Jack, really, I don't . . ."

"Mike, I'm gonna be as straight with you as I can," he said.

Given the week he'd had, Hanson found this refreshing. He wanted to trust this man. "Keep talking," he said.

"Listen," Walker began in a hushed tone. "We know Devon has cut a deal with you. We know all about Ariel Fairchild, and we know that the police have you penciled in as their prime suspect."

Hanson almost fell off his chair. The only thing the man didn't seem to know about was the fifteen million. No way was this guy working for Devon, or the cops. He knew way too much. "Who's 'we'? What the hell are you, some spook?"

This reaction came as no surprise to Walker, who simply smiled, thinking of the "quick plant" electronic eavesdropping device he had inserted in Hanson's apartment several days earlier. "Come on, Mike. You know that even if I was I couldn't tell you. But honestly, you should be a lot more worried about being able to arrange bail. In a capital crime, it can get pretty steep. You and I both know that it's only a matter of days before they try to charge you."

"And you're telling me that Devon has something to do with this?"

Walker laughed aloud. "He's up to his ass in the whole thing. Michael, whether you realize this or not, you're smack in the middle of a war between the FBI and the Chinese government. None of these players are to be taken likely. Devon's behind the whole thing."

"What the hell are you talking about?"

"Wake up, Michael," Walker said, looking meaningfully at Hanson. "Devon's their lobbyist, for chrissakes!"

Hanson felt his face turning red with rage. He rubbed his eyes. "Are you telling me that bastard is setting me up?"

Walker nodded. "What I'm telling you is that Devon has made a number of bad moves lately, not the least of which is pissing off Beijing in a major way. He's taking no prisoners, and the only thing, and I mean the only thing that links him to the murders is you. And trust me Mike, Devon is well aware of this. What I can't figure out is why you are still alive."

Hanson felt sick. He didn't know who to believe anymore. He downed his beer in an attempt to calm his stomach, and looked at his watch. "Unfortunately, I gotta get going."

"Yeah, I know. But I'm available if you need me," he said, handing Hanson his card. "That number will forward to wherever I am. And Mike, I'm not kidding you, Devon can take you out anytime he wants. Watch your ass!"

As Hanson got up from the bar stool he was in a daze, his legs feeling wobbly as he walked to the door.

"Say hello to CeCe for me," said Walker.

Hanson looked back at this man who seemed to know everything about his life, and wondered if Walker would prove to be his savior or his executioner. Why this was happening to him, he had no idea. The only thing that he was certain about was that he had to see CeCe—and warn her.

Chapter Thirty-one

Abe fidgeted in his seat as he and Marlene waited in the psychologist's office. Despite the fact that he owed his life to a team of skilled surgeons, Abe hated doctors in general. He hated this guy and he wasn't even an M.D. After six long months of being cut, poked, probed, catheterized, and impacted, he was sick of the medical profession. And as irrational as it sounded, the part he hated most was that everybody with whom he came into contact—doctors, nurses, physical therapists, orderlies—smelled like antiseptic soap and seemed to wear the same uniform—white coats and green scrubs. Worst of all was the PBA psychiatrist, who Abe was convinced only dressed the part to remind him that he was, in fact, a real doctor. It had gotten so bad that Abe couldn't even look at the Good Humor man or a car wash attendant or a chef without an overwhelming feeling of angst that another dreaded procedure was imminent. No, the walls of the office—festively adorned with diplomas and posters ranging from Barney proclaiming that "You Are Special," to one of Michael Jordan doing a 360-degree dunk—were definitely closing in on him.

"Stop looking at your watch," commanded Marlene. "You've known about this appointment for weeks."

"I know, I know. It's just this case I'm working on . . ."

"Abe, you are a homicide detective. It's not like anybody's going anywhere. Believe me, an hour from now, every one of your murder victims will still be dead. You'll have plenty of time for your investigation when this appointment is over," she said.

There were no two ways about it. Abe was stuck. If he tried to duck out early, Marlene would have his bags packed by the time he got home. Ironically, the one silver lining was that the much unwanted Inspector Lisagor had enthusiastically offered to cover for him at the Georgetown stakeout. Maybe the guy was a real cop after all, he thought. "Marlene . . ." he began, before being interrupted by the doctor's arrival.

"Sorry to keep you folks waiting," he said as he entered the office and took a seat behind his desk. Tall, late forties, with a close-cropped salt and pepper beard, he immediately impressed Abe, as he was wearing a sport jacket and tie. "I'm Dr. Lippman. Let me begin by telling you that I'm a big fan of your son. He's quite a kid."

Marlene blushed at the compliment. She had done her best to conceal her feelings of anxiety about A. J.'s problem. On the outside she was telling everyone that things would work out fine. But on the inside she was terrified. Her sweet child was disappearing right before her eyes and there was nothing she could do to stop it. It was nice to hear someone say something nice about her baby boy. "Th-Thank you, Doctor," she began. "Until lately, we've been very proud of him."

Abe looked at his wife and felt her pain like no other time in their marriage. All of a sudden he felt like the world's biggest shit heel. This had been building for weeks, and he was too consumed with his own recovery to even notice. He had let Marlene carry the burden all alone and had never even asked if he could help. "Doctor," he said, taking his wife's hand, "please help us. Tell us what's wrong with our son."

"Detective Kennedy, I'm not gonna kid you. A. J.'s got his share of problems, most of which concern you. But as far as the big picture goes, he's pretty normal."

"But his grades . . . he never talks anymore. The outfits he wears are ridiculous. His teachers are sending notes home about his behavior," explained Marlene.

"He's always been a model student."

"It's that damned crowd he's running with," she said.

"Okay, okay. Everybody take a deep breath. Let's start by talking about what's not wrong with A. J. As far as his health goes, we tested him for everything under the sun in his workup. Hypoglycemia, hyperthyroidism, Epstein-Barr, mononucleosis, anemia."

"And?"

"And he's as healthy as a horse. Next, we had our psychiatric team evaluate him. The good news is that he isn't ADD. He also shows none of the classic signs of dyslexia or a language processing disorder. We also checked his hearing. Again, everything checks out normal."

"So what's happening?"

"Did you run a tox screen?" demanded Abe, vocalizing his worst nightmare.

The doctor looked at Marlene. By now her eyes were full of tears. "Mr. and Mrs. Kennedy, A. J.'s bloodworm tested negative for cocaine, marijuana, alcohol, and nicotine. He's not using drugs."

"Thank God!"

"We did find one thing, though . . ."

"Yes?"

"Your son needs glasses. His vision stinks."

"Glasses?" exclaimed Marlene. "That's impossible. Up until this fall, A. J. was a straight A student. How could he?"

"My guess is that he's always needed them. Sometimes very bright children can compensate for their physical limitations and you can't even tell. If anything, this is an indication of how bright your boy is."

"So that's it then. We'll get A. J. glasses tomorrow," said Abe.

"Uh, not so fast, Detective Kennedy. His vision only speaks to his physical challenges. What is causing A. J.'s erratic behavior is almost entirely emotional, and it's mostly about you."

"I knew this was coming. I'm never there for him. All I did for the first twelve years of his life was work. Then I got shot. Then all I did for almost a year was rehab. No wonder he hates me."

"Detective Kennedy, if there is one thing that I am certain of it is that your son A. J. doesn't hate you," said the doctor. "Quite the opposite in fact. You are his hero. What is hurting A. J. is kind of complicated."

"We're listening. We'll do whatever it takes."

"Well, after about ten sessions with him, this is what I've pieced together. About a year or so ago, A. J.'s eyes started deteriorating so badly that he couldn't fake it anymore. At the time, he really didn't understand what was happening to him and he doesn't now. Then you get wounded and his world falls apart. In short, he gets scared to death. As for you, Mrs. Kennedy, the kid figures you just don't need any more problems."

"And then I disappear in rehab," snapped Abe.

"No, Detective, that's not it. He doesn't blame you for working so hard at your job or throwing yourself into rehab. He's an incredibly sensitive child. He's knows what makes you tick. He truly believes that someday you'll have time for him."

"Then what is it?"

"Well, as near as I can tell, his problems really got out of hand right after you two had a pretty intense argument about money."

"Excuse me, doctor, I don't know what line of hooey my boy has been feeding you, but the Kennedy family is just fine financially. I make a good living and we practically own our home free and clear."

"Besides, we never argue in front of him."

Abe glanced at his wife and rolled his eyes. "Well, almost never . . ."

"Let's try to maintain some perspective here. What I'm saying is that this is A. J.'s truth. To him it's very real," said Dr. Lippman. "Do either of you recall a discussion not long after the shooting about not being able to send A. J. to a decent college on just your disability pension?"

"Of course not."

All at once Marlene Kennedy's eyes lit up. "I remember it like it was yesterday. Abe, it was when I was trying to convince you to take an early retirement."

"Oh god . . ."

"Well, A. J. must've overheard you. His reaction was classic. He'd nearly lost his father, and he blames himself for sending his dad back to a war zone."

"Are you telling me that our son is dumbing himself down to take financial pressure off me?"

"Yes sir, that's what it looks like. He'd much rather be a D minus student and have you alive than make the honor roll and see you get shot again. What can I say? Kids are funny."

For several seconds no one spoke. Both Abe and Marlene sat holding hands as tears streamed down their faces. Three times Abe started to speak, but he couldn't get the words out. On the fourth try he succeeded. "So what can we do?"

"There is only one recommended course of treatment. Communication," declared Dr. Lippman. "I suggest we start with two sessions a week. And that includes the whole family. I figure that once I get you folks talking to each other, the rest will work itself out."

"And what if A. J. can't get past the fact that I'm back on the job?" asked Abe.

"Then you'll have a choice to make. Which is more important to you, your son or your job?"

"All right. Let's begin the sessions as soon as possible," said Marlene.

Abe stood up. Amazingly, he hadn't so much as peeked at his watch during the entire appointment. "Thanks for everything, Doctor. We are a good family. After a little time with us, you'll begin to see that."

"Detective . . . Abe. I know that the Kennedys are a good family. I just want *all* of the Kennedys to start believing that. Especially A. J.," he said.

"Fair enough," said Abe, finally looking at his watch. It was 4:15 P.M. He still had time to make the stakeout. "See you in a few days . . ."

"Uh, there is one more thing. It's not all that important, but still, you're his parents. You should know."

Abe and Marlene looked at each other. What could be next?

"Your son, A. J. He's color blind." said Doctor Lippman.

"That's so kind of you to say," began Marlene. "In this day and age it is tough to raise a child free of prejudice."

Lippman laughed. "Well, I'm sure that's the case. But that's not exactly what I mean. Your son is really color blind."

"What the hell are you talking about?" blurted Abe. "Are you telling us that he's half blind and can't tell the difference between black and white?"

"Actually, black and white he can handle. It's red, white, blue, green, and yellow that he has trouble with . . ."

"I don't understand."

"It's simple, Detective. Take a look at this," said the doctor, handing Abe a glossy 8 × 10 graphic.

"What is this?" asked the detective.

"It's a hologram. The same kind optometrists use," he said. "Hold it up to the light. Look for the figure eight. Do you see it?"

"Yeah. It jumps out at you."

"Maybe for you. But to a person with color blindness, it's practically invisible. They would completely miss it. It works like a mosaic. Just like the picture on a television screen, or an impressionist painting."

In a flash, Abe's face turned to stone. "What did you say?"

"I said the hologram works a lot like a television . . ."

"No, the other part."

"You mean like a painting? Yeah, the impressionists were masters at using thousands of dots and blotches of color to construct an image. It is truly fascinating."

"Yeah, fascinating," said the detective. "Well, we gotta get going. Thanks for everything, Doc."

Abe made a quick exit, leaving Marlene behind to schedule the first family counseling sessions with the receptionist. Hurriedly he made his way to the unmarked police car. It was 4:33 P.M. He had an outside chance to make the stakeout. As he pulled out, he gunned the engine, stomping the accelerator as he made his way down P Street. For several blocks it was clear sailing as he somehow made every light. Within minutes he was in Georgetown. As he turned down 28th to pick up M, he grabbed his cell phone and punched number 3 on the speed dial. It rang only once.

"Julian Cole," came the answer.

"Hey Jules, it's me, Abe. I got a question."

"So what else is new?" said the Coroner.

"Bear with me. Does the Forensics Lab have the capability to provide blow-ups of photographs?"

"Of course. How large?"

"Big. Really big. Maybe a hundred times normal size."

"Well, it wouldn't be cheap, and it depends on the type of film and its speed, but we could do it. Where are you going with this?"

"I'm not sure," began the detective hesitantly. "It may be only a hunch, but I may have a break in the Ariel Fairchild case."

Chapter Thirty-two

It was the beginning of rush hour, and the mass exodus out of the district had already begun. Traffic was already bumper to bumper on M Street as drivers fought their way towards Key Bridge and Canal Road, headed for their homes in the suburbs. There was about thirty minutes of daylight left. CeCe knew exactly what she was doing. If anybody was going to grab her, they'd have to do it in broad daylight.

From their perch inside an orange-colored Potomac Electric utility truck, kitty corner on Wisconsin Avenue, Murray and Lisagor had a perfect vantage point to observe the meeting. It was 4:55 P.M. and still no sign of anybody. No Hanson nor anyone close to CeCe Fairchild's description, and still no word from Abe. Both men were getting worried. Maybe it was the lack of ventilation in the van, or perhaps yesterday's dressing down from the brass, but the tension was so thick it was palpable. Two dead kids and no witnesses. The clock was ticking, reputations were on the line.

"So, any progress on finding your art terrorists?" asked Ira, breaking the silence.

Lisagor chuckled. "Art terrorists. I love it," he said. "No, Ira, frankly I'm still hoping that something breaks down here. Otherwise, I'm about tapped out."

"It must be frustrating, a high-profile crime like that and coming up empty-handed."

"You know what's the worst part? It's that the damned desecrations make absolutely no sense. The paintings, every single one of them, was a masterpiece. Every one had its own special history. And now they are gone forever. And for what reason god only knows. I'm no closer to figuring out a motive than I was weeks ago."

"So you think we're getting stood up, Inspector?" asked Ira, peering out the rear window through binoculars.

"It's too soon to tell," said Lisagor. "Logic tells me that Hanson's got no other option. If he doesn't play ball with us, he goes to jail. It has been my experience that threats of jail generally motivate people."

Ira smiled, but felt uneasy. This situation just didn't feel right. "Hanson could skip town. Then we get to report to the commissioner with jack shit to show him."

"Hey, he's your boss, not mine."

"Tell me about it," said Ira.

Suddenly the rear door of the van opened. "Relax, fellas. They're gonna show," pronounced Abe Kennedy, with all the conviction of a minister on Sunday morning.

"How did you know what we were talking about?" said Lisagor. "What are you, some kind of psychic?"

Abe grinned broadly as he climbed in the back of the vehicle. "Inspector, I've ridden with this guy for over fifteen years. Every time he works a stakeout he thinks he's gonna get stood up."

"Watch it there, partner. I may be old, but I carry a firearm," said Ira.

"Fine. Do you mind if I borrow those?" said Abe, referring to the binoculars.

"Be my guest," said Ira. "Here, take my seat. I've been staring at the same pavement on the same corner for hours. I hope you have better luck than I did!"

"I intend to," Kennedy said, taking Ira's place. "By the way, Inspector, I got a hunch about your art forgery ring."

"Hunches are good. I'll be glad to take a hunch."

"You don't by any chance have recent photos of the damaged paintings, do you?"

Lisagor really had no idea where Abe was going with this, but indulged him anyway. "Some we do and some we don't. It depends on the museum. Why?"

Abe began to explain when suddenly he noticed something. "Sonofagun . . . Boys, I think it's show time."

"I hate it when he does that," said Ira. "He always does that, the damned showoff."

At first Abe wasn't positive it was CeCe. He looked closer. It was a close call. He picked up his walkie talkie and alerted the other units in the area that a woman generally meeting CeCe's description had arrived. He described her pink suit and blond hair.

Ira joined Kennedy at the rear window of the van and they watched her walking quickly across the street, stopping at the corner. She carried shopping bags from pricey downtown boutiques, but she appeared wobbly on her feet and kept looking over her shoulder. Seconds later, Hanson came into view.

"This is it," Kennedy said softly. "Let's hope he can talk her in."

Hanson was nervous as he approached CeCe. He knew that Kennedy was somewhere in the vicinity, but he couldn't tell where. For all he knew, Devon could be watching the whole thing, as could Walker. Hanson didn't know whether to believe a word that Walker had said, and even if he did, there was still a lot that needed explaining. As he got closer, he was startled by CeCe's appearance. The last time he'd laid eyes on her, she was still ravishing, as sexy as any woman he'd ever known. Not now. She looked nothing at all like the beautiful girl he'd taken to his prom. Something more than just the passage of time had taken its toll on the woman who'd stolen his heart when he was so young. CeCe didn't just look older, she looked sickly, almost like she was dying. "CeCe?" he asked, uncertainly.

When she heard him call her name she was startled, then saw it was Hanson. "Michael, my god, it's you. I wasn't sure you'd get the message, or that you'd come," she said, running into his arms.

Hearing the fear in her voice, he held her for a second as he scanned the area nervously. She was all skin and bones. He was astounded by how frail she was. "What, are you kidding me? I get a call from you like that, how can I not come?"

"Michael, I know it's been years, but I'm in trouble. I need your help. You're the only person who ever really cared about me."

Her words stung. He felt sorry for her, guilty for what he was about to do. "No problem. Do you want to go somewhere and talk about it?" he asked, his voice gentle and consoling.

"No, actually I feel safer out here in the open. Michael, that bastard killed Ariel, he killed my little girl!" she said, fighting back the tears.

"Who did, CeCe? Who killed Ariel?"

"The Chief. Who else could do something so cruel? I know I'm next. I'm afraid, Michael, I'm afraid." CeCe started trembling in Hanson's arms.

"The Chief, who the hell is the Chief? What's his name?"

"It's no use, Michael, it's no use . . ."

"CeCe, get hold of yourself, damn it! You have to go to the police, for your own protection."

CeCe chortled. It was a strange, ugly sound. "Michael, you're still just as naive as ever. I can't go to the police. The people I deal with own the fucking police!" she said. She looked up at him defiantly and stepped out of his arms.

Hanson looked down at her, puzzled by her wild mood swing. "CeCe, then what do you want from me?"

"I need you to help me get away from this place, far away."

"Consider it done. But first you've got to answer a question for me."

"What choice do I have?" she asked.

"Why would Ariel list me as her next of kin?"

Instead of being surprised by the question, CeCe seemed ready for it, and her voice became hostile. "Why Michael, I thought you'd be flattered. To her, you were the only man in her life. What's wrong, are you afraid you might have accidentally fucked your own daughter?"

Hanson was enraged. He had a vague recollection of meeting a girl who would have been about Ariel's age at one of CeCe's parties years back, but he hadn't quite made the connection until now. Most of what he remembered from that night was how disgusted he was by CeCe's new profession. Now her words made him want to tell her to go to hell and deal with her situation on her own, but he didn't get the chance.

CeCe wasn't through. "Why do you care, Michael? You didn't want anything to do with me when you found out what I did for a living," she said, her voice growing harder. "I didn't think you'd really want anything to do with a daughter that came from me. You thought you were so perfect, so above it all."

Hanson didn't know what to say. He felt tears in his eyes. "CeCe, I'm sorry. I know it's too late, but I'm so, so sorry."

CeCe's mood suddenly changed again. "I know," she said, touching his face delicately with her fingers. "You were the kindest person I've ever known."

Hanson blushed and started to reassure her, but his words were drowned out by the surging growl of an engine. He raised his voice, shouting, but the roar grew louder and louder as it seemed to be getting closer. Hanson turned around and looked frantically in every direction. Where was it coming from? Something was wrong. Then, in a flash, as he looked back down Wisconsin Avenue across M street, he saw it. The Harley's rider was dressed in black leather from helmet to toe and speeding up the bicycle lane at him at more than 100 mph. With the detectives' eyes glued to CeCe, no one had spotted the Harley. In seconds the rider was upon his prey, gripping an Ingram M-1 submachine gun tightly in his right hand. All of nine inches long, it was the smallest and most concealable automatic weapon on the market. Perfect for a job like this.

He took aim and squeezed the trigger.

"It's a hit! All units move!" shouted Abe into the mike, as he burst out of the van.

The warning came too late. It took the assassin all of about three seconds to empty his entire cartridge, painting the sidewalk with bullets. Instinctively, Hanson threw CeCe to the ground, covering her body with his own. As gunfire whizzed by his head, Hanson became acutely aware that the same bullets were coming back at him as they ricocheted off of the concrete pavement and steel door frames behind him. Where was Detective Kennedy? was all he could think.

In the blink of an eye, the Harley was gone, zooming up Wisconsin Avenue. A cop dressed as a homeless man futilely gave chase on foot, and two patrol cars pulled out of parking garages only to get stuck in the traffic. Drivers tried to get out of the way of the sudden sirens, but there was nowhere to go. People along the street were running everywhere, screaming. The assassin weaved and zigzagged through the traffic, disappearing up the road from the chaos he created.

CeCe was hit countless times. As Hanson held her in his arms, blood gushed from her multiple wounds.

"Michael, I'm sorry," she said in a barely audible voice.

"CeCe, hang on, please hang on!" he screamed. Her eyes fluttered and he feared she wasn't going to make it. Desperately, he asked, "CeCe, I have to know, who is the Chief? Who is he?" he pleaded.

CeCe looked up at him with lifeless eyes that had seen far too much pain in her life. Tears rolled down her face. She tried to speak, but the only thing that came out of her mouth was blood. She was dead.

"You all right, Hanson?" came Kennedy's voice.

"Where the fuck were you guys?" Hanson shouted, his eyes welling up with tears.

"No one could predict this, not in the middle of goddamn rush hour, for chrissakes," said Ira.

"Bullshit, you sonofabitch. It's your job to predict this. I trusted you bastards and now she's dead!" Hanson sat on the ground, rocking CeCe in her arms.

Abe's eyes narrowed. All of his frustration boiled over. "Don't be pointing fingers, Hanson," he yelled. "If you'd been honest with us from the beginning, this wouldn't have happened." He found himself shaking, and Murray grabbed his elbow and pulled him away. The detective stood and composed himself as a flurry of activity ensued while the police cordoned off the area. After a few minutes the paramedics from Georgetown University Medical Center showed up. "I shouldn't have exploded like that," Kennedy said to Murray.

Murray just nodded. "It's okay. You were right. Why don't you try to talk to him now? We should try to get him away from the body."

Detective Kennedy walked over to Hanson. "Mike, why don't you come with me while these guys do their thing," he said. Hanson stood, in shock, allowing the detective to lead him away, not knowing what else to do. "Ira, you make sure nobody touches anything until Julian Cole gets here," Kennedy instructed. Murray nodded.

Hanson leaned up against a squad car, facing Kennedy. "You know, Detective, it was like she knew it was going to happen."

"Are you sure you're okay?"

Hanson nodded as he stared blankly.

Kennedy was worried about him. He was covered in blood, but otherwise he didn't have a scratch on him. Whoever killed CeCe had to think he'd gotten Hanson too. When the killer found out otherwise, he'd be back. "Look, I hate doing this, but while it's still fresh in your memory, did CeCe tell you anything?"

"You don't give a damn about the fact that she's dead, do you, Detective? All you care about is your fucking investigation!"

Kennedy didn't have time to play around, no matter what condition Hanson was in. "Mr. Hanson, I want you to understand one thing clearly. I give a damn about every murder victim, whether it's some poor black kid shot in a drive-by or some lily-white uptown whore. They're all the same to me. But the difference here is we know this animal is going to kill again, and we have a chance to stop him. Now give me something I can work with or I'm taking your ass in!"

"The Chief."

"What'd you say?"

"The Chief. CeCe said that's who killed Ariel. All she said was the Chief," said Hanson.

"Got a name?"

"I don't know."

"Mike, for your own protection, you have to start trusting me," pleaded Abe.

"Detective, I'm a hundred percent sure that if I tell you any more than you already know, then they'll kill you. Hell, I'd be surprised if they're not watching us right now," Hanson said.

Detective Kennedy just stared at Hanson, wondering if he was still in shock.

Hanson knew Kennedy was right about one thing. If he hadn't been so worried about his reputation, if he had just told the detective the truth from the beginning, CeCe might still be alive. He was silent for a moment, weighing his options. "Okay, Detective, I'm gonna be straight with you. A lot of weird shit has been happening the last couple of days. I'm not sure I can make sense of it. Maybe you can help me, I don't know."

"Try me."

"I can tell you one thing about the killer," Hanson said.

"What's that?"

"I work with guys like this every day. Men who survive at the most predatory levels of politics and business without even breaking a sweat. A breed of animal that stalks its prey in courthouses, boardrooms, and other halls of power. It feeds on fear and gets its rocks off during the hunt."

Kennedy stared at Hanson. He had to still be in shock. Yet there was something unsettling about the way he described the killer—as if he knew him personally. "Come on, Mike. Let me take you home."

After watching the paramedics load CeCe's body into the ambulance, the two got in a cruiser and headed for Hanson's townhouse. It was a short drive and neither man said anything during the ride. Once they arrived, Hanson, for some inexplicable reason, felt compelled to talk. "I knew CeCe back in high school," Hanson said.

Kennedy nodded, keeping his eyes on the road. "I kind of figured it was something like that when I saw you two together on the street back there."

"You got any kids, Detective?" he asked.

"Yeah, a son. Abe Jr.," Kennedy answered.

Hanson smiled sadly. "Really? How old?"

"Thirteen going on thirty. He's giving his mother and me fits."

"That must be great—having a son I mean."

Abe was relieved that Hanson was finally opening up to him. "For me, it's the only thing that makes any sense in this goddamn city."

Hanson stared out the window with a faraway look in his eye, wondering what Ariel was like growing up.

"You still aren't sure, are you Hanson?"

"One more time?"

The detective knew Hanson was dying to talk to someone, anyone, about his past. "You still aren't sure whether Ariel was your kid?"

Try as he might, Hanson couldn't hold back any longer. Slowly his eyes teared up. Memories that had been buried for ages were all coming back. "It all happened years ago, just before the Dems took back the White House. Washington was a strange town back then. Everyone was doing a lot of coke and washing it down with Dom Perignon . . . it didn't matter if you were a Republican or a Democrat, the place was pretty much out of control."

"Believe it or not, Mike, we had our share of that in the department," added the detective.

Hanson nodded. "So, anyway, it's springtime and I get retained by this law firm which needs a Democrat to work the Ways and Means Committee for this big oil client. Things are going well and one night the client comes up from Houston and we all go out. After dinner and way too much to drink, the partner who hired me takes us to this party at one of the fancy downtown hotels. We go up to this private suite and man, like I've never seen so many women in one place. It was wall-to-wall beauties, all dressed to the nines, every one of them flirting and fawning over a bunch of old farts. You know, well-to-do business types. They were like kids in a candy store. I'm there about ten minutes when I run smack into CeCe. It was unbelievably awkward for both of us."

"So what happened?"

Hanson had no idea why he was pouring his heart out to a man that was ready to arrest him a day earlier, but it felt good just the same. "As usual, I said something obnoxious and she stormed out of the place. So I'm standing there, hating life, and I see this face, this face with eyes just like mine staring back at me. She couldn't have been more than eight or nine years old, and absolutely gorgeous," said Hanson, with a pained look on his face. "Well this kid comes right up to me and says 'You're Mike Hanson, aren't you?"

"So what did you do?"

"I'll tell you what I did. I got that child the hell out of there before some rich old bastard decided to teach her the facts of life. I checked her into a separate room, ordered room service, watched "Saturday Night Live" and basically got to know a sweet little girl named Ariel. Unfortunately, I made the mistake of leaving word for CeCe where I'd taken her, and she shows up about two in the morning all wired on coke, making all kinds of threats, accusing me of abusing her daughter and so on. Meanwhile, Ariel is asleep on the bed—fully clothed I might add. I left without even saying goodbye," said Hanson.

"Sounds pretty ugly."

"You don't know the half of it!"

"Trust your heart, Michael. Deep down you know."

"Yeah, maybe you're right," he said with a big sigh as he started to leave the cruiser.

Before Hanson could exit, the detective said, "Mike, I don't have to tell you that your life is in danger, do I?"

"What was your first clue, Detective?" Hanson said. But he smiled at Kennedy.

"Do you have protection? You own a gun?" asked Abe.

"Isn't it illegal for a civilian to own a handgun in D.C.?"

"Hanson, let's not bullshit each other. Everyone in D.C. owns a fucking gun except you! The fact is, I need you alive."

"Relax, Detective, guys like me have nine lives."

"Maybe, maybe not. Now I want you to call me if any more shit happens. I mean it. You say the word and I'll arrange for protective custody," he said. Kennedy paused and looked Hanson straight in the eye. "And whoever the Chief is, we'll get that sonofabitch."

Hanson nodded and got out of the car. Leaning down, he said, "Thanks, Detective. And what happened to CeCe wasn't your fault. It was mine."

Kennedy shook his head. "Mike, for what it's worth, I'd have done the same thing you did to Kassendine, maybe worse."

"And they would have declared war on you just like me. In Washington, no good deed goes unpunished. Those guys up in the Senate, they protect their own, no matter how sleazy," he said.

"Just the same, I'm sorry for what happened to you. Get some sleep," said the detective as he pulled slowly away from the curb.

Hanson walked up the steps and entered the townhouse. After splashing some cold water in his face and fixing a drink, he went to the phone. Wiretaps were of no concern to him at this point, particularly given the number he was calling. He could hear the phone ringing several times as it rolled over from line to line, and finally a man answered. "Walker, it's me, Hanson . . . no, obviously I'm not dead . . . I'm ready to talk. . . . The National Cathedral, fine. Main entrance . . . right . . . see you in an hour," he said, hanging up the phone.

Chapter Thirty-three

The National Cathedral is a magnificent structure that towers over several square miles of prime Washington real estate in upper northwest. At night, illuminated by a geyser of floodlights ascending from the ground, it is absolutely breathtaking. As the moonlight reflects off the stained-glass and granite structure, the church has an almost otherworldly quality that would humble virtually anyone. Hanson, an ex–advance man, knew that this effect was not lost on Walker, who undoubtedly chose this location with a specific purpose in mind. It was obvious that he was about to receive a "try to see the big picture" pep talk.

Hanson approached the meeting site cautiously, fumbling his way through the darkness of the November night. At about two hundred feet the glow of a cigarette in the darkness caught his attention. As he got closer he could see the outline of a man, but couldn't tell if it was Walker or not. If Devon wanted him dead, this would be the perfect opportunity. Other than he and the man with the cigarette, the place was deserted.

"Glad you could make it," said the man.

The sound of the wind cutting through the trees made it impossible for Hanson to discern whose voice it was. "It's not like I have a lot of options."

"No, I guess you don't, do you? Come closer."

Even though Hanson was scared silly and couldn't see more than a few feet in front of him, he decided to go for it. What the hell, if this was an ambush, he was already as good as dead. He took a few tentative steps, getting to within ten feet of the man when he heard the distinct sound of a metal click and dove to the ground. He lay there for several seconds, expecting to hear the muffled sound of a silenced gunshot. When none came, he looked up slowly to see Walker's face lit up by the flame of his metal tobacco lighter.

"What the fuck are you doing down there?" he asked.

Hanson, who was at once embarrassed at hitting the ground and relieved at not urinating in his pants said, "I must've tripped."

"Yeah, whatever. Come over here and sit on the bench before you kill yourself," ordered Walker. After dusting himself off, Hanson joined him, pleased at still being alive. "Were you followed?"

"How the hell would I know? I have enough trouble paying attention to what's in front of me when I drive, let alone what's behind me."

"Well, let's hope you weren't. So you're ready to talk?" asked Walker.

"Yeah. I assume you heard about CeCe?"

"Yes. And I am truly sorry. But frankly, I'm a lot more concerned right now with keeping you alive."

"Me too. I'm definitely open to suggestions in that area," said Hanson.

"Good, then you'll help me stop Devon."

"Not so fast. If I'm gonna do this, I need to know more."

"How much more?" demanded Walker.

"Everything."

"Mike, by law I can't tell you everything."

"Well then, I guess it's no deal," said Hanson matter-of-factly.

"Mike, you gotta listen to me. You are in so far over your head it's scary. Whether you realize it or not, you need us."

"No, excuse me, Mr. Walker, but you're confused. You tell me that Devon should have already killed me by now. It so happens that I'm also a murder suspect. So if I help you stop Devon and I live, guess what? I'm still a murder suspect. Some choice. Either way I'm fucked. On the other hand, you need a fresh face to stay close to Devon. You want my help, you tell me the whole fucking story," he demanded.

Walker gritted his teeth, knowing Hanson had him by the balls. "All right, Mike, but keep in mind that I'm violating about ten federal laws and the National Security Act by doing this."

"Start talking," Hanson instructed.

Walker looked around, wary of eavesdroppers despite the remoteness of their location. "Devon first came to us over twenty years ago, at the tail end of Vietnam. He'd already established a successful lobbying business by then. He told us he had this client, an ex-diplomat, who knew the whereabouts of several million dollars in gold bullion hidden away in the basement of the French embassy in Saigon." Walker paused for a second to take a long drag on his cigarette, glancing up at the stars in the night sky as though he actually missed those days. "We were intrigued. Not by the money, mind you, but by the fact that this successful, seemingly straightlaced Washington operator had this appetite for the rough trade. It's just not every day that a guy like Devon walks in off the street and offers to lead the Company to a king's ransom in gold."

"What did he want in return?"

"Not much. Just a piece of the action," said Walker, shaking his head in amazement. "It was so perfect I thought he was setting us up. Devon was a real risk-taker."

"The genuine article," said Hanson.

"Ain't that the truth," said Walker, almost grinning. "In the beginning, I was his 'handler,' and he and I enjoyed a mutually productive relationship for over a decade, especially during the years that Casey was CIA director. Devon provided us entrees into circles it would have taken us years to penetrate. Wealthy businessmen whose interests were threatened by the communists—Europe, Central America, the Caribbean Basin. We dealt with everybody on every side. Guatemalan death squads, Sandinistas, the Shining Path, you name it. But around the time of Iran-Contra we started getting reports that Devon was freelancing, taking on his own projects. Quite frankly, some of these conflicted with our own operations."

"So you all split up?" asked Hanson.

"Not quite. By that time, Devon had managed to parlay his relationships into a sizable fortune. He'd become far too powerful to let go. The real problem was that he'd also become way too visible to officially embrace. . . . I mean his client list reads like a who's who of international arms dealers. Just check with the House Clerk's office if you don't believe me. Until last year he was a registered agent for the People's Republic of China, not to mention Iran, Yemen, and a shitload of multinational conglomerates like Shanghai Electronics, El Banco National de Cali, Copenhagen Digital . . . honestly, the fucking list goes on forever."

"I know lobbyists in this town who would kill for a client list like that," said Hanson.

"And what makes you think Devon hasn't? If you haven't figured it out by now, every single one of these companies is a front, a laundromat, existing first and foremost to sanitize illicit profits. Blood money," said Walker.

"But Devon says that he's out of the lobbying business."

"And he's telling you the truth. Oliver Devon severed his ties to Beijing more than a year ago. These days he has only one client, he answers to only one god . . . the Investors."

Hanson felt a chill run up his spine. "Okay, Mr. Walker, you got me. I'm ready to bite. What can you tell me about the Investors?"

At that moment, Walker not only stopped talking, but he stopped breathing as well. It wasn't so much a cardiac arrest, or even hyperventilation. Rather, it was just Walker's way of managing stress. For several seconds he would slowly expel all the air from his lungs until he felt fully and totally cleansed. His yoga instructor promised that the oxygen purge would enhance his clarity of thought. And at that moment, he desperately needed clarity. He was about to cross the Rubicon with Mike Hanson and was prepared to tell the younger man everything to gain his allegiance. On the other hand, there was a very real chance that the truth would backfire. After several seconds, he allowed himself the luxury of a deep breath. "Mike, I work with a project out of Langley called ECHELON. You don't know about it yet, but in time you will. It's a joint effort by the intelligence services of the U.S., Britain, France, and Israel to track the flow of international criminal activity . . . particularly anything that has to do with the world wide web."

"What's so special about that? The Feds have been doing stuff like that for years."

"Not like ECHELON they haven't," said Walker. "This program has ultra-high-tech cyber-monitoring stations all over the world, and can eavesdrop on over a billion e-mails and fax communications a day."

"It doesn't sound exactly legal," said Hanson.

"That's because it isn't. Everyone from the ACLU to Hezbollah are terrified of it. Don't get me started about the New York crime families. But the point is that it works! It gave us the breakthrough we needed to finally identify the Investors."

"I'm listening . . ."

"The Investors are a group of international businessmen. It's a diverse group. Brits, Germans, Japanese, Saudis, South Africans, an Israeli, even one American. They number about a dozen. The one thing they have in common is that each has access to ungodly amounts of capital," explained Walker in a plaintive tone. "Since the end of World War II, they have been assuming increasingly aggressive financial positions in assorted corporations, countries, even bankrolling an occasional revolution. Their distinctive trait, you know, the one thing that sets them apart from every other player in the financial markets is that they seem to thrive on instability and chaos. You see, it doesn't matter much to the Investors whether it is political or economic or environmental. The greater the havoc, the bigger the profit."

"Doesn't exactly sound like Business Administration 101, does it?" said Hanson.

"Not on your life," Walker said, laughing aloud. "These bastards, they violate every sound rule of business theory over and over again and they always win. Take Kosovo for example. They have dummy businesses all over the region spreading Investor money around like it's candy. By the time the dust settles and the natives get sick of fighting or run out of bullets, the Investors will own a piece of every building, business, and politician in the region."

"Is that such a bad thing? I mean places like that need all the help they can get, don't they?"

"You'd think so, wouldn't you, Mike?" he began. "But the trouble is that the Investors don't care who they deal with, whether it's some right-wing butcher like a Slobodan Milosevic or the fucking Pope. They only care about profit and control. Period. Their next target is Asia."

For several seconds, Hanson fidgeted on the bench. Finally he asked, "I assume Devon is the American?"

"Negative. The American Investor makes Devon look like an altar boy," said Walker.

"Who is it?"

"Don't go there, Michael, you have enough problems."

"So what about Devon?"

"There's no question that he desperately wants in. Devon has run the Investors' operations in the U.S. for years and is supposed to be the next in line for membership. Make no mistake about it, regardless of his official status, the Investors listen intently to his every word. They definitely follow his lead. He's made them billions. That's why they green-lighted Devon's scheme to funnel all that Asian money into the '96 campaign."

"Oh, I get it now, the China connection again . . ."

Walker looked at Hanson in disbelief. "Come on, Mike, you guys didn't really think you were raising all those millions without a little help, did you?"

"We have before . . ."

"In what century? Don't kid yourself, there never was a campaign like '96 and there never will be. Neither party will ever get close to those kinds of numbers again and you know it."

"Okay, Walker. You've got all the answers, so tell me this. Why? Why on earth would the Chinese spend so much goddamn money? That's the one question nobody can figure out. Not the White House, not the press, none of the investigative committees. Even if Beijing wanted to steal the last election, why would they take such blatant, naked risks? Shit, you could spend a tenth as much with some fancy PR outfit and get the same results. What could possibly be so fucking important to make them spend this kind of money?"

Walker looked at Hanson curiously. He couldn't tell whether Mike was having some kind of catharsis or finally voicing long-festering doubts bottled up inside him. "Mike, what the Chinese really want is a cache of nuclear weapons stolen from the Soviet Red Army almost ten years ago."

"How many weapons are we talking about?" said Hanson.

"About a hundred . . ."

"Jesus Christ!"

"The plan is vintage Devon. He's been working on this for years. In a strange way, he thinks of it as his finest moment."

"A hundred nukes disappear from the Soviet Union and it doesn't hit the papers. Sorry. I don't buy it," said Hanson.

Walker was pleased. Hanson was cautious, not easily duped—precisely what he needed in an operative. "Mike, I never said that the weapons just disappeared, I said they were stolen. Let me explain . . ."

"It's your nickel," said Hanson, skeptically.

"Thanks so much for being reasonable." Back in '81, at the height of the Cold War, the KGB came up with this ambitious scheme to smuggle compact nuclear weapons into the United States. The project was called "Red Locust." The plan was to place these so-called suitcase bombs in secret locations all over the country. According to several defectors that worked on the project, these "tactical" nukes were mostly stashed in large cities near key points of critical infrastructure . . . you know, dams, power plants, airports."

Despite the darkness, Hanson stared Walker in the eye, trying to take measure of the man. "My god, you are fucking serious!"

"Deadly serious, Mike. I hope you are finally beginning to appreciate the gravity of the situation. God knows, the stakes couldn't be higher. Today there is only one superpower. The day after the site locations are delivered to Beijing, there will be two."

"Leave it to Devon to find a way to make a buck by resurrecting the Cold War. So how does Beijing figure in all this? Is China the buyer?"

"Not exactly. Despite the fact that Devon and the Investors have been working together on this deal ever since the Soviet Union imploded on itself, they still have only half the puzzle," explained Walker. "You see, Mike, during the attempted coup against Gorbachev back in 1991, Devon ran an Investor operation that stole the Red Locust file right from under the Kremlin's nose. The good news was that the file contained the longitude and latitude coordinates for all one hundred weapons. But the bad news for Devon was that the detonation codes were missing."

"So basically the weapons were useless."

"No such luck. The fact that the codes were missing made Devon more determined than ever. He spent millions trying to get his hands on them. Even worse, unlike other nukes, the suitcase bombs don't use conventional detonation codes, but a newer technology called 'Permissive Action Locks.' They were designed to be easily armed or disarmed by a single person, and are also almost impossible to circumvent."

"Obviously Devon didn't think so . . ."

"Not for a second. As you might expect, a lot of people in the intelligence business are aware of the Red Locust project. In fact, during Reagan's last year he tacked on an extra two hundred fifty million to the CIA's budget to fund an R&D program at Los Alamos National Laboratories to develop a bypass technology for PALs and other unorthodox technology."

"And lemme guess, Devon stole that too."

Walker laughed. Hanson was actually catching on. "No, Mike, that is where the Chinese come in. For years they have had operatives all over the Energy and Commerce departments. Their deal with Devon is pure quid pro quo. He delivers the site locations of the weapons and they steal the bypass programs, something called "trivialization software."

"The stuff on laptops?"

"Exactly. The place burns to the ground and suddenly the hard drives with PALs turn up missing. Go figure."

"But what about the guys the FBI arrested out there?"

"The people being investigated at Los Alamos are scapegoats. The real bad guys are long gone."

"That certainly explains all the Chinese money floating around Washington. So what's the endgame?"

"It plays out like this," began Walker. "Instead of selling his share to Beijing, Devon and the Chinese have become partners. Together, they intend to use Red Locust to strong-arm the U.S. on every issue from Taiwan to membership in the World Trade Organization. It's like they are holding a loaded gun to our temple and there is nothing we can do about it."

"And the Investors?"

"So far they're clueless, completely unaware that Devon is trying to cut them out. He's playing the China card for all it's worth."

"How was he able to hide the Red Locust file from the Investors and the CIA for so long?"

"This is one area I really have to take my hat off to the old bastard. He knew that even if he could fool the Investors, Langley and M16 would be hot on his trail. That's when his training as an art trader came in handy."

"How so?"

"It's no secret that 30 percent of the masterpieces bought and sold on the open market are fakes—a fact not lost on Oliver Devon, who has every top art forger in the hemisphere on retainer. When it came time to bury the Red Locust file, he enlisted the best men in his organization and figured out a way to log the coordinates directly onto the canvases of the forged paintings."

"Isn't that a little obvious?"

"No, not at all. At any given time most of the forgeries in Devon's inventory were Impressionist pieces. You know, Monet, Chagal, Matisse. Knowing that the technique used by the Impressionists was effectively a mosaic, Devon's technicians inserted the coordinates as holograms. You could only read them under black light."

"Not too paranoid, huh?"

"Completely. He even gave the order that the fakes were to be donated and hung in all the best galleries, including the Louvre," said Walker. "Frankly, the plan worked like a charm."

"You mentioned the paintings. I assume the art slashings in Paris and New York are connected to all this?"

"You assume correctly," began Walker. "The Chinese are growing impatient. The delivery should have happened back in '96. But the campaign finance scandal made it too hot. Back in '97, when the Select Committee made the claim that the Chinese were attempting to steal the American elections, that put the project on hold. The Los Alamos indictments didn't help either."

"They've waited this long, why not just a little longer?"

"Because they don't want to take a chance on the outcome of the elections. For the most part, this president has left China alone. Albert and Prescott are sort of neutral on Beijing. But fucking Thurman scares them to death."

"He's the Reform Party guy. He can't win!"

"No, but he is militantly pro-Taiwan, and if he cuts a deal with Prescott and joins his cabinet, that could present a major problem. The word is that he's angling for Secretary of State. If that happens, the China bashing will heat up all over again, which translates to a media circus over everything from human rights to fair trade. No, Beijing wants the deal done ASAP!"

"So one more time, what do you want from me?"

"Mike, the key to this whole thing is Devon. We need your help to stop him. It's not like the old days when we had leverage over the sonofabitch."

This last comment puzzled Hanson. He'd found Devon's world to be impervious to attack, completely bulletproof. "How so?"

"Mike, this is a little difficult for me. Devon . . . uh, how should I put it? Devon has, shall we say, some unusual appetites."

"How unusual?" demanded Hanson.

"Well Mike, the truth is that Oliver Devon likes girls, little ones. The younger the better."

Hanson's insides turned, immediately thinking of Ariel. "What is it you're saying?"

Walker, for whom manipulation and exploitation was a way of life, knew he'd hit Hanson's weak spot. "I'm saying that over the years a number of people in our employ have made sure that Devon has been able to satisfy his unusual cravings. For a time he was virtually dependent on us. Imagine, a man of his position and stature. Talk about a potential scandal. Our people provided him discreet liaisons, usually outside the U.S., in places like Cali or Santiago or Managua."

"You sick bastards!"

"Mike, I know how this must sound. If it makes any difference to you, I stopped being Devon's 'handler' before this weirdness ever started. I would never have signed off on it. I know for a fact that is what tore a hole in his relationship with CeCe," explained Walker.

The last comment went through Hanson like a knife. "Walker, what the hell are you trying to say?"

"Good god, Mike, don't tell me you didn't know! Geezus. CeCe was Devon's mistress for years, you know, for when grown-ups were around. The trouble started several years back when Devon started to get a little too friendly with Ariel. . . ."

Hanson's head was spinning, feeling incredible anger, revulsion, and sorrow all at once. He didn't want to believe Walker, but the aging intelligence operative just knew too much about him and the murders, as well as CeCe and Ariel. Most of all he seemed to know Devon like the back of his hand. The sick thing was that the whole improbable scenario was the first thing that seemed to make any sense after the most bizarre week in Hanson's life.

"I'm sorry to be the one to tell you, but that's the connection, Mike. Like I said, you're the fly in the ointment."

"Why me?"

Walker didn't mince words. "Because you are one of the few people who can get close to him without raising a red flag. He sought you out, remember?"

"Don't remind me . . ."

"The good news is that Devon's guard is down a little. He knows that ECHELON is watching his every move. And he is completely over the edge on the committee hearings. He's obsessed with his ex-wife and the direction she's taking her investigation. He knows she's getting close, but he's stuck. If he has her whacked, the Investors will have the FBI and Justice breathing down their necks so fast you wouldn't believe it."

"So why don't you guys just kill the bastard?"

"I wish it were that simple. You can't just kill men like Oliver Devon. If we take him out, the Investors will retaliate just to send a signal to our boys at Langley. Worse, that alone won't help us get our hands on the coordinates. Believe me, they have every backup plan you could imagine. No, we need you to take the assignment and find his Achilles heel, something that we can use to torpedo the delivery to the Chinese, and we don't have a lot of time."

"So in other words the Agency is shifting from pimping to blackmail, is that it?" asked Hanson.

"Which would you prefer, Mike, just tell me," responded Walker.

Hanson couldn't believe the conversation had taken this turn. As far as he was concerned, Investors or no Investors, Oliver Devon already had one foot in the grave. It would only be a matter of how and when. "So what's in it for me?" he asked.

"First, we guarantee that your name disappears from the police blotter—there will be no connection between you and the murders. Second, your life expectancy, as well as that of Ms. Harris, will increase by about thirty years. You help us get the goods on Devon and he will no longer be untouchable and neither will his operatives."

"Even the Chief?"

"So you know about the Chief, do you?" said Walker, somewhat surprised at the mention of his name. "Well, rest easy, Michael, we've wanted to bring him in for years."

"Who is he?" asked Hanson.

Walker had to be careful. He was not pleased about having to discuss this agent, who had been classified as "beyond salvage" over two years earlier. Nevertheless, he figured that Hanson would demand to know more about the man who was stalking him. "The Chief, aka Sam Belarus, is a deep cover operative for the Company, an expert in trade craft, as well as the most effective killer Langley has ever encountered. There was a time when he was our best deep penetration agent, that is, until Devon left the fold and took the Chief with him as his head of security."

"Somehow I knew there would be a connection."

Hanson made Walker laugh. He'd never met someone who could maintain such a consistent level of sarcasm, regardless of the circumstances. He liked this young man and felt badly that he'd become caught in Devon's web. "Michael, you seem like a nice guy. The trouble is that in Washington nice guys don't just finish last, they end up dead. Make no mistake about it, even in the unlikely event that Devon decides not to kill you, there's no way the Chief will let you live. Trust me, I know the way his mind works. Belarus is a top operative, but the thing he enjoys most is killing. Having a psychopath as part of an Agency operation is one of the necessary evils of the intelligence business. He's been useful to Devon, so the Agency has looked the other way. But believe me, when this is finished, he'll be recommended for termination," he said.

"Walker, you seem to take this all kind of personally. How come?" asked Hanson.

After three decades of playing spook, there must be a few chinks showing in his armor, thought Walker. In the old days he could have taken a polygraph and no one would've had any idea what he was thinking. "I guess that's because part of this is personal, Mike. Had I stayed on as Devon's case officer, I doubt that any of this would be happening. There's even a chance that Ariel and CeCe would still be alive. I guess you could say he's my responsibility.

What I'm asking you to do is to help me stop Devon before any more innocent people are killed. So are you on board?"

"Do I have a choice?"

"No, son, not really."

"I should be hearing from Devon anytime. I'll call you with an update later."

"Good," he said, not sure that Hanson appreciated his own jeopardy. "Be ready to move fast. We've learned that all of the coordinates have been downloaded to CDs from photographs taken of the paintings. They arrived in Washington by special courier a few days ago."

"Where are they?"

"That's what we need you to find out," explained Walker. "Here, take this, you'll need it," he said, handing Hanson a small box. Hanson opened it to find a sleek, nine-millimeter handgun and two full clips.

"This is the second time today someone has thought I needed a gun," said Hanson.

"Mike, that's a Glock nine-millimeter semi-automatic pistol, the Austrian model with no serial numbers. Practically untraceable. It's made mostly of fiber-reinforced plastic and can get by most metal detectors. If you want to be extra safe, just remove the slide pin. I've also enclosed two fifteen-round clips of hydro-shock hollow-point bullets. They're perfect for your mission."

"A little much for self-defense. Don't you think?" he asked in disbelief.

"Michael, you're not understanding me. If you don't succeed in stopping the delivery of the site coordinates, Devon's people will be coming after you. You are already part of the money trail. He'll have you terminated to insure that there is no trace whatsoever of this operation. Besides that, you've got to worry about the Chief, not to mention the fact that the Chinese intelligence service almost certainly has their own people following you. Trust me on this one, if somebody you don't know looks at you cross-eyed, start firing and ask questions later. Are you getting the message yet, son?"

Unfortunately, Hanson understood Walker all too well. "Loud and clear . . . loud and clear."

Chapter Thirty-four

Hanson hurried along the dimly lit path toward his car. The Cathedral's brilliant lights loomed far behind him and the grounds were dark and wooded, but his only thoughts were of Danielle. He had to get to her before Devon did. Hanson jumped into the Jag and pulled out onto Wisconsin Avenue. After a few blocks, he punched in the number to Danielle's hotel on his car phone. Getting no answer at her room, he waited for the front desk to pick up. "I'm sorry, Ms. Harris doesn't appear to be in," the operator said.

"Operator, it is extremely important that I get in touch with her." Hanson knew he sounded hysterical. He tried to take a deep breath and steady his voice. "Did she say where she was going?" he asked.

"Well, she did leave a forwarding number for committee staff . . . are you with the committee?" the operator asked.

"Yes, absolutely, without me there would be no committee," Hanson said. "What's the number?"

The operator hesitated.

"It's an emergency. I need her number now!"

She reluctantly gave it to him and Hanson dialed it into the phone.

After several rings, another voice answered. "Children's Hospital, how may I direct your call?"

Children's Hospital? thought Hanson. "Uh, yes, I'm trying to reach a Danielle Harris," Hanson said.

"Hold on, sir, I'll connect you through to Neonatology," said the operator.

Hanson breathed a sigh of relief and hung up as he turned left on Mass. Avenue to head for Northeast Washington. Even though he had no idea why on earth she would be there, he assumed she would be safe at the hospital. Devon wouldn't try anything with a lot of people around. Then he thought of Walker's words. Devon was over the edge, and would stop at nothing. Hanson sped up and kept praying that he would get to Danielle first. When the hospital's white towers came into view, Hanson screeched across the emergency room entrance and left the car in the parking lane. Taking advantage of the chaos inside, Hanson ducked into a stairwell and climbed the five flights to Neonatology.

Hanson ran down the hallway and then realized he had no idea where Danielle might be. He looked into each room until he heard a voice behind him.

"Can I help you, sir?"

"I'm looking for a Danielle Harris." Hanson said. "Is she okay? Has she had some type of accident?"

"Did you sign in, sir?" demanded an iron-haired nurse looking curiously at him.

Hanson ignored her and kept running down the hallway.

"If you don't stop right now, I'm going to call security," the nurse said, yelling now.

Hanson desperately kept running, pushing open doors, looking for Danielle. He was crazy with worry. If Devon had touched a hair on her head, he would kill him. Then Hanson stopped abruptly, the nurse close behind. He peered through the glass wall of an incubation room. Danielle sat inside, holding the tiniest infant he'd ever seen.

Just then, the nurse caught up with him and grabbed his arm.

"No, just let me see her," Hanson yelled, and Danielle looked up with alarm in her eyes. The nurse stepped back away from Hanson as soon as he yelled. She waited for Danielle to take charge.

Danielle's eyes took everything in, and she carefully returned the baby to its incubator. As she came out of the nursery, she took off her surgical mask and said, "Michael, my god, is everything all right?"

"Yes, fine . . . I mean no, everything's not all right. Can we sit down somewhere?" he said awkwardly.

"I'll take care of him," Danielle said to the nurse, as Hanson muttered an apology. The nurse just stared at the two of them and walked away.

"Mike, follow me," Danielle said, leading him to a vacant room. She saw the anguish on his face. "Talk to me, Michael."

Hanson was just relieved that she was okay. He didn't feel like telling her the whole story quite yet. "Danielle, what on earth are you doing here?"

Danielle simply raised an eyebrow at him. "Michael, I've spent almost every Thursday night for the last five years in a place like this. It doesn't matter where I am. One night a week I volunteer in a children's ward." She sighed. "Most of the babies here are called border babies, some of them are addicted to crack, some of them have AIDS. Once in a while I play doctor, but most nights I just hold them, you know, rock them to sleep. I guess it's my therapy."

"For what?" Hanson asked.

Danielle smiled. "For personal reasons. And what about you? Do you make a habit of stalking all the women you sleep with?" she asked pointedly.

"Danielle, I'm sorry, I know how this must seem. But it's not what it looks like. Your life may be in danger."

"What are you talking about?" Danielle asked, horrified. She had seen enough violence on the streets to believe him.

"Listen, I don't know how to say this, and I understand completely if you hate me for what I'm about to tell you, but I gotta come clean."

"Go on, Michael," Danielle said. Her face was calm and curious, which only made Hanson feel worse.

"I don't know how to say this, but Devon has tried to retain my services," Hanson began, bracing himself for the worst.

"Since when?"

"Since the day we met."

"I see."

"No, you don't. I had no idea I was going to see you last night."

Danielle looked confused. Disdainfully, she said, "Leave it to Devon. I meet one guy in five years that makes me smile and waddaya know, he's a spy for my ex-husband. . . ."

Hanson just stared at her, feeling unbelievably guilty. "That's not what's happening."

"Okay. So how much is Devon paying you?"

"He offered me more money than I've ever seen in my life, but I turned him down."

Danielle smiled. "I'm sure. So what are you supposed to do for all that money, Michael?"

Hanson took a deep breath. "Next time I testify before the committee I'm supposed to read a dossier into the record. It says that you and the White House are working together to whitewash the whole investigation. That you are setting me up as the fall guy."

Danielle's mouth dropped, and Hanson thought he saw her eyes mist over. Then she set her jaw defiantly. "I can't say that I'm all that surprised. What you've told me is classic Devon."

"Look, I was absolutely, absolutely never going to take the assignment. Especially not after the other night."

Danielle looked away. "Is that why you came back to my hotel room with me?" she said, her voice hard.

Hanson took a deep breath. Knowing it was no time for sarcasm or excuses, he said, "Danielle, it's just that I don't get involved with that many women like you. I suppose that's because there just aren't that many women like you available. Anyway, I don't seem to get close to women who, besides being a knockout, also turn out to be super people. At the risk of being totally shot down, you are what I've been looking for my whole damned life," he said, shocked as the truth came out of his mouth. "I wouldn't blow this for a lousy client, no matter how much money he paid me."

Danielle was unexpectedly moved by Hanson's words. Softly, she said, "Michael, I'm not going to pretend that what you've told me doesn't hurt. It does. But the truth is, I'm way past blame. Washington is such a strange place. This town has a funny way of bringing out the worst in people. I'm not all that surprised that

Devon wants to destroy me, just that he chose you as the executioner."

"Danielle, speaking of bringing out the worst in people, what really happened between you and Devon?" asked Hanson.

"Hold that thought," said Danielle as she got up from her seat and disappeared down the hallway. About a minute later she returned, carrying her purse. As she sat down beside him she began. "In light of the fact that Devon tried to put you on his payroll, I'm sure he's given you an earful about my role with the committee. And the truth is that he has reason to be concerned. But the committee is only part of his concern."

"Trust me, Danielle, he's plenty worried."

Taking a moment to scan up and down the hallway, Danielle spoke in a whispering tone. "Michael, the truth is that Devon has had the committee wired from the beginning. Outside looking in, my hire appears totally legit. I mean, on paper I'm completely qualified. In reality it was a strategic ploy. As long as I stayed away from him and his dealings, everything ran smoothly. On the other hand, if I found out anything new, say on China, then I was his insurance policy."

"How so?"

"Even though it was ages ago, he is still my ex-husband. It's an instant conflict. He knows that he can destroy my reputation in the time it takes to issue a press release."

"Didn't you know this when you took the job?" asked Hanson. "What were you thinking?"

"Considering the scope of his immunity deal, I never thought we'd butt heads. Couple that with calls from eleven U.S. Senators—I was persuaded," she said. "But like I said, he's got other things on his mind."

"Meaning?"

"Meaning this," she said as she pulled out her wallet from her purse. Slowly she opened it and took out a photo. "Michael, look at this . . ."

Hanson took it in his hand. He'd seen it before.

"You asked me about this back at my hotel. Obviously you recognize Devon and me. But look closely at the young boy in the background. Look familiar?" she asked.

"Now that you mention it, yes, he does."

"He should. He was an intern for the Foreign Relations Committee back when you worked on it. His name was Billy, and he was my stepson. Devon was his father."

Hanson stared at the picture closely. After a few seconds he made the connection. "I actually do remember him. He was a great kid. How old is he now, twenty-five, twenty-six?"

Danielle looked away, putting the photo back in her wallet. Slowly the tears came. In a halting voice she said, "Billy was diagnosed with AIDS not long after he left the committee." She leaned into him as Hanson put his arm around her. "Devon hired you to destroy my credibility before I could play my trump card."

"I don't understand."

"Billy knew he was gay by the time he was a teenager. His father, who I eventually learned had this uptight macho attitude about nearly everything, was determined to change him. Devon made the kid's life a living hell trying to change him; military school, the church, countless psychologists. Finally, Devon sent Billy to Washington to work for an old college buddy, Larry Kassendine, figuring a summer in D.C. around dozens of young coeds would be good for him. But instead of finding the girl of his dreams, Billy came out of the closet."

"I'm sure Senator Kassendine's exemplary behavior was a huge help to the situation," said Hanson.

"It only added to Devon's rage. He went on a rampage, hiring private detectives to investigate every gym teacher, coach, or male role model that Billy ever knew. I can't begin to tell you how many lives he ruined during his vendetta. No one was spared, not even Kassendine," explained Danielle.

"Devon's son was gay, that was your trump card?" asked Hanson. "Would you really go public with that?"

"Of course not, Michael," said Danielle. "I loved that boy with all my heart. But that's not how Devon thinks. I was with him at an AIDS hospice in Florida, praying for a miracle. He was down to eighty pounds, dying of pneumocystis, barely alive. All he wanted to do was speak to his father one last time, to make peace. So I called Devon. It was the first time I'd spoken to him in months. I'll never forget his reaction. Devon told me that as far as he was concerned his son was already dead. He told me to have them just burn the body and throw away the ashes, that he didn't want the 'queer's remains' to contaminate the family cemetery," she said in sadness as her voice trailed off.

"What a bastard," said Hanson, not believing that anyone could be so cruel.

"I can honestly say that there is nothing Oliver Devon despises more than homosexuals. His hatred is absolutely pathological!" said Danielle. She paused for a moment to compose herself. All of a sudden she noticed that Hanson had turned white as a ghost. "Michael, are you all right? Michael?"

"My God . . . Adam!" was all he said as he ran down the stairwell.

Chapter Thirty-five

Hanson had the Jag at full throttle as it roared down Constitution Avenue, making the turn north on Connecticut. The Mayflower was about a mile away, which, at his rate of speed, left him about a minute from his destination. Under the circumstances he didn't give a damn about cops, stop lights, or speed limits. The only thing that mattered was getting to Adam before Devon did.

After nearly causing a three-car pileup as he pulled up to the hotel, Hanson screeched to a stop in the middle of the driveway. He sprinted out of the car, blew past the doorman, and headed for Adam's suite. When he got to the eleventh floor, he noticed that it seemed strangely deserted, as though no one else was staying there. Arriving at room 1133, he knocked loudly, screaming for Adam to open up. When no one answered, he rattled the door handle and was surprised when it opened. Slowly he entered the suite, scanning the room. What he saw made him swallow his heart. The suite was ransacked, furniture overturned, and clothes strewn about the floor. Hanson knew he was too late. Making his way down the hallway, Hanson could hear the static of the radio as he neared the bedroom. He entered, half expecting to find his client oversleeping. Instead, he saw Adam lying facedown on the bed, naked. On the wall above the headboard, written in blood, were the words *Die Faggot* and *Death Cures AIDS*. Devon was smart. By making it look part–hate crime, part–hustler murder, the D.C. police wouldn't have a clue.

As Hanson approached the bed, he could see the pool of blood surrounding his client's body. Turning him over, he found Adam's throat slit ear to ear. "Godamn it, Adam. No!" he bellowed. Finding no pulse, he tried to stop the bleeding, but it was no use. Adam was gone forever. For several minutes Hanson held his old friend in his arms, waiting until Adam's body went cold. Finally, he laid his body down and covered him with a blanket. The strange thing was that Hanson finally understood why gay men stay in the closet. There would always be Oliver Devons out there, powerful men who refuse to tolerate the existence of people like Adam.

Despite his grief, Hanson's instincts took over, telling him to get out of the hotel as fast as possible. He was covered in blood, and his prints were all over the suite. The police could be on their way. Worse, Devon or the Chief could be waiting in the hallway for him. Knowing that it was more difficult to kill a moving target, he made a run for it, using the stairwell to make his escape. Taking the fire exit to avoid the lobby, he dashed around the building to his car and sped off.

The time was 8:35 P.M. With no sign of Devon or the Chief, Hanson figured he might have just enough time to formulate a plan. And while he wasn't quite sure what that would entail, he knew the first step was to assemble his troops. His first call was to Tom Griffin. After first retrieving the nine-millimeter from the glove compartment and resting it on the passenger seat, he pressed number 2 on his speed dial. Seconds later, his buddy answered the phone.

"So, still talking to me?" said Hanson.

"Mikey, hey man, am I glad to hear your voice. The question is, are you talking to me?" said Griffin.

"I called you, didn't I? Listen brother, I don't really have time to go into it, but I need your help. It's pretty serious."

"Name it. Whatever you need."

"Meet me at my house in about half an hour, I'll explain everything then," he said.

"Mike, you sound terrible. What's this all about?" asked Griffin.

"Oh, you know, the end of life as we know it, World War III, the usual shit," said Hanson, hanging up.

Next up was Kennedy. After digging his card out of his coat pocket, Hanson punched in the number. The detective picked up almost immediately, saying "Kennedy here."

"Detective, it's Mike Hanson."

"Hanson, I was gonna call you later. It looks like we got a make on Ariel's killer. You'll never believe who . . ."

"Sam Belarus," interrupted Hanson.

"Yeah. How the hell did you know that?"

Hanson massaged the pistol on the seat next to him. "It's a long story. We gotta meet."

"I can't now. We're waiting on the warrant for Belarus. Anyway, it looks like you're in the clear, Mike."

"I don't give a shit about that right now, Detective. Adam Melrose is dead. Those bastards killed him. Go to suite 1133 at the Mayflower. He's been dead less than an hour. They made it look like a hustler murder. By the way, my prints are all over the place."

Detective Kennedy was puzzled. What Hanson said didn't make sense. "Mike, you gotta listen to me. Whoever killed your friend, it wasn't Belarus. We've had him under surveillance for the last few hours."

Kennedy's response only confirmed Hanson's suspicion. "Detective, you aren't getting it. Belarus is just a hired gun. This thing is way bigger than a couple of dead hookers. Whether you want to admit it or not, we're both in way the fuck over our heads."

"How do you know all this?" he asked.

"I'll explain it all to you when I see you."

"All right, we should be able to execute the warrant sometime in the next couple of hours. How can I get in touch with you?"

"The Hamilton, room 821," said Hanson.

"I'll be in touch, and you watch your ass 'til I get there," said Kennedy, hanging up.

With one call left, Hanson pulled over in search of a pay phone, knowing he couldn't really call a CIA number from a cellular without inviting half of Washington to listen in. Finding one on the corner, he pulled over and ran to it. Anxiously, he deposited a quarter and a dime and dialed Walker's number. As the phone rang, Hanson could hear the number roll over several times through the intricate phone network out at Langley. Finally, the aging spy answered. "Hanson, are you okay?"

"Don't talk, just listen. They've killed my friend Adam, but you probably know that already. I've thought it over and I'm going after Devon myself."

"Don't be a fool, you'll need some kind of backup!" he warned.

"Forget about it, this is my party. I can't guarantee that I'll be able to recover the coordinates. But I promise you one thing, by this time tomorrow, Oliver Devon will be a dead man!"

Chapter Thirty-six

By the time Griffin arrived, Hanson had almost finished his assault on his home entertainment system. Various stereo components were strewn about the floor of the living room, lying on a blanket of CDs, cassettes, and vintage long-play albums. The fact was, Hanson's apartment was generally a mess, so its current state of disarray really came as no surprise to Griffin. But the nine-millimeter handgun resting on his friend's coffee table was another matter. "Mike, what the hell are you doing?" he demanded.

"I'll explain later. For now, just take this," he said, handing him an old briefcase. Then, going to a nearby bookshelf, Hanson grabbed a box of CDs, numbering three to four dozen. He quickly put it on the couch and opened it. "All right, start taking those out of their cases. . . ."

"Lemme guess, the folks at Columbia House are finally on to you" said Griff.

"Probably, but that's not the point," chuckled Hanson. "Just take 'em out and hand them to me."

"Whatever."

As Griffin quickly removed each CD, Hanson placed them inside the briefcase, securing them with old newspaper.

"Man, what the fuck is going on?"

"I'll tell you in the car. Come on, let's get outta here," said Hanson anxiously, pushing Griffin out the door. After putting the briefcase in the backseat, the two got in the Jaguar and sped off. For the first ten minutes Hanson said nothing as they headed down Canal Road. Finally, as they crossed Chain Bridge into Virginia, he said, "Griff, I'm in trouble, serious trouble!"

"I gathered as much. So what is it, that police detective? Are you caught up in that girl's murder? Talk to me."

Hanson looked straight ahead. He couldn't believe what he was about to admit. "Of course I am, the trouble is, I can't really figure out how."

"Mike, you're not making sense. Either you're involved or you're not."

"Goddamn it, Griff, you're not listening. I know I'm involved. People all around me are dropping like flies! I even think I know who's doing it."

"Mike, don't fuck around with this. If you know anything, you gotta go to the cops!"

"Don't you get it? This thing is way too big. The cops can't touch these guys. They killed CeCe and Adam and you're probably next," said Hanson.

"CeCe, Adam, dead? My God! Are you sure they know I exist?" said Griffin in a panicked voice.

"Griff, believe me, these bastards know exactly who you are."

Once they reached the Parkway, Hanson turned around and headed back downtown. With the Potomac on their left and the lights from the monuments dead ahead, Hanson recounted everything to his best friend: his connection to Ariel, how CeCe died in his arms, and how he found Adam gruesomely murdered in the hotel suite only hours earlier. After giving him a few moments to take it all in, he told him about Devon and the "nature" of the project he was working on. Finally he told him of the meeting with Walker and about the Swiss accounts. "That's how I got the gun," he said.

"I'll say one thing about you, Mike, when you step in shit you really step in shit."

"Thanks so much for pointing that out."

"What about the Feds?" asked Griffin.

"Walker is the Feds. Look, there's no other way around it. Unless I stop the handover of the codes, I'm a dead man."

"I can't believe I'm hearing this. You're being stalked by Chinese hitmen and other assorted Cold War types who are killing everyone you know, and you're actually thinking about going through with this?" he asked.

As he turned right up the ramp to Key Bridge, Hanson continued to check in both rear and side mirrors in search of anything suspicious. He didn't really know what to look for, but he nevertheless remembered Walker's warning. Satisfied that they weren't being followed, he continued on across the bridge toward M Street. "Listen, I've only got one hand to play, and that's the codes for the suitcase bombs. That's what the briefcase is for. Until I can get Devon to lead me to the real thing, there might be some percentage in making people think that I already have them."

"Michael, you've absolutely lost your fucking mind."

"I honestly wish that was the case. But the truth is that this is all way too real. Man, I hate to ask, but I need your help."

Hanson never got to finish his thought. The black BMW roared up on his left, entering his lane. "Move over, asshole!" he screamed as the car's passenger side window lowered just enough to reveal the barrel of a Tech-9 submachine gun. Without thinking, Hanson pounded the accelerator and yanked the steering wheel as far to the right as possible, narrowly missing several cars on the crowded bridge, coming within inches of a retaining wall. Amid the sounds of car horns blaring and automatic gunfire behind them, the Jaguar sliced through traffic, heading east on the Whitehurst Freeway. Knowing that there was virtually no way to pass on this narrow highway, Hanson top-ended at about 120 mph, attempting to put as much distance as possible between himself and the BMW. With their pursuer nowhere in sight, Hanson headed towards Danielle's hotel. Looking to his right, he noticed that Griffin was white as a sheet. "You okay?"

"Of course not. But at least now I see why you have to do this. So what do you need from me?"

"What I need is for you to stash my car somewhere it won't get spotted. Then I need you to go someplace where you'll be safe and just wait. Check into a hotel or something. Make sure you aren't followed. Don't try to call me. I'll leave a message on your pager with instructions. Oh yeah, here, take this," said Hanson, handing him the gun.

"Mike, really, I don't . . ."

"Just do as I say. Most of all, be careful!" he admonished.

"Okay, are you sure that's all?"

Hanson thought for a moment. "Yeah, there is one more thing. You don't happen to know anybody at the Israeli Embassy, do you?"

"As a matter of fact, I met a couple of their guys at a seminar a couple of months back. Rabbi Meyer introduced me. Why?"

"Good. Give 'em a call," he began. "Tell 'em I'm gonna make 'em an offer they can't refuse."

Chapter Thirty-seven

Hanson had Griffin drop him off a couple of blocks from Danielle's hotel, thinking that if he were still being followed, he would stand a better chance of shaking his pursuers on foot. No matter what else happened, the last thing he wanted to do was put her in danger. The sad thing was, before this was all over, he would have no choice.

The Jag was barely out of sight when Hanson spotted the car inching down the street, less than a hundred feet behind him. From where he stood, he couldn't tell whether or not it was the black BMW. All he knew was that its headlights were out and that he was being followed. Every time he picked up his pace, the car would speed up. Every time he slowed down, it would slow down. Undoubtedly, if he decided to run directly towards it, the car would go in reverse. It was about this time that Hanson wanted to kill himself for handing the Glock over to Tom Griffin, a liberal's liberal who would probably use it as a doorstop.

He continued to move at a brisk clip up 25th Street, using all his self-control to resist the urge to run into some alley in search of someplace to hide. Finally, after several seconds, the car passed under a streetlight and he realized that it wasn't the BMW. Worse, it was Devon. Hanson realized he had two choices: He could make a run for it, knowing that it would be only a matter of time before he and Devon would have their confrontation, or he could change the rules of the game, turning the hunter into the hunted.

Hanson stopped. As he turned and approached the limousine, he remembered Walker's warning that delivery of the codes was to happen any day. What the hell, he thought, at least this way he could keep track of Devon's whereabouts.

Devon's limo came to a stop and pulled over. Hanson expected either a barrage of gunshots or several large men to leap out and grab him. Instead, the front passenger window lowered. From inside came a familiar voice. "Mr. Hanson," began Lonnie as he pointed a gun directly at him, "Mr. Devon has given me instructions to bring you to him. Son, please don't make me use this. Just come along now, nice and quiet, and no one will get hurt."

Rumors of an exclusive after hours club located near the Washington Harbor had circulated around town for years. Catering to the decadent appetites of its elite clientele, it purportedly offered everything from high-stakes gambling to live sex, as well as the best booze, drugs, and women money could buy. All things considered, just a little too hot for a town like Washington. It was kind of ironic that Hanson, with his legendary reputation as a good-time guy, was asked on an average of at least once a week about the club. Most of the guys in his crowd figured that if anybody would know about it, he would.

With Lonnie gripping his arm tightly, they passed the gauntlet of security guards at the entrance of the club. Their reaction betrayed the fact that Devon had been something of a regular at the establishment. As they made their way through the ground-floor casino, Hanson saw some of the city's most prominent faces in the dim light. Arriving at the elevator, he turned to survey the scene, figuring the collective net worth of just the men he recognized to be at least a billion dollars. Someone was making a mint off this setup; roulette, baccarat, craps, blackjack, and of course no betting limits. "What, no slot machines?" he said.

Lonnie shot him a dirty look as the elevator arrived. "Too low-rent," was all he said as he pushed the button to the third floor. Upon exiting the elevator, they were met immediately by a gorgeous redhead in a low-cut dress. "Come this way," she said. "Mr. Devon is expecting you." They followed her through a doorway, entering a large room even more dimly lit than the casino, set up like a cocktail lounge, with a dozen or so tables surrounding a small stage. As they approached Devon's table, Hanson could see that the room was almost empty except for two women—one Asian, one blond—clad in only the scantiest of lingerie, kissing and groping each other on the stage while an 80's retro house-track blared on the club's sound system. Despite the obvious distractions, his blood began to boil when he saw his nemesis seated, back to the wall as usual, at the far side of the room.

"Quite a floor show, huh, Michael?" said Devon. "These two are just auditioning. You should see our regular girls!"

Hanson was in no mood for games. "What the hell is this, your intern training program?"

"Sit down, Michael, sit down, you and I need to have us a little talk."

"I'll stand. I don't intend to be here that long."

Hanson didn't get a chance to finish the sentence before Lonnie used all of his 250 pounds to muscle him into the chair. He began to resist, when Devon intervened. "Thank you, Lonnie, that'll be fine. I think Mr. Hanson is beginning to realize that he'll be staying awhile. Isn't that right, Michael?"

Knowing he was outweighed, outnumbered, and, for now, outsmarted, Hanson replied, "Sure, whatever."

"Good," he said, waving Lonnie away.

No sooner did he leave than yet another luscious woman arrived with a Chivas on the rocks for Hanson. "Drink up, son. Believe it or not, you're among friends."

"I don't drink with murderers!"

"Don't be so self-righteous, Michael. Adam's blood is on your hands as well as mine. To be perfectly honest, I can't help but wonder how you could have exercised such poor judgment."

"Excuse me?"

"Don't play dumb with me, Michael. By bringing that queer friend of yours into the equation, you made this whole thing extremely awkward for me. Nevertheless, I've explained to my colleagues that you couldn't possibly have known. But, my young friend, I'm warning you in no uncertain terms that if you fuck up like this again, our relationship will be severed instantly. And I shouldn't have to tell you that such an occurrence will end up costing you much more than just a client," said Devon, making a not so veiled threat.

Hanson couldn't believe what he was hearing. Devon had as much as admitted killing Adam, and worse, justified it as though it were merely some business deal that didn't work out. While he wanted to rip the old bastard's heart out, Hanson restrained himself. The good news was that Devon apparently had no idea that Hanson knew about his whole operation.

"Anyway, on to other business. I'm probably pulling the plug on the Danielle Harris project," he said.

This was weird. Realizing that it might be a trap, Hanson proceeded cautiously. "And why is that?"

Devon looked at Hanson with surprise, as he wasn't used to being questioned by subordinates. "Well, I have it on good authority that Ms. Harris will be resigning her position with the committee."

"That is inconsistent with my information. I hear she's there for the long haul. Who's your source, anyway?" Hanson demanded.

At this point the questioning was getting irritating. "That doesn't concern you. However, as for your fee, my suggestion is that you hold on to it. Think of it as sort of an advance against future services. If you play your cards right, there may be a long-term opportunity in it for you. Meanwhile, drink up, enjoy the view," he said, referring to the women on stage. Hanson looked over at the two women, as the Asian was now performing acts that almost certainly violated several laws in the District of Columbia. "Would you like one of them, Michael? I'm taking the blonde back to my compound for the night."

"Thanks, I'll pass," said Hanson, concluding that delivery of the codes would not happen until tomorrow.

"Come on, Michael. What's wrong? You guys are in power and all of a sudden you forget how to have a good time? Relax. You and I aren't so different. You do know that, don't you?"

"No, Oliver, you're confused. You and I are as different as two people could be," said Hanson.

"Michael, come on," he began in a fatherly tone. "Look, you don't think I feel bad about Adam? Well, I do. But you know as well as I do that sooner or later your association with that homo would have come back to haunt you," reasoned Devon.

"What exactly are you saying, Oliver?"

"Michael, my colleagues and I have big plans for you. We need a front man to deal with the new administration and you are the logical choice. As a sign of our good faith I have wired an additional ten million to your Hanson & Associates corporate account. How you move it into the campaign is your business."

"You what?"

"You heard me. Oliver Devon always keeps his word," he boasted. "You might have a few problems with the tax man down the road, but I'm sure you'll handle it. At any rate, you'll be a wealthy man before the midterm elections. You see, son, I didn't give the order to terminate Adam because of my personal feelings. I did it for you."

The sound of Devon's words stung Hanson like a wasp. He began to sweat, and felt like he was going to throw up. "You what?"

"Relax, Michael, one day you'll understand. It was for the best."

This last remark was too much for Hanson to take. On instinct, Hanson grabbed his drink and threw it in Devon's face. "Fuck you and fuck your money!"

In a matter of seconds, Lonnie and several security guards were on Hanson, forcing him to the ground. After wiping his face, Devon intervened, saying, "Let him go!" Once Hanson stood up, Devon got right in his face. As they stood chin to chin, he said, "Man, is this gonna cost you."

Hanson knew that the first rule of survival was to never show fear. Over the years, he'd seen the same axiom applied in street fights, politics, and marriage. With that in mind, he played the only card he was holding. "Come on, Ollie, cut the macho shit. Isn't it about time you stopped overcompensating for that fag son of yours?"

Devon was taken aback, shocked by Hanson's statement. How could this two-bit political hack have such information? Either there was a mole in his organization or Hanson was the best undercover operative he'd ever encountered. Both theories made him furious. "Get this piece of shit out of my sight!"

Lonnie and the cadre of bouncers were only too glad to comply with Devon's order, dragging Hanson down three flights of steps, physically throwing him out the back door of the club into an alley. Dizzy and with the wind knocked out of him, Hanson still managed to get to his feet and stagger out of the alley to the street. He knew Devon's outburst of temper had granted him a temporary stay of execution. As soon as Devon had a chance to collect himself, he would almost certainly order his goons to track down Hanson and effect his termination. His only hope of staying alive was to keep moving.

Unfortunately Hanson was only able to move another few blocks before, out of nowhere, he was nearly run down by a late-model Cadillac. After staggering to his feet and dusting himself off, he saw the silhouette in the moonlight of a large man exit the driver's side of the car.

"Mike, get in the car," said the voice. "It will be only a matter of minutes before they come after you. . . ."

"Who the fuck are you?"

"Gosh, Hanson, how soon we forget," said the man as he stepped forward. "Now let's get moving!"

"Walker?" exclaimed Hanson, in a voice filled with relief. "How did you . . ."

Before Hanson could finish his question, a black sedan with diplomatic tags came careening around the corner. As it screeched to a stop, several Asian men brandishing handguns leaped out of the car. Walker turned to him and screamed, "In the car. Now!" With Hanson making a beeline for the passenger-side door, Walker wheeled and got off several shots, pinning down the Asians before they could return fire. After several seconds, his clip empty, he leaped back into the car. No sooner did he stomp the throttle than a torrent of bullets followed. "Mike, next time I tell you to get in the car, just get in the fucking car!"

"Not a problem," said Hanson. "Were those Devon's security people?"

"Nope. Different bad guys. It seems that the Chinese are pissed off and growing impatient," he said as he turned the corner, checking his rearview mirror for company. "Our sources tell us the money transfer is scheduled for tomorrow night. By the way, did Devon tell you where the codes are stashed?"

"No, it didn't come up."

"Don't worry, it will . . ."

Chapter Thirty-eight

Danielle and Griffin waited anxiously for Hanson. Despite being furious with him for lying, they couldn't help but worry. There was no telling what kind of trouble he could be in with Devon on his trail. He'd headed out to meet Walker hours ago and they'd heard nothing since. Finally, about midnight, Hanson knocked on the door of suite 821. "Michael, what in god's name happened to you?"

Bruised and battered, Hanson entered the suite. "Oliver Devon happened to me," he said.

"I was afraid of this," said Danielle. "Let me have a look at you."

"Listen to her, Mike," ordered Griffin from inside the suite.

"People, relax. I just need a stiff drink to calm my nerves."

Griffin quickly obliged, fetching his buddy a scotch on the rocks from the honor bar.

Hanson took a long sip and, looking around the suite, said, "Where the hell's the detective?"

"We were wondering the same thing," said Griff. Just then, there was a knock at the door. Danielle went to the peephole and peered through. It was Kennedy.

Once Abe stepped through the door, Hanson immediately perked up. "Detective Kennedy, I can't believe I'm actually glad to see you," he said. He stopped in midsentence when he saw the look on Kennedy's face. "Detective, what's wrong? Are you okay?"

Kennedy looked like a shadow of his normal self in the stark light of the hotel room. His shoulders were rounded over, and his face looked deeply lined and weary. He usually looked trim and ready to go, but now his clothes were rumpled and disheveled, his eyes bloodshot. He mumbled something, but Hanson couldn't make it out.

"Come in, Detective," he said softly. When Kennedy just kept standing there, Hanson got up and gently guided him into the room.

Kennedy sat down, not sure of his balance. How in Christ's name could this be happening, he wondered. He was the best fucking homicide detective in the department, as well as the most careful. Not the type of cop to lose a partner. Finally the words came. "They got him, Mike."

"Detective, what are you saying?"

"The bastards got Ira. He was pronounced dead at Sibley Hospital an hour ago. The goddamn bastards! He was going to retire at the end of the year."

There was silence in the room for a moment. Danielle got Kennedy a glass of water. "If you'd like something stronger . . ."

"No, no thanks. Still on duty."

Hanson paced the room, and Griffin took it upon himself to convince the concierge to bring them several pots of hot coffee. He knew that the group wouldn't be getting much sleep that night.

Halfway through his second cup of coffee, Kennedy finally started speaking. "We'd just finished putting a mountain of paperwork to bed," he said, fighting to get the words out. "I went back to my desk to review my notes on Ariel's murder. Since he was done for the night, I told Ira to go home and get some sleep. It was my night to take the cruiser home, you know, we'd alternate. But seeing how late it was, no one much cared about that. We shot the bull for a few seconds and he left. That was the last I saw of him. About a minute later I hear this explosion, it sounded like someone dropped a bomb on the station house. By the time I got outside, it was too late. The cruiser looked like a Roman candle. Ira never had a chance."

Hearing this made Hanson cringe. "God, Abe, I'm so sorry," he said.

"Nothing I can do now but catch the killer," Kennedy said. He looked squarely at Hanson. "Can I count on you, Mike?"

Hanson reached for the pot and refilled their cups. "Drink up, Abe, you and I got a lot to talk about," he said.

"I had a feeling."

For most of the next hour, Hanson told them everything he knew about high school girlfriends, madams, dead prostitutes, and about how Devon was up to his eyeballs in Nazi war profiteering. He made sure to include the details of a meeting with a strange man named Walker who seemed to know everything about everybody. Most of all, he made sure they all knew that a money transfer was about to happen.

"I gotta get goin' . . . to see Ira's family," Kennedy said, suddenly overwrought with grief. "Devon's going down, I promise."

"Abe, before you go, I gotta get this off my chest," said Hanson. "Look, except for having broken a few moral laws in my time, I don't know shit about law enforcement, but I do know a little bit about the way this town works. What I'm saying is, if what you want is to arrest Oliver Devon for Ira's murder, then forget about it, because it just ain't gonna happen. Washington used to be a town where all that counted was who you knew. These days, who you know isn't enough. Power depends on who you own, and Devon owns almost everyone in this town."

"He doesn't own me," Kennedy said.

"I know, Abe, but he's already killed Ira, and lord only knows who else he's capable of hurting."

"Meaning?"

"Meaning I remember you bragging to me about a kid you've got at home named A. J. Let's say you arrest Devon. Great. What do you think is gonna be on his mind when he's sitting in a holding cell waiting for his bail hearing?" said Hanson.

Kennedy looked disgustedly at Hanson. "And what if I don't want to do it your way?"

"Then I suggest you go home right now and attend to your affairs. You know—your will, life insurance, funeral plans, because if we don't stop Devon, we're all as good as dead." Hanson looked at Detective Kennedy. He could see the bloodlust in his eyes. Devon had killed his partner, and there was nothing on earth that could make him walk away from that.

At this point Danielle, who had remained silent so far, interrupted. "He has a weakness. . . ."

"What did you say, Danielle?" asked Hanson skeptically.

"He has a weakness, an Achilles heel," she said. "I lived with the man for years. I know almost everything about him."

For the detective, this was the break he was praying for. Coldly and directly, he zeroed in on Danielle's words. "Miss Harris, this ain't the time for maybes or gut feelings. Am I clear? Tell me exactly what you mean."

"I mean I know a way to stop Oliver Devon dead in his tracks. . . . Is that clear enough for you?"

Chapter Thirty-nine

For the better part of an hour, Danielle outlined her plan of attack to the others. As expected, Kennedy—who spent his entire career going by the book—offered the most resistance. For Hanson, the only down side was that the scheme would put Danielle in harm's way. Her rebuttal pretty much summed up the group's feelings. "I stepped in harm's way the moment I met that man. As long as he and I exist in the same world, that won't change." And as for the Messiah of Money, his reaction was vintage Griffin.

"Whatever it takes. I'm on board. Oliver Devon's ass is mine, goddamn it!" he said.

Well past midnight Griffin left, taking the nine-millimeter with him, promising not to chance going home, that he would stay the night at a girlfriend's. Kennedy, on the other hand, stayed the night on the couch in the suite to make sure that Hanson and Danielle would be safe. By the time Hanson and Danielle woke, Kennedy had already gone, leaving only a short note to Hanson, telling him to stay out of sight until he returned.

Kennedy had many things to do, but only one really mattered. As he entered the Murray home, he was met at the door by Ira's brother Frank, who flew up from Miami as soon as he heard the news. "You must be Abe," he said warmly. "Come in, come in."

After hanging up his coat and setting down the spice cake he'd brought over at Marlene's direction, the detective walked down the hallway toward the living room. The deafening quiet of the usually noisy Murray home struck him. The somber mood of the shivah house was unmistakable. Finally he saw Ira's widow, Freda, seated on the sofa surrounded by grandchildren, looking as though she'd aged ten years in a single night.

Freda's face lit up the second she saw him. "Abe, thank God you're here, please sit down, right here by me. Can I get you something to eat?" she said warmly.

The detective went to her quickly, taking her hands in his, feeling a great sense of relief at the welcome. "Freda, how are you holding up? Are you okay?"

"Oh, I'm as well as can be expected. The rabbi has already been by, and my girls, they haven't let me lift a finger," said Freda, referring to their two daughters, who were milling about the house, putting out food and playing hostess as visitors began to arrive to pay their respects. "And A. J. has been wonderful."

"A. J.?" Kennedy asked, startled.

"Yes, he was the first one here this morning. He's been a great help to the girls. I think he's resting now upstairs in the extra bedroom. He's a good boy."

Kennedy just nodded, filled with hope for the first time in a while. But he didn't come to make himself feel better, he came to try to ease Freda's pain.

"Freda, I'm just so sorry, he was only out of my sight for a second . . ."

"Shh," she said softly, squeezing his hands. "You don't have to explain anything to me."

"Is there anything you need?"

The dignified woman thought to herself for a moment, finally saying, "Yes, Abe, there is."

"You name it," said the detective eagerly.

"Not here. Come with me into the den so we can talk before it gets too crowded."

Kennedy followed her into the family room. Once inside, Freda closed and locked the door behind them. Then, going to a bookcase on the far side of the room, she removed a single volume and took a seat. "Come here, sit by me. Abe, there are a few things I want to say to you. First, I don't blame you at all for what happened to my Ira. I know you were always there making sure he was safe. God only knows that the only reason I was ever able to sleep alone at night was that I knew he was with you."

"Freda, you have no idea how badly I needed to hear that, I just couldn't live with myself if I thought you blamed me."

"Well, I don't, and neither would Ira, so stop blaming yourself," she said, holding his hand tighter. "Abe, as far as my husband was concerned, he was closer to you than to his own brother, and he would want you to be okay about this for Marlene and A. J."

"I know, and I will be, just as soon as I get the bastard that did this."

Freda stared intently at him, and although she didn't speak, her eyes said it all. She, like any other widow, wanted to know.

"I'm getting close, Freda, I really am. We think we know who did it. I'm just putting the pieces together for the bust."

"I know you're doing your best," was all she said. Then she opened the book on her lap. "Here, take a look at this."

The detective took the book. Inside was a passbook for a savings account. On the inside flap were the names of Ira and Freda Murray, as well as a third: Abraham L. Kennedy, Jr.

"I don't understand," he said.

"Abe, I hope over the years you've come to realize how Ira and I feel about your family."

"Of course."

"You know that we never had a son, and even though Ira loves his daughters, well, he always looked at A. J. like one of his own," she explained.

"I'll say. He had more pictures in his wallet of the kid than I do." Kennedy smiled.

"Well, over the years he wanted to do something for him, so about ten years ago we set up this account for him, you know, to help with college, or however you want to use it."

Kennedy was stunned. He looked a second time at the bankbook. "Freda, there's a lot of money in here! We can't take this."

"Nonsense. You take it and use it for A. J."

"But what about your daughters?" he asked.

"What about them? One's a doctor and the other married one. They're both fine."

"What about you?" he asked.

"Not to worry."

"I don't know what to say," he began, as his pager went off. He jumped up, wondering if it had anything to do with Ira's killer. "Sorry, it looks like there's a problem back at the station. I probably oughta get back."

"Don't say anything," Freda said. She smiled sadly. "Go do your work."

With that they got up and walked to the front door. Frieda waited with the detective while he put on his coat. As he opened the door to leave, she followed him outside in the cold morning air.

Afraid she would catch her death of cold, Kennedy tried to be brief. "I'll stop by later, and I promise to let you know as soon as we make a collar. Are you sure I can't do anything for you, Freda?"

"Abe, I need to say one more thing before you go. God, please forgive me for what I'm about to do. I know there was something funny about the way Ira was killed. I know because he's been talking about this weird case you two have been working on all week. His last case. It breaks my heart."

"Freda, I promise you."

"Abe, don't patronize me just because I'm old and supposed to be some helpless widow," she said.

"I'm sorry."

"I know, you're only trying to protect me, but I need you to listen to me."

"Go ahead," he said, walking back up the steps to her.

"The people who killed my Ira are probably after you next. There's nothing you or anyone else can do to bring him back. I know that, but the one thing you can do is to make sure that Marlene doesn't end up alone for the rest of her life, like me.

"What I know in my heart is that Ira would want you to do whatever it takes to protect yourself and your family. Abe, what I'm telling you is to find the animals that killed my Ira and get them before they get you."

Up to that moment Kennedy was genuinely torn between tow-ing the line, trying to bring in Devon by the book, and opting for old-fashioned frontier-style justice. But Freda Murray's warning had changed all that. Finally, he understood that he really had no choice. It wasn't so much about vengeance as about self-preservation. For the first time in his career he was going to take off his badge to stop a killer. Mike Hanson, of all people, was right.

The time had come to either kill or be killed.

Chapter Forty

By the time Kennedy made it back to the station house, the place was in an absolute frenzy. Word had somehow leaked to the press that there was a serial killer out there killing young prostitutes, and the place was overrun with reporters and camera crews. To make matters worse, two women's groups and several members of the D.C. city council had shown up, sound bites prepared, ready to ride the coattails of the guys in the homicide squad.

After making his way through the gauntlet of media, Kennedy finally found the desk sergeant. "What the hell's going on?" he asked.

"Press finally figured out about the hooker killer out there. Must be a slow news day. Or maybe everyone's tired of hearing about the presidential race."

Kennedy groaned. "That's just great. Just what I need right now."

The desk sergeant looked sadly at Kennedy. "I'm sorry about Murray. He was a great guy. How's his wife holding up?"

"Okay. She'll be all right. You know how it is."

The desk sergeant nodded. He leaned closer to Kennedy and started talking in a low voice. "They're trying to keep this quiet, but I just heard that some silk-stalking lawyer has arrived, some K Street asshole name Falmont, Arthur Falmont. It looks like he's representing the guy you're trying to catch. The hooker killer."

"What are you talking about?" Kennedy shouted. "Did the killer turn himself in?" His mind was reeling. He couldn't imagine Oliver Devon ever doing such a thing.

"No, Falmont is here to discuss the terms of his client's surrender," the sergeant said, sneering with disgust.

"Arthur Falmont, Esquire," Kennedy muttered. "Shit." Kennedy, like most other cops in the department, knew Falmont's reputation. He was generally regarded as the best criminal defense lawyer in the city—particularly if his client was guilty. Kennedy had followed several cases in which Falmont had represented especially reprehensible criminals: a blue-blooded English teacher who had molested countless students at a prep school, a serial rapist who preyed on illegal aliens at a downtown hotel, and a wealthy doctor who routinely violated his female patients while under anesthesia. Falmont got them all off—less on technicalities than by completely overwhelming the pitifully undermanned prosecutor's office with countless exhibits, psychological workups, jury selection specialists, and highly paid expert witnesses. Kennedy had observed that Falmont liked to represent two types of men: wealthy guilty clients, and notorious guilty clients. He was a large, florid, and ostentatious man and a relentless self-promoter. He made tons of money off his rich clients, and had written books about representing his less wealthy but not less despicable ones. He was a regular on daytime talk shows, the more sensational the better.

"Do we have a name?" Kennedy asked.

"No, nothing. I heard Falmont won't say a word about who it is," the desk sergeant said. "But sooner or later, we'll know." He voice turned bitter. "The guy will come in, on his own terms, with fancy-ass Falmont representing him."

Kennedy just walked away.

Damned if Hanson wasn't exactly right. There would be no justice if they didn't take matters into their own hands.

Having read Kennedy's note, Hanson and Danielle piled back into bed to "stay put" as the detective had instructed. About 2:30 P.M.,

Hanson awoke, jumped into the shower and, despite Danielle's protests, headed out to meet Griffin.

After first placing a call to his buddy's pager from the hotel lobby, Hanson grabbed a cab in the direction of Capitol Hill. Just past the Rayburn Building, he got out and walked a couple of blocks and hailed a second cab. Once inside, he made the unusual request to be driven to Dupont Circle via Constitution Avenue, a route three times longer than usual.

Along the way, he stopped at his bank and withdrew $10,000. He hailed another taxi to Dupont Circle. He didn't think anyone was following him, but he figured it was better to be safe than sorry. Just below N Street, Hanson got out and slipped into the eclectic crowd of businessmen, street people, and bicycle messengers at the park at the Circle. He sat on a bench across from the fountain, eyes scanning the crowd for anything out of the ordinary, and then quickly walked across to Kramerbooks & Cafe at 17th Street. There, seated alone at the bar, his face buried in the latest issue of the *New Republic*, was Tom Griffin. "Boo!" said Hanson as he poked his old friend in the ribs.

"Mike!" Griffin jumped. "Man, am I glad to see you. I thought they'd have killed you by now."

Hanson stared. Griffin's face was bruised and he had a painful-looking black eye. "My god, Griff, who did this to you?"

"The guys who were going through my apartment, obviously looking for something," said Griffin. "I went by my place on the way here and interrupted them."

"You what? Are you fucking nuts? I told you not to go near there," Hanson said.

"Well, I did, okay, Michael?" said Griffin. "Anyway, the bastards kicked the shit out of me. Luckily, my landlord and his two sons just happened to drop by and scared them off. Now I look as bad as you do."

"Trust me on this one Griff, you look a whole lot worse. My guess is that they were only following you because they've linked you to me. They're probably watching us right now," Hanson said, looking around nervously.

Griffin looked around too. "I guess I'm not really cut out for this shit."

"Relax, will ya?" said Hanson. "Griff, do you still have the gun I gave you?"

"Armed and dangerous," said Griffin, pulling back his jacket to reveal the gun tucked in his waistband.

"Wonderful. Now hand it to me under the table, slowly, before you shoot yourself."

After taking the gun, Hanson reached in his pocket. "Here, take this," he said, handing Griffin a fist full of bills.

"Michael, there must be over a thousand dollars here. What am I supposed to do with it?" Griffin asked.

Hanson leaned over to Griffin and whispered, "In a few minutes I'm gonna get up and bolt out of here. Watch to see if anyone follows me, but don't do anything."

Griffin nodded.

"As soon as I'm out of sight, I want you to head out the back. Grab a taxi and get out of the city. You know, Chevy Chase or Bethesda or something. Check into a hotel. Don't use the phone or talk to anybody. Just stay out of sight. I'll try to page you, but just in case we don't connect, this thing's supposed to go down about nine o'clock, which means you need to be somewhere in the vicinity of the Hamilton no later than eight. Make sure your pager's on and bring the car. The car's still okay, isn't it?"

"Mike, I'm afraid I have bad news."

"What are you talking about?"

"It's your car, Mike. The Chinese have killed your car. It's dead."

"You are such an asshole. Really, how is it?"

"Don't worry Mike, your precious Jaguar is fine." Griffin grinned. "I had them put cardboard over the bullet holes. It looks almost previously owned."

Hanson grimaced. "My poor car. It's only two years old."

"Relax, it's safer right now than we are. It's parked in an underground lot on K Street."

"Okay then. In a few seconds I'm gonna get up. Give me a minute or so, then haul ass!" said Hanson.

"Be careful, Mike," warned Griffin.

"I intend to," he said, slapping his best friend on the shoulder as he got up from the bar stool and walked out of the restaurant.

Getting lucky, Hanson was able to hail the first taxi that came his way. As he expected, no sooner had his cab pulled away from the curb, than a black, late-model sedan appeared out of nowhere and pulled up closely behind the cab. As the two cars maneuvered through the dense traffic, the showers that had been predicted all day finally began to fall, just in time for the evening rush hour. "Head up Mass. Ave.," said Hanson.

The cab driver shook his head. "Excuse me, sir," he began. "But that will take us right into the demonstration."

"Just do it," insisted Hanson, knowing full well that they were headed straight for the weekly anti-Saddam protest at the Islamic Center. Massachusetts Avenue would be a virtual parking lot. Hanson smiled to himself. He would never have guessed that someday he would literally be counting on Washington gridlock to save his life.

With the sedan right on their tail, Hanson's cab approached Embassy Row. By the time they reached the turnoff to Rock Creek Park, traffic was bumper to bumper, moving at a snail's pace in what had become a steady downpour. Hanson kept craning his neck to see the driver, but he wore a low hat again, and the rain made it visibility difficult. When thunder shook the cab, and lightning cut across the sky, Hanson decided he was ready. He handed the driver a twenty and leaped from the cab, sprinting back down Massachusetts toward Dupont, passing the sedan along the way. Zigzagging like a halfback through traffic in the driving rain, Hanson looked over his shoulder to see a large figure pursuing him.

As Hanson turned right on 21st Street, salvation appeared to him in the form of a Metrobus, which came perilously close to hitting him as it pulled over. Wasting no time, he climbed on board and quickly moved to the back. There, he took a seat and peered out the bus's back window, where he could see the solitary figure sprinting frantically down Massachusetts in a vain attempt to locate him. To Hanson's dismay, he still couldn't identify him. He was tall, and looked relatively fit, but that's all Hanson could see. It was possible it was Devon, though Hanson doubted it. More likely it was one of his hired men. Lonnie came to mind. It was even possible that it was the Chief.

Hanson stayed on the bus long enough for his heart rate to slow to normal. After about twenty minutes he got off a block and a half away from the Hamilton. Arriving at the hotel's entrance, he scanned the street for any sign of trouble. His watch said 5:47 P.M. Satisfied that, at least for the moment, he had successfully eluded all those trying to kill him, he entered the building. Just to be on the safe side, he avoided the elevator, opting instead to climb the stairwell until he reached the eighth floor. Proceeding cautiously, a soaking wet Hanson made his way to room 821 and, looking very little like the man of Danielle's dreams, he knocked on her door.

After checking through the peephole, Danielle opened the door and, throwing her arms around his neck, said "Michael, thank God it's you. I've been so worried."

All of a sudden, as he took her in his arms, Hanson realized that risking one's life did have some benefits. His bliss was short-lived, however, as Detective Kennedy peered out from behind the door.

"I hate to break this up, but would you two mind getting your asses back inside?" said the detective. Realizing that they were sitting ducks out in the hallway, Hanson and Danielle quickly complied. Once everyone was back in the room, the detective locked and deadbolted the door. "So Hanson, how the hell is it you're not dead?"

"What's got a bug up your ass, Detective?" asked Hanson.

"You wanna know what's bugging me? Fine, I'll tell you," Kennedy began angrily. "First, you did exactly the opposite of what I told you, going out playing cowboy. That by itself was just stupid. Even worse, you not only put yourself in danger, but left Miss Harris here, completely unprotected."

"I can take care of myself, Detective, thank you very much," said Danielle, defensively.

"Funny, that's the same thing my dead partner used to say."

"Detective, look, first of all, I didn't leave Danielle unguarded. And I didn't go out playing cowboy, as you put it. After thinking it over, I figured that if we were gonna pull this thing off, we needed Griffin's help."

"Well, that's just fucking great! Now you're running the whole fucking investigation."

"Come on, Abe, I didn't mean it that way," said Hanson.

"Hanson, you may trust Griffin with your life, but does he trust you with his? Have you even bothered to tell him how much danger he's in?" pressed Kennedy.

Hanson decided to change the subject, thinking of Griffin's black eye. "I know I need a drink. Anyone want to join me?" he said as he poured himself a Dewars on the rocks. He took a long sip and said, "Detective?"

"Don't play with me, Hanson. The fact is, I'm just not all that comfortable with how you want to handle this whole thing. I'm a cop, for chrissakes! I don't give a damn about CIA agents or drug cartels or any of that shit. All I care about is getting the sonofabitch who killed my partner. If I'm not gonna bring Devon in on murder charges, I might as well just take the bastard out myself!"

Hanson's eyes narrowed. "So, Abe, what the hell is this really about? What's going on here?" asked Hanson.

Kennedy took a couple of steps and collapsed into a chair. "Hanson, it looks like the killer's hired a hot-shit lawyer, some bastard named Falmont."

"Arthur Falmont?" asked Hanson.

"Yeah, you know him?"

"Intimately."

"How?"

"It's an unbelievably long story," said Hanson, scornfully. "Falmont is a major scumbag."

"That's one thing we agree on," said Kennedy. "Look, I need some air. I'm gonna head down and check out the lobby one more time. It might be a good idea if you two order up some room service. We've got a long night ahead of us—and Hanson, take a shower, you look like a drowned rat," he said, smiling, as he started for the door.

"Hey, Abe," said Hanson.

"What now?"

"Thanks for not shooting me," he said.

"Don't tempt me, Michael," said the detective as he walked out the door.

Chapter Forty-one

With only a few hours remaining, Hanson still had some unfinished business, not the least of which involved winning a presidential election. While trying to hail a cab, he grabbed the cell phone from his breast pocket and punched in a number. It rang several times. Finally, someone picked up. Hanson listened for a second and then said, "Bundlemeister! It's Mike Hanson calling I'm sorry about the short notice, but I need to talk with you real bad. . . . Bundles, listen, I know it sounds crazy, but how would you like to make a million dollars?" he asked. "No, I'm not kidding. Good, I'll be right over! What's the building called again? The Cairo. Great, see you in a flash."

Minutes later, Hanson arrived, without having had to provide the cabbie with so much as an address. "This building is some kind of haughty-taughty place, huh?" said Hanson as he paid the fare.

"The most expensive address in town," said the cabbie, who looked at Hanson as though he really didn't belong. Hanson entered and asked the concierge to direct him to David Falcone's unit. What seemed like an otherwise reasonable question was met with a rather unexpected answer. "Mr. Falcone doesn't own a unit in this building, sir. . . . Mr. Falcone owns the building. He resides in the penthouse, of course."

"Of course," said Hanson, somewhat amazed. "Why don't you buzz Mr. Falcone and let him know that Mr. Hanson is on the way up."

"Very good, sir. If you wait, I'll announce you."

After about a minute of waiting in a lobby fancier than most people's dream homes, Hanson was cleared to go up. As he rode up a few floors on the elevator he suddenly noticed that he was alone with his thoughts for the first time in days. With the passage of each floor, and the penthouse only seconds away, he realized that finally, after years in the business, he was knowingly about to cross the line. He knew damned well that the Democrats had no chance of legally raising the money needed for the media buy. Without it, they were screwed. For Hanson it was an ethical Rubicon. Either accept defeat or go to Plan B, and Plan B meant dirty tricks. The dirtier, the better. The part that bothered Hanson the most was that the choice was a no-brainer.

Once he arrived at the top floor, he exited the elevator to find that the Bundlemeister's flat occupied not only the penthouse, but the entire floor. Ringing the doorbell of the only door on the hallway, he waited anxiously. After several seconds the door was answered by a gorgeous young blonde in a green silk robe. "Hi, there," she said in a bubbly voice. "You must be David's friend. My name is Nikki. Come on in. Forgive the mess, we weren't expecting company. . . ."

Mike entered to find a flat decorated a lot like how most people would picture the Playboy mansion. "David is in the shower. I'll tell him you're here. He'll be out in a jif," she said, walking down the hallway.

"Oh, I'd say I've got a jif to spare," said Hanson, in awe of all the scenery. "Perhaps even two jifs," said Hanson, spying at least two living rooms, a formal dining room, a den, and at least four televisions. Does everybody make more money than me? he thought.

Nikki returned, announcing, "David said to make yourself at home. Can I get you anything?"

As tempting as the offer was, Hanson resisted. He had to keep a clear head. "So, are you and Bundles an item?" he asked, making small talk.

"I still can't get used to that nickname," she said, laughing. "And no, I'm just one of David's harem."

Hanson started to speak when a familiar voice interrupted. "Mikey, Mikey," came the sound of the Bundlemeister from down the hall. Falcone, still wet and in a less revealing silk robe than his young concubine, was caught just a little off guard by the surprise visitor. "So what's up? It isn't every day I'm honored with an actual visit to my home. You're here uninvited, although not unwelcome. So what's wrong? Who's being indicted? If it's me, I'm gonna be pissed," he joked.

"No one yet, Bundles," said Hanson. "But the campaign needs your help, and well, it isn't exactly . . . well, you know . . ."

"Legal? Is *legal* the word you're looking for, Mike?"

"Yes, *legal* would be the correct term," said Hanson.

"If you don't mind me saying so, you look like shit. So what are the stakes?"

Hanson knew time was running out. "Thurman's gonna endorse the Republican ticket Monday morning. We want to fuck it up."

The Bundlemeister was amused. "Sounds good to me. Just tell me what you need and you got it."

Hanson loved David Falcone, the ultimate go-to guy. "We want to wire-transfer ten million dollars from an offshore bank into the Thurman for President bank account."

"Oh sure, piece of cake. Got it on you?"

"Yes, I do," said Hanson. "Actually, I have a whole lot more . . . but most of it's in the bank."

The Bundlemeister was taken aback. He looked around. "Come on, Mike, who's wearing the wire? I know it's not Nikki, she's almost naked. What's up, Mike?"

"Here, look at this," said Hanson, handing Falcone an ATM printout from his bank account.

"Jesus Christ, you're not kidding!"

"I have another ten million in my corporate account," Hanson continued. "For this to work, we also need the bank account numbers of the Thurman for President campaign."

"That's it?" he inquired.

"Yeah."

"Which one?"

"I don't really care. One will do," said Hanson.

"Done," said Falcone, with a shrug of his shoulders.

Hanson leaned over, shaking his head. "Excuse me, but I just gotta know, Bundles, you're on our Finance Board. How many Thurman campaign account numbers do you have?"

"All of 'em," he said.

"How?"

"Mike, don't be so dense. I have my people contribute small amounts to everybody. When the checks clear, the account numbers are on the back of the check."

"But why would you do that?" asked Hanson, incredulous.

"Oh, just in case we need to trigger an audit or tip off the FEC about some irregularities they might have missed. Or in case somebody like you asks me for a favor. Go have a seat in the den and I'll pull up a couple on the computer. Nikki!" he called out. "Get my friend a drink. Scotch okay?"

"Scotch is perfect," said Hanson, concluding that abstinence was highly overrated.

As the Bundlemeister disappeared somewhere in the cavernous apartment to retrieve the account numbers, Hanson and Nikki retired to the bar. "He's a scary guy, isn't he?" said Nikki as she poured a pair of drinks.

"Not really. He loves us. He's on our side," said Hanson. "A fact for which I thank god daily."

"You ever stopped to think what life would be like if he wasn't?"

"Then I guess I'd have to switch sides," joked Hanson.

Soon, the Bundlemeister returned, laptop in hand. "Good, you've got your drinks. Give me a second while I plug this in and hook up the modem. While I'm at it, could I ask if there is anything special in this for the ol' Bundlemeister?"

"Like I said on the phone. A million dollars."

"Come on, Mike, quit fucking with me."

"Is that gonna be enough, Bundles? I mean, I know you're going to a lot of trouble for us."

Falcone didn't know what to make of Hanson. He regarded him as one of his best best friends and trusted him completely. It was all just so unexpected. "Yeah, Mike. A million bucks will do just fine. But I'm warning you, if we end up as cellmates in fucking Lewisburg, I'm the man. Got it?"

"I wouldn't have it any other way," he joked as he blew Falcone a kiss.

"By the way, does Griff know about this?"

"Not enough to get indicted."

"Well, lucky him. Okay, let's get started. You want to transfer ten million dollars. I assume because that's about how much the Thurman campaign is in debt. Correct?"

"Right you are."

"Okay, from where?"

"From this account in the Caymans," said Hanson, handing him the wire transfer slip from his initial fee from Devon.

"Oliver Devon? So you are gonna be the one to kill the Tyrannosaurus rex, huh, Mikey? Well good for you."

"Will that work?"

"Okay so far. Is there ten million bucks in this account?"

"My guess would be no. But I can get you ten million by morning if you can make this happen."

"Hmm. Here's what I can do. I'll call one of my guys in Hong Kong as soon as the sun is up. It will already be tomorrow there. On my marker, he'll arrange to move ten million into the Caymans account on Monday morning. Once that's done, we'll move it into the Thurman account. It shouldn't be a problem."

"When can you get us copies of the wire transfer transmittal slips?"

"About two seconds after the transactions go down. I'll e-mail them to you by seven-thirty Monday morning."

"Well, that about covers it. Thanks, Bundles, you're the best."

"What can I say? . . . It's what I do."

Part Five

"The illegal we can do immediately, the unconstitutional takes a little longer."

—Henry Kissinger

Chapter Forty-two

When Hanson called earlier that day, Devon was encouraged. He'd worked his magic easily on dozens of younger players in the past, but Hanson was a hard case. Sure, Hanson was a little older, and presumably somewhat wiser than most, but still unusually tough to impress. After all the fine wine, the fancy lunches, the Cuban cigars, not to mention millions of dollars in wire transfers, it was about time he came around.

At exactly 9:00 P.M., Devon arrived at the President's Box at the John F. Kennedy Center for the Performing Arts, a spectacular, bleached-white monolith sandwiched between the Watergate and the Memorial Bridge. Following Hanson's instructions, he'd stopped by the will-call booth on the way to pick up his ticket, and, having been informed by an extremely pushy usher of his tardiness for the evening's performance, was immediately escorted upstairs to the most exclusive theatrical perch in Washington. For Devon, a guest in the Box on countless occasions, this was a humiliating experience. Not because of the indignity of fetching his own ticket or the uncharacteristic rudeness of Kennedy Center personnel; but rather because, the instant Devon arrived at the Center, it dawned on him why Hanson had selected this setting. The President's Box, elegant in its decor, complete with velvet seats, brocade framed portraits of recent presidents, and paneled mahogany dating back to the days of Eleanor Roosevelt is, by design, a dimly lit, somewhat narrow cocoon in the middle of the 4000-seat concert hall. Accordingly, it offers theatergoers the unique privilege of complete visibility and almost total privacy. What's more, there is only one way in and one way out. Ordinarily, all guests are screened through the White House Office of Public Liaison and are required to be present at the Box no later than thirty minutes prior to all performances. Upon arrival, they are met by someone who appears to be an usher but who is really a member of the Uniformed Secret Service. Ironically, once a guest enters the Box, they have virtual carte blanche to take advantage of the many niceties that go along with one of politics' more enviable perks—including a fully stocked wet bar offering a wide assortment of aperitifs, gourmet finger food, as well as a healthy selection of desserts to satiate one's sweet tooth. But best of all, the fact that the Box had been soundproofed back in the 80's to prevent nearby patrons from listening in on a president's conversations, offered yet another advantage. The actual sound from a live performance could be heard through a high-fidelity set of speakers in the rear of the box. Translation: unless a guest stood and shouted at the top of his or her lungs, they could be as raucous as they liked and still not risk offending nearby theater patrons.

As Devon stood outside the entrance to the Box, he was overwhelmed by a feeling of anxiety. He tried to keep himself calm. This was all just a mistake. Some carelessness, some miscalculations on his part. Nothing he couldn't fix, he told himself. Devon wasn't used to losing, and he didn't intend to end his lifetime winning streak now. Especially not against a loser like Michael Hanson. Yet, as Devon stood alone and prepared to enter, his instincts told him to be cautious.

There were eight seats in the private box, set up in two rows of four. Once inside, Devon found it difficult to make out the images in the dim light. As best he could tell, Hanson, and a large black man whom he didn't recognize at first, occupied two of the seats in the back row.

"Nice of you to show up, Oliver," began Hanson in a soft voice, not certain until that very moment that his nemesis would take the bait. "Please, take a seat. Right here, in front of me if you don't mind." No sooner had Devon complied than Hanson leaned forward and discreetly placed the barrel of the nine-millimeter in the small of Devon's back. "Oliver, I think you know my friend, Detective Abe Kennedy of the Metro police . . ."

Staying cool in the face of enormous pressure was Devon's forte. It didn't matter whether it was politics, business, or even a negotiation with a special prosecutor, the rule was always the same: never, ever show fear. Tonight would be no exception, despite the fact that the detective was glaring at him with a palpable hatred that made Devon queasy. He coolly eyed Kennedy. "Whoever you are, it is obvious that you have no idea with whom you are dealing."

"Shut your fucking mouth!" ordered Kennedy. "Or I swear I'll blow your goddamn head off," he said, driving the point home by pulling back his suit jacket to reveal the glimmer of his unholstered, nickel-plated service revolver.

"When I'm through with you, you'll wish you were never born," Devon retorted. Then, looking at the detective closer, he said, "Now I recognize you. You're that homicide detective who's been making himself a pain in my ass. I thought I had you killed."

Kennedy went rigid. "Pay attention, you sonofabitch!" he said through gritted teeth as he went for his gun, placing it squarely between Devon's ribs. "I told you to keep your mouth shut." His trigger finger wavered, as he thought about Ira.

"Abe, keep the goddamn gun out of sight!" admonished Hanson.

"What exactly is it you want, Detective?" asked Devon, without a trace of nervousness.

"What Detective Kennedy wants is five minutes alone with the man who killed his partner. As I understand it, that would be you," said Hanson. "Fortunately for you, Oliver, my agenda is more ambitious, which means you get to live a little while longer. Have a seat, the National Symphony is about to start the "Funeral March" from Wagner's *Twilight of the Gods*. I'm sorry it's not something more hip, like *Rent.*"

Devon's jaw dropped. It was clear he'd underestimated his opponent. Hanson either had incredible balls, or had lost his mind.

Hanson smiled. He knew that Devon, despite being one of the most powerful men in the world, was nothing more than a bully. As the cadence of the Prussian rhythms rose in the auditorium, Hanson said, "Oliver, let me make a couple of things real clear. If you get lucky, you may end up killing me, but until you do, I'm running things. Got it?"

Devon started to get up, but was quickly restrained by Kennedy. With the detective's powerful hand holding him in his seat, he hissed, "You're dead, Hanson! *Dead!*"

"Oliver, let's cut out the macho shit, it's really getting us nowhere," said Hanson.

Devon was frustrated. He was used to giving orders, not taking them. As much as he hated to admit it, he knew the upstart was right. Hanson, indeed, was calling the shots. For the moment, Devon was helpless. "Okay, Michael, you're in control. Happy now? Why don't you show me something tangible for once?"

"That depends on what you mean by tangible."

"You could start by delivering one Danielle Harris, like I asked. On the other hand, if this is just some kind of cheap shakedown . . ."

"Oliver, you insult me. This is a very, very expensive shakedown, in case you haven't noticed."

Despite the fact that a gun was pointed right in his back, Devon would not be intimidated. The fact was, he had grown sick of Hanson's game, not to mention his condescending attitude. "Michael, I warn you one last time not to overplay your hand. I mean, there is no reason to get emotional. Business is business. You saw your chance to make a big score and you went for it, albeit somewhat recklessly. To be perfectly frank, I'm actually a little impressed."

Out of the corner of his eye, Detective Kennedy looked at Hanson, trying not to be too obvious. The plan was going better than expected. Devon seemed to think this whole thing was a naked grab for power and profit by Hanson. The good news was that the sonofabitch was playing right into their hands, the bad news was that they were running out of time—they had to finish their transaction before the end of the second act. Ever so subtly, the detective held out his arm so Hanson could see his wristwatch.

Without saying a word, Hanson acknowledged the signal with

a quick wink. "Good lord, Oliver, you aren't serious, are you? I mean you are talking to the ultimate bleeding heart liberal. I could never do something just for money."

"Then why are you doing this?" asked Devon impatiently.

Hanson took a deep breath and leaned up against a chair. The intensity of staying in character during the charade was taking its toll on him. Fortunately, his next statement didn't involve any acting. "See, Oliver, it's all pretty simple. I don't really give a shit about your money or your fucking power. That shit doesn't really impress me a whole lot, particularly when somebody comes by their wealth and position the way you did. Hell, if I was a billionaire I could buy half the elected guys in this town, the same as you."

"Michael, I'm surprised. I never thought I'd hear sour grapes coming out of your mouth," said Devon.

"Well, you shouldn't be. After twenty years in this business, the one thing I've learned is that all men are not created equal. All most people want in this town is a level playing field. Democrats, Republicans, it doesn't matter, we just want a chance to do our fucking job. But see, it never works out that way. Every time something bad happens in this town, the real bad guys walk. Watergate, Iran-Contra, the S&L scandal, they're all the same. Dozens of people have their careers ruined while guys like you sit back calling the shots, and no one can touch them. You know damned well that you're above the law, and you flaunt it. Most of the time you can get away with murder and no one ever makes you pay for your sins," said Hanson, growing angrier with every word. "But not this time!"

"And how do you propose to accomplish that, Michael?" asked Devon in a defiant tone.

"Simple. I've got something you want. And you're gonna pay dearly for it."

Devon was beside himself. Hanson was proving fearless. Knowing he was powerless to stop them, he instinctively began to issue threats. One in particular, concerning Kennedy's wife and child, provoked an unusually strong reaction by the detective.

"Are you threatening my family, motherfucker? Are you?" he said, nudging him with the barrel of the revolver.

"Come on, Abe, don't kill him yet. Wait until we get the fucking codes for chrissakes," lobbied Hanson as Kennedy focused his icy stare on the hapless Devon.

"The codes?" remarked Devon.

"That's right, the launch codes. We know all about Beijing, the Red Locust project, all your illegal shit."

"Well, well, well, Michael. We have been a busy boy, haven't we," said Devon. "All this time I thought you were just an extortionist. I had no idea that your goal was to become the next fucking 'Master of the Universe.' "

"Shit happens, what can I say?" said Hanson with a smirk on his face. "Now listen up, this is the way it's gonna be. You cooperate, that means you hand over the codes like a good boy, and I deliver the goods."

"Meaning?"

"Meaning not just Danielle Harris, but a whole lot more than you ever bargained for."

"Intriguing . . ."

"Groovy, I'm glad that I've finally got your attention," snapped Hanson. "But here's a dose of reality. Either you turn them over or Detective Kennedy takes you for a ride, a long ride. At the end of that ride you will be delivered to our new friend. What is it you call him? . . . Oh yeah, the Chief."

Devon was stunned. Hanson had said the one thing that could shake his facade. "How do you know the Chief?"

"I've been talking to his lawyer all day," said Kennedy, continuing the ruse. "A silk-stalking shyster named Falmont. Your buddy is scared shitless. My guess is that he's pissed you off in a major way. . . ."

"You're bluffing."

"Try us. Either we deliver you to him or we deliver him to you. Frankly, it doesn't matter that much to us, as long as we get results."

Sometimes in life, settling old debts takes precedent over practicality, or even reason. The Chief had killed the only thing Devon had ever loved, and making him pay was more important than anything. Just hearing the name was enough for Devon. "Let's get on with it. I find your offer extremely interesting. Deliver the goods as you say and you will have my full cooperation. You can name your price."

* * *

A full three hundred feet underground, the parking garage beneath the Manchester Presidential offered more than just a secure safe haven from downtown traffic. With its first four levels reserved for hotel guests, and a fifth for valet parking, the section designated as G-6 VIP was cordoned off by a security gate manned by a full-time armed guard. In certain sensitive situations, VIP patrons could even access the G-6 level via a little-known hidden entrance. The idea was simply to offer discreet access to Washington's most exclusive hotel. Notwithstanding the minor inconvenience that the lot was so far beneath the earth's surface that it qualified as a bomb shelter according to the Nuclear Regulatory Commission, hotel patrons at the Manchester could count on as much privacy as money could buy.

Shortly before ten o'clock, Messrs. Hanson, Kennedy, and Devon made their appearance, slowly trolling their way via rental car down the garage ramp. It was hard to tell which was more unpleasant for Devon—being the victim of a kidnapping or the ordeal of having to ride several blocks in a midsized Pontiac Bonneville. About, fifty feet down, they stopped as Detective Kennedy jumped out of the car and sprinted back several feet, blocking off the ramp with a long strip of yellow police tape, providing one last measure of insurance against interlopers. Quickly, he returned to the car, and the three headed on. Waiting for them at the bottom was supposed to be Peter Lisagor, who had arrived two hours earlier and made good use of his time, conducting a full sweep of the VIP level, evicting any unwanted vehicles in the process. Additionally, the inspector stopped in on the hotel's monitoring center and made sure that the closed-circuit television cameras that patrolled the perimeter of the building, as well as the entire garage, were dark for the next several hours. An FBI matter, he explained to the guard at the security desk.

As scripted, only three vehicles would be allowed on G-6: Hanson's rental, Danielle's BMW, and a black 1999 FWD Dodge Durango. By the time Hanson and crew showed up, the other two vehicles had already arrived through the secret VIP entrance, and were parked about a hundred feet apart in the darkest corners of the lot.

With no clue as to the ins and outs of running an ambush, a

drop, a handoff, a drug deal, or any other kind of meeting that involved large sums of money and illegal firearms, Hanson enlisted his new ally, Jack Walker, for advice. The truth was that the gristled old spook had only marginal faith in Hanson, and made it clear that he thought his plan was borderline insanity. Even so, he still offered a few time-tested pointers. According to agency guidelines, only two factors mattered: time and place. First, hold the meeting early enough so that bail money can be wired from the west coast or some other time zone, if necessary. Second, whatever location you choose, make it a home game. Make sure you know the site better than your enemy. The more familiar the turf, the greater the edge.

As the Pontiac came to a halt, Hanson spoke. "Detective, if you wouldn't mind babysitting Mr. Devon here for just a few minutes while I take a look see . . ."

"Not a problem," said Abe, his gun pointed at Devon's rib cage.

Slowly, Hanson got out of the driver's side of the car, warily scanning the dimly lit garage. He took a few tentative steps and, seeing that the BMW and the Durango were in place, looked around for any sign of Inspector Lisagor. At first, he saw nothing. This was not good. They had been very specific about where they would rendezvous. Lisagor was supposed to be right here waiting. Suddenly, the sound of footsteps coming toward him made the hair on the back of Hanson's neck stand up. He looked back and signaled Abe to be ready. Devon undoubtedly had his security people tail him both to the Kennedy Center and on to the hotel, that much was expected. What Hanson and company didn't know was how many. For him, this was about an 8.5 on the pucker factor. Anxiously, he massaged the barrel of his nine-millimeter, pointing the gun in the direction of the footsteps. Deep down, Hanson was terrified, virtually certain he didn't have the will to take the first shot. Hopefully, shooting back would come easier.

Then, without warning, a voice cried out.

"Hey, be careful where you point that thing. You could kill somebody waving it around like that," yelled the inspector.

His heart pounding and the rest of his body sweating in places that rarely sweat, Hanson screamed, "Where the hell have you been?"

"I ran into one of Devon's guys when I was securing the stair-wells. But don't worry, he won't be bothering us anymore."

"Are you okay?"

"Yeah, I'm fine. But we should get started. Before he passed out, Devon's guy said there is one more of his number on the hotel grounds."

"Passed out?"

"Believe me, Hanson, you don't need to know the details," he said. "Seriously, though, we probably haven't got a lot of time."

"I hear ya. Go roust Danielle and I'll signal Abe."

Hanson quickly returned to the car, opening the rear door to the Pontiac. "Showtime, fellas," he said, reaching his hand in and pulling Devon out by the arm. "Come on, Oliver, I know a whole lot of people that have been just dying to meet you."

"I'm counting on it," he replied.

"Everything secure?" asked Kennedy.

"According to Lisagor it is," began Hanson. "Hey, by the way, are you sure that guy is really a postal inspector?—I mean, he's kind of scary."

Abe took a deep breath. "Hanson, I'm not sure anybody is really who they say they are anymore. Anyway, let's do this!" he said, pointing the gun at Devon.

Hanson nodded. "Okay, Oliver. Listen close. The three of us are going to walk to the middle of the garage. A few seconds later, I will produce Danielle Harris as you have requested. You will then keep your part of the bargain and disclose the location of the launch codes," he said firmly. "If at any point you bluff or even hesitate for a second, then Detective Kennedy will take over. Got it?"

Devon just stared ahead, saying nothing, to the complete annoyance of the detective. "Signify yes by saying yes, you sonofabitch," ordered Abe. "Do you understand?"

Glaring at him, Devon muttered, "Yes, goddamnit, I understand."

"Okay, now that we're all working so well together, let's take a walk," said Hanson.

Together, the three walked slowly to the center of the garage. There they waited for Danielle's signal. A few moments later, the BMW flashed its headlights twice. After taking a moment for one last look around, Hanson waved them over. First came Inspector Lisagor, looking like a teenager wearing his father's oversized trenchcoat. A few steps behind him Danielle strode confidently, dressed to perfection in winter white, head held high, eyes straight ahead. As she came closer, Hanson looked at Devon's face, seeing him shrink before his very eyes.

Once they were assembled, Hanson began. "Okay, people, let's get started. Oliver, I believe you and Ms. Harris are well acquainted."

"Danielle, I see that Washington agrees with you," said Devon, awkwardly.

Instantly, she laughed. "That's certainly one way to look at it. And you, Oliver, how are things in the ever exciting world of the Devon Group?"

"Things will be going a whole lot better once I lose my escorts," he said, glancing in Kennedy's direction.

"In time, Ollie. In due time," said Hanson. "Now, as negotiated, Ms. Harris here has agreed to issue her resignation to the Select Committee, condemn any investigation concerning Chinese espionage in the United States, and accompany you anywhere you desire. All we want are the launch codes."

Devon couldn't take his eyes off Danielle even for a second. In a resolute tone, he said, "As soon as Danielle and I are safely aboard one of my jets to a destination of my choosing, I will provide you with the codes. Not one second before."

"Oliver, I warned you not to do this," said Hanson.

"I'm not doing anything other than covering my flank," he said.

Hanson began to walk around in an agitated fashion, screaming profanities. "Goddamn you, Oliver, goddamn you! This could have all been so simple. Unfortunately, now I have to go to Plan B."

"I'm impressed, Michael, I wouldn't have figured you were sharp enough to have a Plan B," snapped Devon.

Hanson continued his angry rant, actually glad that Devon was going to make this easy for him. "Oliver, let's start with some introductions. Meet Postal Inspector Henry Lisagor," he said, gesturing to his right. "Inspector, meet the man who is responsible for ordering the slashings of the Weisel collection at the Louvre, as well as those at the Met, the Hyde, and all of the others."

"I didn't give the orders directly, Michael."

"Cut the crap, Ollie. You were the brains behind the operation, and you know it," said Hanson.

"Good enough for me," said Lisagor. "Mr. Devon, under my authority as a United States Postal Inspector I am charging you with twenty-two counts of trespassing, one hundred fifty-nine counts of vandalism, seventy-one counts of income tax evasion, and one count of unlawful flight to avoid prosecution."

"Go ahead, inspector. Take your best shot. Over the years, I've had my fill of FBI agents, U.S. Attorneys, special prosecutors, even a couple of television networks. You want me, come get me, you little pissant," said Devon defiantly.

The inspector didn't flinch. "You have the right to remain silent."

Hanson and Kennedy looked at each other. Both their faces had stunned expressions. Obviously Inspector Lisagor was taking this case much more seriously than he was letting on.

"Hey, Inspector, could you lighten up just a little?" said Hanson.

"Yeah, like at least until we get our hands on the codes," added Abe.

Lisagor stepped back, somewhat contrite. "I'm sorry guys, it's just that I've been chasing these guys for ten months. If you two can't finish the job, I will. . . . For now I think I'm gonna go up top and check out the perimeter."

"Probably a good idea," said the detective.

As Lisagor made his way up the ramp, Hanson turned to Devon. "Like I said before, this could have been easy. But since you insist on being a prick, let me continue," he said, motioning in the direction of the black Durango. Almost as soon as Hanson made the gesture, a large, hulking figure emerged from the SUV. For several uncomfortable moments, the figure lumbered through the dark light towards them. As he got closer, the click of the man's hiking boots grew louder, until the glimmer of the dim light on the porcelain dome of his bald head became visible.

"Yo, Hanson. It's a 'war party,' baby!"

"Seltzer, my man!"

Rick Seltzer walked into the small group and grabbed Hanson with both arms, almost picking him up right off the ground.

"Good to see you, brother. So where's the prick?"

Hanson, who had little experience being hoisted in the air by bodybuilders, humbly said, "The prick would be the man with the silver-gray hair standing right over there."

With that, Seltzer returned Hanson to the ground and turned, leveling a dead stare right between Devon's eyes.

"Oliver, this is Rick Seltzer. He's a reporter newly assigned to the national desk at the *Post*. Before that he worked in what you might call the alternative press. You know, rags like the *City Paper*, the *Advocate*, the *Blade* . . ."

"With that kind of a resume, I don't think I have much to say to your friend," said Devon.

"Actually, I'm here for an interview," said Seltzer.

"Is that so?"

"Yeah, that's so. I'm doing a profile on one of the most powerful men in the country. He's the kind of guy who is equally comfortable with Presidents, Popes, and prostitutes. But wait 'til you check out the back story. It turns out that this cat is this sick homophobe who kicked his own son out of his life just for being gay. According to my sources, this guy abandoned his own child when he found out he was HIV-positive. Care to comment on that, Mr. Devon?"

Devon looked at Hanson with disgust. "Is this honestly the best you can do? Do you think I care if some gay rag runs a story attacking me for being pro-family? Michael, as I'm sure you are aware, I don't really plan on staying in town that much longer."

"Oliver, would it change your mind if Rick disclosed his sources? I mean, between Danielle, Senator Kassendine, and me, the story begins to add up."

"So what if it does? I'll just deny it. Everyone thinks that my boy died of a drug overdose," said Devon defiantly. "Besides you liberals, who'll read the story anyway?"

"My guess is everybody," said Danielle, looking off into the darkness.

"Well, no dice. I've worked a lifetime on this deal and there is nothing you or anybody else can say. I will not be intimidated, do you hear me?" Devon warned.

And then, just as Devon seemed completely emboldened, it came.

"Dad . . ."

In seconds, the group fell silent. Although Hanson and Kennedy had no way of knowing if the voice was authentic, the look on Devon's face said it all. It was one of absolute terror.

Again the voice sounded. "Dad, is that you?"

As a shaken Devon turned, he saw a miracle emerge from the darkness.

"Billy?" he said.

Even though Hanson knew what was coming, he really couldn't believe his eyes. Oliver Devon's humanity was about to be tested once and for all. Coming towards them was a handsome young man about thirty years of age, looking to be the spitting image of Oliver Devon, minus at least twenty-five years and twenty-five pounds.

"But, the last time I saw you, you were . . ."

"Dying," he said, as he walked past his father, putting his arm around Danielle. "Came pretty close that time. But what can I say? Protease inhibitors and AIDS cocktails did the trick. My T cell count is over five hundred . . ."

Both Hanson and Kennedy marveled at how the boy's existence riveted Devon's persona. This was truly his Achilles heel. "Oliver, I would have to say that this changes things a bit. . . ."

"Hanson, pardon me for being blunt, but how is this any of your fucking business?"

"Allow me to explain," interrupted Rick Seltzer. "As a journalist, this whole psychodrama is my fucking business. See, when this thing started out, it was strictly inside, maybe A-8 to say A-15 of the *Post*, maybe even Metro or Style. But now, with the arrival here of young Mr. Devon, I think we're talking more like special to *USA Today*."

"Don't forget a book deal with serial rights to *Time* or *Newsweek*," said Hanson.

"Hell, this will be the first time I've outed a whole family!" exclaimed Seltzer.

At this point, Devon was desperate, in search of any port in the storm. "Danielle, please, can't you help me stop this?"

Danielle took a long hard look at her ex. In so many ways he used to impress her, but now he seemed crippled, a shell of the man who once controlled Washington. He was broken, and she was the one who had administered the fatal blow. Strangely, it made her sad. "Devon, the only way to keep this quiet is to co-operate with them," she said. "I beg you, please just give them what they want. Otherwise, they will kill you."

"And you, son. What is it you want from me?"

"*Son.* It's been a long time since anybody called me that. Honestly, all I wanted to do was see you one last time," he said, appearing to get a lump in his throat. "I'm sorry, but I wanted to hang out with the guy who taught me to play ball, who used to be my best friend. But don't worry, I don't really expect anything anymore. Hell, last time we saw each other, you said I was dead to you."

"Man, Oprah's gonna love this one," said Seltzer.

For several seconds, Devon looked like a dead man walking. With the detective's gun still trained on him, he moved slowly. He was sweating profusely and appeared about to faint. He looked like a man who was about to lose everything. "Hanson, would you mind telling your friend there to point that thing somewhere else?" he asked plaintively.

"Waddaya say, Abe?"

Reluctantly, the detective backed away a few inches, giving Devon slightly more breathing space. "All right, let's have some answers."

"Oliver, its simple. All a man really has is his family and his reputation," explained Hanson. "Now, to me it's pretty obvious that you've destroyed any semblance of family you might have had. Do you really want the Devon named dragged through the mud, your deepest, darkest secrets exposed like that? I don't think so. You give us what we want and I have Rick kill the story. Otherwise your life becomes a public spectacle."

Devon began to speak, but realized there were no clever words left. It was in that instant that he became familiar with defeat. "The account codes are on several CDs in a briefcase at National Airport," he said through gritted teeth.

"Which one?"

"The American terminal, number 007."

"Stop fucking with us," said an irritated detective as he pressed his weapon against Devon's throat.

"I'm telling you the truth, that's the number of the locker. One of my operatives has a sick sense of humor."

"Well, that's it then," said Hanson.

"Not quite," said Devon. "Now what about your end of the bargain? I demand that you release Ms. Harris to my custody and that you disclose the whereabouts of the Chief."

Hanson couldn't believe this guy. He had balls the size of coconuts. "Not so fast," he said. "What about the key?"

"Be smart, don't make us get ugly," said Abe menacingly.

"Detective, I've indulged your frontier justice approach for the better part of an hour. Frankly, I'm getting just a little bored with it all. I don't know anything about a key," said Devon.

"Hold this for me," said Kennedy as he handed his service revolver to Hanson. Then, removing his jacket and rolling up his sleeves, he paused for a second to look around. "You have five seconds to hand over the key or I am going to conduct a full-body strip search on you . . . including body cavity inspection. Are we clear?"

Devon could see that Detective Kennedy had a take no prisoners look on his face, and that a strip search was probably only the beginning. "All right, it's obvious that you people are a bunch of fucking psychopaths. The key is right here, taped to my chest."

"Hanson . . ."

"Got him covered, Abe. Go for it."

Knowing this, Kennedy leaned over and ripped open Devon's shirt to find a small locker key taped just above his abdomen. It took him only seconds to rip it off his body.

"So this is it? No more games?" said Hanson.

"You now hold the key to this nation's future in your hands, Detective," said Devon, his voice betraying a sense of loss.

"It's almost eleven, we gotta keep moving," said Hanson. "Oliver, if your story checks out, you might actually live long enough to ruin a few more lives."

"And if it doesn't?"

"Then I will kill you myself," warned Danielle in an icy tone.

"Not if I beat you to him," countered Seltzer.

Chapter Forty-three

According to the plan, Kennedy and Danielle went first, taking the elevator directly to the hotel's lobby. There they exited, making their way on foot a block and a half to the detective's cruiser, and driving to the rendezvous point.

After several minutes, Hanson and Devon emerged from the hotel's underground parking lot, cautiously heading for the revolving doors of the lobby's entrance. Both men had plenty to fear. For Hanson, it was an ambush by any number of foreign agents. For Devon, it was the gun pointing at his back.

"All right, Oliver, listen close," began Hanson. "It's about a hundred feet to the exit. I want you to stay about three feet ahead of me. My gun will be right here in my coat pocket. If you so much as even think about making a run for it, I swear I'll put a bullet in your brain. At this range, even I won't miss."

"Relax, Michael. As we speak, you have control over everything in the world I care about—my money, my son, not to mention my ex-wife. Why on earth would I run away?" said Devon incredulously.

"Whatever. Just stay close," he said.

They were outside just a few moments when Hanson was startled by the sight of Devon's limousine. It appeared that somehow Walker and his friends had failed to neutralize Lonnie. As they approached the car, Hanson gripped the handle of the gun tightly, ready for a shootout. Just then the passenger side window lowered. From inside came a familiar voice. "Mr. Hanson, Inspector Lisagor, U.S. Postal Service. Detective Kennedy has asked me to give you a lift," he called out from the driver's seat with a smirk on his face.

Suddenly overwhelmed with relief, Hanson took a deep breath. He scanned the area, looking for any sign of Devon's cohorts, not to mention the Chinese. Satisfied that things were secure, at least for the moment, he shoved Devon towards the limousine. Lisagor jumped out and opened the rear door. As they climbed in, Hanson said, "Oliver, I believe you remember the inspector. I have a feeling that you two maniacs have a lot to talk about."

"I'm looking forward to it," said Lisagor. "How about you, Ollie . . . you feel like chewing the fat?"

Taking his seat in the right rear of the limousine, Devon grumbled something about the inspector's family lineage, making it clear he was in no mood for chitchat.

"That's okay, Inspector, if Oliver doesn't cooperate, I strongly suggest that you just shoot him," said Hanson.

The inspector made no attempt to conceal his contempt for Devon, thinking back to the corpses found outside of at least a dozen of the world's greatest museums. "Hey, I'm up for it," he responded as he pulled back his jacket to reveal his handgun.

Once all were aboard, the limousine quickly sped off, reaching its first destination in minutes. At the corner of 24th and N Streets, the car slowed at the sight of a dark sedan parked halfway down the block, flashing its headlights in their direction. As they got closer, Hanson could see that it was his Jaguar, and told Lisagor to pull over. "Inspector, keep an eye on this guy for me, I'll be just a minute," he said as he got out of the limousine. No sooner had he closed the door than Griffin was out of the Jaguar, jogging his way across the street.

As the two men stood in the mist of the light autumn rain, Hanson went over the plan. "Listen up, we haven't got much time. First, you have to do exactly as I say. Do not, I repeat, do not improvise. Understand me, Griff?"

Griffin was taken aback at Hanson's demeanor. "Talk to me."

"We know where the Investors stashed the launch codes of the bombs."

"You what?"

"You heard me. They are in a briefcase at National Airport, in a storage locker," he said, reaching into his pocket and taking out the locker key. "Here, take this."

"What's this for?"

"We need you to pick it up for us. It'd be a good idea if you called your friends at the Israeli embassy and let them know you're comin'."

From inside the limousine, Devon could see the two men discussing the final details of the plan. Try as he might, he couldn't think of a way to stop them. He considered offering Inspector Lisagor a substantial payment to betray Hanson, but the postal inspector's cold stare told him that such an attempt would be fruitless. As for Hanson, it was clear he was beyond bribery, almost as though this whole thing had become personal. No, for the first time in his life, it appeared to Devon that he had run out of options. The only question that remained was what Hanson would do with him when this was all over.

Hanson opened the door, still carrying on his discussion with Griffin. "Okay, so you understand? No questions?" he said.

"Nope. I got it."

"You're sure?" pressed Hanson.

"I'm sure."

"Remember. When you get in front of the Embassy, just park the car, reach in the backseat, and grab the suitcase. Don't waste any time, just hand it over and get out of there."

"Hold it. I don't understand." said Griffin.

"You understand fine. Get goin', you don't have much time," said Hanson, shaking Griffin's hand. "I owe you."

"But Mike . . ."

Without responding, Hanson turned and reentered the limousine. For a few seconds, they waited in silence for Griffin to drive away. When he was gone, Lisagor said, "Where to, Mike?"

"There's only one stop left," he said, looking Devon dead in the eye. "Take us to the White House."

Chapter Forty-four

Following Hanson's instructions to the letter, Griffin ended up taking the most circuitous route imaginable to National Airport. After first valeting the Jaguar at the Capital Hilton, he grabbed an airport limousine to Dulles Airport. Along the way he slipped the driver a C-note to let him off about a mile short of their destination. After a few minutes, he grabbed a cab and headed back downtown, getting out in Georgetown, where he hailed a second taxi, which took him to the Hilton. Once inside the Jaguar, he picked up the Whitehurst Freeway to Key Bridge and, instead of driving straight to National, he took the scenic route through Arlington, weaving his way through the Vietnamese section, called Little Saigon, then Fort Myer, eventually ending up near the Pentagon. Up to this point, he wasn't sure whether or not he was being tailed, but nevertheless followed Hanson's instruction to use a little-known shortcut through the famed military installation's civilian parking lot. Entering through the south gate, Griffin turned right on a service road that completely encircled the enormous structure and came out on the building's north side. From there he had easy access to Jefferson Davis Highway, which, conveniently, went right past his destination. Knowing that there was no way anyone would have followed him into the lot, Griffin let out a sigh of relief, as he could see the beacon lights of National Airport ahead of him.

Finally, around 10:25, Griffin arrived. Again, doing exactly as Hanson had told him, he double-parked the Jaguar in front of the main terminal to minimize the risk of getting nabbed by the Investors or the Chinese on the way back to the car. Griffin moved quickly, knowing that by this time the airport was closed to air traffic and he had precious little time to retrieve the codes before airport security would begin to question anybody entering the terminal.

Once inside, Griffin did his best to look inconspicuous, which was no easy task for a man of his size. Trying to act as though he was there to pick up an arriving passenger, he paused to check the flight information log at the first ticket counter he came to. Then, walking slowly in the direction of the storage lockers, he stopped at a pay phone and dialed the Israeli embassy, telling the military attaché to expect a delivery within the hour. He pressed the disconnect button to end the conversation but continued to talk into the receiver as though he were still on the line for several seconds, during which time he anxiously scanned the terminal. Amazed that he'd actually made it this far, he hung up the phone and headed for the lockers.

After walking a few hundred feet, he removed the key from his pocket to check the locker number. When he saw "007" he had roughly the same reaction that everyone else did. "Funny, funny," he said to himself. "I guess these guys want me to die laughing."

Finally, arriving at Locker 007, Griffin stopped and looked around one last time. He took a deep breath. All of his life he'd been drawn to challenges. Whether it was football or a presidential campaign, the greater the risk, the more he liked the action. Besides friendship, this, more than anything, was why he had said yes when Hanson asked him for help. The truth was, though, that this was a little more than he could handle. It wasn't the threat to his personal safety that bothered him. In a weird way the action junkie in him sort of liked that part. Rather, it was that the stakes were just too high. Unlike sports or politics, it wasn't about winning or losing. This time, if he fucked up, the fate of the world could be changed forever.

Taking a deep breath, Griffin inserted the key and turned it. "Here goes nothin'," he muttered, shutting his eyes as he opened the locker. He opened them to see a slick, silver, Haliburton briefcase with French lettering near the handle. Covering the lock was a broken wax seal, indicating that it had recently been opened. His concern that the CDs had been removed was quickly allayed when he hoisted the case out of the locker. "What the hell's in this thing, rocks?" he said. The weight of the case caused him to rest it quickly on the floor.

Concluding that the briefcase was definitely not empty, Griffin figured the worst part was over, and hurriedly closed the locker door. It was then he received the shock of his life.

"Excuse me, sir, but what's your business here at the airport this time of night?"

A startled Griffin stood there, his heart pounding under the menacing gaze of an airport security guard. "Uh, uh . . . I . . . I . . ."

"Is that your bag, sir?" said the guard.

Griffin was freaked. "Uh yes, yes, it's my bag. Actually it's my briefcase, but yes, it's mine."

"You don't look so good, you know that? Are you feeling okay, sir?" he said.

The truth was, Griffin was feeling terrible. He was sweating, his mouth was dry, and he was only moments away from losing his dinner all over the guard. "I . . . I have the flu. . . . Uh, don't get too close," he said as he grabbed the suitcase and began to walk away.

"Not so fast," said the guard. "Let's see your claim check."

Claim check? Hanson hadn't said anything about a claim check. Think fast, Griff, think fast. "I don't have one. See, uh, I missed my flight and well . . . I never checked it in."

The guard looked at him skeptically, rubbing his chin as he eyeballed Griffin up and down. "Oh yeah, what flight?"

"What flight?" Griffin asked.

"Yeah, what flight?" he persisted.

This was a disaster, thought Griffin. They hadn't planned on this happening. Hitmen, Chinese intelligence, sure, but not a bored security guard with nothing else to do but bust his balls. "Uh . . . American, number 247 to Miami," he said, blurting out the only flight he could remember from the flight information log.

"Number 247. That flight left hours ago."

"Tell me about it, I arrived late and they bumped me. I figured as long as I was here, I'd have a couple of cocktails. Instead of lugging this thing around, I threw it in the locker. And, well, you got this barmaid over in the Delta terminal."

"Oh yeah, I've seen her, I hear she's a Scorpio."

"Well, then, you know what I mean," said Griffin, who in reality had no idea what the guard was talking about.

"What's her name?" pressed the guard.

Who the hell was this guy? "Uh . . . Hillary," he said, picking the first woman's name that came to mind.

"You mean like . . ."

"Exactly. Ain't that somethin'."

The guard seemed intrigued. "Are you two . . . you know?"

"No way. We're just friends," he said.

"Do you mind . . . if I?"

"Go for it," said Griffin, patting the guard on the shoulder.

"Cool," the guard said, grinning from ear to ear. "You take care of that flu now, ya hear?"

"Will do, officer," Griffin said, giving the guard a two-finger salute as he picked up the briefcase and walked away. As he did so, he seriously wondered which would be worse, being shot by the Chinese or having to listen to that guy for another five minutes.

After several minutes of carrying what seemed like the heaviest piece of luggage in the world, Griffin arrived at the terminal exit relieved to find that the Jaguar had only been ticketed, not towed away. Wasting no time, he sprinted through the sliding doors threw the briefcase in the trunk of the Jag and, gunning the engine, sped off. Within seconds he was on the George Washington Parkway, headed for downtown. So far so good, he thought. What Griffin didn't know was that about the time he reached the Memorial Bridge, he'd been spotted both by the Chinese and by Walker.

* * *

About halfway across the bridge, the Chinese made their move, approaching the Jaguar on the driver's side in an attempt to force Griffin to pull over. What they didn't bargain for were the two cars under Walker's command, one of which was right on their tail. "Red Dog One, we've got 'em both. Primary target vehicle, along with one intruder, please designate preferred target. Repeat, please designate."

"We copy, Red Dog Two. Focus on the intruder. Over. We'll handle primary target from here, do you copy?" Walker said.

"That's a Roger, we own this bastard!" came the reply from the lead car as they stepped up their pursuit. Accelerating, they got within several feet of the Chinese agents, just in time to see the barrel of an AK-47 assault rifle protrude from the passenger-side window.

Before they could radio for instructions, Walker was already screaming, "Intercept! Intercept!"

Knowing that the primary target had to be protected at all costs, the driver of the lead car punched the throttle until the speedometer hit 110 mph as he attempted to wedge himself between the intruder and the Jaguar. Unfortunately, the operatives from Beijing had other ideas. Spotting the lead car as it approached from behind, one of the Chinese agents took aim and unloaded a barrage of automatic weapon fire in its direction, hitting the driver several times. Critically wounded and bleeding profusely, he steered the car towards the rear bumper of the Chinese vehicle. Then, as he felt the life bleeding out of him, the driver hit the gas pedal one last time, accelerating into the back of the intruder, causing it to spin out of control. Along the way, it took out three of the passing vehicles. Fortunately for Griffin, the Jaguar was unscathed by the accident which, ironically, afforded him an opportunity to escape his pursuers.

Griffin continued to speed across the bridge, veering left at the Lincoln Memorial, taking 23rd Street to Washington Circle. Some distance behind him was Walker, who caught a glimpse of the Jaguar as it went right off the Circle to K Street. For several blocks, the veteran spy weaved in and out of the dense Friday night traffic, desperately trying to catch Griffin, eventually closing in on his target as he turned left on 16th Street. Reacting instinctively, Walker turned the corner at breakneck speed, spotting the

Jag about a hundred feet in front of him. For about another block and a half he continued the chase, when suddenly Griffin did something that totally stunned him.

"Oh my God!" he screamed as he saw the Jaguar cross over to International Drive, and slow to a crawl in front of the Israeli embassy. Fearing the worst, Walker slammed on the brakes and leaped out of his car, giving chase on foot. Pulling his gun, he yelled, "Stop, you fucking traitor!"

Spotting the military attaché standing at the front gate, Griffin parked the Jaguar directly under the NO PARKING—TOW AWAY sign near the entrance. Wasting no time, he reached back and grabbed the briefcase and jumped out of the car. In one motion he pressed down the automatic locks and slammed the door shut Then, with all the speed his 240-pound frame could muster, he sprinted around the rear of the car to the embassy gate. There, he was greeted anxiously. "Come inside quickly," said the Embassy official.

"No time for that," Griffin said. "Here, just take this, it belong to you."

The Israeli took the briefcase and said, "Tom Griffin, I canno adequately express the gratitude of the Jewish people."

But before he could finish, Griffin turned and ran back into th street, where he frantically tried to hail a cab. In a matter o seconds he was interrupted by an angry voice yelling, "Freeze you sonofabitch! I mean it. I will blow your fucking head righ off."

Griffin put his hands up and slowly turned to see Walker stand ing about ten feet away, a .45 automatic aimed right at his ches "Do you have any idea what you've just done? I should just finis you off right here," he said as he fingered the gun's trigger.

Suddenly, out of nowhere, a late-model sedan parked acros the street gunned its engine and peeled out into traffic. The soun of its tires squealing filled the air as the car pulled a complet 180-degree turn and headed right for them. Walker took aim an tried to get off a shot, but it was too late. At the last second, h dived out of the way as the sedan kept coming, screeching to halt right between the two men.

Griffin, at this point, was too scared to jump out of the way anything. He stood frozen as the driver's side window lowere cringing in anticipation of yet another encounter with the Chinese. But instead of hearing gunshots, Griffin recognized what was at that moment the sweetest voice he'd ever heard.

"Griffin, get your fucking ass in the car, *now*!" screamed Detective Kennedy.

Without thinking, he dove into the backseat of the police cruiser.

Lying facedown in the back, he felt the detective hammer the throttle as they pulled away. They drove for about a minute as the sound of gunfire in the background slowly faded away. At last, the only sound he heard was his heart pounding.

"You all right back there, Griffin?" Kennedy asked.

"Yeah," Griffin said, sitting up. "I think I wet myself, but I guess that beats getting shot."

"No, not really, they both suck," the detective said. "You know Danielle Harris, the mastermind of tonight's little escapade."

"Oh, hey there, Danielle, I didn't know you'd be along for the ride. What a surprise—"

"Excuse me! But would you two mind holding old home week some other time?" yelled the detective impatiently.

"Sorry," Griffin said.

"Did you make the delivery?"

"Absolutely!"

Danielle, who was riding in the passenger seat, punched in a number on Kennedy's portable phone. "Here," she said, handing it to him.

"Thanks," he said, waiting for Devon's limousine to answer. "Yo, Michael, I picked up your boy . . . yeah, he's alive . . . we'll be there in five minutes."

"Where are we headed?" Griffin asked.

"The White House," said Kennedy as he looked at Griffin in the rearview mirror. "Hanson and I have some unsettled business with Devon. I suggest you two just sit back and enjoy the view."

Part Six

"Don't get mad. Get even!"

—Robert F. Kennedy

Chapter Forty-five

At 11:01 P.M. Devon's limousine circled the White House for the third time. The rain, which had come and gone most of the night, showed no sign of letting up. As they started loop number four, passing the Ellipse, across from the South Lawn, Inspector Lisagor said, "All clear, Mike."

"Sounds good. Let's go around one more time . . . this shouldn't take long." As they made the turn down 15th Street, past the Treasury building, Hanson said, "So Oliver, it looks like this all comes down to you and me."

Devon looked furious as he sat facing his captor in the back of his own limousine. Over and over again, he kept asking himself how he could have let this happen. He realized he had made two deadly mistakes—first, he had let things get personal, second, for the first time in thirty years, he'd let his guard down and lost control. In Washington, mistakes like these were equivalent to suicide. He looked over at Hanson with contempt, certain that his opponent couldn't be nearly as shrewd as circumstances might suggest. This had nothing to do with Hanson. He had just gotten too comfortable, too lazy, Devon told himself. "Excuse me for asking, Michael, but what exactly do you have in mind for me?

You have a bunch of my money, you have the Red Locust file. What else could you want?"

"Sorry for the inconvenience, Oliver," Hanson snapped. "My town, my game . . ."

"Honestly, is killing me really going to serve any purpose?"

"Killing you? What makes you think I'm going to kill you?"

"Oh, I don't know. Maybe it's the fact that I've been kidnapped and held at gunpoint for the last two hours," Devon said snidely.

Hanson loved it. "You got me all wrong, Oliver. Murder is your specialty, not mine. Personally, I don't have the stones for that sort of thing. Tell me, what is it like to beat the life out of a seventeen-year-old girl?"

Devon raised an eyebrow. Hanson thought he killed Ariel. He almost smiled, then caught himself. "Well, then, if you don't intend to kill me, what is it you're after?"

"Believe it or not, Oliver, I'm still trying to figure that out myself," Hanson said. "Part of me wants to play by the rules—you know, to see you tried and convicted in a court of law. But we both know that ain't gonna happen. And then there's the part of me that wants an eye for an eye, my proverbial pound of flesh. The truth is, I haven't decided what to do. For now I'd just like some answers."

"What kind of answers?" asked Devon cautiously, figuring the more he could keep Hanson talking, the better his chances of survival would be.

"For starters, I'd like you to tell me why the hell I'm involved in any of this. I wake up one morning and there's a cop on my doorstep telling me I've been identified as the father of some murdered teenage hooker—"

"She wasn't a hooker, Michael," interrupted Devon, flinching at Hanson's choice of words.

Hanson couldn't believe it. He had made Devon react. Completely by accident, he'd pushed one of Devon's buttons. With a little luck, he would be able to push a few more. "Whatever you say, Oliver. Anyway, before I know it, you're in my life."

Had things gone according to Devon's plan, he'd intended to clear everything up for Hanson sometime after the inauguration. By that time his young consultant would have grown accustomed to the lavish lifestyle that went along with being part of Devon's universe, making the power broker's extraordinary revelations more palatable. Unfortunately, it was now or never. "Michael, while I'm sure you had no idea, the fact is I've been involved in your life for years now."

Devon's statement was so incredible, so ludicrous, that it made Hanson laugh out loud. "Pardon me, Mr. Devon, but I must have misunderstood you."

"It started almost twenty years ago, when CeCe Fairchild came to New York. I guess she was still CeCe Farentino back then. She had dreams of becoming a model."

"I remember," said Hanson as his eyes grew wide with anticipation. "Keep talking."

As the limousine turned right on E Street, Devon paused as he studied Hanson. Gun in hand, he seemed transfixed by Devon's every word. Continuing, he said, "Well, back then the top agencies used to hold these outrageous parties to show off their new crop of girls. That's where I first met CeCe. We began an affair almost immediately. It was around that time when I first heard of the infamous Mike Hanson. You were in college at the time. I can still remember the way CeCe would go on and on about you; how you were going to be a lawyer and how you were going to run for Congress by the time you were twenty-five. It was amazing. I was actually jealous of some kid I'd never even met. Well, as you know, she got pregnant."

"No, actually I didn't. The only thing I knew was that she disappeared from my life about the time I graduated from college. No phone call, no letter, nothing," Hanson said.

Despite the circumstances, Devon was actually savoring the moment. For years he carried this part of his life around inside him, haunted by the need to confess his complicity in the destruction of Hanson's career. "Well, you didn't disappear from hers—at least not in her heart. I swear, that girl carried a torch for you for years. In fact, I was so concerned about it that I intervened on your behalf about the time you got out of law school."

"Come again?"

"I realize this is difficult for you to understand, but by that time my marriage had fallen apart and CeCe and her daughter were extremely important to me. I admit it, I felt threatened by you,

Michael. To protect myself, I hired a private investigator to keep tabs on you."

"You've got to be kidding."

"Unfortunately, I'm dead serious. When the P.I. told me that you were interviewing with some Wall Street firms, I had to put a stop to it. There was no way I could allow you to move to New York," Devon said.

About this time, the limousine approached 17th Street, where it was supposed to head north towards Pennsylvania Avenue. Instead, Hanson asked Lisagor to pull over. With his appetite whetted, he wanted to hear everything Devon had to say. "Are you saying you had me nixed?"

"Yes, the fact is I did. But in my defense, I did take steps to make sure that you landed on your feet, far away from us. In Washington."

Hanson could swear he saw traces of a smirk on Devon's face. "You sonofabitch!"

"Come on, Michael, stop being so naive," Devon said. "I'm curious. Do you even remember how you got your job on the Foreign Relations Committee?"

This was about the last question Hanson expected. In fact, after spending years trying to block out the whole experience, most of the details had gotten a little murky. "Not exactly."

"Well, I'm not surprised. Michael, the truth is, you never even applied. I know for a fact that you got a call from the Chief Counsel of the committee, and that during your interview he offered you a job on the spot. No transcripts, no references, nothing. Didn't that ever strike you as just a wee bit strange?"

Hanson mulled the question over for a second before answering. "No, not really. I guess I just thought it was my winning personality."

Laughing heartily, Devon said, "Not hardly."

"So that was all your handiwork?"

"Of course it was me. Remember, Michael, this is Washington. Nothing ever happens without a reason. In your case, I actually came to admire you. All CeCe's bragging turned me into a fan."

Hanson couldn't believe what he was hearing. Getting fired from the committee sent his career into a tailspin from which he never quite recovered. In spite of the circumstances, he still blamed himself for years. All the while it was Devon playing puppet master. "Tell me, Oliver, if you were such a big fan of mine, then why the hell didn't you do something when Kassendine tried to hang me out to dry?"

Devon shrugged. "Well, that was unfortunate. Make no mistake about it, I have no great love for Malcolm Kassendine. Quite honestly, when word got around that you kicked his ass, no one was more pleased than me. The trouble was that the senator was about to enter the New Hampshire primary. It was one of the few times in my life that my hands were tied. C'est la vie," Devon sighed.

"And now?"

"The truth is, my young friend, you shouldn't be involved in any of this, but when Ariel named you as her next of kin I had no choice but to get involved."

"I'm underwhelmed," said Hanson. "So let me ask you, with all the consultants in this city, why the hell did you hire me, anyway?"

"Actually my reasoning was quite simple. By hiring you I was killing two birds with one stone. I was able to keep an eye on you while using the time to figure out why Ariel listed you as her father. My guess is, it was because of things that her mother said after we split up. But the main reason was, I really did need someone to torpedo Danielle and her rather untimely crusade against the so-called 'Chinese espionage connection' . . . not just anyone, mind you, but a gentleman. She was my ex-wife, for godsake!"

"You always were Mr. Sensitive."

Devon continued stone-faced. "Michael, make no mistake about it, I wanted the inquiry stopped dead in its tracks. That way there's a lot less controversy and, you know, a lot less media. The trouble was that you took so goddamn long to take the assignment that we lost our window to do the job right. Even so, I still saw some advantage in keeping you around. You know the old saying, keep one's friends close and one's enemies closer. Besides, I always wanted to see how much it would take to buy ff the honorable Michael Hanson."

"Honorable. Yeah, sure," Hanson scoffed, holding the gun ghter.

"Actually, despite your best efforts, you still have a reputation as a stand-up guy. Quite frankly, until I saw you back at the Kennedy Center I couldn't picture you ever going for the jugular. Obviously, I misjudged you."

"I learned from the master," Hanson said as he fingered the trigger of the gun. "So tell me about the murders."

Once again, Hanson had pushed a button. Devon's voice rose slightly, filled with anger. "Michael, whatever else happens, goddamnit, you have to believe me. I had nothing to do with Ariel's death, or CeCe's for that matter! I'm sure it was the Chief."

This time Hanson wasn't going to let Devon pass off the blame. Pointing the nine-millimeter right between Devon's eyes, he said, "The fact that you let that monster anywhere near her makes you guilty, you well-heeled piece of shit!"

"I didn't let him near her, for god's sake. It was CeCe's fault. Stupid bitch. I could never—"

Devon's continued denials enraged Hanson. Summoning all his self-control to not pull the trigger, he shouted, "You shut your fucking mouth right now. Stop saying you couldn't. The fact is you did . . . and you gotta pay!"

"Enjoy this while it lasts, Michael, paybacks can be hell, you know."

Hanson laughed. "Yeah, Oliver, they sure can. Speaking of which—Inspector, if you don't mind, let's take one last drive by the White House."

"And then what?" asked Devon.

"And then nothing," he said. "That's where you get out."

"I don't get it."

"You don't have to, just do like I tell you."

As the limousine slowly made its way up 17th, Hanson noticed something on the face of his captive that he hadn't seen in their previous meetings: fear. A fear born out of powerlessness, the same kind of fear that average people have every day over things they can't control, like crime, or the economy, or when they get laid off. For the first time in his life, Oliver Devon had no power, and seemed lost. To Hanson it was truly a sight to behold. "Listen, something's been bugging me. I know you're caught up in all these deals with the Investors, and god knows who else. If you ask me, you seem a little power mad. But somehow I've got to think it's more complicated than that. If you want to set the record straight, this is your chance."

Devon looked taken aback. "Why do you care, Michael?"

"Because you're Oliver Devon and to me it doesn't make sense that a man who already has all the money and power anyone could imagine would do the things you do."

"Michael, how could you have spent so many years in this city and still be so goddamn naive? The world is a scary place, son, and it's changing all the time. If guys like us don't evolve, we become an endangered species, the prey instead of the predators."

Hanson was puzzled. "By evolving you mean jumping in bed with the fucking Chinese?"

Devon looked at Hanson incredulously. "I'm saying that evolving means recognizing that the rules have changed permanently. Take that wonderful President of yours, for example. The Republicans lost and they never got over it. They were so pissed they decided to impeach his ass. And guess what, the press loved every minute of it, so they went along. Just you wait, in a few days, when Prescott wins—"

"What, like you have some kind of fucking crystal ball?"

"Michael, mark my words, he's gonna win," Devon said officiously. "Anyway, like I said, next time around, you guys are gonna pull the same thing. You may not think so right now, but you will. After four or five years out of power, you and the rest of your tree-hugging buddies will get so antsy that you'll concoct some kind of fucking scandal to hurt Prescott. And just like last time, the press and the networks will jump on the bandwagon."

"I'm looking forward to it," said Hanson.

"As well you should," Devon said. "Washington has become a brave new world. The politics of personal destruction has become the natural order of things. The only way to survive is to anticipate the worst and get them before they get you. Politics will never be the same. Every election will now and forever be a war of total stakes. I don't know, maybe you're too young to really remember the Cold War. . . ."

"I'm not that young, Oliver. Cut the fucking history lesson and make your point already."

"In the old days, the world was divided between East and West. But since the fall of the Soviet Union everything has been up for grabs. And, notwithstanding what the Japanese or the Brits may think, the only two real major powers in the world are the United States and Beijing. As for the rest of the fucking world, most of it is made up of third-rate economies just waiting to be exploited. Unfortunately, the American government hasn't had the balls to take advantage of the opportunity. So I went to the Chinese and offered them a way restore the balance of power. Believe it or not, in the long run it would have had a stabilizing effect on the arms race, not to mention being good for the world economy."

"I suppose any guy who is able to leave his own son on his deathbed can rationalize pretty much anything," said Hanson, almost stunned at Devon's earnest demeanor.

"Cheap shot, Michael," Devon retorted. "But geopolitics is extremely complicated, I don't really expect you to understand."

"I understand just fine, Oliver. I was all wrong about you. Your problem isn't that you're power mad, it's that you're deluded, deluded by your own arrogance! How is it that no matter which party is in power, every four years or so a few guys like you always crawl out of the woodwork? You come to my town from places like Wall Street or Palm Beach or Beverly Hills with your own agendas and act like our rules just don't apply to you. When your President violates the Constitution, you call it leadership. When your operatives commit war crimes you say it's a matter of national security. And now you've committed about a dozen felonies including murder and you call it business!"

"Spare me the moralizing, Michael. I've heard the 'no man is above the law' speech before . . . from better men than you, I might add."

"You still don't get it, Oliver. What bugs me about guys like you isn't that you have no regard for the law. It's that you are just so goddamn lame."

"I beg your pardon?"

"Not that you could ever appreciate this, but it takes a certain amount of talent and guts to get things done in this town. Since thugs like you have neither, you just throw your weight around, bullying people until you get what you want. And when you get caught breaking the law, you cry foul and scream that you're being targeted by the liberal media or the religious right or whatever plays best to your audience. The fact is, Oliver, that you and your operation are a fucking joke. The Washington press corps would have a field day with you if they ever found out."

"So is that your plan, Michael? To go to the media? Well, go right ahead. Tell fucking Woodward and Bernstein for all I care," barked Devon defiantly. "Trust me, son, no one, and I mean no one, will believe a word you say. I mean who the hell are you? Some lightweight political hack is gonna expose the arms deal of the century? You're dreaming."

"I'm not gonna tell 'em. You are!"

Then, as the limousine stopped at the signal on E Street, Lisagor said, "The White House is just around the corner."

"Good. Now, Inspector, I want you to just idle the rest of the way. About thirty yards past the South Gate, come to a stop so we can let Mr. Devon out."

"No problem."

About that time, Devon's carphone rang.

"Answer it, Oliver, and act like everything is just fine." Hanson raised the barrel of the nine-millimeter for emphasis.

Devon picked up the phone. "Yes?" He paused for several seconds, and then, handing the phone to Hanson, said, "It's for you."

Hanson smiled, knowing it had to be Griff. "Hello," he said. "Good, good. Okay, just hang in there. I'm almost done. See you in a little while." After returning the phone to its receiver, Hanson turned his attention back to Devon. "Oliver, I want you to listen to me closely. In a few seconds the limo will pull over and you're gonna get out. Don't look back or hesitate even for a second. I want you to haul ass straight toward the White House fence . . . then I want you to climb it."

"You want me to do what? Are you fucking crazy?" Devon said, shaking his head in disbelief. His face turned ashen.

"Once you're on the other side, I want you to start running in the direction of the White House. And no, I'm not crazy."

"Good God, Hanson, think about what you're saying! I won't make it a hundred feet before the snipers take me out."

"That's not my problem. The truth is, I'm giving you a lot better chance than you deserve."

"So much for our deal."

Hanson laughed. "Our deal is still on. I'm a man of my word. If you survive this, then you get Danielle Harris as promised. By the way, that was Griffin and he's got the file. Thank you very much."

"Michael, please," pleaded Devon.

"I have no choice, Oliver. After all, you're the one who said it. I'm a lightweight, remember? If I tried to take this story to the *Post* or the *Times* or the networks, they'd laugh in my face. But that doesn't change the fact that you're guilty as hell of murder, treason, obstruction of justice, and God knows what else. On the other hand, think about what'll happen when word gets out that a prominent Washington power broker inexplicably invaded the White House grounds, hurdling the security fence in the middle of the night. I know the White House press corps. It might not happen right away, but little by little they'll ask questions. And if they don't get the answers they want, they'll keep asking until they do. I mean, if there is one thing you and I should agree on its the fact that those bastards never quit. It'll be only a matter of time before one of those bloodsuckers uncovers the whole conspiracy. You see, Oliver, it doesn't matter whether you live or die. Either way, you'll be exposed for what you are."

"And what if I refuse to cooperate?"

Hanson smiled and held up the gun.

"You wouldn't," Devon said, but his voice was trembling.

Hanson continued to smile. "Maybe not. That's why Inspector Lisagor has been kind enough to give us a lift. He and I have worked out an arrangement."

"Just say the word, Mike," said the detective.

"But why?"

Hanson thought for a second. He wanted Devon to understand with absolute clarity why he was taking it this far. Pointing the gun straight at him he said, "Why? For CeCe, and Adam . . . and Ariel, that's why."

"And Ira," Lisagor called out.

"That's right. And for Ira Murray."

"You're not hearing me. I told you, I had nothing to—"

"Cut the crap," yelled Hanson, taking aim with the Glock. "I've only got one more question to ask. Tell me the truth and I'll let you walk."

Devon was shocked. The last thing he expected was an eleventh-hour reprieve. "You have my full cooperation."

"Who is the American?"

"I beg your pardon?"

"Don't play dumb, Oliver," Hanson said. "The American Investor?"

In a flash, Devon's stoic countenance wilted. Hanson could have asked any of a hundred questions about scams and operations all over the world and Devon would have been only too glad to oblige. Under almost any circumstance, Devon would have eagerly compromised any colleague or client to save his own skin. Unfortunately, Hanson had asked him the one question he was absolutely forbidden to answer. He took a long deep breath, and then in a quiet voice said, "Sorry, Michael, I can't really help you there."

"Come on, Oliver, its your only way out!"

"Maybe so, but I guess I'm gonna have to take my chances with the snipers."

Hanson was stymied. "Are you fucking nuts, Oliver? I'm giving you a way out, for godsake."

"Nuts may well be an apt term for a man in my circumstance," Devon said.

"Insane seems even be more apropos," said the Inspector.

"Whatever, just give me the fucking name already," Hanson demanded.

"No dice," Devon chuckled. "No dice. I'll say this once. I cannot, under any circumstances, reveal the name of the American Investor. And even if I could, I doubt seriously that you would believe I was telling the truth."

"Try me."

"Michael, I swear to you on all that is holy, the American is someone you should avoid at all costs. Someone evil, someone to be feared. You are simply better off not knowing." Devon's resolve was clear. He would never talk.

"Okay, I guess we're back to Plan B," said Hanson. "Get ready to run, Oliver."

Suddenly, as the limousine passed the South Gate, the White House came into view, the pristine aura of its brightness lighting up the November night.

"This is ridiculous. I won't do it."

Without responding, Hanson called out, "Inspector, you still ready to kill this motherfucker?"

"At your service."

"Five seconds, Oliver!"

"You're dead, Hanson!" screamed Devon, enraged.

"Okay, Inspector, you win. We've got the codes. He's yours. Just drop me off before you whack him."

"With pleasure. By the way, Mr. Devon, there are a few of Ira's friends I want you to meet before I kill you. Detective Kennedy will be bringing them. Lord knows they want to meet you."

"All right, goddamnit! Pull over," Devon relented.

Lisagor quickly brought the limousine to a halt, unlocking its electric doors. Devon, his eyes glassy like a prize fighter who was out on his feet, said, "See you in hell, Michael!"

"Get out of my sight, motherfucker!" Hanson said, the venom in his voice almost palpable.

Slowly, Devon exited the limousine. Almost as soon as he got out, he violated Hanson's orders and looked back at him.

Hanson lowered the window and looked Devon dead in the eyes. It seemed strange that the man he once regarded as the most powerful player in Washington could suddenly appear so weak. For a brief moment, he wondered how he or anyone else could have ever feared the pathetic figure cowering in the rain outside the car. He had mortally wounded his enemy and now it was time to finish him off.

"By the way, Devon, Ariel wasn't your daughter, *she was mine*!"

Devon said nothing as the words went through him like a saber Hanson had beaten him and he knew it. Realizing it was over Devon turned away, accepting his fate. In seconds, he was over the fence.

"Get us out of here! *Now*!" screamed Hanson.

The limousine pulled away at full throttle, turning left up 18th Street as the sound of automatic weapon fire filled the air. Soon the Tomahawk helicopter gunships dispatched from Fort McNair could be heard patrolling the skies above the White House. And then came the piercing scream of the ambulance's siren. There was no denying it.

Devon was gone.

Chapter Forty-six

Having rendezvoused earlier that morning at the Hamilton with Danielle, Griff, Billy, and Rick Seltzer, an exhausted Mike Hanson was barely able to make it through a well-earned Dewars on the rocks before he crashed. Suddenly, international arms deals, geopolitics, and presidential elections took a backseat to a more pressing imperative: sleep. And sleep he did, enjoying a record four hours until his bliss was interrupted by a predawn rousting from Abe Kennedy. As a result, Hanson found himself in the detective's police cruiser watching the sunrise in Washington's most exclusive neighborhood. Between sips of weak 7–11 coffee and bites of doughnuts, Hanson asked, "So is this like a stake-out?"

"Uh, technically yes," the detective said.

"Wow, I've never been on a stakeout before."

Kennedy shook his head. "Actually Hanson, you still haven't. I've had Kassendine's place under surveillance for the last twenty-four hours. I just called you because I thought you'd want to be in on the arrest."

"Hey, I've got coffee and a nosh. I have as much right to be part of this stakeout as anybody," joked Hanson.

"Don't push me, Michael," said Abe, trying to keep a straight face. "Now explain to me one more time what the connection is between Kassendine and the Chief."

"All I know is that when I worked for Kassendine there were all these rumors flying around."

"You mean about him being gay?"

"Yeah, that was part of it. But there was one that stood out. As I recall, there was this one rumor that the Senator and some big-time intelligence guy were supposed to be an item. I've got a hunch it was the Chief."

"What makes you think so?"

"Well, I didn't think about it until yesterday, but this guy would call the office almost every day, just before quitting time. He would never identify himself, never a first name, never a last. But one time, right before this big fund-raiser, the Senator comes up to me and asks if the Chief had checked in. I didn't understand, until Kassendine's personal secretary clued me in that this was the guy who called every day. I only heard the name once. Apparently, he and the Senator were real buddy-buddy. It slipped my mind until you mentioned Arthur Falmont."

"I don't understand."

"See, after Kassendine and I had our little altercation, his people were determined to sweep the whole thing under the rug, insisting that I sign a settlement agreement. Otherwise, they would prosecute. It said I couldn't go anywhere near the Senator or ever discuss the matter. The lawyer who put the whole thing together was this real big-time asshole named Arthur Falmont."

"Coincidence?"

"Not in Washington," said Hanson, recalling Devon's admonition that things never happen in this town without a reason.

"What the hell, it's our best shot. Let's check it out."

"Abe, I think we should call the Senator's bluff. My guess is that if I'm right, he'll cave in quick."

"And what if you're wrong?"

"If I'm wrong, we're fucked," he said. "But in my situation, what's a few thousand more in legal bills?"

"So, are you sure you're up for this?"

"I've been waiting fifteen years. If I'm not ready now, I never will be."

"Boy, it's funny how things work out. I mean this was supposed to be my first case back on the job and Ira's last. And now, it turns out to my last case too."

Hanson was puzzled. "What are you saying, Abe?"

"What I am saying, Mike, is that after we take the Senator in, I'm turning in my badge. This is it. I'm not a cop anymore."

"What are you talking about? You're the best cop in the whole city. You can't quit!"

"Good cops don't go letting suspects get killed no matter how much they hate them. Good cops don't let their partners get killed either. Any way you look at it, I've crossed the line," said the detective.

Hanson was shocked. "Not so fast. Think of what Ira would say. Cops like you are out there every fucking day, holding the line. Every time someone like you turns in his badge, the bad guys win!"

"My mind is made up. Come on now. Let's do it," said Kennedy.

Together, they walked up through the gate of 84 North King Street, just off Foxhall, otherwise known as the Kassendine Estate. The eight-bedroom, Tudor-style mansion was completely dark except for a light in an upstairs window. Hanson got out first and took measure of the regal setting. "So, who says there's no royalty in America?"

"So waddaya make of it? Is he still up?" Hanson asked.

"Trust me, he's awake. He's only been home an hour or so."

Slowly, the two men made their way across the yard. Arriving at the front doorstep, Kennedy ignored the doorbell, rapping his knuckles loudly on the door. Finally, Kassendine answered, characteristically adorned in ascot, silk pajamas, and smoking jacket. "Detective Kennedy! Somehow I knew we'd be seeing each other again," he said. Then, noticing Hanson, the Senator paused, betraying only the slightest feeling of surprise. "And that wouldn't be my favorite pugilist, Michael Hanson, now would it?"

"Mr. Hanson has a personal interest in an investigation I'm conducting. He's here at my request," said Kennedy.

"Well, I'm sure he will prove to be quite an asset to you. Although, just between you and me, I wouldn't piss him off."

Hanson shook his head in amazement. Malcolm Kassendine

was truly the most natural political animal he'd ever seen. Who else could answer a knock on his door at the crack of dawn, only to find a homicide detective and the man who cost him his presidential bid waiting on the other side, and still manage to be charming? After all these years, the Senator hadn't changed. The only way to catch him with his pants down was to catch him with his pants down.

"Would you gentlemen like to come in?" Kassendine said as he took a step back and gestured for them to enter. Once they were inside, he led them into a sitting room just off the foyer, where he went straight to the bar. As he poured himself a brandy he said, "I'd offer you fellows a drink but I assume this isn't a social call."

Kennedy was growing impatient. He took out his handcuffs. "Senator, I need for you to assume the position. I'm placing you under arrest for the murder of Ariel Fairchild. Now please just turn around."

"On what basis?" The Senator demanded.

"On the basis of this," said the detective, holding the presidential cuff link in his hand.

The Senator turned white as a ghost.

"We found this in the victim's hotel room."

"Good Lord, but that isn't even mine. I gave a set of those to a friend years ago."

Kennedy smelled blood, knowing Kassendine would crack any second. "Senator, we got your prints, as well as plenty of blood and semen samples."

"That's impossible!" Kassendine said defiantly.

"By the way, Senator, would you mind telling me what blood type you have?"

"None of your damned business!"

"Most of all we have a witness," said Kennedy.

Finally the detective had cracked Kassendine's polished veneer. With a stunned look on his face, the Senator exclaimed, "That bastard!"

"Who are you talking about?" Kennedy pressed.

"Don't fuck with me, Detective. We both know your department is looking for Sam Belarus in connection with the girl's murder. It's all over town."

"I'm not at liberty to disclose—" began Kennedy.

"You're not, but I am," interrupted Hanson.

"Hanson!" the detective barked.

Hanson had waited years to see Malcolm Kassendine sweat and he wasn't going to pass up the opportunity. Ignoring the detective, he continued, "Listen up, Senator. Belarus signed a sworn affidavit telling us everything about the Investors, your relationship, and most of all, about how you killed the girl!"

"Detective, if you don't object, I think I should speak with my lawyer before this goes any further," Kassendine said.

"There's no time for that. At this very second, your lawyer is back at my station house, arranging the terms of your friend's plea bargain," the detective said, stretching the truth just enough. "In a few minutes all we'll be left with is his sworn affidavit and you."

"And the prints," added Hanson, going along with the bluff.

"That's hardly enough to make a case."

"Not if you throw in Rene LaSalle's murder. You're already tied to that one. That shows pattern. The prints put you at the scene, so there's plenty of opportunity. And we already have motive," Kennedy explained.

"What motive could I possibly have to harm that girl?" the Senator asked.

"Jealously. Plain and simple," said Hanson. "At least that's what Belarus said."

"Pattern, motive, opportunity. To me that spells life without parole."

Kassendine looked nauseous and walked to a chair and sat down. "Detective, what is it you want me to do?"

Holding his watch in front of the Senator's face, Kennedy said in a stern tone, "You have five minutes to tell me how the girl died. If you didn't kill her, then I need to know who did. Otherwise you're going down whether you murdered her or not!"

Looking every bit as humiliated as the day Hanson kicked his ass years before, Kassendine told his story. "As I'm sure Hanson here has told you . . . uh, I am a . . . I'm a homosexual. I have been all of my life. You know it's not easy."

"Senator, I don't care about any of that. What happened to the girl?" asked the detective.

"It happened Sunday night. Sam and I, that's Sam Belarus, well, we'd had a personal relationship on and off for years, and that night we had this argument . . ."

"What about?"

"Oh, something stupid. Actually it was my fault. See, unlike me, Sam is something of a switch-hitter and, well, once in a while he'd want a woman."

"So how did you end up at the Capital Pavilion?" Hanson asked.

"It was Sam's idea of humiliating me. He knew about the party and wanted to go there. His plan was to screw one of the hookers right in front of me."

"What went wrong?" asked Kennedy.

"Well, we were in the suite having a few drinks and we each did a couple of lines. Things started to calm down between us. I guess Sam was looking forward to having a little female company more than I realized. Around nine, this beautiful young hooker shows up. Sam seemed to know her, but she wasn't in the room more than a minute when they began to argue. First, she refused to do a three-way, and then it was about Sam using a condom. Finally, he got sick of her lip and tied her up . . . and that's when it happened."

"What do you mean?"

"I don't know if it was the booze or the coke or what, but Sam couldn't get it up. The girl, Ariel, was tied up at the time, lying on her back. But even so she began to laugh out loud at him. He kept trying but nothing worked! The angrier he got, the more she seemed to enjoy it, taunting him over and over again. Finally he lost it and started beating the hell out of her."

"And what were you doing all this time?" Hanson asked.

"I tried to stop him, and for a minute or so we went at it pretty good. Some of the blood you found in the suite had to have been mine. He hit me over the head with something during the fight. That's when I passed out."

"Is that everything?"

Kassendine hesitated. It was clear that he didn't enjoy recounting the next part. "No. When I came to, Sam was on top of Ariel, having intercourse. She wasn't moving. I stood up and could see the blood all around her . . . and on the walls. I got close enough to see how badly he'd beaten her. The poor kid's skin was already turning blue, and her eyes were still open. The animal didn't even have the decency to close her eyes, for chrissakes. Lucky for me, Sam was in some kind of a trance and didn't even seem to know I was there."

"What did you do next?" Kennedy asked.

"I grabbed my jacket and got the hell out of there."

Wanting to be sure, the detective asked, "So to the best of your knowledge, was Ariel Fairchild alive or dead when you left the hotel suite?"

Kassendine looked at Kennedy strangely. "Detective, I must not be making myself clear. I got a real good look at that poor girl before I left. She was definitely not alive."

"Are you saying that Belarus was having sex with her after she was dead?"

"Yes, unfortunately, that's exactly what I'm saying."

Detective Kennedy was about to explode with anger. "Senator, please assume the position. I'm placing you under arrest as an accessory to murder."

"But I thought—"

"You thought wrong. I still have to arrest you. Now if you're a good boy and tell the DA exactly what you told me and are willing to testify, my guess is that you'll probably walk. Just the same, I wouldn't plan on running for reelection anytime soon." The detective walked over to Kassendine and turned him around. After patting him down, he started to putt the cuffs on, but suddenly stopped. Then, looking at Hanson, he said, "So, Mike, you wanna give me a hand with this? Lord knows you earned it."

"Do I want to?" said Hanson excitedly. As he walked over to Kassendine, he thought of all the years of pain he'd been caused by this man's vindictiveness and how he was powerless to fight back. For so long he'd dreamt of turning the tables on his long-time nemesis, and now it was about to happen. He took the handcuffs from Kennedy and firmly secured them on each of the Senator's wrists. Then, as he gripped Kassendine's arm, he said, "What goes around comes around, huh Malcolm?"

Seeing that Hanson was getting a little carried away, the detective, using his most fatherly tone, said "Take it easy on him, Mike, we still want him to testify."

Hanson was savoring the moment and refused to be denied. "Sorry, Abe, I lost my head there for a minute. Senator, I apologize. Where are my manners?" he said as they started to walk towards the door. But once they were outside, he couldn't help himself. "You have the right to remain silent. You have the right to get your ass kicked. You have the right to burn in hell . . ."

Chapter Forty-seven

No matter where you are from, whether it's a small town or a big city that wraps itself in pomp and circumstance like Washington, nothing quite affects the mood of a community like the funeral of a police officer who dies in the line of duty. Never was this more apparent than on the afternoon of Ira Murray's memorial service. By dawn, the caravan of state police cruisers representing New York, New Jersey, Pennsylvania, and Delaware was already crossing the Bay Bridge. From the south, state troopers from Georgia, North and South Carolina, and Mississippi rendezvoused at the steps of the state capitol in Richmond to make the ride up I-95 together. At National Airport, uniformed officers in dress blues as well as detectives began arriving en masse on the shuttles from Boston and New York. Meanwhile, at Dulles and BWI airports, fellow officers flew in from places as diverse as Cheyenne, Muncie, Cleveland, and Miami. But perhaps the most striking of all these tributes was the contingent of motorcycle patrolmen, ten wide and thirty deep, from the metropolitan police departments of Philadelphia, Baltimore, and Washington, D.C., which led the funeral procession that arrived at Washington Hebrew Congregation at noon.

The memorial service itself was officiated by the temple's rabbi, with eulogies delivered by the Chief of Police, the head of the Policemen's Benevolent Association, as well as Ira's two daughters. Rabbi Meyer of the Holocaust Memorial also said a few words as a special favor to Hanson after he had called that morning and poured his heart out. Detective Kennedy was offered a chance to speak but declined, preferring instead to save his remarks for the interment. Although Hanson, Danielle, and Griffin made it in time for the service, they couldn't get anywhere near Kennedy, who was seated in the front row. So, just like everyone else, when it was over they followed the enormous funeral procession across town to Arlington Cemetery. As it turned out, Ira Murray wasn't just the most loved homicide detective in the department, he was also a Marine Corps veteran, who rarely spoke about his own experience in Vietnam with anyone but Abe.

The procession itself took over an hour to make the trip to from upper Northwest to Arlington. When they arrived, the place was so mobbed that the young military sentries began to direct the mourners to park their cars along the shoulder of the narrow road leading from Fort Myer to the cemetery. After parking, Hanson, Danielle, and Griffin made the long trek on foot to Ira's gravesite. Like many who visit Arlington Cemetery, it didn't take long before they were overcome by the sheer enormity of the setting, with nothing but thousands upon thousands of headstones of dead American soldiers as far as the eye could see. "I never understood how big this place was," said Danielle, who'd never visited Arlington before.

"That's the trouble, no one does," said Hanson.

By the time they reached the gravesite, the burial ceremony had already begun. As they got closer, they could see Detective Kennedy standing next to Ira's flag-draped casket, surrounded by dozens of fellow police officers. Seated in the background were Freda Murray and her two daughters. Then Hanson spotted someone he didn't expect to see. White House National Security Advisor Todd McCartney.

Dressed in what had to be his best blue suit, the detective spoke in a soft voice. "For those of you who knew Ira Murray, a lot of what I'm gonna say isn't gonna come as anything new. But for those of you who didn't, you might be surprised that there really was a man who was as good a husband, a father, and a cop as Ira." Kennedy paused for a moment to compose himself. He'd been through a lot in his life, but this was about as hard as anything he'd ever tried to do. "Like I was saying, Ira wasn't just a great husband and father, he was the best partner a guy could have. He not only taught me everything I know about being a cop, but more important, he taught me everything I know about being a good cop."

Then inexplicably, Kennedy looked up and somehow spotted Hanson among the enormous crowd of mourners. As they made eye contact, a slight smile became visible on the detective's face. "Best of all, Ira Murray always got his man," he said, giving Hanson a quick wink in the process. "For fifteen years, I rode as Ira Murray's partner. In that whole time I never once saw him lose his temper, violate procedure, or fail to give at least a hundred and ten percent. See, to me Ira was much more than my partner and my best friend, he was my brother. As the father of a teenage boy, I can honestly say that if my son grows up to be exactly like Detective Ira Murray, then I'd be the proudest papa in the world."

Kennedy's emotional tribute struck a responsive chord throughout the crowd. Many of the officers present, men and women alike, were crying openly, while others seemed lost in quiet reflection on special moments they had shared with Ira Murray. Seeing this, the detective decided to lighten things up a little. "You know, what's really ironic is that I'm sure almost everyone who knew him would agree that if there was ever a guy who would go straight to heaven it would be Ira. Now imagine that, one of the best homicide cops ever to walk a beat stuck in a place with no crime."

Kennedy's attempt at humor got the desired response, with the laughter starting slowly and becoming more contagious as people in the crowd got the joke. "Seriously, though, as Ira's partner I've been trying to think of the best way to honor his memory. Believe it or not, I haven't had a whole lotta luck figuring this out on my own. And then this morning on the way here I remembered something this new friend of mine told me." He paused for a second. Then, looking at straight at Hanson, he continued. "He reminded me that every time one of us quits trying, the bad guys win. You know, after Ira died, I didn't want to hear any of that talk. I was just so angry that I wanted to give up. But what my friend said was right. If we throw in the towel then the bad guys really will win and we just can't let that happen. As cops, we all took an oath to protect and to serve. Ira Murray gave his life upholding that oath and by God I refuse to let him down. Make no mistake about it, this city is a dangerous place, and with Ira gone it's gonna be that much more dangerous. So it's time for us to honor our brother. We gotta all suck it up and try that much harder to do our jobs, no matter how tough it gets, because that's the way Ira would have wanted it." Then, stooping to one knee, Kennedy reached out and touched Ira's casket. With tears running down his face, he said gently, "So long, partner. I'm gonna miss you more than you'll ever know. But you know how it is . . . I got a job to do."

Kennedy stood up and walked over to Freda, taking her hands in his while she thanked him. He then stepped to one side as members of the honor guard carefully lifted the flag from the casket, folded it in a precise triangle, and returned it to her. Following protocol, the seven-man honor guard fired three rounds into the air, delivering the customary twenty-one-gun salute. Finally, as the echo from the gunshots started to fade, a young officer in dress blues began to play "Taps" as the detective and his fellow officers stood at attention, saluting Detective Ira Murray one last time.

After several minutes, the crowd slowly began to disperse. With a number of people trying to get near Freda Murray to pay their respects, Kennedy used this opportunity to speak with Hanson, whom he saw standing under a tree about a hundred feet away with Danielle and Griffin. "Hey, thanks for coming," called the detective as he approached them.

"Waddaya kiddin' me?" said Hanson as the two shook hands. "So, are you still a cop?"

Kennedy hesitated for a moment and said, "Yes, Michael, I am."

"What changed your mind?"

"Well, the truth is, I couldn't get what you said out of my mind no matter how hard I tried. And then I talked it over with my wife, who reminded me what Ira would've thought about the whole thing, and then I made the mistake of going fishing."

"Fishing?"

"Yeah. I've been promising to take A. J., my son, fishing for a while now. The kid is really good. I mean he's like a fish assassin. I've never seen anything like it."

"What's that got to do with your decision?"

"See, after our little talk yesterday morning, I got home around noon. I was way too hyped up to sleep, so I decided to gather the family up and head out to Sandy Point," explained the detective, referring to a jewel of a fishing spot less than thirty minutes from downtown Washington.

"Yeah?"

"Well, we get there and we're freezing our tails off. My wife won't even get out of the car. So A. J. and I start talkin' about me quitting and he sides with his mother, so we decide to have this bet. If he catches the most bluefish I stay a cop, if I do, then I can do whatever I want."

"So who won?"

The question seemed to embarrass the detective. "Uh, it's kind of complicated, see I had trouble with my reel."

"You couldn't catch a cold!" came the voice of young Abe Kennedy, Jr. out of the crowd.

As they looked up they could see Mrs. Kennedy and A. J. walking towards the cars. "We'll see you back at the Murrays'," Marlene called. A. J. on the other hand just made mock choking motions with his hands around his neck in an apparent attempt to needle his father.

"It wasn't even close, Michael. If fish were people, my son would be a mass murderer."

The three of them tried hard to contain their laughter, but to no avail. "I don't mean to laugh, it's just that—don't most people go fishing to relax, not to get their butts kicked?" asked Hanson.

"I know, I know, joke's on Abe," said Kennedy. "Listen, Mike, I'm glad you're here. There's something else I wanted to talk to you about."

"Sure, go ahead."

"Not here. Meet me down the hill by my car. I'll be along as soon as the grave is filled in."

"It sounds serious."

"Believe me, it is," said the detective.

Chapter Forty-eight

Although completely unaware of it, Hanson, Danielle, and Griffi had been followed for most of the morning by a shadowy figur in a business suit. The man did his best to blend in with the othe mourners, but nevertheless seemed rather menacing as he traile his prey down the hill in the direction of the detective's cruise Up to this point, he'd taken great care to avoid detection. Bu now, as the threesome approached Kennedy's vehicle, he decide to make his presence known.

Spotting him first, a couple of hundred feet away, Griffin sai "Uh-oh, trouble!"

"Goddammit, don't bad guys ever take a day off?" said Har son, still not having spotted their pursuer.

"Relax, boys," Danielle said. "There must be two thousan cops here today. What are they gonna do?"

"Man, am I glad you came along," said Griffin, who by thi time had become Danielle's biggest fan.

"Not to worry," Hanson said, recognizing the man. "It look like our buddy Jack Walker has decided to pay his respects."

"I don't know, last time I saw him he was pretty pissed," Gri fin warned.

"Well, let's see . . ."

"What happened, Michael?" Walker asked as he walked closer.

"The meet went just like you planned. No glitches," said Hanson.

"I'm not talking about the meet, Hanson," Walker said angrily. I'm talking about the goddamn stunt outside the White House. Are you nuts? Where do you get off freelancing like that?"

"You said stop him. I stopped him."

"Yeah, you stopped him all right. I got word the bastard took over twenty shots to the torso before he even hit the ground. Anyway, I haven't got much time. So where the hell are the codes?"

Hanson thought it strange that Walker, a guy who liked to work in the shadows, would ask such a bold question in such an indiscreet setting. "Look, Jack, I know you're pissed about the Israelis . . ."

"Mike, I'm pissed that you're yanking my chain. I checked with Israeli intelligence. All they received were a bunch of music CDs. Incidentally, they don't think your prank was very funny," Walker said sternly. "We both know you didn't hand over the codes."

"You didn't?" said Danielle, shaking her head in disbelief.

Hanson stood there amazed at how Walker was connected. "All right, I'm busted. But you should be happy. You obviously didn't want Red Locust in the hands of the Israelis anyway."

"You're right, I'm overjoyed," he said sarcastically. "But in case you don't realize it, there are one hundred tactical nukes scattered all over the country and that poses a huge threat to national security."

"You yourself said that they're useless without the PALs. . . ."

"Let me worry about that, Hanson. So what's your game? Do you honestly think a lightweight like you can suddenly go into business for himself and play arms dealer?"

"It honestly never crossed my mind."

"I'll bet. Now tell me where you hid them, goddamnit. I've got a plane to catch."

Something was wrong, Hanson thought. Normally, Walker was a cool operator. Now he seemed agitated, even a little afraid. "Okay, we'll go in a few minutes," he said, trying to gauge where the veteran spy was coming from before telling him any more "I've got to talk with Detective Kennedy about something first.

"Do it later," Walker ordered belligerently. "We've gotta ge moving. Now."

Walker's attitude immediately got under Griffin's skin. "Hey slow down, Jack. I know you helped us out and all, but you don' get it. We just buried someone important to us."

"No, you are the ones that don't get it. Before this whole thin is over, ten years of Agency relationships and operations are go ing to be exposed, with hundreds of agents compromised. Yo don't know the kind of heat that's coming."

"So what's the goddamn hurry?" asked Hanson.

"None of your business. All you need to know is we had bargain. You stop the delivery of the Red Locust file to the Ch nese and we make sure you walk on the Fairchild murder. Nobod said anything about cutting yourself in for a piece of the actio Now let's get moving," he said, grabbing Hanson by the arm.

The two men began to struggle when suddenly, out of nowher came Kennedy's voice. "*Freeze!* Nobody move! Hanson, g away from him. Now!" screamed the detective, who was pointi his gun right at them from about twenty feet away. Right behir him were Todd McCartney and Inspector Lisagor, weapons al drawn.

For a split second, everyone stood still. Hanson couldn't mov frozen with fear. Walker, on the other hand, was trying to buy few seconds to calculate his next move. Finally, after sizing the situation, he went for his gun. Immediately Kennedy and cor pany opened up with a barrage of gunfire, hitting Walker with least a half dozen shots. As he fell to the ground he tried to retu fire, but couldn't find the strength. He lay there bleeding profuse as the multitude of policemen and military personnel in the ar converged on the scene. Hanson, who was in shock, quickly kn down, attempting to assist the dying man.

"Detective, are you crazy? This guy tried to help us, he pro ably saved our lives!"

Danielle quickly rushed over. "Somebody call the paramedic she screamed.

Then Walker, who was seconds away from death, grabb Hanson by the hand to make sure Mike heard his last wor

Looking up with lifeless eyes, he said, "... okay, Mommy.... I'll do it for you ..."

Hanson's head was spinning, not understanding what had just happened. Then the detective, who was now at his side, said, "Mike, this is not Jack Walker. That's just an alias." Pausing to pull Hanson to his feet, he continued, "Meet Sam Belarus, aka the Chief. This is the guy who killed Ariel."

"Kassendine matched a picture with his Black Ops file this morning," said McCartney.

"I don't understand, he tried to help us ..."

"He wanted the launch codes, Mike. Devon was double-crossing the Investors, and Belarus was double-crossing Devon. My guess is he'd have have killed you as soon as he took delivery."

"This can't be the same guy," Hanson said.

Kennedy bent down to search the Chief's body for identification or any other personal effects. "Oh no, what do you think this was for?" he said, holding up a syringe.

"What's that?" Griffin asked.

Kennedy held the syringe to his nose and smelled it. "Hmm. Almonds. Looks like the Chief was getting ready to give you a cyanide cocktail."

"I gotta sit down," said Hanson. Slowly, Kennedy and Griffin walked Hanson over to the hood of the detective's police cruiser. For several minutes, Hanson tried to take it all in. Not only was Walker really the Chief, he was Ariel's killer, and Hanson had very nearly become his next victim. On top of everything, he'd almost made the Chief a billionaire in the process. Danielle handed him a glass of water, which he immediately gulped.

"Sorry it's not something stronger," she said.

"Believe me, this will do just fine," he said, beginning to calm down. "Why didn't Belarus just steal the Red Locust file himself?"

"It would have been too obvious," said Abe. "That's why he needed you, to make it look to the Investors like you stole it."

"So I assume that's what you wanted to tell me."

"Correct."

"You think maybe next time you could send me an e-mail or something?"

"Let's hope there isn't a next time."

"Uh, Hanson, I realize you're a little distracted right now, bu would you mind telling us what you did with the files?" aske Lisagor.

"It would be my pleasure," Hanson said. "But not here, not ou in the open. For now, just know they're in a safe place."

Todd McCartney, who had been attending to Walker, inter rupted. "Well that's it, he didn't make it. Mr. Hanson, my peopl will be following up with you in the next several days for de briefing. I want to caution everybody that this incident is likel to cause a real media frenzy. I suggest everyone lay low for few days."

"Your wish is my command," said Hanson.

Before leaving, Abe put his hand on Hanson's neck. He leane in and said, "Now look, I gotta get back and check on Freda. want you to call me later and let me know how you're doin', yo got that?"

Hanson nodded, still stunned.

"All right, and don't forget, we beat the bad guys this time."

As the detective turned and started to walk back up the hi Hanson called out, "Hey Abe, did you really mean what you sai back there?"

"You mean about not giving up?"

"No, I mean about us being friends?" he asked awkwardly.

Kennedy stopped and looked at Hanson. Then, smiling ear ear, he said, "For life, Michael . . . for life. Just please try to sta out of trouble so I can get some rest."

As they waved goodbye, Detective Abe Kennedy disappear over the hill. Hanson knew that it wasn't the end of his associatic with the finest of D.C.'s finest, but only the beginning. He di however, plan on taking Abe's advice and avoiding trouble for while.

"So, anybody need a drink?" asked Griffin, playing his usu role of enabler.

"How about it, Michael? Anything you want," Danielle sa nurturingly.

"Absolutely," said Hanson. "And then we gotta get back work . . ."

". . . And win us a goddamn election!"

"So much for laying low," said Danielle, shaking her head.

Part Seven

"Follow the money."

—Deep Throat

Chapter Forty-nine

Gopey and the Republicans waited as long as possible before confirming the exact time of Monday morning's press conference. Their idea was to delay the formal announcement as long as possible to give the Democrats virtually no time to put their "rapid response" machine into motion. This was a risky strategy. On the one hand, they wanted the event to be massively attended by the media. They also wanted it timed right so there was plenty of footage for the evening's newscast. On the other hand, if they tilted their hand too early, then the Democratic nominee would be ready and waiting come prime time, sound bites in hand, to bury the opposition.

Thus, at 9:05 A.M. on election eve, an army of volunteers at the RNC mounted one of the more heroic fax and e-mail campaigns in recent years. Using a dozen or so Pentium computers equipped with state-of-the-art modems, this group of young, clean-cut, true believers in the conservative cause tried in vain to deliver the press release announcing the 10:00 A.M. news conference at the National Press Club. Try as they might, though, each volunteer kept getting the same response. E-mail all over the city was being returned as undeliverable and fax machines all over the city were busy.

What Gopey's volunteers didn't know was that Hanson and Griff had been up all night planning an e-mail and fax campaign of their own. After receiving a copy of the wire transfer transmittal earlier that morning, they went right to work. Knowing they couldn't do any of this at campaign headquarters, they commandeered the fax machine at the Hamilton. Then, after loading Griffin's entire e-mail directory into a laptop with a multi-use fax modem—the list included at least a thousand reporters—they were ready. In a matter of seconds, copies of the incriminating document were in the hands of journalists and news services all over the city. Griff, for his part, did much the same, cherry-picking his favorites, including Eleanore Savoy of the *Post*.

Operation Smoking Gun was well underway.

By 10:00 A.M. the lower-level conference room of the National Press Club was so mobbed that photogs with minicams were simply holding their cameras aloft directly over their heads, attempting to get some footage. Whether or not a shot was in focus didn't seem to matter a whole lot. At this point, just about any shot would do. If the capacity of the auditorium was 250 people, as rumored, the good people of the NPC were in for a big fine from the fire marshall. Hanson and Danielle entered the crowded venue right behind Tom Griffin, who used his size and football instincts to forge a path. Together, the three went to the rear of the room and waited.

Finally, at approximately a quarter past the hour, Gopey Taylor flanked by Thurman and the Republican nominee, stepped to the podium. He wasted no time as the explosion of flashbulbs made the otherwise drab room seem to glow. "Ladies and gentlemen of the press, I want to thank you for coming here on such short notice. I am pleased to say that, with the election only hours away you are all about to witness an historic event in our country's pursuit of democracy."

"Yeah, yeah, Gopey, get on with it. Shut up and introduce Thurman, will ya?" said Griffin, loud enough to draw stares.

"So without further ado, the Reform Party's nominee for President, Ben Thurman!"

As Thurman came to the podium, Hanson could see several reporters holding single sheets of paper in their hands. He could only hope they were copies of the wire transfer slip. He knew that Thurman would open up the floor to questions after a brief statement. With any luck, they were laying in wait to nail him, he thought.

Thurman spoke longer than expected, almost thirty minutes, apparently savoring the last minutes of his candidacy just a little too much. It was a moving and heartfelt talk, albeit from a complete egomaniac. Hanson was pleased to see that the press seemed to be getting restless, chomping at the bit to ask questions. Finally, Thurman made Griffin's day by concluding, "And I want all of you out there to view this election as a referendum on the Republican Party. It's a time for a new beginning, where we put old differences aside. And if you don't mind, I want to personally thank Gopey Taylor for making me see the light. Thanks a million, Gopey!"

Gopey stepped up to say something into the mike, but never got the words out. "Mr. Thurman, Eleanore Savoy of the *Post*. What can you tell us about a secret deal between your two campaigns on debt retirement?"

"There was no deal," began Thurman. "I'm supporting the Republican ticket because I think it is best for our nation's future."

"Come on, Eleanor, follow the money, follow the money," Hanson chided under his breath.

"Mr. Thurman, are you categorically denying that your campaign has received any sort of financial assistance from the Republican Party in return for your endorsement?"

"I deny that categorically. Such an arrangement would be highly illegal. Now, next question," Thurman said, feeling ambushed.

"Be tough, Eleanore, be tough, be tough," called out Griffin.

Another reporter tried to ask a question, but Eleanore Savoy would not be denied. "Mr. Thurman, or any of you gentlemen up there, what would you say to the charge that bank records prove conclusively that there was in fact such a deal?"

"Miss, I've tried to answer your question . . ."

By this time, the Republican nominee, who was supposed to speak last and appear as though he were the great unifying force of the GOP, was beginning to sweat visibly. Finally, Gopey stepped to the mike and, in an angry tone, challenged the reporter.

"Eleanore, if you've got some type of evidence about some dea then I demand that you produce it right now!"

"Thank you, Gopey, thank you, thank you, thank you," Griffi said.

"We can leave now. Our work is done," Hanson said.

As the three walked out of the crowded chamber, they coul hear Eleanore Savoy still at it. "Mr. Thurman, is there any cor nection between this illegal money transfer and the suicide c Republican financier Oliver Devon."

"That's it. Follow the money. Follow the money," said Hansor over and over to himself.

Chapter Fifty

Election Day

Hanson looked at his watch for what had to be the fifteenth time. It read 5:43 P.M. The polls would close on the east coast in just over two hours. He was growing impatient. After days of forced separation from bed and board, he was just beginning to enjoy his digs again: his bar, his badly mangled stereo, his few remaining CDs. That was until Inspector Lisagor, Todd McCartney, and what seemed like the entire staff of the National Security Council showed up on his doorstep earlier in the day.

"Look, Mr. McCartney, I've told you everything. What else could you possibly want?"

"Mr. Hanson, let's not play games. I know exactly who you are. You are a guy who has a lot of powerful friends, not the least of whom are the President and my good friend Abe Kennedy. Because of that, I'm not going to play rough. But I cannot minimize the seriousness of the situation. What the NSC and everybody else wants is the Red Locust file," he said. "It is in your best interests to cooperate with us."

"Like I've been telling you, it's in a safe place."

"Mr. Hanson, you're not getting it. There is no safe place, not anymore," said McCartney. "Make no mistake about it, the United States government intends to treat this as a matter of national security."

Hanson was miffed. The truth was, he wasn't exactly sure what to do. Without asking for it, he controlled a nuclear arsenal that held more destructive power than the strategics munitions of Britain, South Africa, and Israel combined. And, contrary to what the NSC might think, all he wanted to do was give it back. The question was to whom? Now he was getting strong-armed by his own White House. Turning to Lisagor, Hanson asked, "So, Inspector, what's your angle?"

Lisagor treaded carefully. He, like Kennedy, had crossed the line in the investigation and knew that Hanson was well aware of it. "Mike, I'm here because the Postal Inspector's office wants to close this case. We've broken the art forgery ring. To a reasonable degree, we've identified the killers of the photographers in the various cities here and in Europe. The only thing left to put to bed is the Red Locust file," he explained. "I've assured the National Security Advisor here that whatever you've done with the codes temporarily, you will cooperate and hand them over to the government."

Hanson studied the two men. Obviously they were both just doing their jobs, although Lisagor was going the extra mile to cover his backside. The disturbing thing was that Abe appeared to be suddenly out of the loop. "What does Detective Kennedy think about all this?"

"Detective Kennedy is a homicide detective, and no longer has any jurisdiction in this case," said McCartney in a strident tone.

"Mike, this is now a federal investigation into possible illegal arms smuggling, money laundering, racketeering, tax evasion, and conspiracy. Besides my office, Justice, Treasury, and State are also tracking it. The pressure is coming from pretty high up," the Inspector said.

"Mike, honestly, this is really no time to be a hero," said McCartney.

Hanson smirked. "Please, this is Washington. They outlawed heroes here years ago."

Seeing that they were getting nowhere, McCartney interrupted. "Mr. Hanson, I'm gonna lay it out straight for you. If you don't hand over the Red Locust file soon, and by that I mean like in the next twenty-four hours, you will be called before a grand jury. In all probability you will be indicted. On top of that, you had better be prepared to present testimony to a congressional investigative body to explain your actions."

"I'm sorry, but you must have me confused with someone that gives a shit," said Hanson facetiously.

McCartney gave Hanson a cold stare. "All right, people, we're done here," he said, giving his staff the signal to exit.

"Mike, make this easy on yourself. It's time to move on with your life," Lisagor said.

"Nice working with you, Inspector. Honestly, I mean it. You've got my number if you're ever in town," Hanson said as the two hook hands.

McCartney waited several minutes as his team piled out of lanson's townhouse. After the last man left, he abruptly closed he front door and locked it. Then he turned to Hanson. "Okay, Aike, I've given you the 'come to Jesus' talk for public conumption. Now let's you and I get real. So much for God and ountry. Abe Kennedy warned me that you were a hard case, that wouldn't get anywhere by bringing up the grand jury or even ndictment. He said you've heard it all before . . ."

"Unfortunately, that would be a true statement," Hanson said.

"Well, then, let me give you one last dose of reality. Personally, don't care if you testify before the grand jury or anybody else.)uite frankly, I don't have time to worry about whether or not ou do jail time. What is important to me is that whatever you ecide to do, you understand that the major imperative here is ssentially about one thing."

"And that would be . . ."

". . . protecting the President. What else?"

"Funny how it always seems to come around to that."

"Understand me. This is absolutely no time for jokes," said 1cCartney. "If word gets out how close the Chinese came to ealing the Red Locust file, the press will absolutely bury the resident."

"But I thought the White House had nothing to do with this."

"As far as I know it didn't. But with all the investigations into Democratic fund-raising, do you think it really matters whether or not it is true?"

"No, probably not."

"Look, I gotta get back. We still have a country to run. Whatever you decide, at least buy yourself some time. While you're at it, don't forget that your President needs you. Not tomorrow or in a couple of weeks, but right now."

"FYI, McCartney, I don't need a fucking lecture. I've been watching this guy's back for eight goddamn years!"

"You and me both. But this is something different. The press won't know what to do with this story for a while. Use this to your advantage."

"Thanks, you have my word. I promise to give it my best spin job."

"Forget spin, Mike. This is Damage Control 101. Just follow Standard Intelligence Protocol—first, admit nothing; second, deny everything; and third, if cornered, attack with countercharges. You got that?"

Hanson listened to the words, but wasn't certain he heard them correctly. "McCartney, would you mind repeating what you just said?"

McCartney let out a deep sigh. Hanson wasn't only bullheaded, but was suddenly hard of hearing. "I said, 'if cornered, attack with countercharges."

"No, no. From the beginning."

The National Security Advisor, who had ongoing problems in Kosovo, the Sudan, and Iraq, found himself near the breaking point with Hanson. "Look, it's very simple: just follow Standard Intelligence Protocol—"

McCartney had promised Hanson a dose of reality and had absolutely over-delivered. "All right, all right, I've got it. Thank you, Mr. McCartney. Let me contact some people and I should be able to straighten this out in a few hours," Hanson said.

"For your sake, I hope so," said McCartney as he headed for the exit. "If you need me, contact White House signal and they'll track me down."

"Gotcha."

As the slam of the front door resonated through the townhouse

Hanson made his way to the bar. Sadly, upon arrival, he found only the smallest remains of an eighteen-year-old bottle of Glenlivet. Knowing it would only offer a short-term respite, Hanson poured the mouthwatering brown liquid into a glass and slumped down on his couch. There, he sipped his drink as he tried desperately to hold it together, weighing his options. Out of nowhere he had become the central player in the Investors' ultimate conspiracy, as well as Devon's final power play. And while McCartney didn't come right out and say it, Hanson knew that there were still two or three major reptiles lurking about the West Wing, the type that were sleazy enough to offer up some type of sweetheart deal to smooth things over with Beijing. All in the name of national security.

Just as Hanson downed the last sip of whiskey, the phone rang. After the week he'd had, he really didn't want to talk with anyone, with the possible exception of Danielle, and that was limited to non–working hours. By this time, it was about ten minutes after six, so he decided to pick up the phone. "This is Mike."

"Man, you are like the missing link!"

"Hello there, Mr. Griffin. I was wondering how long I was going to be able to avoid you."

"Hey, maybe it's me, but since you work for the campaign and today being Election Day and all, did it ever cross your mind that it might be a good idea to come to the office?" Griffin said in a sarcastic tone.

"I'm officially retired. Besides, I'm sure you have it all well in hand."

"Not exactly. Turnout is extremely light, and the exit polls say it's a dead heat," Griff said. "By the way, did you even vote today?"

"No, haven't had a chance. McCartney and Lisagor showed up here a few hours ago to debrief me. I've been stuck here all day," said Hanson.

"Shit, Mike, I'm sorry. I didn't know. For once you have a decent excuse. So when are we hooking up? Name the time and place."

"There is no time or place. As much as I hate to break it to you, you and I are not hooking up. I am staying home. Maybe if

I'm lucky I can get Danielle to come over and make me her Democratic love slave."

Griff laughed aloud. "Mike, you can't do this to me. This is Election Day! There will be parties all over town. Besides, the President has invited us all over to watch the returns."

Nice move, thought Hanson. Devon's words came to mind: Keep your friends close and your enemies closer. "No can do, amigo."

"Damn you drive a hard bargain. Hey, how about I become your love slave?"

"Pass."

"But seriously, Mike. I'll have nobody to hang with . . ."

"Bullshit."

"Nobody fun."

"Hang out with Bundlemeister. You guys love each other."

"Bundles isn't coming either. I spoke to him this morning. He said he's headed out of town on holiday."

Hanson shook his head. "Griff, what the hell are you talking about?"

"Like I said, Bundles is going on vacation. . . ."

"That doesn't make any sense. Besides you and me, David Falcone was the top fund-raiser in the Democratic party this year. Election Night is his chance for a victory lap. I know Bundles; he lives for this kind of shit. You must have misunderstood him," said Hanson.

"No, I didn't. The lucky bastard is taking a client's private jet out of Reagan National in the next couple of hours."

Suddenly, Hanson had a sick feeling in the pit of his stomach. For a few seconds he was queasy, almost paralyzed with disbelief as McCartney's words came back to him—Just follow Standard Intelligence Protocol." After several deep breaths, Hanson composed himself. Finally the picture was clear. "Griff, I want you to meet me at the private airstrip at Reagan National in thirty minutes."

"Mike, I don't understand. What's this all about?"

"The American Investor," he said as he hung up the phone.

Chapter Fifty-one

The newly renovated private terminal at Reagan National Airport was designed to offer the elite traveler quick and discreet access to the nation's capital. As Hanson and his group walked onto the tarmac, he could see several dozen small corporate jets parked in an interlocking wing formation awaiting clearance to taxi onto the runway. Hanson panned the area, spotting countless Gulf Streams and Learjets, but still no sign of the Bundlemeister.

"Are we too late?" shouted Griffin over the noise of the jet engines.

"We shouldn't be," Hanson called out as he looked at his watch.

"What are we looking for?"

"Falcone is supposed to be on board a Citation X business-class jet. He's asked the tower for a seven-thirty departure."

"Look, there it is up ahead," said Griffin, pointing about a hundred feet away.

There, they could see David Falcone standing at the bottom of the portable stairs leading up to the jet's cabin, speaking with a uniformed member of the flight crew. Standing in the background was an extremely large man in a dark suit, presumably a bodyguard, who immediately spotted them.

"Call off your dog, Bundles," Hanson yelled as the bodyguard started towards them.

Somewhat startled, Falcone looked around and signaled the bodyguard to keep a safe distance away. "That's okay, these guys are my friends. . . . We are still friends, aren't we, fellas?"

"Oh sure, best buddies," Hanson said as he walked closer. "In fact, I have lots of new friends that want to meet you."

"So, Mike, how did you know?"

Hanson smiled to mask the hurt he felt inside. The whole episode was sad. He truly cared for the Bundlemeister, but his hands were tied. "You know, a couple of things, like the fact that your ego would never let you pass up a chance to watch the election returns with the President. And there was that other little thing . . ."

"What thing?"

"Don't play games, Bundles. You were very specific. "Admit nothing, deny everything. . . . What is it called again? Standard Intelligence Protocol?"

"You've obviously had some coaching," Falcone said. "So why are you guys here? My guess is this isn't a bon voyage party."

"Sadly, no. The way I figure it, you are the last link to the espionage operation at Los Alamos. If anybody knows what happened to the bypass software—what do they call it, uh, 'trivialization programs,'—it's you."

The Bundlemeister studied Hanson for a minute before responding. "Mike, word has it that you still have the Red Locust file. Are you suggesting some sort of partnership?"

"Bundles, I'm saying that you have to give back what you stole from Los Alamos."

"I didn't steal anything."

"But you know who did," Griffin said.

"Fellas, as a member of the bar, this seems like a good time for me to ask to see my lawyer," said the Bundlemeister.

Hanson noted the whereabouts of the bodyguard, who seemed to be looking for any chance to intervene. "Bundles, you aren't getting it. Take a look around. Do you see any cops? We're not here to arrest you."

"What we want is some answers."

"Make this easy on yourself," said Hanson.

"Easy! Do you think any of this has been easy?" Falcone screamed. "In a few minutes I am gonna get on that plane and leave my country . . . forever! I will never see any of my friends again. I won't be able to walk down the street of my own neighborhood, go to a ball game, even vote, for chrissakes."

"If you cooperate, I'm sure that Justice will cut you some kind of a deal."

"Justice is the least of my worries. Mike, the Investors spent millions of dollars to get the Red Locust file. They spent at least as much to get the bypass programs from Los Alamos. Right now they have very little to show for their money."

"The bypass programs don't belong to the Investors. You have to hand them over."

"I'm sorry. It's not up to me."

Hanson was determined to get through to Falcone. "Bundles, are you thinking straight? The spooks at Langley are hard-core. They will hunt you for the rest of your life if need be. They will never let you get away with this!"

The Bundlemeister looked at Hanson and suddenly realized that his buddy was actually trying to save his life. "Mike, I'm not sure you have a clear picture of what's really going on. Before you go too far with this, I suggest that you climb on board the plane and take a look around."

Hanson gave Falcone a puzzled look.

"Just do it, Mike!"

For some strange reason, Hanson sensed that Falcone was being sincere, trying to do the stand-up thing. He turned and slowly made his way up the steps. Once he reached the top, he paused and looked back at the Bundlemeister and the rest of the group, bewildered. Then, ducking his head, he entered the cabin. Not knowing what to expect, he braced himself for the worst. And while he might have been able to handle anything from a process server to automatic weapon fire, nothing could have prepared Hanson for what was waiting for him in the rear of the jet. There, seated all alone, both beautiful and sad in a winter white pantsuit, was Danielle Harris.

"Hello, Michael . . ." she said, refusing to make eye contact as she looked out the window.

"Danielle? What are you doing here? I don't understand . . ."

Finally, she turned and looked at him. "Isn't it obvious?"

"No, not exactly. Are you and Falcone . . ."

"Lovers?" she said, pausing for a second to let the word register with Hanson. "In a manner of speaking, yes. But a more accurate description would be partners."

"Since when?"

"Oh, Michael, I feel so bad telling you this. I've only known you a short time. I mean, you deserve some answers, but you're probably better off not knowing."

"I'll be the judge of that."

"Have it your way then. David and I met about ten years ago at an ABA conference. We've been lovers on and off ever since my marriage started to break up. When Devon wouldn't let me alone I went to David for help. He has been a great friend. We have a deal. He agreed to help me set up Devon, whatever it took. In return I promised that, if we were successful, we would pool our winnings and blow this godforsaken town once and for all."

"But why? Why didn't you just resign the committee job?"

"Michael, you don't understand. Taking the committee job was part of the plan. That way I could control the direction of the China investigation and keep pressure on Devon."

"He thought he was setting you up and all the while you were laying a trap."

"Don't make it sound so sinister. Devon had made it his life's work to ruin me. Sometimes he was incredibly obvious. Other times he was more discreet, like when he hired you. But whatever the method, his wrath was never-ending. It started back when I was still with the U.S. Attorney's office. It was about 1990–91. At the time, I was still prosecuting drug cases in Miami. That was when he first told me about the Investors. As it turned out, one of the original twelve had died and it was Devon's turn. The only problem was that he didn't have a spare billion dollars to buy in."

"A billion dollars? He's worth five times that much."

"He wasn't ten years ago," she said. "That was the entry fee. The number was non-negotiable. So he came to me for help."

"You had that kind of money?"

"No, but as a specialist in tracing drug money I knew where billions of dollars were stashed by the Cali and Medellin cartels. A lot of it was in accounts frozen by the DEA," she explained.

"So, you turned him down, right?"

"Not exactly, Michael," said Danielle uncomfortably. "The fact was that Devon, my husband, who I knew was cheating on me at the time, asked me to destroy my own career to help bankroll his criminal bullshit. I just couldn't get past it. I knew that the second he got the money he would walk out on me."

Hanson knew where this was going. One thing he'd learned from being close to the President was that there was absolutely nothing as lethal as a woman scorned. "So what did you do?"

"I did what I had to do to protect myself."

"Meaning?"

"Meaning I strung the bastard along just long enough to meet the other Investors," she said. "Then I cut my own deal."

"Excuse me?" he said in disbelief.

"Sorry to disappoint you, Mike. I guess I'm not one of those girls with a heart of gold after all."

"You are the American Investor?"

"Yes, Michael. I am the American."

All of a sudden Hanson knew what the rawhide of a baseball felt like when Mark McGwire hit it into the nosebleed sections. Almost in shock, he reached out to grab the back of one of the jet's passenger seats to steady himself. "Danielle, I honestly don't know what to say. Are you telling me that your marriage to Devon didn't break up because of what he did to Ariel?"

"Michael, my marriage broke up because Devon couldn't handle being married to his boss. The fact that he was a disgusting pervert and homophobe was why I wanted him killed," she said coldly.

"But you didn't kill him. I did."

"I know, and for that I will always be grateful."

"You weren't even going to say goodbye, were you?"

Once again, Danielle looked away. "You would have received a telegram saying I was on holiday, that I needed to get away. An accident would be staged. I would not survive. You would spend your life blaming the Investors."

Hanson shook his head. "Not bad. A damned good plan if I do say so myself. But just one thing. Aren't the Investors gonna be just a tad pissed about the Red Locust file? What about that?"

Danielle laughed at the question. "I hope to god they are pissed. That's part of the plan. Once everything is sorted out, they'll blame Devon for everything. He was double-crossing us and I stopped him. The bottom line is that I will be viewed as a hero."

"And what about me, was I just part of the plan?"

Danielle knew the question was unavoidable, yet she dreaded having to answer it. "At first you were just a convenient target, someone to use to achieve an end. But then you became important to me."

"I'm touched."

"I'm telling you the truth."

"Whatever," said Hanson in a disgusted tone. "Where will you go?"

"I honestly don't know, Michael."

"You know I can't protect you. . . ."

"I know. Just try to forget we ever happened. Promise me—"

"I gotta get going," he said coldly.

With that, Hanson exited the jet, sprinting down the stairway. First, he went to Falcone. "You take care of her, you fucker," he said, pounding his finger in the Bundlemeister's chest. "Otherwise, I will track you down and kill you!"

"You can count on it."

Hanson walked briskly past Griff, who called out, "Where are you going?"

"Leave it alone, Griff," Hanson screamed. "It's over."

As Hanson stormed away, Griffin ran after his best friend, finally catching up with him in the parking lot. "Mike, what happened back there?"

"Same old story. No good deed goes unpunished in this fucking town!" barked Hanson.

Griffin grabbed his buddy by the arms. "Look, man, whatever it is we can talk it out. Come on, lemme buy you a drink."

"Griff, the last thing I want right now is a drink."

"Fine, then just hang with me while the returns roll in. We don't even have to go to the White House if you don't want to. You really shouldn't be alone," he pleaded.

"Well, alone is about all I can handle right now," Hanson said. "Besides, I've got to handle something I've been putting off."

"Mike, the polls in California are going to close in less than an hour. What do you have to do?"

"Something important, for once in my life."

Chapter Fifty-two

Never in a million years could Hanson have imagined spending the last Election Night of the twentieth century completely alone, surrounded by death in the absolute worst part of town. He'd seen this place once before and vowed never to return. But tonight he knew in his heart there was nowhere else he could have been.

"Can I help you?" asked the desk clerk at the D.C. morgue.

"Uh, yes," he began nervously. "I'm here to arrange for the transportation of a body. I also need to claim her personal effects."

"Name?"

"Hanson. Michael Hanson."

"Is that the name of the deceased?" said the clerk.

"Oh, no. I'm sorry," Hanson said. "I've never done this before. The deceased's name is Ariel Fairchild."

"I'll need to see some I.D."

"Of course," he said, reaching for his wallet and taking out his driver's license. "Here ya go. I've arranged to have her taken to Murphy's Funeral Home in Arlington. The Hansons have a family plot just a few miles away."

"Fill out this form to authorize pickup and discharge." The

clerk sounded as though she'd given the same instruction several thousand times. She gave Hanson the form and began to enter his name into the computer. "Uh-oh," she said.

"What do you mean, uh-oh?"

"What I mean is that we don't have you in our computer."

"That's impossible, I know for a fact that I'm listed as Ariel Fairchild's next of kin!"

"Mr. Hanson, please calm down. We have the entry listing you as next of kin. But without more information, we can't release the body."

"You gotta be kidding me."

The clerk, who clearly had no patience for Hanson or anyone else, said, "Mr. Hanson. Exactly what was your relationship with the deceased?"

After all of his self-inflicted recriminations and soul-searching, at that very moment there was simply no worse question to ask Mike Hanson. He took a deep breath, then another, and another, in an attempt to keep his Irish temper at bay.

"Mr. Hanson, I asked you a question. What was your relationship to the deceased?"

Hanson could no longer resist his impulse to bite the clerk's head completely off. He started to speak, but before he could utter a word, he was interrupted.

"He's her father! Does that answer your question, or do I have to spell it out for you?" boomed Abe Kennedy's voice.

"Detective Kennedy?" said the clerk, who recognized Abe's face immediately.

"Mr. Hanson is Ariel Fairchild's father. Now do me a favor and speed up the paperwork. Mr. Hanson is grieving and doesn't want to be here all night," he ordered.

"Yes sir." The clerk began to scurry behind the counter.

"Abe, what are you doing here?" Hanson asked.

"Tom Griffin called me in a panic," said Kennedy. "After checking every bar in the city, I figured this was the only place you could be. How you holding up?"

"Pretty lousy. Man, this is hard."

"Don't even bother trying to make sense of it, Mike. You'll never get used to this, at least I hope you won't."

"Thanks for coming down."

"Hell, after all you've been through I just couldn't leave you hanging. Besides, I wanted to bring you this." He handed Hanson an overstuffed legal-sized envelope.

"What's this?"

"During the investigation we conducted a search of CeCe's condo. Ariel lived there for a while. The envelope contains some of her things. Including a diary."

"A diary?"

"Yeah. A young girl's diary. It makes for interesting reading. You take up about ten chapters."

"But she didn't even know me . . ."

"Well, that didn't stop her from writing about what she thought you'd be like. And you know what, that girl of yours didn't miss the mark by much," said Abe.

Hanson was so taken aback by the detective's words that the lump in his throat made it next to impossible to say anything intelligible. After several seconds, he was able to manage the words, "Thanks, Abe. Thanks. You have no idea what this means to me."

Abe took Hanson's hand in his, squeezing it hard. "Yes I do, Mike. Yes, I do."

"So how come you haven't asked me what I did with the Red Locust File?"

Abe smiled. Hanson never missed an opportunity to bust his chops. "Mike, the way I look at it is that you have this insurance policy, that so long as the file is unaccounted for, nobody in spookland can touch you. Am I right?"

"Pretty much."

"Well, good for you," he said, laughing.

"Would you believe me if I told you that I loaded the whole file into the disc changer of my Jag's CD player?"

"And the notebook. There was a notebook . . ."

"Yeah. It was old and in Russian. Barely legible. I'm sure it'll turn up in the right hands in due time."

"I never doubted it for a moment," said Abe.

For the next hour or so the two men talked nonstop until the hearse arrived to pickup Ariel's body. After a goodbye filled with hugs and not a few tears, Hanson jumped into his Jag and followed the hearse to Virginia, making sure that Ariel's body arrived without incident. Then, after reviewing the funeral arrangements one last time with the parlor's director, he headed home.

It was almost midnight by the time Hanson walked through the door of his townhouse. He wasted no time before he emptied the contents of the envelope onto his coffee table. Then, knowing that his bar was empty, he ran to the refrigerator and poured himself a glass of milk. Returning, he started with her birth certificate and worked his way through middle school report cards and old tattered photos of Ariel with her mother. He couldn't believe how beautiful they both were once upon a time. Finally, it was time to open the diary. But Hanson, who believed Abe's critique included some well-intentioned bias, was nervous. He thought of how great it would have been to actually have known his little girl. He remembered that special night several years back when he met her for the first time, how she was so young and so beautiful and so adoring. Knowing that he would have only that memory to hold onto for the rest of his life, Hanson slowly turned to the first page. And then, suddenly, the telephone rang.

Picking it up on the second ring, Hanson said, "This is Mike."

"Great, you're still alive."

"Yeah, Abe found me. Sorry I scared you."

"Are you watching CNN?" asked Griffin.

"No."

"The polls closed hours ago. The election's too close to call. CNN is going first with their projections. Quick, turn it on."

"Sorry there, big guy, I'm gonna have to catch you later."

"Mike, what are you talking about? They're about to project a winner!"

"What can I say? I gotta catch up on some reading," Hanson said as he hung up the phone. Waiting a few seconds, he picked up the receiver and took it off the hook to avoid any more interruptions. Then, after a deep breath, Mike Hanson began to read, taking the first step to connect with what should have been the most important thing in his life.

Dear Diary,

Last night I met my Daddy for the very first time.

He was big and strong and handsome, just like in my dreams. He has big brown eyes just like me . . .

"Oh god, Ariel," he said aloud to himself as the tears ran down his face. "I'm so, so sorry . . ."

Epilogue

was bitter cold on the morning of the inauguration and Hanson 'as up before sunrise. Adorned in a baseball cap and sweats, he rove the Jag down to the Hill to take what would be his only p-close look at the Capitol building all dressed up in the red, hite, and blue trimming for the swearing in of this country's 3rd president. As is typical during inaugurations, the Secret Serce had blocked off more streets than they had left open. Yet om about five blocks away he could still see the familiar twoory stage, carefully reconstructed every four years for this spefic purpose. Draped in American flags and bunting and velvet pes, the inaugural stage is made of structurally reinforced steel support ten times the weight of the country's first and second milies, the members of the Supreme Court, the Senate Majority eader, the Speaker of the House, and about fifty VIPs. As Hann got out of his car to take one last look, the freezing cold air him hard in the face, as did the reality that he used to be one those VIPs and never would be again.

For several minutes he stood there trying to take a mental pice of the setting, the sheer majesty of the city in all its splendor. his political travels, he'd attended coronations and royal weddings, even one state funeral. To Hanson, nothing out there came close to the glory and granduer of an inauguration of a new president. But as he watched the sun rise over the Capitol dome, he knew that it was over for him. After years in the trenches, after years on the inside, after years of experiencing all of the privilege and pain of power, he was now an outsider. The shockwaves from the Red Locust file had overtaken his life in ways he'd never expected. When the *Times* reported Hanson's role in the illegal money transfer into Thurman's campaign accounts, it was no big surprise that the Republicans called for his head. No big deal, just more legal fees. But what he didn't anticipate was the firestorm his dirty trick would cause at the White House, particularly the Vice President's office, which had spent most of the last month calling for his prosecution. It had gotten so bad that Hanson had issued a statement absolving Tom Griffin of any role in the scheme. No sense both of them going down, he thought.

All of a sudden it was 2001, and Hanson was a political hack without a party. Nobody in their right mind would hire him, and with good reason. He had gone from powerbroker to pariah in a matter of weeks. Today the country would inaugrate a new president, and apart from this brief visit to memory lane, Hanson had no choice but to ingore it and, for the sake of his own sanity, stay busy. After returning home for a shower and shave, he went out for breakfast, hit the gym, and headed out to Virginia where, upon finding a movie theater that was actually open, took in a flick. By 4:30 P.M. he arrived home and, knowing that the ceremonies had ended, figured that the worst was over. He was wrong.

The call came from the White House just as he was taking off his jacket. The President needed to see him ASAP, said the new chief of staff. Hanson wanted to know why, but no explanation was given. He wanted to change into something more appropriate, but the COS insisted that there was no time. A car would be by in a few minutes to pick him up, he was told. Trusting no one, Hanson declined, assuring the COS that he could get there on his own.

As Hanson sat in the Oval Office, he racked his brain trying to figure out the timing of his summons. Sure, so long as he retained possession of the Red Locust file, he expected to hear 'om the spooks from time to time, maybe the NSC, but not the resident. Besides, this guy had been in office all of five hours. /hat on earth could be so urgent?

"Mike," said the President as he entered alone. "Thank you for)ming on such short notice. He walked around his desk, extend-ig his hand to Hanson before sitting. As the two shook hands : said, "Can we get you anything? Coffee, soft drink?"

"No, I'm fine, sir."

"Well, don't be shy if you change your mind," he said, trying feign a little southern hospitality. "So, quite a day, huh? Did)u watch any of it?"

"Uh, no, Mr. President. I had some other things to do. I figured at the Republic would survive without me."

"Oh." The President sounded almost disappointed. "Too bad.)r obvious reasons it was the best inauguration I'd ever been vited to."

"I'll bet!" said Hanson, laughing aloud. "So tell me, sir, what's urgent?"

Instantly the President's tone turned serious, as if he were ving to deal with a subject he dreaded. "Mike, this is rather fficult for me, particularly in light of some of the things my pporters have said about you over the past couple of weeks."

Hanson had no idea where this was going. It was a big enough ɔck that he'd been called to the Oval Office in the first place. ɔw it looked like he was going to get an apology from the big ın himself.

"But I want you to know that none of those attacks came from : or had my blessing," continued the President.

"Of course not, Mr. President," Hanson said, knowing that the v Commander in Chief was full of shit.

'Mike, to cut to the chase, we received these official commu-ations in the last few hours from both Beijing and Moscow." e President handed Hanson two letters. "Both of them ask the ne thing."

'And what's that?" said Hanson as he studied the letters.

'That I appoint you as the U.S. Ambassador to their respective ıntries," he said.

'Excuse me?"

'I also received a congratulatory phone call from the Israeli ambassador, who asked which inaugural ball you'd be attendin and that they would welcome your getting the post in Jerusalen We have had similar communications from the Brits and th South Africans."

"That's ludicrous."

"Mike, it might be ludicrous, but it's true," said the Presiden "Frankly, I can't figure it out. I don't know what cards you' holding, but everybody seems to want you on their team. So that why I called you in."

"You're losing me, sir."

"Mike, let's not dance around this. I want to know what yo want."

"Want? I don't want anything."

"Come on, Mike. The way I look at it, if you're in such demar abroad, it might make some sense to keep you closer to hom working on our team."

"Meaning?"

"Meaning on my Cabinet. You know, Secretary of Commerc Treasury, whatever."

"Mr. President, respectfully, even if that made political sen for you, which it does not, I would never make it through co firmation."

"Don't worry about that. I can handle the Senate."

What Hanson didn't know was how much the President kne about the Red Locust file. It was obvious that he was concern enough to start off his presidency with a risky appointment tl was sure to backfire. But what else did he know? Had he be briefed by McCartney? Before Hanson could even respond, had to know more. "Mr. President, I mean no insult to you, t I have no interest in taking a job with this administration. I j want to quietly get on with my life, and I'm not so sure that ev that's possible."

"You'll be getting other offers, I assure you. . . ."

"I hope you're right," he said, standing. "Sir, it's been a pl sure. But I know you have lots of other things on your schedu I think it's time that I let you get to them."

The President came out from around his desk, and put his ha on Hanson's back as they slowly made their way to the door the office. "I hope you'll think about my offer."

"I will, Mr. President. I will," said Hanson.

As the two stood there, the President paused and gripped Han-on's hand tightly. "Mike, if I can just offer one piece of advice, urge you to take great caution in accepting an offer, especially rom a foreign government."

"Thank you, Mr. President. I will keep that in mind," said Han-on awkwardly.

"Good. You know, I remember when I was young and I used talk politics with my father, he would tell me about what it 'as like to deal with the Soviets. He would say that the most alued asset we had in handling the Soviet Union was Red hina."

"Is that so?"

"Oh yes. He really believed that so long as we were able to pit eijing against Moscow we would have the upper hand. Playing e 'China Card' he would call it, the most dangerous hand in litics."

Hanson studied the President, who was clearly sending a signal. Why is that, sir?"

"Because, Mike, whoever controls the China Card is the most werful man in the world. He is also the most hated."

"Lucky the Soviets aren't around anymore, huh, Mr. Presi-nt?"

The President smiled. "There are plenty of evil empires out re, my friend, and they all fear Beijing. The good news is that People's Republic still wants a whole lot from the U.S., and m me. For now I control the China Card, and I don't intend share it with anybody. Do we understand each other, Mike?"

Hanson felt the hair stand on the back of his neck. "Yes, Mr. esident. We do."

"Great," he said, as he guided Hanson out the door. "And re-mber, you always have a home here."

"That's good to know, sir. And thanks."

As Hanson made his way through the West Wing and across White House grounds, he knew he was being watched. Not y that, but he was certain that he was going to be watched so g as this President was in office. While neither man had said ut loud, a deal was offered by the President and Hanson, by silence, had signaled his acceptance. In the ways of Washington, when you make a deal with the devil, its terms are veiled i secrecy and enforced according to the odd cultural mores of th power elite. The price of silence was high indeed. Acting in hi own self-interest, the President would mobilize his allies, wh would make sure that Hanson had plenty of business opportuniti and plenty of perks. They would make sure that his every nee was fulfilled, that he should want for nothing. And this would g on indefinitely . . . so long as Hanson continued to possess h very own version of the China Card.